THE STONEHOLDING

Legacy of the Stone Harp: Book One

THE STONEHOLDING

James G. Anderson
& Mark Sebanc

THE STONEHOLDING

A Baen Books Original

Baen Publishing Enterprises
P.O. Box 1188
Wake Forest, NC 27588
www.baen.com

ISBN-13: 978-1-4391-3299-9

Cover art by Todd Lockwood
Maps by James G. Anderson

First printing, September 2009

Distributed by Simon & Schuster
1230 Avenue of the Americas
New York, NY 10020

Library of Congress Cataloging-in-Publication Data

Anderson, James G. (James Gideon), 1967–
   The stoneholding / James G. Anderson & Mark Sebanc.
      p. cm.
   Based on: Flight to Hollow Mountain, 1996.
   ISBN-13: 978-1-4391-3299-9 (trade pbk. : alk. paper)
   ISBN-10: 1-4391-3299-2 (trade pbk. : alk. paper)
   1. Middle Earth (Imaginary place)—Fiction. I. Sebanc, Mark, 1953– II. Sebanc, Mark, 1953– Flight to Hollow Mountain. III. Title.
   PR9199.4.A524S76 2009
   813'.6—dc22

                                                 2009017548

10   9   8   7   6   5   4   3   2   1

Pages by Joy Freeman (www.pagesbyjoy.com)
Printed in the United States of America

To my wife, Joanne, and my children,
Veronica, Dominic, Bernadette, Ben, Roseanne,
Maria, Anthony, Daniel, and Natalie,
who endured much in the making,
with love—MS

To Lisa and our sons,
Stephen, Malcolm, and David,
for their constant and unflagging
encouragement—JA

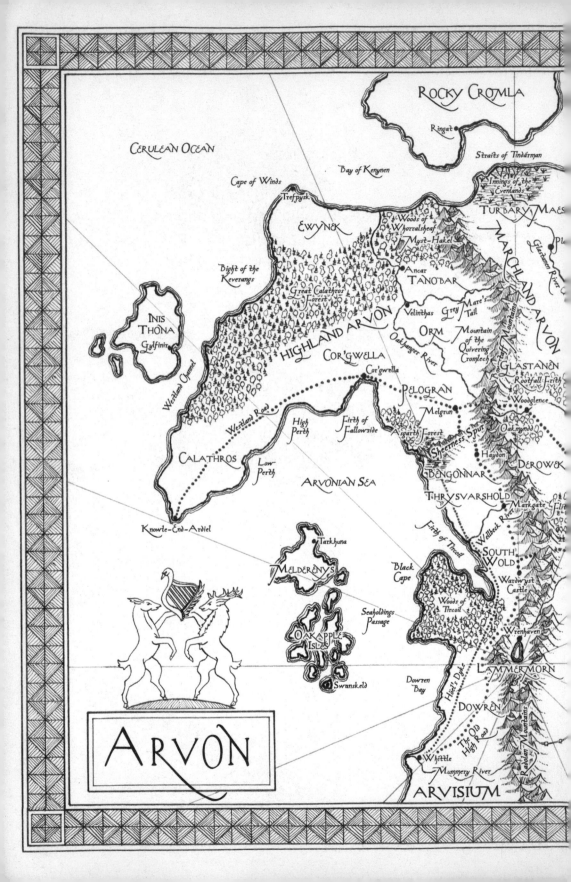

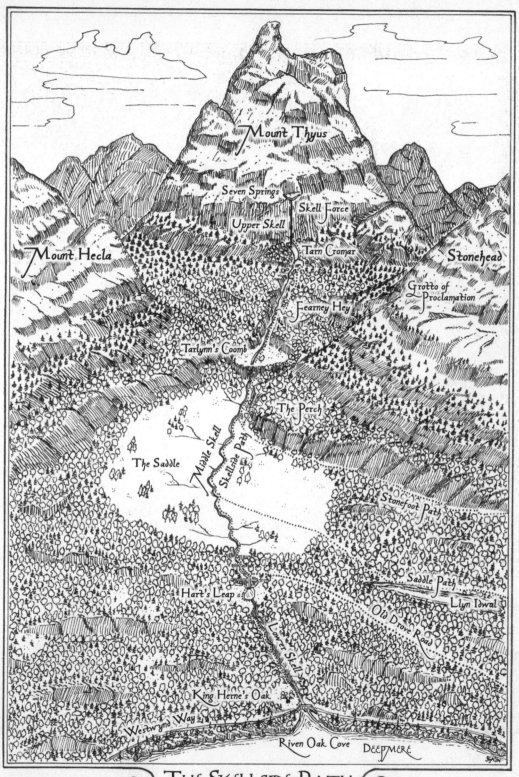

THE SKELLSIDE PATH

THE STONEHOLDING

We have escaped as a bird
from the snare of the fowlers;
the snare is broken,
and we have escaped.

—David, King of Israel

PROLOGUE

The harvest moon had come and gone, leaving only a failing crescent of light to guide them along the river. The air was chill and rife with the smell of leaf mould. The two wherries were now the sole craft on the water, their oarsmen riding the current downstream. Of the river wardens there was no sign. They were busy elsewhere, drawn away by rumours of a planned attempt to break into Tower Dinas. In the stern of the larger of the two boats, Frysan remained alert, for it would be bloody work with sword and dagger if they did chance to meet with one of their patrols. Pulling his ermine-edged cloak more tightly around his shoulders, the slight man peered into the darkness and shivered, steeling himself for the desperate night's work that lay ahead.

The boatmen passed the Hangtree, the city's notorious place of execution. In the freshening wind, the corpse of the river pirate that dangled from the weathered crossbeams began to clank in its shroud of chains. Downriver, in grim keeping with the mournful music of the gibbet, the distant bells of Tower Dinas tolled their final warning. It was curfew time.

By now, the patrons of the Three Cranes in the Vintry would long since have left the tavern to avoid being caught abroad beyond the curfew hour, which was being strictly and oftentimes savagely enforced these days. Besides being their favourite watering hole, with all its hustle and bustle, it had proved an ideal meeting place for Frysan and his men in these perilous times. Earlier this evening, in fact, they had launched their dangerous venture from the quay below the tavern.

1

Not to mention that the Cranes was a good spot in which to spark gossip and foster hearsay—the useful rumour, for instance, that had distracted the river patrols from their normal duties. It helped, too, that the tavern's owner was a trusty highlander, a loyal King's man, although Frysan fervently hoped that they had covered their tracks well enough that no suspicion would later attach to him. Otherwise, like themselves, the man could find himself dangling like rotten fruit from the Hangtree's frame.

Frysan stirred to ease his stiffness and glanced at his broad-shouldered companion. He smiled gravely to himself. Here was Cammas, who was the brawniest jolliest soldier in Frysan's troop of elite Life Guardsmen, dressed in plain coarse-grained trousers and tunic, like one of the many watermen who ferried passengers back and forth along the Dinastor River. Catching Frysan's eye, Cammas swung the oar blades onto the gunwales for a moment and kicked at the lumpy pile of canvas at his feet, where two other comrades lay hidden.

"Ruddy hard work it is making headway with this load of fish bait. Even on a downstream drift."

"It's your own fault, Cammas," humoured a voice from under the canvas. "The ham-handed way you sweep them oars, you'll have sprayed half the Dinastor River aboard before we berth, and the worst of it is, we don't have bailing cans."

"Maybe we can use our scabbards."

"Better your empty heads," Cammas said, poking the canvas again.

For a while Frysan let them banter back and forth, even after Cammas laid his back into the oars again, for such was the timeless custom of fighting men before battle, a way to ease the tension.

The great pile of a building loomed indistinct on the promontory to their right, overtopping the river. They were approaching the extensive grounds of the Silver Palace, which housed the royal apartments. At a signal from Frysan, the second wherry, which although smaller also carried four men, pulled away and beat fast to the shoreline, following a line of rocky bluffs until it came to a halt beneath them.

Some minutes later Frysan could just make out a straggled line of four figures spidering their way on climbing ropes along the face of the rock towards the top of the bluffs. His eyes scanned the brink, probing the scrub brush. Eldor had better be there, else it would be a measure of linked iron chain as a winding sheet for each of them before the night's business was done. But then again, Eldor was the deadliest fighting man in his charge, which was saying a lot, for even a run-of-the-mill highlander was worth at least two lowland rogues.

Now he had Cammas redirect their own wherry across the current towards the rugged heights along the water's edge. The plash of the oars echoed and grew louder as they turned aside from the broad reaches of the dark-flowing river and nosed the boat into the narrower channel of the water gate that cut through a beetling wall of rock. Frysan stared grimly ahead to where the King's Stairs descended to the sheltered moorage. Better to call the place the Mindal's Stairs, he mused, since it was the Royal Council that had a dire chokehold on the city. Here, at the foot of the Stairs, the royal barge was made fast, below the gardens and grounds of the palace.

Even before they reached the quayside, which was well-lit by becketed torches, Frysan could see, in the gloam above, three archers on a landing stooping to span their crossbows. These were men, handpicked by the Mindal, deadly earnest about their duties. That was how the Royal Council always did its business—with ruthless efficiency.

"All right, you two in the boat, in the name of the Mindal, ease up on your oars and state your names. What business brings you here at this hour? Quick now or we'll play it safe and pin you in place with a bolt to the chest." On the alert, the archer had begun descending the stone stairs, his weapon raised to cover the unexpected intruders.

"Ship your oars, Cammas," Frysan whispered to the oarsman facing him. "Dock the boat on this riverward side of the royal barge, if you can . . . My name's Dorassy, Elzemon Dorassy of the Drapers' Guild." Frysan hailed the crossbowman over the water, hoping he had managed to purge his speech of its telltale highland burr. He had even chosen a false identity riddled with perilous "r"s that he had polished well by practice. "By warrant of the Mindal, I'm here with an urgent message for the Captain of the Guard. It's a matter of the highest importance. I must see him. Immediately." He struggled to his feet in the bobbing wherry. "This is Cammas, a most obliging waterman," he said,

throwing off his cloak so they could fetch a look at him in his
finery: a doublet with embroidered sleeves, a long-skirted jerkin,
topped by a linen ruff and a low-brimmed velvet cap, inset with
the jewelled emblem of the Drapers' Guild.

"Come then, Master Guildsman, and we'll have a look, but mind
you make no sudden movements, not you nor the water rat! No,
no . . . Not there, this way. Dock the boat here on the port side
of the royal barge, where I can make certain of you."

With a grimace, his back to shore, Cammas edged the wherry
up to the quay, allowing Frysan to reach out and clamber to his
feet onto the firm ground of the landing. He too climbed out of
the boat and made it fast to a mooring post.

"Now both of you stay right where you are. Easy now, not a
step further. You'll have your chance to see the Captain of the
Guard all right enough. But it'll be the mountain coming to you,
not you to the mountain," said the nearer sentry, and snickered.
The man had come to a halt just above the landing. Keeping
his crossbow trained on the two of them, he looked them over.
His comrades remained rooted in place on the level ground
above. There were three of them spaced neatly apart, making
four sentries in all. Frysan had not noticed the additional man.
He had been hidden from sight before, or else he had come up
at a signal from one of the others, his crossbow still unspanned.
Instead, the fellow had begun to lift a small hunting horn to his
lips. Frysan cringed.

"Never mind the horn, man. We're not under attack," said
another guard. "We'll hold them here, and you go fetch Captain
Baldrick. You know how he is. You'll catch more than just the
edge of his tongue, if you rouse up the whole garrison merely to
bid welcome to an unlooked-for messenger from the Mindal."

"Still and all, you know his orders, 'Anything out of the ordinary and—'"

"Aye, dolthead, but use your sense. There's no need to go
wasting your breath and blowing a great alarm just for a lone
unarmed guildsman and his boatman. Get on with you now and
fetch the Captain."

The man put away his horn and marched off, grabbing hold of
a lantern as he went. At first the minutes spent waiting for him
to return dragged on in awkward silence. The tension that had
settled over the whole city was at its thickest here at the Silver

Palace. These days there was no place in all of Dinas Antrum that was more strictly off-limits and more apt to be tightly guarded. It was here that King Colurian lay comatose and dying, his Queen and infant son gathered to his side, under close watch.

Frysan could make out the winking approach of lantern lights and the dim figure of a huge tun of a man, lumbering his way towards the top of the stairs like an unchained bear.

"Where in creation did he come from? I could fit two of me in his breeches!" Cammas said under his breath.

A mountain indeed, unnerving too, for Frysan remembered vividly that he had met this Captain Baldrick one time before—on parade four years ago when he had been inducted into the ranks of the Life Guardsmen, just before they were disbanded and banished from their barracks, forced to reassemble their ranks secretly in the countryside outside of Dinas Antrum. It was this Captain Baldrick who had personally welcomed the new recruits for King Colurian, taking their oath of fealty on his behalf.

The occasion stood out in Frysan's mind. He had been a smooth-faced nondescript youth then, slighter and less muscular, but hampered by a noticeable limp, for he had badly torn a tendon in his heel during a training session in the tiltyard the day before. When his name was called, he hobbled up to the dais. There had been a moment of discomfort when their eyes met and Captain Baldrick asked gruffly what ailed him, since all the other newly minted guardsmen were stepping up smartly to receive their commission. Frysan's answer was brief—no more than a phrase. The big man nodded and then Frysan placed his hands between the Captain's and swore his oath. He withdrew to let the next man in line do the same. It had been a long and tedious ceremony. There were many that had pledged their fealty that day, including soldiers from other regiments, a great number of them already in the direct employ of the Mindal. Now Frysan hoped he was a long-forgotten face to Captain Baldrick.

"You may lower your weapons and unspan them, men, but stand ready. We mustn't make the mistake of being too trusting. There's an old fool within who could tell you all about the pitfalls of being too trusting, a right royal fool." The big man gave vent to a ferocious burst of laughter, then shed his mirth as suddenly.

"You, Master Draper, come along, step up to me here. We'll speak our business in a better spot, where the light's brighter and

I can see what kind of face you have, whether it's honest or sly. Sly, I'd say, at a venture, for I've never yet met a bearded man who didn't have something to hide. Like the esteemed members of the Mindal. Have you noticed? Every last one of them sports a bird's nest—the bushier the beard the greater the scoundrel." He guffawed again, stroking his own vast comet's tail of whiskers, which swept down to the barrel of his chest. "What did you tell my men your name was?"

"Elzemon Dorassy, Captain. Elzemon Dorassy of the Drapers' Guild. I bear an urgent message for you from the Mindal under seal." Frysan climbed the stairs two steps at a time with scroll in hand. He moved away from the area of the quay, where the rowboat bumped against its moorings beside the royal barge, its dangerous cargo still hidden and undiscovered.

"Hold it! You too, waterman, don't you slip away on me!" bellowed Baldrick, as Cammas made to turn back to where his boat was berthed. "You may wait for us here with my men, while I consider Master Dorassy and this urgent message he brings for me from the Mindal."

Frysan stepped up from the stairs into a large circular area paved with cobbles, from which footpaths led in various directions fingering their way into the splendidly groomed grounds of the palace. To his right, lurking somewhere amid the grove of trees that crowned the edge of the escarpment above the river, waiting and watching, crept Eldor and his men.

At the centre of this open area above the King's Stairs stood a large summerhouse hung with a battery of shining lanterns both inside and out. Trailed by two mail-clad pikemen, Baldrick and Frysan strode towards the structure, leaving Cammas with the sentries. At least Baldrick strode, while Frysan found himself having to feign a light step. The tendon injured four years ago was tightening up again. It pulled like a drawn bowstring against his heel, burdening every step he took with a sharp twist of pain, as it was wont to do whenever he found himself tired or pressed, or when the weather was damp and cold, as it was tonight. The summerhouse lay close at hand. Baldrick ushered Frysan through the entrance, a doorless opening in the circular half-walls, which stood at waist height, allowing the royal family and their guests to look out over the river and enjoy its summer breezes. Light fell from a large lantern suspended from the open beams.

"Here now, let me have a look at that precious missive of yours." Baldrick reached a thick hand out to snatch the sealed page, as he dropped himself heavily into a high-backed chair behind a stout oak table in the middle of the summerhouse. The Captain broke the wax seal. Knitting his brows, he began reading the document they had so carefully forged. Frysan gathered the skirt of his jerkin behind his knees and seated himself across from Baldrick. He let his eyes wander over the sparsely furnished interior of the summerhouse and the thick darkness outside until he ventured a closer look at the man he faced. From the corner of his vision at first, he noted the man's balding neckless head fixed like a tattered bolster on massive shoulders. There was the smell too. He wrinkled his nose at the sour sweat-mingled stench of the wine that flushed the soldier's cruel snub features.

"So they've had some trouble at Tower Dinas?" Baldrick looked up at last from the scroll, regarding Frysan with small piggish eyes.

"Yes, serious trouble, Captain."

"The clay-brained fools, I warned them they'd need to post more men there. Although the plain truth is that it wouldn't make a jot of difference how many men you posted there so long as they insist on retaining that foppish thin-faced charlatan they've put in charge of the place. Why, I wouldn't trust the man to clean a latrine."

"You may rest easy on that point, Captain. After tonight the Mindal has seen fit to withdraw his commission." Frysan lied glibly. Better to make it seem like the Mindal was bowing to some of Baldrick's suggestions—it might make him more pliable when the question of evacuating the King and Queen was broached.

"Plague on him! It's about time, seeing as it's all our necks that are like to get stretched if we let the old-guard rabble take Tower Dinas."

"The situation would be even worse if they took the Silver Palace. Precisely the reason why it's you they've put in command here." Frysan leaned forward in his seat. "Let Queen Asturia and her son manage an escape and you'll ignite whatever resistance there remains in Arvon, like pouring oil on fire. As far as the Queen and baby are concerned, the Mindal's taking no chances."

"No chances! How do you mean no chances?" Baldrick struck the table with his fist. "If they were serious about taking no chances, they'd be coming to me with the order to blood their throats!"

"Not yet, Captain, you know the time isn't ripe for that yet."

"So instead they want me to move the wretched termagant and her whelp to the Summer Palace and hold the both of them there together with the King. If he survives the trip. 'Take the royal barge,' they say—" He lifted the document and let it drop onto the table. "—'And a dozen of your best men for escort' . . . with Elzemon Dorassy of the Drapers' Guild to hold her hand and humour her."

"If you wish to put it that way, Captain, yes, precisely. Now that you have some idea of the arrangements, perhaps we can move along now to the royal apartments and collect the royal family. The sooner we set off upriver the better."

"Very well, Master Dorassy," said Baldrick, as he steepled his fingers, flexing them, his elbows on the table. "One last question. Why you? How is it they've sent you to fetch this pestilent battle-axe of a woman? I don't know that I've ever met you or even heard mention of your name. And it's my business to know all the scavenger fish that feed on scraps from the Mindal."

"Because they needed someone who'd not raise the Queen's hackles. Someone not known to swim with the scavenger fish, as you call them, but trustworthy all the same and sympathetic to their designs. It so happened that I had been invited to their meeting tonight for the first time, and they asked me to undertake the task. I'd had some friendly dealings with the Queen when I was but a journeyman draper newly arrived in Dinas Antrum from my hometown."

"What hometown is that, may I ask?" Baldrick had unsheathed his dagger and fell to paring his nails with its razor-sharp edges.

"Woodglence, on the upper Dinastor."

"I thought I noticed a touch of an accent . . . almost took you for a highlander for a moment there." He looked up squint-eyed at Frysan. Light perspiration began to gather on Frysan's brow. His foot began to throb. He knew the heel was soon bound to hurt worse.

"No, I'm from the marchlands this side of the Radolan Mountains, a lowlander when all is said and done."

"Good, come along then," said Baldrick, as he rose. He held out his dagger pointing to the doorway, then slid the blade into its sheath. "We'll let you wheedle the woman with your soft graces, Master Merchant, although if it were up to me, I'd not stand on ceremony but bind and gag her and throw her into the boat's bilge, her and her whining imp. And I'm willing to bet you a full month's wages you'll be hard put to get her to agree that her husband should be moved in his death pangs."

Baldrick and Frysan left the summerhouse and turned onto a flagged footpath towards the buildings of the Silver Palace itself. The two pikemen provided them with lantern light, one ahead and one behind. They threaded their way across the grounds, where the sculptured hedges threw strange shadows in the flaring light, past flowerbeds and terraced gardens, their plants now faded with the summer's passing. Wincing at the surging stabs of pain, Frysan started to favour his left foot, lagging a step behind the Captain, who more than once cursed and prodded the pikeman who led the way in an effort to quicken their pace. Without warning Baldrick turned his head.

"What ails you, man?" he asked, stopping to regard Frysan with a narrow eye. Frysan's heart skipped a beat.

"Oh . . . nothing, just turned my ankle when I jumped onto the wharf from the boat, that's all."

"Aye, it can be hard to find your footing in the dark. Those stones are slippery, awful slippery. A man can't be too careful, can he?"

"No, never too careful," echoed Frysan, stiffening at the remark, which had been delivered with a wry smile, almost a leer. The Captain was reputed to be the Mindal's spymaster, deeply involved in their scheming and intrigues. Ah well, there was no going back now. All he could do was grit his teeth and carry on, although suddenly he found the feel of the sheathed knife resting between his shoulders profoundly reassuring. He cast a glance upward, as they neared the shadow-draped face of the grey-stoned palace building, to where its turrets and chimney stacks stood lost in darkness.

At the postern gate they came to a halt, facing a massive oaken door with heavy steel hasps and rivets. Over the door, which stood flooded by light from two torches fixed in wrought-iron cressets, there curved a stone arch adorned with the royal coat of arms. Overhanging the arch was an embrasure that bulged out from the wall, its floor and each of its three sides having grated openings, which afforded the guards inside an unencumbered view of anyone who might approach the palace seeking entry. Baldrick pulled on a rope that dangled down from the embrasure. From within they heard the harsh clang of a bell, followed moments later by a clipped voice that challenged them from behind the crisscross grillework.

"Password!"

"Terrible trials trouble robin redbreast's roosting rest," Baldrick replied in his rough baritone.

Frysan smiled. A curiously whimsical kind of password, as well suited to the stalwart Captain as a girl's lace-edged frock.

"And what about him too, the fancy-dressed gentleman behind you, sir?"

"He's with me, soldier, can't you see?"

"Aye, but orders is orders, sir. We ain't supposed to open the door for nobody who ain't said the password. You said so yourself, Captain. Not even if Lord Gawmage hisself was to come and beg admittance, him and all the Mindal."

"Very well done, soldier. I am impressed." Baldrick's words were cold, spoken with steel-edged menace.

"Th-thank you, sir. Now you, gentleman, you've got to give the password."

"Now surely Captain, there can't be need—we've orders from the Mindal—let's move along, it's late enough as it is." Though he feigned impatience, a chill passed down Frysan's spine. It was clear to him why they had resorted to such a password. No highlander, no matter how long he had been resident in Dinas Antrum, could pronounce "r"s like that without giving himself away with some hint of a telltale burr.

"But it's just a short phrase, Master Draper Dorassy, ever so short and easy. And I mustn't always be overriding my orders. Not good for the men. I can't have them getting the notion that when I issue an order I'm not serious, dead serious."

Frysan stiffened. His foot ached.

"Here, I'll make things easy for you. I'll speak the password again and you can say it directly after me. That way you won't tax your memory. We all know how you merchants feel about taxes. Come now, repeat after me, 'Terrible trials trouble robin redbreast's roosting rest.'"

"Very well then, Captain, since you insist," said Frysan with an air of gracious resignation. If he made some move now, he might still escape, especially if Eldor and his men lurked anywhere nearby. The mission, however, would be ruined, Arvon's last hope gone. It would be best to play along, to play mouse to Baldrick's cat for as long as he could, biding his time, waiting for a chance to salvage his mission. He must let Baldrick admit him into the palace first, to the Queen's apartments, if possible, and then he'd deal with the man—somehow.

Taking a breath, Frysan repeated the tongue-twisting syllables of the password phrase. He had been in Dinas Antrum for six years now on and off and had always possessed a good ear for language, passing for a lowlander readily enough with most of the people he encountered in the city. But that slightest bit of a brogue, he knew he'd always have it in a pinch. It stuck to him like burdock seed. Here it was, dogging him again, putting his very life in the balance. He stumbled pointedly, trying to unclick his tongue and round out the sounds. He cringed at the reaction he expected from Baldrick as he finished.

"Oh mercy on me, you can take the boy out of Woodglence, but you can't take Woodglence out of the boy!" Baldrick guffawed, pulling at his beard. "Come, soldier, open up. We'll let him pass. It's just his marchland accent." Again there appeared a gleam of mockery in his small sable eyes, but no longer as veiled as before. They waited for the huge door to be unbarred and unbolted by the sentries on duty within. The Captain bade the pikemen resume their post as guards outside the gate. The door swung open.

"After you, Master Draper Dorassy," Baldrick trilled with leering gusto.

The door banged shut behind Frysan. He was now sealed into the Silver Palace.

Frysan swallowed hard and fell in behind Baldrick, nursing his limp. He followed the big man's swift step down a barrel-vaulted corridor of rough-hewn stone, glancing at the guardroom adjacent to the great oak entrance door where the two gatekeepers had returned to their game of dice. From this passageway he and Baldrick emerged into the heart of the Silver Palace, an enclosed courtyard lit bright by lanterns fixed atop fluted stone posts. These were spaced at even intervals around a magnificent fountain in the shape of a harp that splashed crystal jets of water from its forepillar into a wide marble basin. They reached a covered portico at the far end of the courtyard, where a doorway opened into an elegant parlour with a lofty ceiling that rose into one of the palace's turrets. They passed through this room, then turned in to another hallway with smooth marble floors and elaborately wainscotted walls that boasted beakhead mouldings in silver leaf beneath a frieze of river scenes.

They had reached the royal lodgings. Baldrick had remained silent, almost pensive. Frysan would need to take some kind of decisive action fast, but it would have to wait until he gained admittance to the Queen. No other way.

Midway down the passage, hazy with the soft light of low-trimmed oil lamps, two guards dressed in the livery of the Mindal stood before a closed door marked with the royal insignia, a rampant stag clutching a golden harp between outstretched hoofs. The armed men at the door slipped smartly to attention as their superior officer approached. From within could be heard a baby's restless wailing.

A nod from Baldrick permitted the guards to stand easy.

"On my word, sir, but the brat's been mewling the whole day long. And most of the evening too," said the huskier of the two, rolling his eyes.

"Oh, it's a hard life of plaguing mischief you've got, soldier, but it's his mother the Queen that spoils my nights with her colic spite. In any event, it won't be long before we're quit of the woman and her bawling babe, isn't that so, Master Draper?"

Frysan cursed the man's hard-nosed insolence.

"You, soldier," he continued to the same man, "go find Sergeant Cuff and bid him meet me here on the double!" Baldrick turned to the remaining guard. "Now stand aside and let us enter. Leave the bolt of the door unshot."

Without ceremony Baldrick wrenched the door open and stomped into a large antechamber. Hung with fading old tapestries, its walls were lined with richly upholstered chairs. The figure of the Captain of the Guard seemed outlandish in the room—brute and uncouth, a formless lump of tallow encased in armour. He closed the door behind Frysan.

"Woman, are you in your chamber? I've brought you a visitor. A friend of yours, or so he claims," he barked above the baby's crying and swaggered towards the velvet curtain that covered the entrance to the royal bedchamber itself. For a brief moment

Frysan considered pulling out his hidden dagger. The temptation was strong to plunge it full into Baldrick's back—or his neck, if he could find it. With all his girth this man would not die quickly or easily. The blade would have to cut through the chain mesh of his hauberk and mounds of flesh to reach the vital organs. All the man had to do was cry out once to pull the whole garrison down on Frysan's head. Better to wait until they penetrated farther out of earshot into the royal apartments.

"Come along now." Baldrick craned his head back and scowled at Frysan, as he parted the curtain before him, revealing a large bedchamber. Stepping in, he moved aside, distancing himself from Frysan.

He was being careful all of a sudden. Frysan would have to show his hand and strike soon or risk being taken.

At the far end, before a bed that was recessed into the wall under a splendid tester, there knelt a woman stooped over a cradle, rocking it gently and crooning a lullaby, her face hidden by a cascade of auburn tresses. The wails of the baby who lay in the cradle had subsided to pitiful wheezes. The woman lifted her head and recoiled at the presence of Baldrick, who obviously frightened her, although she made a brave attempt to hide it. Now a look of puzzlement crossed her face at the sight of an unknown stranger in the garb of a merchant. The closely guarded confinement was taking its toll of her, streaking her hair with grey and adding careworn wrinkles to her finely chiselled features.

Frysan felt an upwelling of pity. Clearly the Queen was reaching the limits of her strength. The weary days had stretched into weeks, into months. It had begun with the hunting accident in the Deer's Slunk. The King had been gored by a stag, an injury from which he never recovered. He had grown steadily worse. Now he lay dying. Dinas Antrum was awash with rumours, dark hints from the Mindal that the day of reckoning was at hand. Rumours that soon the Queen would consider herself fortunate to be sharing a small cell in Tower Dinas with her daughters and the infant Crown Prince. Rumours that by one means or another the King would be dead.

Frysan stepped past Baldrick to approach the Queen, who lifted her hands from the cradle and rose, straightening herself to full height. It was the first time he had seen her at close quarters. No diamond-studded tiara or beautiful gown set her apart. Instead she was dressed in a loose blue smock embroidered simply at the neck and girdled with a narrow white belt. Her baby began to whimper again. She picked it up, kissed and soothed it, clutching it with both hands to her bosom. Frysan made a courtly bow.

"Your Highness, your humble servant, Elzemon Dorassy, Master Draper, as ready to be at your service as ever I have been all those many occasions in the past. The years since we last met have not dimmed your splendour," he declared, seeking to lock eyes with hers. He winked. She stood there baffled. Again he winked.

Everything within these walls smelled of a closing trap. He chafed at the unbroken tension, calculating his chances if he were to wheel around and close with Baldrick all of a sudden, armed only with a dagger. Frysan resisted the impulse to look over his shoulder. The Queen remained wary. He had come to her with the Captain of the Guard. She must suppose he was one of the man's cronies. A wise assumption, but a very awkward one at the moment.

"I don't understand." Ignoring his pleading face and gestures, she looked past Frysan to Baldrick for an explanation.

"Oh, but you will, you will, Your Highness," he said with an unusual deference. He edged his way to the curtain, resting his left hand on the pommel of his sword. The fingers of the other caressed the dagger strapped to his belt. "I'll leave you now with Master Dorassy for just a wee bit of a moment. Don't go away, he'll answer all your questions quite handily, I'm sure." Baldrick smirked as he backed his way out of the bedchamber past the drawn curtain and then disappeared. They could hear a scuffle of sounds and then the faint rattle of the door latch. Queen Asturia retreated a step or two from Frysan, holding fast to her baby, all swaddled in blankets.

"No, no don't be afraid, Your Highness. Don't worry, I'm not here to hurt you. Listen closely, we haven't much time," he whispered, casting a nervous glance over his shoulder in the direction of the antechamber. "I'm Frysan Wright, Captain of your highland Life Guardsmen, loyal to a man." He had slipped into his highland brogue. It seemed to reassure her, just as it had betrayed him to Baldrick. At once he could see the painful look of doubt begin to lift from her eyes. "My men and I—we're here to set you free, to take you and the Prince to safety, and the King too, but our ruse has failed. Baldrick has sniffed me out. There, the open door there, where does it lead?" He pointed with his finger to the looming darkness that lay beyond a door that was flung wide open on its hinges, two lamps on either side.

"It's another bedchamber. It's where the King lies, close so I can tend to him. The windows have bars just like this room. There used to be another door in that room, but they've bolted it fast."

Frysan flung aside his draper's cap and his cloak and reached back over his shoulder to pull the dagger from out of the sheath next to his skin while he kicked off his boots with an inward sigh of relief. They had pinched and hobbled him, making his aching tendon worse. Now in stocking feet at least he could fight and manoeuvre.

"There's no way out except the way I've just come?"

"Yes. But wait, put that weapon away. It won't do you much good against a sword. I can give you something far better. Here, hold my little Starigan for a moment." She entrusted the child to him, while he managed with one hand to slip the dagger back into its hidden sheath. She hurried over to the bed and began feeling with her fingers at the base of one of the elaborate spiral posts that held the canopy.

"Hurry, please hurry, as you value your life, somebody's coming." Encumbered by the child, Frysan made shift to lay it on the bed, but stopped short.

"There!" she said.

There had been the slightest of clicks and then half the bedpost flew open on unseen hinges bringing to light a superbly tooled leather scabbard, open end down so that it rested against the quillions of a sword laid upright. It was made of steel so finely tempered and so sharp that she had to take care not to nick herself as she drew it forth from the scabbard and held it out to Frysan, glinting in the lamplight. The thing was marvellously wrought.

"But m-my lady . . . th-this sword?" he stammered. His eyes gazed upon the strange runic characters scored across the length of the blade.

"Don't ask questions, Master Guardsman. Here, take it quickly."

No sooner had they exchanged sword and baby between them than Baldrick burst into the bedchamber and pushed past the curtain, sided by a tall rangy soldier with a dour face. Both wore helmets and had entered with swords drawn. Baldrick's was a great double-edged broadsword that he held lightly before him, two hands on the grip.

"On my heart! Look what our limping young Guardsman found for himself while we were gone. Very naughty of him, wasn't it, Cuff? Good way for a fellow to get hurt. And his manners too! Imagine that? Strewing the floor with his draper's rags. And worst of all, lying to his sweet uncle Baldrick, who's been the soul of kindness, who's done everything he can to make the lad's visit to the palace such a pleasant one. Tsk, tsk, I am disappointed, nephew, gravely disappointed." Baldrick laughed without losing any of his steely aspect, for he stood ready, regarding Frysan with chill eyes.

"Oh, strange. Look at the sword he's got. Not your everyday blade, is it?" the sergeant said.

"Aye, so the rumour was true. They'd found it."

"What do you mean, sir? Who found what?"

"Never mind. You'll learn in due course, once we nail his hide to the floor."

"Shall I call out the garrison, sir, now we see he's a fighting cock and armed?" Cuff looked askance at Frysan, as the Guardsman sliced the air, measuring the heft and feel of his new weapon. The Queen, clutching her baby, who had begun to whimper, backed off towards the door of the King's sickroom.

"No, no. Are you daft, man? Spoil a perfect chance to be rid of the witch and her spawn. As for her husband, we'll speed him on his way too. The beauty of it all is that they're going to think it was done by this fop of a draper—or Guardsman. And death gnaw our bones, if the two of us can't carve him up and lay him in his grave."

Frysan leaped forward to the attack, slashing at Cuff's shoulder, forcing him to parry backhanded. He wheeled back, feeling the wind of Baldrick's great blade, which came crashing down on the spot he had just vacated, even as Cuff swung his sword around, regaining his guard position. Cuff was a warier fighter. Frysan made to lunge at Baldrick, but pulled back when he saw how quickly the man had managed to recover. He backstepped to the centre of the room.

Frysan's neck hairs prickled and he could almost hear his heart thumping against his rib cage. Baldrick advanced. Here was a more dangerous adversary than he had expected. For a man his size, armed as he was, he was showing himself to be amazingly sure-handed and nimble on his feet. He would have to use his own speed and footwork to good advantage if he were to stand a chance against this deadly pair.

His opponents separated, trying to circle him. Baldrick moved in directly upon him, his face cut by a cruel mocking smile, while Cuff stalked his way sidelong, weaving his sword, forcing Frysan to divide his attention and shift his eyes back and forth from one man to the other, even as he continued to retreat before them. If he could find a corner, he could at least cover his back. He would have to dispose of one of them quickly—probably Cuff. He appeared to be the lesser swordsman. Otherwise he had no doubt they would be feeding the dogs with his carcass.

Catch him off balance and run him through, that was what he had to do. Then somehow he would tackle Baldrick. Overconfidence would be his weapon. Lead them on a bit, make them think he was easy pickings, and that they had as good as finished him, and then strike back, fast and hard, before they knew what hit them.

Without warning he took a quick flurry of steps backwards as if seeking to escape, sidling to his right, which brought him in line with Cuff. Without thinking the two soldiers were drawn into his wake, their first instinct being to match the pace of their lone opponent and keep up the pressure they were exerting on him. Cuff stood closer. He was caught leaning forward, slightly overbalanced, when Frysan stopped short and sprang to the attack once more. A quick feint to the head brought Cuff's arm up, exposing his side. Before he could recover, Frysan slipped below his guard and thrust his sword point full into the man's ribs, skewering him through from side to side.

Cuff groaned and collapsed, looking dumbly at the red pool of blood welling from his side onto his quilted tunic. Frysan pulled his sword clear and leaped back stumbling, tripping over the leather boots he had cast off earlier. He scrambled to regain his footing, relieved to have trimmed the odds. Baldrick stepped in with a slashing side cut that would have sliced him in two if he had been just a moment too slow in reacting. Again Baldrick moved in, this time with a downward clout, grunting loudly as he delivered it. He missed. He brought his sword up from where it had thudded into the floor and tried again. His stretched tendon forgotten in this fight for his life, Frysan ducked and dodged the blows, scrambling over the Queen's four-poster bed to evade his big assailant. Baldrick was puffing now and so drenched with sweat that he flung away his helmet and mopped his brow with his free hand.

"Why, you little dog-fox, you'll get tired of dancing your little jig, and I'll split you open from crown to groin!"

"You'll have to catch me first, you boorish hell-kite." Frysan returned to the middle of the bedchamber, watching for some opening in the man's defences. He was a formidable adversary, no doubt about that, quick and strong for all his suet-like girth. And no fool, for he paused now to catch his breath and marshal his thoughts, a smug smile playing on his lips.

"Very well, then, a thousand plagues on you, dog. You can go on playing soldier with your toy sword and marching backwards when you fight . . . Like a true and trusty Life Guardsman. That's all the energy I'll spend on you now that I've limbered up the old sword arm. My men will be more than pleased to take care of you . . . after I've finished the business that you, my friend, will take the credit for. Imagine your fame in the chronicle books of Arvon . . . Mighty Slayer of Kings, Queens, and baby Princes," Baldrick said, still catching his wind.

Half-turning, he backed his way to the lamplit entrance of the King's sickroom. All that could be heard now was the snorting wheeze of the heavyset man's breathing. For all his taunts, Baldrick was playing things very carefully, never letting his eyes stray from Frysan.

A flicker of movement erupted from the shadows of the sickroom just inside the door. Someone lurked there, creeping up ever so silently behind Baldrick. For the briefest of moments Frysan's eyes widened in surprise. Then shifting his gaze, he narrowed them again to focus on Baldrick.

Out of the corner of his eye, he saw the Queen and what she intended. With her hand extended to the right side of Baldrick's waist, she was reaching for the hilt of the dagger sheathed at his belt. She had moved so close to Baldrick that Frysan saw her wince at the sour reek of his unwashed body. She had the dagger, was lifting it free. The slightest of steps backwards and he would stumble on her. He would cut her down without hesitation. The Queen would not stand a chance.

"Come then. Bodes well for the Mindal, putting its trust in

a hedge-born fishmonger like you," Frysan said. It was now or never. He had to close with Baldrick. Anything to move him away from the Queen back into the open area of the bedchamber. "Come get me. I'll wait for you on this spot—right here, like a rooted tree," he shouted, brandishing his sword, tight with the expectation of combat.

"Crows and daws! You're looking at a fellow that's not stirring an inch. If you think I'm playing your game again—I've given you enough chances to oblige me. You come here to me! Come fetch your treat from Uncle Baldrick, or shall I tell Their Royal Highnesses you've wet your breeches and are indisposed?" Broadsword held with two hands before him in a guard position, ever watchful, Baldrick made a little half-turn and lurched back a step.

"What's this?" he exclaimed in mid-stride, his progress blocked, feeling the jab of the dagger as nothing more than a pinprick at first, a tear in his hauberk. Thrust into his side by the Queen, the keenly sharp dagger sliced viciously through the protective chain mail. Baldrick's own momentum helped drive the thing into his flesh hilt-deep. Groaning with pain and rage, he twisted, tore free of the blade, and caught sight of the Queen, still clutching her bloody weapon and wide-eyed with horror. Not wanting to lay open his back to an opponent like Frysan, he resisted the impulse to lunge headlong after her, even as she withdrew, back-stepping out of his reach towards her husband's sickbed in the corner of the room. Frightened by the fresh outbreak of noise, her baby started wailing again.

"Why, you grey-coated leprous witch!" Baldrick roared, ignoring the blood that oozed from his wound. He backed his way into the bedchamber, pivoting around in order to cover Frysan while he advanced on the Queen, his eyes glaring deadly hate.

"Now I'll fix you and yours for good. Blood for blood, my Queen."

Frysan kept pace and stepped warily into the sickchamber. The King lay on a simple bed, his infant son swaddled at his feet. With Baldrick's gory dagger held before her, the Queen took her stand by her lord, like a cornered animal, mindful only of fending off harm from her husband and child. Now her baby had worked himself into a frenzy of crying, letting loose at the top of his lungs, as if he sensed his mother's fear and the imminence of the danger.

"Stand off, get away! Help, someone, help, for the love of heaven! You, Guardsman there, do something, stop him!" Her voice quavered, while Baldrick came on slowly, holding his broadsword at mid-body, seeming to take gruesome relish in prolonging her horror and fear.

Frysan moved closer, calculating his chances of evading that wicked blade in these smaller quarters, making ready to feint and lunge—one last desperate bid to save the royal family.

"Aye, come, my light-footed friend," Baldrick beckoned, a scowl on his face. He stopped for a moment, shifting the point of his weapon, lifting it to shoulder level. "Let's see what you can do on a smaller dancing floor. A dashing figure wouldn't you cut with a peg leg, my limping Guardsman?"

Quick as a coiled snake, he sent the blade of his broadsword whistling through the air in a deadly arc that would have severed Frysan's knees had he not leaped aside like a cat. As he fought to regain his balance, his feet shot out from under him on the polished marble floor, slipping on a small pool of Baldrick's blood, as slick as mutton grease. The shock sent Frysan's sword flying out of his hand right to Baldrick's feet, who stopped it with his boot. No way could Frysan retrieve it. Grinning mirthlessly, Baldrick kicked it behind him, like a bull pawing the ground. It rattled to a stop under the window of the sickroom, its dark steel bars visible in the dim light. Frysan rolled to evade the big man as he closed, skittering across the floor spider-like. The baby's cries grew shriller yet. Baldrick swung his body around, aware of the Queen's deadly rage behind him, fearing yet another cold prick of the dagger.

But it was not the Queen that met his eyes as he turned. The King himself in nightshirt tottered towards him gaunt-faced, his cheeks sunken and right eye drooping. With two hands he bore the sword lost by Frysan.

"Stand, Asturia . . . Back, Guardsman . . ." commanded the King, his voice weak and breaking.

Baldrick froze in place. From the King's sword there emanated a faint glow. The soldier rubbed the back of his hand across his eyes. He took a deep breath. Then again his eyes narrowed as a cruel grin played across his face.

"Why, if it isn't our anointed sovereign of sighs and groans come back to life. Arvon's very own lump of gilded clay ready for battle! And most becomingly dressed. I'm shaking in my boots, sire. Well, we'll just take care of first things first, kings before commoners and all that." Despite the jeers his eyes betrayed a hint of doubt. His face grown pallid, he winced at the searing pain of the knife wound. The advancing sword kept its glimmer.

"For all that, I am King."

Fear shadowed Baldrick's face. King Colurian shuffled closer. Baldrick raised his broadsword over his head, preparing to throw all his might into one lethal swing, a blow so powerful no smaller sword could hope to parry it, one that would cleave the frail King's torso in two.

The King closed with him.

Frysan edged his way towards the unevenly matched combatants, his own dagger now in hand. He found himself assailed by questions, entranced by the unearthly gleam of the King's sword, now grown more luminous still. Queen Asturia cried out.

Looming over the King, Baldrick abandoned all thought of subtlety. He roared, his rage boiling over, and down fell the broadsword like a bludgeon.

Up came the King's sword to block, his arm slow and palsied, but quick enough to meet the blow. Frysan tensed for the brief clang and the murderous cut that would follow, ready to leap to the attack and plunge his knife into the king-killer.

His ears filled with the sound of shattering glass.

The King reeled, his sword unscathed, even as Baldrick stared dumbly at his own weapon, now reduced to a mere hilt. Shards of the blade lay strewn across the chamber. The big man's knees buckled and he slumped dazed to the floor. The trickle of blood from the wound in his side now became a flood.

Frysan sprang forward with his knife.

"No, Guardsman, stay your hand. I'll not pass from this world in a welter of needless slaughter. Leave the man be! He's dying, as am I . . . Come, help me to my bed." The King's voice slurred like that of a drunk man, weaker now and cracking with strain, as he too sank to the floor, letting his sword fall with a clatter.

Queen Asturia rushed to her husband's side, but by the time Frysan laid him on his mattress, the King was dead.

It was dusk, and damp too with a raw edge which boded the coming of winter. Sharp-set to reach Ashwood Hall before nightfall,

Frysan pushed on numbly through the Deer's Slunk, leading the party down the lonely stretch of royal forest. This had been the king's chase. Threaded with tangled thickets and beaver meadows, it was a well-favoured refuge for game.

Frysan lapsed into a daydream, his senses lulled by weariness and hunger and the confident knowledge that they had come almost to the end of the first and most critical leg of their journey. One night's welcome rest in Ashwood Hall and then tomorrow they would set out again, taking backcountry trails in order to achieve safe haven in Arvon's highlands.

Frysan stifled a yawn. Getting away from the Silver Palace with the Queen and Prince had been surprisingly easy and uneventful. Between Eldor's modest detail of men and the Life Guardsmen hidden under the tarp in the wherry, they had managed to overcome the small contingent of soldiers placed by Baldrick on night watch in the grounds above the King's Stairs, taking them unawares. The only casualty was that headstrong fellow who had ignored Eldor's call to surrender and had brought the horn to his lips to blow an alarm. Eldor had choked him of his wind with a well-placed arrow. Determined to play the hero, that one. Cost him his life. Frysan shook his head and grimaced. And the two men-at-arms who controlled the postern gate, they had shown precious little fight, letting themselves be locked into a small armoury closet with scarcely more than a murmur. Hard to blame them, faced as they were with the naked steel of Lightenhaft—a sword with a highly persuasive edge, even when it did not glow.

Frysan's left hand slipped to the pommel of the blade that hung by his side, his fingertips tracing the finely tooled leather and metal of the hilt. A wonderfully wrought piece of work. Like any Arvonian, Frysan knew the ancient lore attached to Lightenhaft, that it underwent a transformation only when wielded by one of royal blood and anointing. The King had found it by chance just over a year ago. Frysan recognized the sword for what it was as soon as he laid eyes on it.

It had been a great discovery, to find the sword of Ardiel, the first High King of Arvon, when for countless ages it had been thought lost. Queen Asturia had explained the story of the sword in detail to Frysan earlier. The times being what they were, the Queen bade her husband tell no one, but to keep the famous weapon hidden, a secret shared between the two of them. Better to hold it in reserve, she had argued, depending on how events unfolded. Thankfully Colurian had been content to heed her advice. It helped matters that by that stage even he, for all his earlier blindness to what was happening in Arvon, had begun to suspect that the Mindal harboured treasonous ambitions.

Frysan fought to stay in his saddle. Exhaustion swept over him in waves.

The worst part of the escape from the Silver Palace had been having to hoist the body of the dead King over his shoulders and carry it out of the bedchamber to the royal barge even as he kept a firm grip on Lightenhaft in readiness. He had laid down the King's body only for the few minutes it took to deal with the guards at the postern gate.

Once he and his fellow Life Guardsmen, together with the Queen and her infant, had all boarded the barge moored at the King's Stairs, they eased the high-prowed craft out into the wider reaches of the river. More than once they had been forced to douse their torches and sit at anchor in a reedy bend of the Dinastor in an effort to evade the Mindal's patrol boats. They manoeuvred the barge upriver by slow stages under power of its oars as far as the Queen's Hythe, a sheltered landing in a calm sidewater. There the party disembarked amid fields and forests well outside the city of Dinas Antrum. They were met by their escort, a troop of Frysan's comrades led by Mactrin, Eldor's second-in-command.

Frysan had never understood what Eldor saw in the fellow—a brooding grumpy soul with mutton-chop whiskers and a dogleg nose in a furtive cockeyed face, always disgruntled about something or other, forever cursing the air blue under his breath.

Mactrin's troopers, in all a good score of them, were mounted on horses and dressed unobtrusively in leather jerkins and leggings, like simple men-at-arms. They had brought a covered wagon, so crude, with its ill-greased wheels and rickety side panels, that it seemed hardly fit for a woodcutter or charcoal burner, let alone the Queen of Arvon and her newborn son. Still, it had allowed the two Life Guardsmen who had been charged with procuring it to slip out of Dinas Antrum in disguise and make their way to the Queen's Hythe without drawing unwelcome attention to themselves.

And the wagon would hold together long enough to bring a woman and her child to the Summer Palace, even on this stretch of ill-kept trackway—a less frequently used approach to the palace grounds, one normally reserved for the King on his hunting forays. It had been decided that, as they drew nearer to their destination, they should swing off the main road and take this route northwards into the Deer's Slunk. That way Frysan and his men could make a discreet reconnaissance of the Hall first, check to see if it was all clear, starting with the abandoned gamekeeper's cottage nestled in a coppice on the edge of the Slunk, where if all went according to plan Wilum would be waiting for them.

Frysan rode ahead in advance of the escort. He made yet another effort to stave off sleep, straining to keep his eyes open, fighting to remain alert. The trouble was that, after the tumult and strife in Dinas Antrum, the wooded depths of the Deer's Slunk in their shrouded fall colours reminded him too much of his home far away in the highlands of Arvon. He thought of his wife and infant son. It took the edge off his watchfulness, gave him a deceptive sense of security.

Otherwise he might have noticed with alarm the weasel on the moss-grown log preparing to spring viciously on a hapless rabbit that stood mute, too frightened to squeal or run from its doom. Or the sudden absence of birdsong. It should have filled the thick veil of brush crowding the trackway here on either side, which was carpeted with a ghostly profusion of corpse plants, an ill omen, their creamy paleness like a winding sheet in the lengthening shadows cast by the trees.

Frysan glanced back wearily at the slow-moving wagon as it clattered over stone and root, its driver slumped with fatigue, while a packhorse plodded alongside. Smiling to himself at the thought that they had kept one step ahead of the Mindal and its armed thugs, he felt his roan gelding misstep and lurch out of control. He heard a crack as he whipsawed forward, like dry kindling being snapped. Something sped at him, flew past him, brushing the nape of his neck.

Pitched out of his saddle, he tumbled headlong into the thick clump of bushes crowding the edge of the pathway. Had his horse not stepped into a frozen rut and stumbled just at that moment, the arrow would have ripped a hole in his face instead of crackling to a stop in the brittle autumn foliage of the trees beyond.

"To arms! To arms! Ambush!" Eldor's shouts were the last words he heard, before a sharp blow to the head stopped him short and sent the world around him spinning into darkness.

✧   ✧   ✧

The moans of wounded men . . . his fellow Life Guardsmen . . . and others at hand too, a great many voices, speaking harsh words in a strange tongue. Swords being slid from scabbards . . . men trampling the undergrowth . . . the hustle and bustle of movement. A baby crying. And cold, how he was stiff and cold.

Groping his way as through a slowly thinning mist, Frysan struggled to lift himself up on an elbow, dazed and groggy, so deep in a laurel thicket that he felt smothered. The stiffness. It was all he could do to summon any real response from his limbs. And the jabbing pain in his ribs. The hilt end of Lightenhaft. He was sprawled awkwardly over the sword. Shifting his weight with a grunt, he moved the weapon. His head throbbed.

How long had he been unconscious? A few minutes maybe? Couldn't be hours . . . He should have worn a heavier cloak.

They had been attacked. That much was clear. He shivered.

The ambushers had carried the field. Torches and lanterns everywhere. Too close.

He sensed danger and stifled a groan as fresh throbs of pain flooded his wakening brain. Gingerly he touched a gash just above his temple.

"So what is the final count? Have we caught them all in our net, your comrades-in-arms? Good fighters. They mounted a stout resistance, it must be said to their credit."

Frysan tensed. Someone stood near, his words carried by the stiffening breeze. Strange sort of accent. A cultivated, formal Arvonian garnished with a sinister oiliness. He could not place it, although in his mind's eye he imagined the speaker as a slender elegant figure—but dangerous, smoothly dangerous.

"Not surprised. I trained most of them, never got no credit for it." It was Mactrin. "As for netting them all, there's one man missing."

"Which one is that?"

"Frysan Wright. Wee Tot I calls him."

Never to my face, you snivelling piece of worm meat. Frysan bit his lip.

"Aye, Wee Tot, the esteemed leader of our happy little troop of loyal Life Guardsmen. The one what donned the draper's rags and snatched away the woman and her babe. He's got to be hereabouts. Can't have gone far, what with the lake and a pond blocking his escape on either side. Not to mention them guards of yours—"

"It was an ideal location that you chose for us to make the ambush, Guardsman."

"Didn't I tell you it was near perfect?"

"Nevertheless, if this captain of yours did manage to escape?"

"No, impossible, he's still here right enough. Must be dead or wounded for him not to be showing his face. Either way, it don't matter. We'll find him. Puffed up young woodcock he may be. A perfect little eight-penny counterfeit, taking it on himself to be captain over us older men and him but an unlicked lad. All the same, one thing's sure, he'd never take flight to save his own hide. Not our Wee Tot. Leave the Queen and her princeling to their own? Not on your life. Not a fellow like him, what with his self-important notions of honour and duty to King and country. Knowing Wee Tot, I'd lay heavy odds he's dead or wounded mortal."

"We must find him, Guardsman, else the agreement we have between us stands null and void. There must be no witnesses. There will be no witnesses if all these brave comrades of yours lie silent in their graves. The Mindal, astute men they are, will suppose the obvious, that it was your stalwart companions that stole away the Queen and her son. Oh, how they will fret and fume, the petty burghers of the Mindal! We must cover our tracks and bury their bodies where no one will ever discover them—"

"The Charnel Pit. So I said, right by here. A place so deep that no one's like to find their bones in a thousand years."

"The survival of even one man could spoil it. It would make all these elaborate arrangements of mine pointless or doubtful at best, something I will not tolerate . . . You are right, I am certain. No doubt the fellow is near. All the same, my men will find him. I will have them scour every inch of the area until they root him out."

Frysan hardly dared to breathe, let alone move. Where were the Queen and Prince Starigan?

Again he considered the weird accent, so overlaid with a sneering contempt for Mactrin, the foul traitor. He could almost picture Mactrin's shifty-eyed smugness. The intonation and colour of the other man's voice struck Frysan as enigmatic, archaic somehow, but with a creeping, shadowy quality. Different from anything he had heard in Dinas Antrum, one of the great cosmopolitan cities in Ahn Norvys. His mind fumbled and groped as he tried to place the oddly formed syllables. The frustrating thing was that there was a thread here—something tantalizingly familiar in the accent. The man's words carried a recognizable ring. If he could just make the connection.

Like the tumblers of a lock falling into order, his thoughts slipped into place. His mind flashed back to his days as a schoolboy learning the Old Tongue. This fellow talking to Mactrin, he was like . . . like someone from Ardiel's time all those centuries ago coming back and trying to speak present-day Arvonian. Hard to explain, but that was the impression the man's voice gave—of someone ancient and not only ancient but anciently cunning. Deviously, malignantly cunning, with a mind that bore the long subtlety of a time span calculated in centuries, not years.

"First I shall have my men finish piling the rest of the bodies onto the wagon," the stranger said. "It will not take but a few more minutes. A tidy load of offal to tip into the pit, once we have found your Guardsman friend."

"He ain't no friend of mine!"

"Good. I would scarcely have guessed it. In the meantime, I shall take a moment to see to the comfort of the dowager Queen and heir apparent, such important royal personages. We must take care to make certain they are properly prepared for the long journey ahead and not too severely inconvenienced by the conditions of their capture."

"How about I have a look around for him myself while you're doing what you're doing? Starting in the bend of the road there in all them bushes. He might have crawled in there if he was wounded."

"By all means, Guardsman, make yourself useful until my men are ready to hunt."

There was a further brief exchange of parting words that Frysan could not make out, as the wind had shifted.

Frysan struggled to his feet, slowly pulling Lightenhaft from its scabbard. Not fifty yards off in either direction, armed men clustered the road with lanterns that cast a flickering glow into the darkness. Frysan stood silent for a moment.

He considered the situation. Behind and ahead, the attackers choked his routes of escape. They had been set on by a small army, first-rate fighting men who made no mistakes and knew exactly how to plan an ambush. Besides that, they plainly out-numbered the convoy of Life Guardsmen. Cammas, Eldor . . . they had not stood the ghost of a chance. Frysan fought back tears of grief and rage. If only his longbow had not been strapped to the saddle of the roan! He would have no trouble sending at least one or two of these villainous wretches to a well-deserved grave. A light bobbed close along the roadway. No mistaking that gait. Skulking slowly, his sword drawn and lantern in hand, Mactrin probed his way.

"Come, come, my triple-turned knave . . ." Frysan whispered to himself, dropping to a crouch, waiting for Mactrin to approach nearer. Before drawing level with Frysan along the road, however, he stopped for a moment, then turned into the woods, wading through the undergrowth, so close that Frysan might have run him through without warning.

"Psst, psst, here."

"Who-who's that?" Mactrin rounded toward the voice, but too late to bring his own sword into play. "Why, Captain Frysan, you're alive. I've been looking—" he stammered, staring at the blade tip poised at his unguarded chest.

"Cut the drivel, you double-faced botch of nature," hissed Frysan through clenched teeth, "or, I swear I'll fillet you right before your eyes."

"B-but I—"

"By the glence, man, you'd better shut your trap!"

Mactrin recoiled and shook his head.

"That's good. You're not nearly as lean-witted as you look. Now let go your sword. Just open your fingers and let it drop."

Mactrin's sword fell from his right hand.

"There's a smart fellow. Now then, we'll have our talk. To begin, tell me who these men are, where they're from, how many of them there are. Loosen your tongue, man, or I'll gladly loosen it for you."

"I-I don't know. They all jabber in a language I've never heard, on my life, maybe a hundred of them or even two. It's difficult to tell on a dark night like this."

"All right then, let's take another tack." Frysan fought to restrain his anger, trembling as he nudged his sword point deeper through Mactrin's leather jerkin, forcing him back against a large boulder, where the lantern he still held clanged against the rock.

"Stop, stop. You're drawing blood . . . I'll tell you everyth—"

"Their leader, that strange-talking fellow you were just talking to, he speaks our language well enough. Who is he? What's his name?"

"I swear to you, I don't know. Gives me the creeps. He's played it tight-lipped, never named himself, not that I dare ask him. Ain't healthy to know too much—"

"It's not healthy to know too little either. Now tell me straight, how did you turn traitor? Where did you make contact with these men?"

Mactrin let out a sigh of resignation.

"All right, all right. It all started with a chap in the Cranes about a fortnight ago. I'd seen him before in the place, nursing his ale and sitting real quiet and contented like mine uncle on a bench by the hearth. A foreigner, you could tell from the cut of his cloth and the broken manner of his Arvonian. If he was a spy, I thought, he'd have made a better effort to blend in. Anyway, now and again he'd flash me a smile and tip his cap like we was mates from way back. Made me think he was a pleasant sort of chap. All the same, I didn't pay him no heed 'til he and I, we happened to stumble out of the Cranes together one night. As we was making our way down Limehouse Alley, we was set on by four or five footpads. This fellow, Delyddlo's his name, or so he claimed, a mason by profession, he fought them off right handily, almost before I could get my own weapon free. Body o' me, he knew how to fight. A man could see that. Why, he sent them lice-ridden cutpurses scrambling for their lives.

"Well, after that, I'm full of warm fellow feeling for the man, like we was comrades-in-arms, and he gets real friendly, says he's from Sifadda, a stranger to these parts, and wouldn't I stop by with him at his place for a nightcap, meet his fellow countryman who craved company but didn't like going to drinking holes, didn't like jostling with all them hordes of people. So this fellow Delyddlo brought me up to his garret, and it didn't take but a moment for me to get the notion something's out of kilter, for his friend turned out to be the very fellow you inquired about a moment ago, the leader of this gang of men. He's a fine-baited talker who comes right out and says to me with that fleering face of his that he's heard all about me, about what a fine soldier I am, and that he knows full well us Life Guardsmen are busy hatching some plot or other to snatch the King and Queen out from under the very nose of the Mindal."

Frysan, standing easier now, retracted the point of his blade from Mactrin's chest. His anger had lost some of its white heat.

"Listen close, you'd scarcely believe what he told me next," Mactrin continued, his voice grown solemn.

"Go on, then. What did he tell you?"

"Well, he said . . . Do you know what he said? He said . . . He said, you was a dead man!" He yelled, defiant, even as he swung out with the lantern he still held gripped in his hand, knocking Frysan's sword aside while he leaped clear before his captor, reeling and off-balance, could recover.

"To me, to me, I've found him! He's alive! He's here! To me!" Mactrin screamed at the top of his lungs, fighting free of the bushes, heading towards the road, where already the bobbing lights loomed closer, coupled with rising shouts of alarm and command.

For a moment Frysan stood rooted to the spot. Pursuing Mactrin was out of the question.

It was this pause that allowed him to hear it—just the lightest of footfalls rustling in the underbrush at his back. As he whirled around, he raised Lightenhaft point forward at mid-body and lunged with it at a dark figure coming at him in a blur, like a moving fragment of the night, clad wholly in black, a long knife gleaming faintly in the starlight. Frysan felt his thrust connect, tearing through flesh and bone, and quickly pulled his sword free, as he hovered over the body.

He looked back over his shoulder. From every direction armed men were converging on him from the roadway, chain mail glinting in the light that spilled from their lanterns, their swords drawn, egged on by Mactrin's shrieking voice. A glimmer of light caught him, followed by fresh shouts.

Only one way to run—towards the beaver pond. He turned from his pursuers into the woods, tearing through the alders. An arrow swished through the air overhead, rattling branches and twigs—archers. They had brought on their archers.

On he fled, scratched and torn, slashing at the undergrowth with Lightenhaft. He summoned the knowledge about the lie of the land that he had gained from the times his company of Guardsmen had been stationed at the Summer Palace, assigned to watch over King Colurian as he indulged his passion for the hunt.

If he could just skirt the ramparts of the beaver dam, he could lose himself in the woods beyond, or have a fighting chance at any rate.

The ground grew spongy underfoot. He had reached the outlying margin of the sprawling beaver pond. Soon he was pushing aside the withered stalks of cattails and crunching through shallow puddles of half-frozen water. He stopped for a moment to recover his breath. He had outpaced those who followed behind. Their lights shone dimmer in the distance.

To his right sloped a wooded ridge that overlooked the pond. Lots of cover, but too much uphill slogging. Veering left, he found it did not take long for the terrain to rise clear of the sodden bog, becoming more firm. Somewhere ahead—not too far ahead, he hoped—a wing of the beaver dam met the higher ground and closed the outflow of the pond. If he could just turn the corner of the dam and escape the confined stretch of ground between the pond and the road. A tight-sprung trap if there ever was one.

As he topped a small hillock and cleared a belt of trees, a phalanx of armed men with lights came into view. They had plugged the gap, blocking his escape in that direction. The young highlander stopped in his tracks and scrambled to retreat, outpacing the hail of arrows that thudded into the ground at his heels, as the enemy caught him in the outer range of their lantern light.

Panting, he retraced his steps only to find that the original group of pursuers had made up for lost ground. Once again they bore down on him. Running an erratic, darting course, he felt an arrow tear at his leggings and he winced. He stared around wildly. Before him loomed the ridge overlooking the beaver pond, which lay to his left. He scanned its reedy margin. No place to make for but the ridge . . . Or else . . . The idea struck him with sudden force as he ran . . . the beaver lodge, a dark mass of thickly plaited sticks and mud a good twenty-five paces out from the shoreline.

But to what good? Even if he did manage to swim out to the lodge through the ice-cold water, once there he would freeze to death, dripping wet and exposed to the cold. Besides, it would be a dead giveaway where he had headed, leaving a trail of broken ice.

He clambered across the shoulder of the ridge and entered a spinney of oak that fell away to the banks of the pond, so dense he was lost to sight, although those who hunted him washed the heights with their lantern light. Pausing to recover his wind, he glanced upslope and his heart dropped—more light poured onto the crown of the ridge from the other side, casting a crisscrossing maze of lights through the woods below.

The noose was tightening. Unless he found a way to evade them, to escape them as they beat the bushes, he would die this very night.

A kind of madness swept over him, clouding his mind. In a panic he floundered forward through the underbrush.

The ground underfoot changed, becoming clear of vegetation, smooth and well-trodden—a path. Now he broke into a run, until he reached a small clearing fringed with aspens, some of them felled, with stumps that bore the distinctive marks of beaver teeth. He had descended almost to the pond, which lay at the foot of the clearing, its icebound surface pricked with the stiff dry stalks of reeds and cattails—except for a channel, made clear and straight over time by foraging beavers, which led underwater to their lodge offshore.

The whole area of the clearing resembled a sloping shelf, dropping off sheer into a steep ravine along two sides, an ideal spot for the beavers since it afforded them natural protection from their predators while on land. He, however, was trapped in a dead end. No time to backtrack either. His pursuers had drawn too close in the precious moments he had lost, swarming across the flanks of the ridge, hunting for him. Already he could make out the faint glimmer of their lanterns even through the screening trees.

He would run no more. A peace came over him. He had tried escape. Let them come now and he would sell himself dear, as befitted a highlander, one of the King's Life Guardsmen. He stood resigned, his back braced against the trunk of a huge linden tree, as he flexed and turned his wrist, testing the feel of Lightenhaft in his sword hand and steeling himself for the shock of battle.

He looked out over the pond again and regarded the dim mass of the beaver lodge whimsically. He sighed, savouring the calm before the storm.

But wait—

Frysan bolted to attention, abandoned the linden tree, and

strode to the lip of the clearing. There had to be a plunge hole on a ledge like this, otherwise the beavers would have no easy way down to the water. It had to be around here—here in line with the channel. Poking through the tall grass and gnawed aspen branches by the faint light of a slender moon and stars, he looked for the opening the beavers used in order to swim back and forth to their lodge. Glancing up the path, he saw that the enemy's lanterns winked brighter. Where could it be? He grew more frantic. He quartered the ground like a confused hound, then finally discovered the hole, almost falling flat on his face as he stumbled on it. Scarcely more than shoulder width, it was tucked beside a rotting stump, its edges trampled by the coming and going of the beavers.

Here was his sole remaining hope of escape, a way to evade the murderous hue and cry behind him. He did not have the leisure to hesitate, to wonder if the plunge hole would prove broad enough all the way to let him squeeze his body through.

The surface of the water lay some three feet down the hole, yet unfrozen. He slipped Lightenhaft back in its scabbard and knelt at the edge of the opening, which sloped gently to the water. He sucked large drafts of air, priming his lungs for the ordeal ahead.

He launched himself headfirst, every nerve set tingling by the icy shock of the water. Scrabbling with both hands, he pulled himself through the submerged elbow of the passage and gave an inward sigh of relief. The hole's curve downward into the pond was not too narrow or sharply angled. Otherwise, he would never have negotiated it with Lightenhaft belted to his waist—wedged, trapped, unable to retreat, left to drown. He drove himself forward and headed desperately for the pond.

He entered the channel leading to the lodge. He could tell by feel from the cattail stalks on either side of him. Every fibre of his body strained to traverse the space between him and the lodge. So near and yet so far, so measurelessly far. Above him stretched the icy rind of the pond, but to Frysan it was simply a part of the enveloping blackness. Blind, he propelled himself forward through the canal, the supply of air in his lungs affording him less than a minute to make the lodge. He felt his body heat seeping away, his air dwindling, as he swam underwater along the muddy bottom.

The reeds and cattails gave out. He could no longer feel their stalks on either side of him. He felt the grip of panic. He had reached the deeper water. What if he missed the lodge? He was approaching the limits of his endurance. Frysan longed to break the surface ice and take a breath—the sheer bliss of it, one more breath before he let the vengeful cold cradle him in death, even if it meant the hot sting of an arrowhead. He could not hold out much longer. His mind grew fuzzy.

As in a dream, his fingers touched the fretted branches, a large pile of them. Now to find the opening. But how? Should he give up and surface? Only seconds of air left, and cold—cold settling in his bones and sinews like lead. He could barely move his arms and legs. Groping feebly, he sought the submerged entrance to the lodge, willing himself to dive deeper as he felt for the gap, so numb he had almost lost his sense of touch.

Then there came no resistance to Frysan's listless, delving hands. Here was a break in the solid bulk of the structure. He summoned up the last traces of his slackened strength to push his head and shoulders into the opening, driving himself up from muddy footholds within the slanting, water-filled passage, so tight a fit that its side walls tore at his clothes and chafed his insensible body, snagging at his sword belt.

When his head broke the surface of the water, Frysan was nearly unconscious. Sputtering, he gulped the air, sour fetid air rank with the heady smell of beaver musk. He coughed, pushed himself forward. The acrid air burned his throat. The utter darkness of the lodge closed on him—trapped by ice, now trapped by mud. In a delirious attempt to free himself he thrust Lightenhaft once and again and again through the walls of the lodge. It caught and he shook it free. A wisp of cool air came through the holes. His chest heaved and he heard a chittering bark of alarm.

"Stay back . . . stay back . . . must hide here." He was so cold he could barely frame the words.

Shivering, he slashed blindly through the air to keep the animals at bay. With his second pass the tip of the sword made light contact, producing a whimpering squeal of pain.

"Now stay back!" Frysan hissed, hoisting himself out of the bone-chilling water onto a shelf, its bed of dry bark and wood chips only two or three feet from the dome-like roof of the lodge. For a moment he simply lay there, rubbing the circulation back into his legs and relishing the snug warmth of the place.

Without warning, a dim half-light grew in the chamber, allowing him to make out where the beavers had retreated—five or six of them—a huddle of fur and frightened eyes on a ledge-like platform directly across from him, but on a higher level within the lodge. One of the beavers advanced, chittering with agitation, a big buck, threatening. Brandishing Lightenhaft, Frysan prepared to defend himself. Then, to his bewilderment, quick as a flash, the beaver turned and dove into a second plunge hole followed by the others in immediate succession, skittering over the latticework of wood strips and branches.

Darkness filled the inside of the lodge again, as deep as the grave. Were those shouts he heard? Once more a feeble light filtered into the place—from the outside—it came from the outside through the sword holes he had made. Now it faded. In the blackness his teeth chattered as his body adjusted to the stuffy warmth of the place.

Again the light came. His pursuers. They had arrived at the pond, flooding its frozen surface and the lodge with lantern light. Could they know? No, they were just looking, searching.

Frysan listened closely, holding his breath. More cries. Again the light, but coming from the opposite part of the chamber, from where the beavers had huddled. They were checking all approaches to the dome-shaped structure, making certain he had not reached it somehow. They must be standing on that other promontory beyond the ridge, which faced the back of the lodge. Its position in the landscape would allow them to check the whole lodge area for sign of their quarry. Well, they were not going to see much except for unbroken ice and the vault of the beaver dwelling intact.

The darkness returned to envelop him. He could hear nothing more beyond the walls of the lodge. Cramped as he was, he undressed and wrung out his dripping breeches and tunic. Slowly he revived, no longer chilled to the marrow and shivering. After a while he put his clothes back on. No sign of the beavers he had driven from their lair. They had probably retreated to another of their dens.

For what seemed like ages he lay there recovering his strength, Lightenhaft reassuringly at hand, while his clothes turned dry from his own returning body heat. It was a waiting game now. He would have to be patient and allow them time enough to give up their search, clear out, presume he had sneaked past them somehow—at least until nightfall of the next day. No sense in hazarding his new lease on life.

Still he champed at the bit, rehashing the audacious escape he and his men had made from the Silver Palace and their bitter betrayal by Mactrin. Finally, exhausted, he drifted off to sleep, a long sleep ridden by nightmares, haunted by ghostly piteous images of his dead comrades and also more sinister phantoms—Baldrick's evil scowl, Mactrin's sulky face, his nameless enemy's shadowed visage . . .

When he awoke he knew for certain it had to be time to break out of the lodge, its stuffy darkness now oppressive and stifling as a tomb, no longer a haven. Grabbing hold of Lightenhaft he began to hack away at the roof of the chamber, pulling at the roots and branches as they broke free from the frozen mud.

He had waited long enough. Night had fallen once again, the position of the stars showing him that it was close to midnight. He crawled out onto the roof of the structure and recoiled at the chill blast of wind that met him cloakless.

It was a cold night, much colder than the night before. Perhaps it had thickened the ice. At the base of the lodge he tested the surface of the pond warily with the partial weight of one foot, then, finding it held, with both feet. Slowly he ventured another step, then another. The ice started to crack, its hairline fractures spreading in a widening circle around him. Frysan bolted, outrunning the ice as it broke, until he clambered up the bank of the pond and fell sprawling onto grass thick with hoarfrost.

Only then did his eyes stray to the lifeless figure—Mactrin's body, clean without a mark, lying sightless almost next to him on the grass, his face horror-stricken. The abductors of the Queen had gone their way. Frustrated in their search for the sole survivor of their ambush, they had left behind this grim token of their disappointment.

Frysan felt an upwelling of pity, pity for Mactrin and pity for his guiltless comrades—Eldor, Cammas, and the other Life Guardsmen, stalwart friends all, who through no fault of their own had paid the price of another's treason.

After lingering for a moment, Frysan broke his gaze from Mactrin's stiff features, pushed himself from the frozen ground, and sped on his way.

It was time to seek out Wilum.

ONE

Along the Edgemere Road strode a lithe young man of spare build, his cowl pulled back and his tunic unbuttoned, his sparkling blue eyes a sharp contrast to his thatch of thick, sable hair. Morning had dawned bright and clear, heralded by the robin's song, but the air still held a chill which set a tinge of frost on his breath. It was unseasonable, considering they were already more than a week into May. But these were strange days, full of omens and portents not seen in a generation, not since the death of King Colurian and the abduction of his Queen and the Crown Prince.

Take this year's Candle Festival, for example. As usual, the men, women, and children of the remote highland Clanholding of Lammermorn had come together for the Festival on the first day of May, known in the Old Arvonian calendar as Tramys, the Month of Fire. Only the Hordanu, the High Bard of all Ahn Norvys, had been able to keep his candle lit with the new fire on that blustery, sodden evening, but just for a short while after two false starts. Everybody else had been forced to lay aside their candles in favour of sputtering rushlights and flaring links of tow and pitch.

The Festival was followed by eight days of unrelenting rain and wild storms. The constellations wheeled through the sky and formed irregular, quirky shapes that were there for the space of one watch of the night, and then gone the next, blown, it seemed, by the same great winds that were buffeting the whole valley from end to end.

For the first time no one in the Holding could mark the outline of the Longbowman in the spring sky. In its place Sarmel, the Holding's garrulous old pedlar, spent so much time and energy insisting that he could make out the unseasonable outline of the Shepherd that most folk came to agree with him, if only to keep him quiet. Others, more reticent than old Sarmel, murmured that they saw more sinister patterns traced out in the strange new star groupings.

On the horizon, spectacular columns of the Boreal Lights leaped and frolicked like motley giants reaching with long arms for the roof of the world. The air itself was cumbered with a foul, heavy odour like that of ripely fermented must. And more portentous still, despite all the storms and rain, the water level of Deepmere had dipped yet lower, lower than anyone had thought possible, leaving a calcified white ring along the shoreline that gave the ancient lake the look of a grimy, unscoured washbasin.

But the storms had broken, and at long last spring was once again remaking the sheltered valley of Lammermorn. From the south a breeze blew in, freshened by the snowcapped ranks of the Radolan Mountains, bending the grass alongside the hedgerows, wave upon wave. The air smelled pure and clean, full of the sweet heady scent of earth, dew, leaf bud, and the early wildflowers that filled the pastures.

The young man smiled. With a skip-step he picked up his pace, and then broke into full-voiced song.

> "There were three ravens sat in a lone tree
> Downe a downe hay downe downe dee
> There were three ravens sat in a lone tree
> And they were as black as black may be
> With a downe downe derrie downe derrie downe
>   dee—"

"That's a right strange tune to be singing on a bright day, Kalaquinn, lad. Can you find nothing better than 'The Three Ravens' to vent your spring fever?"

"Briacoil, Diggory!" the young man called out the traditional highland word of greeting to a cheerful red-faced man of middling height, built as stout and strong as his team of dapple-grey work-horses. "I do beg your kind pardon for my choice of songs. You should count yourself lucky. I was all set to sing 'The Ferret and the Coney.'"

The older man had been working the headland close by the road and stopped now within hailing distance of the young man, in order to give himself and his horses a much-needed rest after an early morning's start on the day's ploughing. Even as he spoke, Kalaquinn left the road and made for him over a stile in the hedge of hawthorn already growing white in blossom.

"Where's that pet of yours?" said the ploughman, casting an eye towards the sky.

Kal laughed. "Up in the hills, I imagine, hunting for his breakfast."

"Old man Dobbins lost a ewe with lamb night afore last. He's blaming that bird of yours. Says it's not right a body should keep a fellhawk." The ploughman shook his head.

"But, Dhu would nev—"

"Aye, never touch anything he weren't allowed to. So you've told me before, and so you'll tell me again, no doubt." Diggory Clout rubbed the back of his neck. His eyes twinkled in the morning light. "A safe fellhawk . . . I believe you, lad, I do, I do. Though thousands wouldn't, I do . . ." He chuckled to himself, shaking his head, then looked up at Kal. "But tell me now, where are you off to on this fine morning singing away as if you had the entire Holding to yourself while the rest of us sober bodies be busy at our work? It ain't right, by my ten fingerbones, it ain't, that we old ones moil and toil while you young gamecocks walk abroad with not so much as a care in the world to bother you," bantered the stout Holdsman, his broad gap-toothed smile and flashing blue eyes set deep in a ruddy weather-creased face.

"Ah, Diggory, you know full well I hate having to tread this road back and forth all the time, a glorified errand boy. I'd much rather be working with Father in his wheelwright's shop or putting my hand to the plough," Kalaquinn said, as he regarded the bulging shoulders and hindquarters of the powerful workhorses. "I'd step into your shoes and take my place behind your team any time you please. Just say the word."

"I know you would, lad, and I wouldn't be against letting you take a turn or two around the headland. But it be pleasing to our revered Hordanu to have you and our Galli as his helpers, especially you, Kal. He's taken a real shining to you. That's clear. He says you've got an uncommon knack for the strange and foreign ways and speech. He told me once you're right near his equal when it comes to talking the Old Tongue. Sure, he's taken to you, Kal. I think you'd be adding to his hurts, the poor old fellow, if he heard you giving voice to your discontents and with him in such a state, having his head full of all them thoughts about the troubles that are sore afflicting Arvon these days."

"Yes, I know. I wouldn't want to hurt dear old Cloudbeard and make things harder for him. Believe me, I wouldn't. I don't half mind spending time with him and hearing his stories, even though I don't really understand a lot of what he's saying, especially when I'm alone with him in his keeil and his eyes glaze over and he begins reciting those strange songs of his in the Old Tongue. Whenever that happens, it's as if he's entered another world. It scares me. Sometimes I get the feeling that he might never come back. It's happened more than once, let me tell you, that there's a long pause, and I end up tugging gently at his cloak, then a bit more roughly, then as roughly as I dare, to get his attention, but to no avail. I can't get any response from him, and then I feel his hands to find them as cold as a stone in winter, and I begin to think he's gone and died on me, sloughing off that tired old body of his."

Leaning against the plough, Diggory nodded his head, then stooped to pluck a withered stalk of grass that he began to chew.

"At times like that, a cloud'll flit across the sun and the wind'll pick up and I'll feel that I'm the only person left in this whole world. It's so unnerving that I'll set myself to leave him those times, but then all of a sudden his eyes open and he calls me back. 'Come, stay here with me,' he says and then picks up the thread of our conversation, like nothing had happened. After that, it's as if he's making up to me for it. He'll start explaining all kinds of things to me about our history, I mean the history of Arvon and the Holding here, really fascinating things, and the day just races by, 'til he sends me on some errand or other or has me fetch Galli so that the two of us can weed his garden or clean his dovecote or do some other chore that needs doing. And believe me, he's got an endless supply of chores. There's always something." Kal sighed and gazed at a swallow darting in the air over the ploughland. "Re'm ena, I'll never be free. I feel like a serving boy. Look at the other fellows my own age. They're finished their apprenticeships already or clearing their very own farmsteads. Take Galli, setting himself up as a beekeeper in those clover-rich meadows next to Mantling Moss. But here I am, doing all these blasted little jobs, patching the stonework of the Great Glence, sweeping the floor, and running here and running there, rushing to Wrenhaven for this and off to Broadmeadows for that."

"I'd advise you not to get too onion-eyed and sorry for yourself. You think you're not free? Just give a thought to all them hordes of people in the lowlands. They're the ones who've lost their freedom in very truth, swinking and sweating under the overseer's lash. Your father can tell you all about it from his days as a young man in Dinas Antrum, stories that'll curdle your stomach."

"I know," conceded Kal, looking aside again to the fresh-turned soil, "but still . . ."

"Aye, there be a good reason why we call the lowlands the Dungheap. I can think of no better word to give a proper notion of the place. You know it was old Sarmel that came up with it one evening at the Bottle while deep in his cups. About the only sensible thing to come out of the old codger's mouth in an age, save for his talk about strange signs in the night sky, but don't go telling him that.

"Kal, you're a Holdsman born and bred. Be right thankful you're not stuck in them rat-infested lowlands providing another strong young back for them thieving scoundrels. Still and all, we're in a sorry state these days, a right sad and sorry state." Diggory paused, his eyes straying over the younger man's shoulder to the Edgemere Road. "Now look at that! Who's that raising the dust like a windstorm?"

Kalaquinn fetched a look back at a mounted figure who approached, riding furiously in the direction of the clanholding's only town, Wrenhaven.

"Somebody from the court of the Crown-Taker," Kal said. "Can you see the mastiff's head on his surcoat? Yet another unwelcome messenger come from seeing Wilum, I expect, hoping to bend his old bones to their wishes." The rider drew closer. He passed near the two Holdsmen, rounded a bend in the road, and disappeared from sight into the woods. "The fellow does seem in an awful hurry, though, doesn't he? Can't get out of the Holding fast enough, by the looks of it. Heading straight for the Pass, no doubt." Kal looked back at Diggory. "And, no doubt, Master Wilum has sent the man scurrying back to the Mindal with a few threats of his own."

The ruddy ploughman chuckled, then furrowed his brow in thought. He pulled on his jaw and looked to the north. "Now, who's on watch up at the Aerie now?" Kal followed Diggory's gaze to a slight break in the wall of mountains—the Wyrdlaugh Pass. There stood a watchtower—the Aerie to the folk of the Holding—which overtopped a massive iron gate that blocked the only point of entry into the secluded valley. The gate and watchtower, fixed solidly into the flanking granite walls of the Pass, had helped to keep the small highland clanholding free from invaders for years beyond count. "Nemdin, I think . . . Aye, and Drusil, and that young lad, Laggis!" Diggory said, nodding with satisfaction, obviously pleased with himself for his good memory.

Kal looked again to where the rider had thundered into the woods. "I wonder what that old fox Gawmage is up to now," he said. "One more thing for Wilum to worry about, I expect. I should hurry."

"Sure he's up to no good. He and his greedy lot want to set new boundary stones to the Dungheap, bring it all the way to our doorstep and then some. Room to expand, they call it, claim it's their right. A surly lot they are, like those two lowlanders that have been skulking around the Holding for days on end now—"

"Friends of Enbarr's, brought in by him," Kal said. "Aye, they're a suspicious pair."

"Well, I'd sooner give those two scoundrels the back of my hand than the time of day. If it weren't for the fact that they enjoy the protection of Kenulf, that hog-grubbing son to our good thane, they'd have been run out of the Holding long ago. Each as brash as a rooster on a manure pile. Why they even treat our good Thane Strongbow like he was just another flunky." Diggory clucked to himself and shook his head. "The lowland dogs! They're all like their master. And Gawmage's not one to be trusted, not in the least ways. By my ten knucklebones, Kal, I have a queer feeling we'll not be left in peace."

"How's that? They've been threatening and ranting for as long as I can remember."

"And that goes back a far, far ways, don't it, lad?" said Diggory with a grin. "But you're right, you're right, they've been showing us them claws of theirs for some while now. But one day, when the time is ripe, they'll make good on their threats. You know how the old saying goes, 'As often as not it's the sheep what's been warned that the wolf takes for his supper.' Well, Kal," he ended abruptly, returning to his place and balancing the plough point behind the two great horses, "I've had my little rest. It's back to the furrows or I won't get my ploughing done today, and who knows but that it might rain tomorrow."

"Will I find Galli up at the house?"

"Aye, he's expecting you. So's Gammer Clout, clucking and fussing, I'll warrant, like a broody hen about her nest. She's spring cleaning, doing her carpets, and that with a vengeance. I'm glad I've got my ploughing to do. It don't pay to be anywheres near her when she's at her cleaning. Briacoil, Kal—on we go then. Come Sandalfoot! Up Jobber!" he urged the horses.

"Briacoil," Kal said, and, with a final wave, sought his way again. He broke into another song, one which Diggory, if he was cocking an ear in the growing distance, would find much more to his liking. Indeed, Kal soon gave up the song and listened instead to the ploughman, who took up the tune lustily as he plodded along the furrow fresh-turned by his team and plough.

> ". . . Come fellows, and hearken, by the tun or the firkin,
> For I know that you know beyond doubt
> That nought brings as good cheer as good comp'ny
>   and beer!
> So let's drink to Ale, Porter and Stout!
>
> Three damsels come daily, to me they sing gaily . . ."

Diggory began the song again, and its strains faded as Kal strolled out of earshot. He left the Edgemere Road and passed over a stile in the quickset hedge, beyond which ran a path that took him past the woodlot of the Clouts. Along the edge of the woods, Kal came to a cart track that twisted and turned from the main road to the Clout homestead, set comfortably, amid a burst of foliage, on a gently rising hill. He had hardly emerged from a tangle of yellow overwintered grass and set foot on the trackway to the Burrows, as the Clouts called their farm, when he was almost bowled over by Nightshade, Galli's coal-black retriever. A mere few steps ahead of Nightshade flashed a light brown hare, running for its life. The dog was almost on it, only to be frustrated when the animal bolted for the safety of a hare-hole in the base of a drystone wall. At the entrance to the hare-hole, Nightshade began to bark, pressing his snout into the narrow opening, pawing at it in a vain effort to follow his quarry.

"Come here, Night, leave him be. He's long gone. You'd best come along home with me. Come, Night. Come on, boy, let's go! I'm not the only one with spring fever today, eh Night?" said Kal, stroking the dog's head when he had bounded back to him, his tongue lolling and his tail wagging. Even the brindled cow who had been tearing complacently at some meadow grass moved off towards a clump of alder trees to give the energetic dog a clear berth.

The laneway began to mount the rise of land on which the Burrows was set. Kal could now see the house and its outbuildings through a screen of tall poplars that acted as a windbreak. Reaching the farmyard, he decided he'd have a look around before he tried the house. It was likely that Galli was hard at work around one of the barns, getting a new hive ready to set in his tract of meadowland.

"Galli," he shouted, "are you there?" Again he shouted. No answer. His presence caused a flurry of excitement among the clucking chickens and squealing piglets, which had found their way into every nook and cranny of the muddy farmyard. Kal greeted a group of cows who were tugging lazily at a bundled sheaf of winter hay.

"Why ladies, what are you doing with that old stuff, when you've got a whole farm's worth of fresh grass?"

One of the cows started to pull out of the group and lumber towards Kal. But it was not one of the cows at all, rather the bull, and with a look of ill-concealed annoyance about him. Nightshade barked at him.

"That's all right, fellow, no harm meant, honestly—Quiet, Night. Get out of his way, don't bother him—I'm just minding my own business, can't you see? Moving right along, honestly. Good bull . . . nice bull . . . easy bull. That's a good bull—Leave him alone, Night, you'll just get him riled. Get away from him! Quiet! Stop barking!" The bull kept shambling closer, lowering his shaggy head, gently rocking it side to side inches above the muck of the barnyard. Clearly he wanted to show man and dog who was in charge. Kal broke into a brisk walk that quickly turned into a run. Looking over his shoulder, he remembered with dismay the things Galli had said about this ill-tempered monster. Probably it was all exaggeration on Galli's part. He had no intention, however, of staying to find out, for the bull was coming closer and closer, picking up speed along the way. Kal passed near the pond, where a bold gander gave him a violent start when it jumped out from a curtain of bulrushes, hissing at him and buffeting Nightshade with his wings. This aggressive display from the gander checked even the bull, who seemed to have adopted the opinion now that none of this was worth the bother and so pulled away to rejoin his cows.

A few swift strides and Kal was clambering over a lofty stone wall that kept the animals out of Gammer's kitchen garden. He jumped down into a soft patch of garden soil. Nightshade had slunk through a gap in the gate at the far corner of the enclosure. Kal breathed a sigh of relief and smiled at the sight of the dog.

"Did you get some sense knocked into you? It serves you right, you crazy dog. 'Deadly Nightshade' would better suit you. I almost got myself killed there thanks to you."

Kal looked up, and a discreet smile lit his face at the sight of Galli's aunt and her eldest daughter. Armed with thick birchwood clubs, they were both busy beating a brightly coloured carpet stretched out on a long trestle under an apple tree white with blossom. At their backs stood open the door of a thatched cottage of buff-yellow stone trellised with ivy.

"Briacoil, Gammer!" hailed Kal.

"Briacoil, Kal," greeted Marya demurely, to which Kal replied in kind.

"Briacoil! How are things going, young Master Kalaquinn, this fine spring morning, a long overdue one at that?" Gammer peremptorily took up the conversation from her daughter, lifting an eye in her direction. "And what brings you to the Burrows so early in the day? And so breathless?"

"I've come to collect Galli. We're needed by Wilum. He wants us to spruce his place up properly now that the Candle Festival's come and gone. And then there's his garden that needs turning. He said he wanted us to report to him first thing in the morning come rain or shine. 'No sleeping in on the nones of May.' Those were his words, Gammer, no mistake," said Kal. He knew what was coming.

"So they were, and a hard time I had of it keeping my Galli from gloating that Wilum wanted him and you up at the Great Glence and that he'd be having to leave the house just when I'm in the middle of my spring cleaning and me and my four girls in sore need of a man's strong arm lifting these carpets and giving them a proper wallop to get out all the dust and grime of winter!" To give weight to her point, she delivered a flurry of blows to the carpet. Kal, grinning, glanced at Marya.

"He told me of Wilum's instructions this morning," Gammer puffed, "but I told him right crisply, 'A likely story you're giving me, Galligaskin Clout. I weren't born yesterday. Just you wait here and help your aunt Gammer, 'til Kalaquinn Wright comes to collect you, if what you says is honest truth.' Many's the time in the past, old Gammer's had the right notion of things, when my Galli's set his mind on gadding about the Holding, getting into heaps of mischief. Oh, when I think of how often I told his poor old mother, bless her soul, to watch that young one, her little Galli! Mischief-maker he were already even as a child. Little did I ken I'd be left pulling in the reins on him with precious little help from his uncle. Mercy, if it were up to Digg, Galli'd be roaming the Holding without a care day and night."

She stopped abusing the carpets and turned a feigned scowl on Kal. "That's what I said to that young scamp of mine, Kal, and mercy me if he didn't up and disappear on me before I could catch my breath. Next thing I know he's up on yon grassy knoll pointing and waving his arms like a witch-ridden huskin, yelling down to me that he sees something out of the ordinary up in the woods above the Shaad, that he's going to have a look. 'Tell Kal I'll meet him at the Howe,' he shouts and off he goes like a rabbit in fright. Into the woods and he's gone without so much as a 'by your leave.' That's our Galli for you. What's a body to do with a feckless lad like that? Now tell me honest truth, Kalaquinn Wright!" demanded Gammer as the young man fidgeted under the burden of her lighthearted invective.

"Well . . . um . . . I'd best be moving, Gammer, or I'll be late getting to the Howe. I'm sure Wilum has a pile of work for us to do," Kal said, edging away from her.

"And good luck to poor old Wilum if he thinks he can get more out of the lad than his very own flesh and blood can. Tell your friend that he can save some of that armpower for when he gets back home. Mind you bring him home the gainest way, Kal. I'll be counting on you not to let him malinger in the bypaths. There's plenty of things I need lifted and moved and rearranged before the girls and me are done. Oh, woe is me, so much to do, so few hands to lighten my burden, and me getting older, not younger."

"I'll get him back to you as soon as I can, the worthless lay-about," replied Kal with an impish grin, "as soon as we're done at Wilum's."

"You're a good lad, Kal. For that matter so's Galli, most nearly always, except when he's out roaming the hills and dales and keeping other honest folk from their work."

At that Gammer and Kal eyed each other and both broke into broad smiles, while Marya watched with shy bemusement.

"And you're a good Gammer, Mother Clout. And I'm sure Galli wouldn't trade you for any other aunt in the world!" Kal put his arm around the small fubsy matron, whose face shone out from her violet kerchief like an overripe pippin.

"Well then, come in, Kalaquinn, for some toast and tea and thimbleberry jam before you goes your way. Marya, heat up the kettle and get out a tablecloth," Gammer said, her air of pique now gone. "By the gingers, if young Galli can take a break from his labours, then so can we, especially seeing as we've got to leave the lad some work to do when he gets home to the Burrows, don't we, Marya?"

"I'm sorry, Gammer, no thank you, but really I can't stay. I think I'll be late even if I leave right now." Kal began again to turn away. "Perhaps on our way home. Right now I'd best be off to Wilum's, if I'm to get any work done at his place today. Briacoil, Gammer! Briacoil, Marya!" bade Kal, anxious to extricate himself from Gammer's toils, for he knew from bitter experience that she could hold a body up for ages, as she discoursed on her favourite and endlessly various topic—the shiftlessness and misdemeanours of her nephew Galligaskin.

"Ah well, if you must, you must," huffed Gammer, who turned, threatening a carpet with her cudgel. She glanced back to Kala-quinn. "Briacoil, lad. And mind you keep an eye on Galli."

Skirting Gammer's kitchen garden, he made for the edge of the orchard, where there was a swinging wooden gate set in the wall that he had gamely climbed to escape the bull moments before.

The Clout farm was the last farm on the Edgemere Road before the glencelands, which consisted of the lands attached to the Great Glence and Wuldor's Howe. About a hundred hides of land fell to the oversight of Wilum, the Hordanu. This was an immense, mostly forested tract of land that encompassed much of the southern shoreline of Deepmere as well as a sizable swath of the trackless mountain heights. By contrast Thane Strongbow, who oversaw the entire Clanholding of Lammermorn, owned only fifty hides of land, while the average farm in the Holding was just one or two hides in extent. Wilum and most of the Hordanus who had preceded him allowed the Holdsmen to hunt and fish in certain parts of the glencelands. A few folk were allowed to pasture some of their sheep and cattle in the handful of open fields that could be found scattered here and there.

In a hurry to make Wilum's, Kal decided that instead of retracing his steps and following the Edgemere Road he would take a shortcut by a little-used footpath that wound its way through the woods, ending up at the Shaad, a field close by the Great Glence. Leaving the knoll on which the Burrows rested, Kal turned his steps down its eastern terrace of stone, where it merged into a lush pasture that lay within a cordon of hills, brimming with coppice woods. Above the horizon the sun climbed slowly into the cloudless sky, lighting up the snowcapped spires of the Radolan Mountains and beginning to send broad, glistening bands of gold onto their dusky flanks. In places there were long gloomy gashes on the sun-soaked hillsides, where deep ravines and stony river courses gave shelter to woodland creatures.

Kal spared little thought to what might have caught Galli's attention in the distance. He was always chasing after will-o'-the-wisps, ranging up and down the hills of the Holding with reckless energy. After all, the woods were to him what water is to a fish. It was the Telessarian blood that he had inherited from his mother, or perhaps it was his father's wanderlust.

As a young man, Cammas—Galli's deceased father, Gammer Clout's young brother—had up and left the valley to explore the wider world. He was never seen again. A few years later, though, a young Telessarian woman, half-starved and with a babe in arms, surprised the gatewardens, claiming in halting lowland Arvonian that she was the wife of Cammas Cornkister. He had counselled her to take their infant son and make her way to the Clanholding of Lammermorn in the highlands of Arvon to escape the strife that was enveloping the folkdom, as had happened to so many of the lands of the East beyond the protective palisade of the Coolcower Alps, as well as the lands beyond the Great Wall. Cammas was not heard from again. It was thought he had died of the Black Fever.

Cairderga and her son were taken in by the Clouts. The young mother did not outlive her young son's fifth birthday. Gammer had said straightaway, when Cairderga first came to the Holding with her boy, that "her heart's broke, poor thing" and gave out the opinion that "she's not long for this world. Ah, but I'll feel sorry for the wee lad left without mother nor father." And so, lacking sons of their own, Diggory and Gammer took in and indulged their orphaned nephew. From an early age, Galli's Telessarian browmark caused him to stand out from the other boys of the Holding. When he grew older, in his eagerness for understanding of his ancestry, he sought out Wilum, who took him under his wing together with Kal. While Galli was not a particularly good student, he soaked up the lore and legends of his Telessarian forebears that were passed on to him by the elderly Hordanu.

Passing to the edge of the pasture, shrill with the chirping of crickets, and staying within sight of a few scattered head of grazing cattle, Kal came to a very old yew. Its larger branches riddled with holes and cavities, the ancient tree was thick with pairs of starlings busy with the task of nest-building. The air boiled with their ceaseless chatter. Here the pathway turned into the woods and rose to a boulder-studded hillcrest, from which Kal looked across to the Burrows. The lone squat figure of Gammer Clout still beat her carpets. Beyond her, past the winding laneway leading into the Burrows, lay Deepmere, bright and sparkling in the light of the morning sun. Kal waved to Gammer and looked around him, wondering for a brief moment what Galli might have seen. He himself could not see anything. Then again he did not have Galli's keen Telessarian eyes or boundless curiosity.

Kal pressed on through the forest, following the ups and downs and meanderings of the path and breathing deeply the earthy smells. At his feet lapped vivid green bracken fronds that had pushed themselves up through last year's bed of mouldering beech leaves.

Soon, his way took him up a sharply sloping ridge crowned by a grove of trees, the Craythorne Firs. On the other side of them lay the Delf, a deep trench which separated the Clout farm from the glencelands. From the Firs he could see the Great Glence itself, built with granite slabs quarried from the Delf. Adjoining the Great Glence at right angles to it stood Wilum's keeil—his living quarters and scriptorium. Farther towards the west lay Stillfields, which remained the ancient burial ground of the Hordanus from the time of Hedric. Dominating Stillfields were the Haltadans, an avenue of massive towering stones that flanked the entrance to Ram's Knap, the mausoleum where Hedric, the first Hordanu, was interred. Not far from the Great Glence, just below it, could be seen the southern extremity of Deepmere, which gathered itself into a sheltered basin to the lee of Raven's Crag Island. The turreted ivy-clad walls of Owlpen Castle, the ancient seat of the Thanes Strongbow, now deserted, overtopped the thick-growing trees of the Island. At the opposite end of the lake, some four leagues distant as the crow flies, lay the town of Wrenhaven and beside it Broadmeadows, the manorial home of generations of the family Strongbow, Thanes of the highland Clanholding of Lammermorn. Beyond Wrenhaven was the Wyrdlaugh Pass, a narrow breach in the majestic ring of mountains that cordoned the Holding on every horizon. So far as the folk of the Stoneholding knew, this was the only way in and out of their lakeland clanholding, the most ancient and venerable of all of Arvon's clanholdings, and the smallest too.

The Craythorne Firs grew straight and smooth as ships' masts and towered above Kal, as he approached the edge of the Delf, making for a place they called the Channel. Here he slid down a steep chute of scree to the bottom of the deep ravine, about two hundred yards—a good bowshot's distance. Behind him thundered a hail of stones.

He followed the gulch of the Delf farther up into the mountainside out of which it had been hewn by some mysterious force of nature, passing long-disused quarry pits gouged from the flanks of the mountain by pick and shovel. Soon he arrived at some ancient stone steps that had been cut into the granite for the convenience of the pit workers.

The Holdsman mounted these steps, emerged from the Delf, and entered the wooded depths of the glencelands. At first the footpath took him higher up into the hills, but only because a curving ridge of rock had to be skirted before he could strike a downward course towards Wuldor's Howe and the Great Glence. The Howe was a little apron of land at the very southern tip of Deepmere, where Ardiel, the first High King of Arvon, after his great victory at the Velinthian Bridge over three thousand years ago, had caused the Great Glence to be built around the Glence Stone. And even before then, in a mistier time, the Howe was a spot where the echobards gathered to sing their ancient runic lays at the Stone and at the standing stones that towered over nearby Stillfields.

The way broadened, winding down the naturally occurring terraces of the mountain. With its many ancient oak trees, their twisted boles bearded with outcroppings of moss and draped with mistletoe, the forest gave the impression of venerable age. Serenading him was a colony of ring-ouzels with their mellow plaintive whistles. As he approached the floor of the valley, he could see the granite stone cupola of the Great Glence rising above the treetops. To his right grew more mammoth oaks, keeping guard over thick ranks of bluebells, bladder campions, and wood anemones. A field mouse pushed aside the scaly stalk of a fern and scampered quickly for cover. A hawk hovered above the crown of a neighbouring oak.

Soothed by the drifting melodies of warbler and thrush, Kal moved along the edge of Oakenvalley Bottom, an ancient wood that had stood unscathed by woodsman's axe for century upon century from the time of the First Age, the Age of Echoes. None save the Hordanu dared enter its strange depths, where the life of its birds and beasts and flora, as rich and colourful as it was, seemed different, natural and yet somehow wholly out of the ordinary. It was in a brazier set in the heart of the Bottom that the Sacred Fire of Tramys was kept perpetually burning. The Hordanu entered the wood himself on the evening of the Candle Festival to bring the inhabitants of the Holding new fire for their yearly celebration.

Whenever he passed the Bottom, Kal felt its mystery as well as its strange peace. It was a place that the folk of the Holding were forbidden to enter. The few scoffing adventurers who hazarded their way into it were invariably gripped by an overpowering fear before they had trodden more than a step or two of the hallowed ground. Nor were they ever the same after the experience. Indeed, many of them met an untimely death.

The road turned down, clinging fast to the southern margin of the Bottom. Dropping into a hollow, it crossed a small brook over a weathered stone bridge, then rose again steeply. Where the road resumed its descent to the Great Glence in Wuldor's Howe, a branching footpath clung to the steeple of the ridge which overlooked the Bottom. This was the Echobard's Walk, trodden only by Wilum whenever he entered the strange haunts of the wood.

The ground of the Echobard's Walk, made soft by the rainstorm of the previous evening, showed two distinct sets of prints, one far larger than the other. Clearly the smaller set belonged to the Hordanu. But the other?

Kal stooped down to examine one of the big prints, made by someone with an odd cut to his boots and in a hurry. Galli would be able to read much from these tracks. Straightening his frame, Kal set off again, quickening his pace, eager to relate what he had discovered to Wilum.

From the Echobard's Walk the way broadened out again into a wider avenue surrounded by great-boled oak, beech, and maple. It was as if the woods of Oakenvalley Bottom had spilled over their enclosing ridge. In the same way the lone flute-like rolls of some bird, tremulous with mystery, drifted down from the lip of the Bottom. Its soft tones intensified Kal's growing unease. The ancient forest ended abruptly and Kal broke into a run across the Shaad, a field thickly covered with clover and alfalfa.

In the near distance loomed the Great Glence. Set on a low hill, it looked like a massive granite skep, tall rectangular window openings rising at regular intervals along its hive-shaped circumference. The great carved oaken doors of the entrance, rounded to fit the contours of the stone on either side, were shaded by a portico resting on two stout square pillars. As Kal drew closer, he could discern the fragrance of herbs carried on the faint breeze. Master Wilum, he knew, would no doubt have them cleaning the portico, still strewn with marjoram, meadwort, and thyme from the ceremonies of the Candle Festival.

Kal slackened his pace as he made for the long low building

that abutted the Great Glence. Smoke drifted in a thin curl from a chimney set in the slate roof—old Cloudbeard chasing away from his keeil the chill that clung yet to these spring mornings.

Kal's eyes strayed up into the hills. There flashed a glint of what looked like sun on metal. Now gone. Then again. A gleam of light, coming, it seemed, from a dense clump of bushes that crowded a small ledge on one of the forested ridges that overlooked the Howe. "Is that you up there, Galli? What are you up to?" he muttered, as he stopped to scan the area more closely. The light flashed again as the screening leaves were caught in the breeze.

Kal cupped his hands at his mouth, bellowed his friend's name, and paused to listen. No answer came. He called a couple of times more, then gave up to turn back towards the keeil.

As he turned away, something caught his attention in the corner of his eye. He strained now to pick out detail. Yes, there, not two good stone's throws away, still as a hare, a man crouched in the greenery close to a patch of bare rock not far below the telltale sparkle of light. Certainly not Galli, Kal realized with shock from the outline of the man's figure and the colour of his clothes. The man remained bent over, his face turned towards the clearing in the Shaad. Because he kept still, his green tunic hid him against the foliage. As it was, Kal would surely have missed him, if it had not been for the gleam of light drawing his eyes to that spot on the hillside.

Nobody ever skulked around in the woods of the Howe. Kal quashed his first impulse to rush and investigate. That would put the intruder on his guard and might scare him off. Better to carry on in the direction of the keeil. After quickly informing Wilum, he could circle around the Great Glence and scout stealthily back to the Shaad along the edge of the forest.

He shouted Galli's name once more by way of a ruse, indirectly watching the hidden man. Animal or person—it doesn't matter what you're stalking—they'll feel you staring at them, his father had always told him. Use the corner of your eye, he had advised.

It was then Kal saw the spyglass the lurking figure held up against his eye. He swallowed hard, his neck hairs prickled. With a shrug, trying to look carefree, he broke into a loud rendition of "The Three Ravens" and made his way towards the keeil again.

Towards the woods on his left, the Shaad was broken by a stretch of rich dark soil where Wilum had his garden. A wall of mortared stones enclosed it and an adjacent orchard. Kal passed the draw well from which they watered Wilum's vegetable patch. A wooden bucket dangled from its jack-roll, which was covered with an open roof of cedar shingles.

The dreamy sound of cooing pigeons grew louder as he approached the keeil, skirting a six-sided stone dovecote. Before he could reach the door of the building, it swung open, the door-handle clasped in the crook-fingered grip of an old man.

"Well I'm here, Master Wilum," Kal said, relief in his voice, as he sprinted through the entrance.

"Thank heaven, lad!" The old man sighed, pushing the door closed behind the both of them. Bent over with age, he clutched at his staff. A dishevelled mane of hair brushed the collar of his long brown cloak, which swept down to his sandalled feet and was secured by a thick rope cincture around his waist.

"We need to get help—they've quenched the Sacred Fire. I still can't believe it's happened, never, not since Ardiel's time," he said, pulling at the white beard that framed his flushed and deeply lined face. A tremor seemed to run through his body. He gripped his staff more tightly and shook his head.

"Who's they?"

"Gawmage's messenger. He stole into the Bottom. Must have been early this morning before I came to see him off at the guesthouse. When I got there, he was already gone."

"Well then, that's what I saw when I passed by, his tracks. I wonder, I just saw someone up on the hillside above the Shaad, spyglass and all!"

"What are you talking about?"

Kal recounted what he had seen.

"So, that explains it," said Wilum.

"Explains what?"

"The feeling I've had . . . of being watched. But where's Galli?"

"He's not here yet?"

"No, I thought he was coming with you."

"When I stopped by the Burrows, Gammer Clout said he'd run ahead, chasing after something he'd seen in the woods. What if he's up on that hillside and in trouble?"

Wilum looked grim.

"I'm going to sneak out into the woods to where I saw the fellow and try to find out what's going on. Galli may be there."

"Aye, go find him quickly. I hate to send you out alone, but we've got no choice. There's no time to fetch any of the other men. You go look for him. You've got your shortsword?"

Kal nodded, grabbing at its hilt.

"You'd better take my longbow."

"You have a longbow?"

"Right here," Wilum said, as he opened the doors of a large closet built into the wainscotting.

"Really?"

"You needn't act so shocked, young Master Kalaquinn. I was young once too, believe it or not. I used this to lay in my supply of venison for the winter and it wasn't so long ago either." Wilum held out a bow and quiver to Kal.

"Nice weapon," Kal said, admiring the bow's horn-tipped ends and its finely carved grip. He accepted the bow and felt its balance, then unstrung the quiver's leather flap, flipping it back to reveal nearly a score of expertly fletched shafts. No common hunting tools these.

"A gift. These were a gift. But the main thing is it works. I just tried the bow the other day, when I fitted a new string on it," replied Wilum, with a half-smile and one snowy eyebrow cocked.

"Whatever you do, be careful and come straight back to me here once you've found Galli. Don't use the bow unless you've no other choice. No foolish heroics. Do you understand? We've got to get help. We must summon the Thane and the men of the Holding for a folkmoot. The Fire's out. We have grave matters to discuss." Wilum paused, placed his hand upon the young man's raven head, and, looking into his bright eyes, nodded. "Now go."

"All right. Lock your door and try not to worry. I'll be back as soon as I can."

"Briacoil." The old man raised his hand in parting.

Kal opened the door of the keeil and walked out as if nothing were wrong. A cold hand clutched at Kal's insides. Something sinister and threatening hung in the air. He could sense it bearing down on him from the hillside above. He must find Galli. Steeling himself against the looming menace of the watcher, he turned past the gabled endwall of the keeil. The young Holdsman made a wide circle around the Great Glence, aiming for woodland on the edge of the broad clearing that surrounded

the stone structure. To the north he could make out the lofty
battlements of Owlpen Castle, crowning the heights of Raven's
Crag Island, set like a sentry picket in the waters of Deepmere's
narrow southern limits.

Slipping into the woods—unnoticed he hoped—he turned onto
the first footpath going in the direction he wanted. It ran well free
of underbrush at first. As the path rose, the tangle of briars and
brambles became thicker. Finally Kal left it in order to pursue a
straighter course to the hill above the Shaad.

Pricked on by the unfamiliar thrill of adventure, he waded
through the thickets, heedless of the thorns that tore at his leggings.
He slipped down a slope of bracken and dogwood and came to
the banks of a trout brook, where a kingfisher kept up an incessant chatter. In places the ground remained wet from the spring
runoff, and Kal's feet and shins were soon soaked through. He
followed the brook upstream to its source. Dripping with sweat,
Kal paused to take a drink from the cool waters. He climbed up
the ridge from the spring and joined a path that brought him to
the woods above the Shaad. Peering through a gap in the foliage,
he looked down on the dovecote and the keeil.

The green-clad intruder had to be close now, on the other
side of a thin stand of white birch trees to the right. He stole
forward, then stopped for a moment, listening. There was a stir
of movement in the woods and the sound of a voice.

"Hey Grumm, will you look at what we've found us here. Sleeping like a baby. With moss for his pillow." It was a man with a
thick lowland accent, hidden from view by two great oak trees
that loomed ahead.

"Maybe you could speak a little louder, Skrobb, so's everybody
in the valley will know we're here," another lowland voice said.

"It's that black-haired fellow's mate. You know, the two of them,
always together, the old one's men. I don't know how we could
have missed him. He's fast asleep here—or was asleep. Lookee
here, our baby's waking up."

Kal crept closer, guarding his every footfall against any dry
twig, stick, or leaf.

"What do you want me to do? One of us has got to stay put
and keep watching the old man's place. Where's that blasted tracker
gone to? He's supposed to be helping us."

"He's here with me. Weird bill of goods, if you ask me. Don't miss a trick in the woods, though, I'll grant him that. It's him that found this lad here. What do you say I stick this highland scum like a milk-fed pig?"

Kal listened, aghast. He launched himself forward into a run, trying to pinpoint the gruff lowland voice.

"Wh-wh-what's this?" It was Galli, groggy and disoriented.

"No! You no kill. He from Telessar like me. See mark on face," said another heavily accented voice.

"Ah, move out of my way, you idiot! Out of my way, quick, before the piglet gives us the slip."

"Galli!" Kal cried. The scrub caught at his legs and arms as he ran. He stumbled, pitching forward, and the bow was torn from his grip. He threw himself from the ground, regaining his feet, and drew his sword as he broke free from the underbrush. He could see them now, all three of them. They were farther away than he had thought.

Unarmed save for his hunting knife, Galli half-rose from the crook of an exposed tree root. He reached for his sheath and edged away from a huge man who had his sword drawn and was now sparing a distracted glance in Kal's direction. Kal recognized him as one of the lowlanders Kenulf and Enbarr had brought back with them from Dinas Antrum. Facing the man stood a tall rangy figure in green homespun. Kal came at them at full tilt, waving his shortsword.

"To me, Grumm, to me! It's the old man's lackey coming to the rescue! Here, I'll take care of this one first. Let him finish his nap in the grave." The lowlander turned to plunge his sword into Galli.

"No, leave man alone!" The tracker pulled at the lowlander's sword arm this time, even as the big man lunged forward to pin Galli. Deflected from Galli's stomach, the sword point tore instead at his arm, slicing through his tunic, causing him to drop his knife.

"Let go of me, you painted mongrel. Now I've had more than enough of you," the man snarled in anger and brought his sword around in an arc, cutting down into the Telessarian's shoulder where it met the neck. The tracker sank to his knees, blood gushing out from the wound in a flood. Galli clambered up over the thick tree root out of harm's way for the moment. The lowlander turned on Kal, who now confronted him, shortsword at the ready, looking for an opening.

The other man, hearing the commotion, had left his point of vantage nearby and hurried to the aid of his comrade. To Kal's horror, the man carried a crossbow, spanned and ready. Though he was screened by the trunk of the large oak, Galli must have heard the man grunting with the effort of running as he came, for Galli stiffened. From the corner of his eye, Kal watched as Galli peered cautiously around the tree and caught sight of the man stampeding through a patch of fern, clumsily raising his crossbow to his shoulder. He slipped from cover with quick stealth and circled wide. Deftly he stalked the lowland ox, lightly darting forward across the soft forest floor, until he stood close on the heels of his quarry.

"Watch out! Behind you! Grumm!" his companion shouted, taking his eyes off Kal for a brief moment.

Grumm turned, but Galli was ready for him. He pushed the fellow off stride and darted forward alongside him, knocking the crossbow from his grasp. But not before the lowlander had triggered it, letting fly the bolt.

Kal's opponent blanched and swore, bringing a hand up to caress his ear, which had been creased by the quarrel and now dripped blood on his collar.

"Leave him, Kal. Stand off. I'm fine. Let the big lout chase you if he can," cried Galli, as he snatched up the crossbow and smashed it against a tree trunk. Grumm staggered forward towards his partner.

"Let's be gone," he quailed, while backing off into the woods, timid without his weapon. At this, Skrobb also lost the heart to go it alone with Kal. He turned and took heel.

"There they go, Dinas Antrum's best and bravest," said Galli, slumping pale against a tree, favouring his blood-soaked arm.

"Let's take a look at that wound of yours."

"Forget about it. He just scratched me. What about him? A Telessarian."

"What's he doing here?"

"It doesn't matter. He saved my life. Look, I think he's still alive. What should we do?" Galli moved to kneel down beside the man and cradled his head. The stranger's breathing was shallow. Slowly his eyes flickered open.

"Cairderga . . . You face like sister . . . Cairderga . . ." It cost him great effort to give the words voice.

"Let's rig up a stretcher. We'll have to get him down to the keeil fast," said Kal and began a distracted search for something to use for poles.

"Kal . . . Kal. He's dead."

They searched the body, but found nothing to tell them the identity of the strange man, just his Telessarian features, his green homespuns, and a pouch with flint and steel, together with a long cruel knife he had not had time to extract from his belt. They pulled the body away from the path and laid it beneath a gnarled tree.

"Just a moment . . . before we leave him," said Galli. Kal watched his large well-muscled friend. A shadow of grief passed over the pug-nosed face full of freckles, his fair hair tied at the nape of his neck revealing the telltale birthrite tattoo worn by Telessarians over the brow along the hairline from ear to ear. He stooped to pluck a wildflower and touched it to his own forehead. "Let thy browmark be thy warrant," he intoned as he laid it across the dead man's forehead. "We'll come back later and see he's buried decently."

Kal nodded then said, "We'd better report to Wilum and let him have a look at that wound of yours."

"It'll be fine. Nothing but a scratch, only a bit worse than what I'm getting all the time from the nasty spikes on the blackthorns. Hardly more painful than some of the stings my bees have given me. Just a flesh wound, looks uglier than it is."

"Still, Wilum'll have some ointment or other to make sure the wound doesn't fester—"

"Wait, I need to fetch that dagger," Galli said and set off into the woods at a run.

"What dagger?" Kal scrambled to follow him.

"It caught my eye when I followed them up here. I left it lying where I found it . . ." Galli halted in a small clearing where he bent to pick up an object. "Will you look at the workmanship!" he cried, straightening himself out to admire the naked dagger he held in his hand, its beautifully jewelled hilt flashing in the sun.

"I wish you'd tell me what's going on."

"Let's get out of here first. I'll explain when we reach Wilum's."

Galli slid the dagger back into its polished leather sheath, while casting a wary look around him.

Kal stifled his curiosity. "Sounds good," he said, "but first I need to grab Wilum's longbow."

"Wilum's longbow? Wilum has a longbow?"

"I'll explain when we reach Wilum's . . ."

TWO

"Now are you going to tell us how you managed to make such charming lowland friends, or do we have to pry it out of you?" Kal said, as Wilum had his two assistants take their seats on soft leather cushions before a fire that crackled in the stone hearth of his keeil. The old man, holding back his own questions, had finished with Galli's wound, cleaning it gently and applying a soothing herbal ointment.

"Aye, go ahead. Tell us quickly, lad, and then we've other matters to discuss," urged Wilum once he had ushered them to their places, a gaunt hand clutching the staff that he lifted like a pointer, jabbing towards Galli.

"Well, it's like this," Galli said, pulling the jewelled dagger in and out of its sheath, turning it over and around, keeping his hands busy with it. "I hadn't done more than just start shaking a stick at one of Gammer's carpets at the Burrows, when I happened to look up and see a flash of light up in the woods." He made a gesture as if to show the direction with the dagger. "I didn't think much of it at first. Thought it was just a trick of light. You know the way a rock or a tree can catch the sun and glitter sometimes. Well, my eyes kept straying to the spot and, after a while, I got curious. So, I climbed that little hill behind our cottage to get a clearer look. Anyway, I thought I saw something. It wasn't an animal. I decided I'd better go check it out. I wasn't much in the mood for working anyway, what with it being such a lovely day. It struck me as odd that anyone should be up there at all."

Frowning, Wilum rose from his stool and leaned his staff against the corner of the mantelpiece. "Let me brew up some paxwort tea for the three of us. A cup of it would do me the world of good. Calms the nerves. I'm sure it wouldn't sit badly with the two of you either. Go on then, lad." Wilum nodded, as he filled the kettle from a wooden bucket standing by the hearth.

"Well, I headed up there. A blind man could have tracked them, what with the oxpath they'd trampled through the woods. I got to the hill over the Shaad, just above a little ledge that jutted out from the hill, and guess what I found? This dagger lying on the ground." Galli held the weapon out again, running his fingers along the flat of the blade. "The area was strewn with bracken, cut and laid, like it was being used for bedding. And the place was thick with tracks, two sets of them, the same as I'd followed up there. Fellows wearing boots. Lowlanders. Impossible to mistake it from the stitching on the sole, and they were all over the place, some old and some really fresh. Two sets going to and from that ledge. It gave them a perfect place from which to keep an eye on the keeil and the Great Glence. I was all keen at first to keep following their trail and put some questions to them, but then I thought better of it. Lowlanders, I figured they were probably unpleasant types—"

"Or worse still, deadly types," said Kal. "We know that first-hand, don't we?"

"That's why I thought it'd be wiser to wait for you. Also I figured it would be better to leave the dagger where it was. Maybe one of them had unstrapped it from his belt on purpose before he lay down, forgetting to put it back on. Anyway I thought to myself, why don't I find a hidden spot and stay put up here on the hillside 'til Kal arrives at the keeil. Then I could sneak back down and grab him and we could deal with the two lowlanders together. So I settled in silently against the big oak tree root. From there I could easily catch sight of Kal down below. At the same time I could keep watch over their spy post on the ledge perfectly and not be seen. What a comfy little nook it was. Too comfy. You know what, though?" Galli glanced up from the dagger. "All that time I had a strange feeling that I was being watched. But it didn't raise my hackles. Somehow I didn't get a sense of any real danger, just of someone or something being curious about me, looking me over. I'm almost certain now that it was that Telessarian watching me from the shadows."

The boiling kettle fussed over the fire, sputtering.

"Telessarian?" Wilum raised his brows in puzzlement, turning once again from the teapot he was preparing.

"Sorry, I'll get to him in a moment. It's my guess the two lowlanders had him keep an eye on things while they were gone on other business."

"But how come you didn't spot the Telessarian's tracks at all?" said Kal.

"Well, I wasn't looking for anything of that sort, so I missed them. A seasoned woodsman from Telessar can leave a trail that's almost invisible. Anyway, the next thing I know, there's that big lout trying to run me through and the Telessarian trying to stop him for some reason—"

"That's when I came on the scene," said Kal, taking up the thread of the story now, peppered with an interjection here and there from Galli. When he had finished his account, they sipped tea for a moment, left to their own thoughts.

"But this Telessarian . . ." Kal broke the silence. "Where would he have come from? How did he get past the gatewardens at the Aerie and enter the valley?"

"It's plain he was in cahoots with those two spies."

"Which makes it even stranger still why he risked his own life to save yours."

"What about those dying words of his. He mentioned your mother's name, didn't he?" said Wilum as he poured Galli another mug of tea.

"'Cairderga . . . you face like my sister . . . Cairderga.'"

"I think he was trying to say that Galli's face— He must have figured that he and Galli were somehow related. After all, Galli's mother— Well, the man may have been one of her brothers and so suspected that Galli was a son of Cairderga's," Wilum said.

"Which would make Galli a long-lost nephew. That's why the man tried to fend off Galli's attacker! It's the only explanation that makes sense!"

"Even so, the bigger question remains."

"What do you mean, Master Wilum?" asked Galli.

"What were they doing up there in the hills spying? Why were they so quick to resort to violence and murder?"

"Well, I can't say it surprises me." Kal shook his head. "Two lowlanders, no doubt the same two as have been prowling around the Holding for the past few weeks, comrades of Kenulf and Enbarr by all appearances. And you know Kenulf and Enbarr . . . especially Enbarr. The way I gauge it, he's got Kenulf under his thumb, although you'd be hard put to ferret that out judging by the surface of things. Enbarr's too clever, knows exactly when to blend into the woodwork when he needs to. I tell you, Enbarr's the sort who would slit his own mother's throat to go on an orphans' outing."

"Aye," agreed Wilum, "but it's Kenulf the old Thane's sore distressed about. His only son, last of the direct Strongbow line, and doesn't care a mote about the old ways. Why, he looks and acts more like a lowland coxcomb than a proud highland prince."

"Small wonder," Kal said, "when he and that cousin of his spend more time in Dinas Antrum than they do in the Holding. Then they return home to the highlands with those thugs in tow."

"In any case, there's a greater evil afoot here in the Holding," continued Wilum, "the quenching of the Sacred Fire—"

"How's that? The Sacred Fire . . . quenched?" Galli's eyes grew wide. At the same time Wilum's staff slipped from its niche and clattered onto the tiled floor, giving the three of them a violent start. Kal rose to pick it up.

"Ah, yes, yes, you don't know yet . . . Re'm ena, the whole thing's quite unimaginable. I never expected it. Caught me totally by surprise, utterly beyond my reckoning." He shook his head and shuddered, staring blindly out the large window of the keeil towards Stillfields, where his predecessors lay buried. "Aye, the Sacred Fire's been extinguished, for the first time since Ardiel carried it forth from the Balk Pit of Uäm after his great triumph at the Velinthian Bridge. Can you imagine? For more than three thousand years it has burned here in the Stoneholding, time out of mind, but now it burns no more. I can still hardly fathom it."

"But how did it happen?"

"It was Gawmage's messenger who snuck into Oakenvalley Bottom early this morning at dawn. By the time I got there, the coals that feed the Sacred Fire lay dead cold in their brazier. I had called for him in the morning at the guest lodge. He was not there, nor was his horse. The next thing I know, he was thundering down the Eastmarsh Causeway from the direction of the Bottom." Wilum turned his tired gaze back to Galli. "A sly weasel-faced fellow, and bold too, asking endless questions about the Holding. About Raven's Crag Island and the old Castle too. Kept wanting to talk to me about the manor rolls for some reason, slipping in his queries about the Bottom.

"It's really my own fault," he said and paused, cradling his mug of tea with both hands, staring blankly into it. "I should have been more cautious, more vigilant. But I've lost count of the times Gawmage has sent his messengers over the years. Every spring, as regular as swallows, they've come riding into the Holding, shouting down the gatewardens, bearing some proposal or edict that Gawmage has spent the winter months concocting at his palace in Dinas Antrum. And whenever they come, I always feed them and give them shelter, as loathsome as I find the endless bicker of their conditions and demands. That way, at the very least, they can't make me out to be sour and inhospitable." Wilum sighed, glancing up from his tea wearing a wan smile. "So you see, you weren't the only one caught napping, Galli. This latest move of Gawmage's has caught me flat-footed too. While I may not have been short when it comes to hospitality, I've certainly been short on guile." He rose restlessly from the stool on which he had paused to seat himself. "The wily Crown-Taker, he guessed well that after all these years my guard would be down. What better time for him to spring his mischief on me!" The old man halted, his lips tight, as he shook his head, so consumed by his fretting that the tea slopped over the lip of his mug.

"No wonder the fellow was in such an awful hurry to reach the Wyrdlaugh Pass," Kal said. "I saw him this morning galloping down the Edgemere Road as if his very life depended on it."

"Oh, the wonderful clarity of hindsight. What I should have done." Wilum set his tea mug on a sideboard. "Ah, but it's no good moaning now about water that's passed under the bridge, when it's too late . . . much too late . . . But then in the end what could I have done, a doddering old man, invested with an office that is but a shadow of a shade of its olden glory? Shoring up the fragments, that's my lot these days." As he spoke, the morning sun passed behind a cloud, casting a chill over the room. For a moment the old man shivered, leaning heavily on his staff, which he had taken in hand again.

"Listen," he bade suddenly, cocking his ear. "There's my pigeons again. Something's not right. Can you hear them, lads?"

"They do sound different," said Kal. Galli lifted his eyes from where he had again begun toying with his knife.

"There have been other things too," Wilum continued, stooping to warm his hands at the fire of the hearth, his voice grown pensive and brooding. "Last night I heard the greyhen cry and the night before last as well, above the frightened cooing of the pigeons. And my dreams, they've been hag-ridden and storm-tossed. I'm very much afraid that the quenching of the Sacred Fire is merely the beginning of our woes. There's evil abroad, even here in the Howe of all places, and it's crept up on us in tiny cock's steps, so slowly that it's caught us all but unawares.

"Arvon is overspread by lengthening shadows of unrest. Something in my bones tells me that all of Ahn Norvys is in dire upheaval. The deep darkness is casting forth powers that have long lain dormant or have been held in check, at least, in hidden out-of-the-way places. The Great Harmonic Age is ending, even as the Age of Echoes ended many centuries ago. Hedric foresaw it, darkly and in riddles. I sense it now more strongly than ever, I smell its vapours of decay, even in Oakenvalley Bottom, now that alien feet have trodden its hallowed soil."

Still clutching his staff, but now straight and unstooped, Wilum stepped back from the hearth and turned round to the two, his face flushed and resolute. "It was powerful runes that messenger of Gawmage's must have used to broach the boundary of our holy wood. And the means he used to extinguish the Sacred Fire were cunning and far-sought."

Kal looked puzzled.

"Come, Kalaquinn, you know yourself, lad, that the Fire is well nigh unquenchable while it burns in its brazier. But even so there is a way of snuffing it out."

"By using . . . pyraphoric mistletoe, right?"

"Aye, with pyraphoric mistletoe, which grows only on the oaks found in the Atrian Forest."

"The Atrian Forest?"

"Far from here, far from Arvon, on the eastern marches of Ahn Norvys, a place which the sun scarcely touches in its rising and its setting. A wild lawless place that even Ardiel could not fully tame to the measure of the Great Harmony. But very cleverly Gawmage has managed to obtain some of this hard-won herb to force my hand, or so he thinks," the old man said with a strained laugh.

"If he only knew, he wouldn't have been so suspicious all

these years, so frightened of me, thinking that I know where the young Prince Starigan is, that somehow I've secreted the last tender shoot of the Royal House of Ardiel and that I'm protecting him somewhere, waiting patiently for an opportune moment to pull him out from under my sleeve, like some upstart Thrygian magician."

"I don't understand, what do you mean by Gawmage forcing your hand?" said Galli.

"I mean that Gawmage is not an utter fool and he knows as well as you and I do that the Sacred Fire must be rekindled, or else there'll be no Candle Festival as usual next year . . . an unthinkable prospect. And not just anybody can retrieve it. The fact of the matter is that only one of Ardiel's very own bloodline may undertake the task. So ancient tradition has it. Hedric says as much himself in a little-known section of his *Criochoran*, the *Song About the End Age*."

"Galli, do you remember our lessons? Landros was always fond of quoting from the *Criochoran*," Kal said. "I remember him speaking about the lore of the Sacred Fire. You remember, don't you, Galli?"

"I don't, no. But you, Kal, you've got a head for those things. Besides, it was a while ago."

"Aye, it was, and we didn't spend much time discussing it anyway. I suppose he didn't think it was very important."

"It probably never crossed his mind that the Sacred Fire could ever go out. I'm sure the very thought would have struck him as ridiculous," Wilum said, slowly shaking his head. "The worst has happened, lads, what Hedric predicted."

"What was it that Hedric said? I can't remember. Landros only mentioned the lines once, I think, to illustrate a rare point of grammar in the Old Tongue," said Kal.

"Well, the key lines of the prophecy run something like this:

'The Sacred Fire shall soon expire
When darkness light assail.
Will seed alone of ancient throne
Rekindle Oakenvale.

The Kyne-merk true, by darkest ruse,
Obscured by shadows foul,

Shall slip the snare, rise daystar fair,
From up the Glen of Owl.

Royal blood new-found shall trumpet sound
The triumph over dark,
Bring forth relit, from Uäm's far Pit
The Ever-Sacred Spark.'

"That's my own translation from the Old Tongue," Wilum said, after reciting the verses, "although I'm not altogether happy with the first line of it. Needs work."

"What's that word 'kyne-merk'?"

"It means 'a mark or sign of royalty.' A very hard word to translate, so I just left it."

"How about the 'Glen of Owl,' where's that?" Galli raised his eyes to meet the old man's.

"Nobody has figured that one out yet, lad. It's a real puzzle, and the *Criochoran* is full of puzzles. Makes me wonder sometimes just why Hedric ever set himself to writing it, when it's a piece even the wisest of bards haven't been able to make nor head nor tails of, as dense and difficult as a fog in the Breathing Sea."

"So only Ardiel's descendant can restore the Sacred Fire . . . And he will come from some place called the Glen of Owl, wherever that is?"

"Exactly. That's what Hedric is saying, and as I mentioned before, ancient tradition confirms this interpretation." Wilum rose from his stool by the hearth to pour more tea for himself and the two young men from the teapot that he had left perched on a trivet near the flames.

"So where does that leave us?" Galli inquired.

"Not where Gawmage thinks it leaves us, that's for certain. He thinks I know where Prince Starigan is to be found, and that this way I'll be forced to bring him out of hiding."

"I don't understand all this talk about King Colurian's son. None of the family of King Colurian survived," Galli said.

"That's what Gawmage has led men to believe, but it's impossible. You two lads of all people ought to know that," Wilum gently rebuked.

"How's that?"

"Because somehow, some way there must always be a King, a King that has Ardiel's blood coursing in his veins. It was a solemn promise that Ardiel made before he left on his last quest and disappeared from the annals of our history. When I was a boy, we had a little rhyme supposedly coined by Ardiel, 'Through thick and thin, you'll have my kin.'" Wilum afforded himself a whimsical chuckle.

"What about Gawmage? Is he not of the line—?"

"Gawmage? There runs not a drop of royal blood of any kind in his veins! Why, he's no more than a vile power-hungry upstart, a usurper, the distinguished descendant of a long line of Dinasantrian shopkeepers."

"But all the same he thinks some of King Colurian's folk survived?"

"Aye, he does indeed and that bothers him," answered Wilum, "even though he wants men to suppose that the seed of Ardiel was destroyed forever when the Mindal seized power from the faltering line of King Colurian. I think he's haunted by Ardiel's promise, much as he likes to dismiss all the old promises and prophecies as so much rubbish. Also, and this is much more disturbing to him, the fact of the matter is that there's a whole grey area here. Neither Gawmage nor I know what befell the young Prince Starigan or who was behind his disappearance. Gawmage is convinced, however, that I'm somehow privy to this secret, and that I actually had a hand in spiriting the Prince away. Hence has that stolen circlet of royal office perched precariously on his crown these last eighteen years. In addition, the ferocity of our highland archers has kept his crop-eared bullies from marching with main force into our clanholding to root me out of the Howe and put an end to the menace they see in me yet. That and his hope that he could wheedle the information about Starigan from me one way or another by flattery or by guile." Wilum turned to face the fire, seized a poker, and stirred the embers.

"Nonetheless, it's been my fear for some time now that Gawmage has been waxing in strength, growing bolder and more reckless, partly at least because he's brought Arvon into the Gharssûlian League and he can draw on the immense might of the League to buttress his power . . . So there we are," Wilum heaved a sigh and placed fresh logs from a small pile beside the hearth onto the now glowing bed of coals. He returned this attention to Kal and Galli. "We have no choice in this matter. We must find Prince Starigan. It's he who is the rightful High King of Arvon."

"But how? Where do we start?" Kal said.

"I'm not sure . . . I was in Dinas Antrum when the Prince was born, the seventh child of King Colurian, nineteen autumns ago, Colurian's only son," mused Wilum. "I was there by Colurian's side at the Silver Palace in Dinas Antrum as his wasting sickness drained him of the last dregs of life. It was only at the end that he understood in what danger the folkdom stood. That's why he sent for me and I hurried to his side as quickly as I could from Wuldor's Howe, the second and last time I've ever left our little highland clanholding. Alas, there was little I could do against the might and influence of the counsellors of the Mindal.

"They had been growing stronger for years while King Colurian lived for the pleasures of the chase. All real authority had finally become vested in them, and the High King had become little more than a figurehead. I sent him letter upon letter, trying desperately to warn him, for it had grown clear to me that the Mindal was a viper in his bosom. It was they who turned the smallholders of lowland Arvon from their homes to make their sheepwalks and huge enclosed estates, battening themselves greedily, like cormorants, on the misery and helplessness of their fellow folk. It was they who hobbled them with their forest laws and woodmoots. It was they who despoiled the lush valley of the Dinastor, razing the forests and fields to make room for noisome fuming smithies and forges, befouling the air and the water. It was they who ravaged the glences and robbed the orrthon of its ancient glory."

A darkness had passed over Wilum's brow. "Anyway, lads, I don't think I need to go on and list all their evildoings or their latest treasonous alliance with Ferabek and the Gharssûlian League." Wilum sighed, turning to eye Kal, who was held rapt by the old man's account. "I decided that posting letters was no longer enough. The situation had turned so dire that I travelled to Dinas Antrum in person for the first time ever in my life and dared to tell Colurian to his face that on account of his weakness the folkdom stood in the greatest of peril. Well, he flew into a wild rage, threatening me with a dungeon room in Tower Dinas and even worse. I think it was only the influence of the Queen that saved me from suffering harm. All the same, he came close to deposing me then and there as Hordanu, which was what the Mindal in its sly lust for power was pressing for.

"Ten autumns later he lay on his deathbed in the Silver Palace, the victim, some were saying, of poisoning by his counsellors after a hunting accident. And I don't for a moment doubt the truth of that. As far as the Mindal was concerned, he was still too unpredictable and too much his own man. They were ready and eager to assume total power. I think Colurian began to suspect as much himself. These first faint glimmers of suspicion tipped the scales in my favour. That's why he sent for me, hoping the folkdom could still be saved, as late in the day as it was. It was good fortune that the Mindal, in their pride and certainty of triumph, considered me of such small account that they didn't try to stop me from rushing to his side. They did not perceive a threat to themselves in the maunderings of a dying king." Wilum rested again on the stool, his hands clasped around his staff, his eyes closed, and his head bowed forward.

"I still remember vividly his last words to me. He was but a vestige of the man he once was, his royal dignity but a fragile shell. 'Wilum,' he said, 'I looked for peace, but no good came; and for a time of health and harmony, but, behold, trouble and blackest chaos, for they've come, Wilum, they've come. They're devouring the land and all that's in it. I place my family and folkdom in your care. Hurry, Wilum, you must hurry. My last hope rests with you. May Wuldor speed your steps. Briacoil, Wilum, briacoil.'

"But though the Mindal didn't care a tinker's dam about King Colurian in his death throes, they did very much care about his royal line and wanted to destroy the whole Ardielid dynasty, root, trunk, and branch. They needed to pave the way for their elective monarchy, one in which a member of the Mindal, one of their own tight-knit circle of insiders, would be elected by his peers to the High Kingship. Any surviving member of the legitimate royal family was bound to be a threat to them. So, on the flimsiest of pretexts they arrested all of Colurian's daughters, his brothers and sisters, and all their children and threw the lot of them into the dungeons of Tower Dinas.

"As for Queen Asturia, who remained feverish and unwell after giving birth to Prince Starigan, they placed her under house arrest at the Silver Palace. That way they came to gain immediate control over the main bloodlines of the entire Ardielid dynasty. I had a very good idea what was going to happen. They were waiting for Colurian to die and then they would execute a sentence of death on the Royal House of Ardiel, trumping up a charge of high treason."

One of the fire logs crackled in the hearth, sending a shower of sparks across the floor. Wilum lifted his gaze to the raven-haired youth before him.

"It was at that point I conceived the notion of making one last desperate gambit, to try to save the King and Queen along with their newborn child. Thus it was that I sought out your father."

"My father?"

"Aye, your father. In Dinas Antrum. There are parts of this story that you've never heard, I'm sure, for your father and I have kept it a close secret between us—with good reason as you'll learn."

"Father's never spoken much about his years in the lowlands. Only vaguely."

"Having my contacts, I hastened to seek out your father, since he was crucial to my scheme. He lay in hiding outside of Dinas Antrum, a loyal captain of the King's Life Guardsmen—"

"What? My father?" Kal stared at Wilum, wide-eyed, then turned to look at Galli, who shrugged.

"Indeed," Wilum said, chuckling at his young companions' astonishment, "your father, Kalaquinn, he was a first-rate soldier, clever and resourceful. He and some of his comrades who had not shifted their allegiance to the Mindal were waiting for the chance to take up arms and mount some real resistance to the usurpers."

"A captain of the King's Life Guardsmen!" Kal said, recovering himself somewhat. "I had no idea."

"As well you should have had, Kalaquinn. In any case, we talked together, your father and I, and formed a plan. By a clever ruse, at great peril to their lives, he and a handful of his men gained entry one night to the Silver Palace. They managed to free the Queen and her newborn son, but not King Colurian. He died that very night. Commandeering the royal barge, they fled up the Dinastor River. Leaving the river, they headed on horseback for Ashwood Hall, the King's Summer Palace on the Lake of the Swallows, aiming to rest there briefly and then hurry on to the safety of the highlands with mother and child. It had been agreed that I would meet them at an abandoned gamekeeper's cottage near the Summer Palace, but before they could reach it they were ambushed, 'slaughtered' would be a better word, by an unknown group of assailants, aided by a traitor in your father's own troop.

"Apart from your father," Wilum continued, his eyes still trained on Kal, "only the Queen and her son survived. Clearly it was the little boy they were after for some reason of their own. They took him alive, carrying him and his mother with them after they had abandoned their efforts to comb the woods for your father, who escaped by the very skin of his teeth, having salvaged Lightenhaft—"

"What! Lightenhaft! The Lightenhaft!" exclaimed Kal.

"Aye, the one and only, which, thanks to your father, rests now in safe hands."

"But where—?"

"Aye, who's got it now?"

"That's a whole other story. Leave Lightenhaft be for the moment, lads." Wilum raised an open hand. "And your father's past, as well . . . Well, what was I saying? . . . The ambushers, yes." He shook a finger and continued. "They threw the bodies of your father's fellow Life Guardsmen into a deep ravine, practically inaccessible. It's as if they wanted to put people off the scent and remove all traces of the slaughter, making it seem to anyone investigating that it was the Life Guardsmen who had disappeared with the mother and child.

"The next morning, coming from Dinas Antrum, I arrived at that cottage near Ashwood Hall myself, where I waited impatiently, until at last your father managed to arrive and recount his tale of what had happened. With great difficulty and danger, he descended into that horrible ravine—the Charnel Pit, they call it—looking for survivors. But alas, to no avail. Because there were indications that the attackers had passed through Ashwood Hall, we searched every nook and cranny of the place, desperate to unearth a clue about their identity. I remember vividly the ravens, flocks and flocks of jet-black ravens, that croaked at us in bitter mockery from the grove of royal oaks and beech trees that hedged in the Hall like a living tower.

"No sooner had we finally grown tired of our fruitless searching than we heard a clatter of mounted troops. They had come, I think, from Dinas Antrum hot on your father's trail, for they flew Gawmage's mastiff's-head pennant. We were rummaging halfheartedly in the garden, but they came on so fast we had to make a run for it into the woods, although not before they caught sight of us, recognizing me, but not your father. They thrashed around in the forest, trying to find us as we fled.

"But as chance would have it we found a bypath deep in the woods that led us to the dwelling of a humble cottar and his wife, with five young children. Accepting their gracious hospitality, we stayed there for a fortnight, scouting the countryside round about, looking for some clue that would help us unravel the mystery of the strange abduction of Prince Starigan."

Having laid his tea mug aside, still seated on his stool, Wilum traced patterns on the floor tiles with his staff. "There was precious little. We did, however, manage to gather one very striking scrap of information, puzzling though it was. We learned from the cottar's oldest two children that they had been playing in the woods a few days earlier, when they saw from their makeshift hidey-hole a large party of men, most of them clad in black. The men were armed and passed by the hidden children. The little boy and girl cowered in their place of cover. They heard a baby's cry. When the party disappeared from sight, the children fled home to tell their mother.

"I questioned the two of them, taking them to the spot at which they had been playing and discovered from the boy that one of the men, the one who seemed to be their leader, was dressed differently from the rest. He wore a green crosscloth on his forehead matched by a green tunic. Your father and I tried taking up their trail, but, whoever they were, they proved too clever at covering their tracks.

"At a loss, I teased more details from the two children, discovering that on both the crosscloth and the tunic was blazoned a black orb shining forth with rays stitched in gold. Flanking this orb were two dark birds facing one another. So maintained the lad with much sureness, and his sister confirmed it. I had never heard of such an emblem. I made numerous inquiries about it when I returned to our clanholding and pored through *Hedric's Master Legendary* looking for a clue. But to no avail. For the longest time I supposed it was a ruse of Gawmage's, to put loyal Arvonians off the scent, although I couldn't understand why he did not just kill the child straight off. As it turned out, for many years I was none the wiser about it. Until very recently," said Wilum, turning his face again to the fire.

"There was scarcely a thing else to be learned, except that for the first few months the Mindal set about beating the bushes furiously in their desire to catch me and your father's fellow Life Guardsmen, letting out the word that we had abducted the Prince and setting a high reward for our capture.

"In any case, taking our grateful leave of the cottar and his family, your father and I fled across country, making for lowland Arvon's western marches. We skirted the high roads and slept in lonely farmsteads, breathing a sigh of relief when we achieved the safety of the highlands. I remember vividly the day your father and I reached the Aerie and looked down on the town of Wrenhaven snuggled peacefully against the shores of Deepmere. We agreed to tell no one what had happened. You two are the first Holdsmen I've told of this." Wilum eyed them gravely.

"It was soon after this," he continued, returning his gaze to the fire in the hearth, "that the Mindal had Gawmage crowned as High King, his first royal act being to depose me as Hordanu and appoint a new Hordanu to reside in Dinas Antrum. It was decided, too, that henceforth all Hordanus would be appointed by the High King and continue in the office at his good pleasure. Thus they overthrew the custom that we have held from time immemorial, by which we the folk of the Holding, upon the death of a Hordanu, choose the next one for all of Ahn Norvys. As for the young Ardielid prince, who had slipped from their grasp, the first flush of their ardour to lay hands on him waned and they forgot all about him in the intoxication of their newfound power. For a time I speculated that Gawmage and the Mindal had in fact disposed of Prince Starigan themselves and were merely using me as a scapegoat, blaming me for his abduction in order to deceive the people and divert suspicion from themselves.

"Then with the passing of the years I began to suspect that Gawmage was guiltless in this matter, perhaps the only thing of which he stands guiltless, and that he truly believed I was the one who had abducted Prince Starigan. At first, the whole question did not bother him overmuch. He and the Mindal were too preoccupied with the power and wealth they were grabbing greedily in Arvon's lowland counties. It was merely a matter of time, they thought, before the highlands in their wild backwardness gave way to superior force and numbers. And when that happened, and the highland clanholdings, even the Stoneholding itself, fell into their grasp, they would have me at their mercy. Then the secret of Starigan's fate would not matter much anymore."

Wilum rose from his place and made his way to the window of the keeil. "Well, it has not happened according to plan for them. The highlands are too rugged and our fighters too spirited. At first, though, Gawmage sent solemn messengers who presented me with dire ultimatums, demanding me to present myself forthwith before his royal court in Dinas Antrum. Then, as his military sallies failed, his messages became more tempered, more seductive. He began to ply me with smooth lies, promising me safe passage to Dinas Antrum and reinstatement as Hordanu if only I would leave the Holding to pay him homage at his royal seat." Wilum growled, stamping the floor with his staff. "As if I needed his approval to retain the office that belongs to me 'til death divests me of it! And I never worried too much about an attack on my person, because I knew that Gawmage could never be certain what precautions I had taken to ensure that with my death the secret he thought I possessed would not die with me. But recently he's become more brazen and threatening. There's a new confidence about him, and I find that sinister.

"But now I have some notion why. With this latest move he's neatly forced my hand, a cunning scheme to flush out the heir of King Colurian, since he knows well enough that I have no choice but to send Prince Starigan to recover the Sacred Fire. That's common knowledge, Kalaquinn—only an Ardielid can retrieve the sacred spark. At least it used to be common knowledge. Every bard worth his song in all of Ahn Norvys used to be able to recite large parts of *Hedric's Master Legendary* by heart and in their original Old Arvonian, mind you, until now, alas." The old man looked again to Kal, gesturing at him with a bent finger. "That's why Landros sent you to me in the first place, your gift with languages. Even though you're not a bard, at least not yet, I've had you commit so much to memory yourself, before it's lost, you know."

"So they've baited you," said Kal, leaning forward in his seat, "forcing you to show Starigan, and when you do, they'll pounce on him."

"Maybe that's why they've been spying on you here," Galli said.

"Likely."

"So where does that leave us, Master Wilum? What happens next?" asked Kal.

"First things first. We'll need to summon a folkmoot as soon as possible."

"For when? Tonight?"

"Aye, tonight, here at the Great Glence after supper as usual. Let your father sound the summons. I'll explain to the people what's happened, but not everything, not some of the things we've discussed together this morning. There are others in the Holding besides Kenulf and Enbarr whose loyalties are questionable, and it's best to leave them in the dark. Mind yourselves and mark your words with prudence too . . . Kalaquinn, Master Galligaskin." Wilum held the two with a fierce steady eye. "Also, we'll hold court and try the lowlanders, get them out of our valley one way or another, no matter the fuss that Kenulf may make—"

"While Enbarr whispers encouragement in his ear and goads him on, no doubt. But what about finding Starigan?"

"We need a clue, a place to start. I've spent endless days and watches of the night poring over all the old manuscripts to the point of nausea, trying to puzzle things out. But there's hope. I'm waiting for word from . . . from a friend . . . from Aelward."

"Who's Aelward?" asked Kal, getting up to stretch.

"Hard to answer . . . who Aelward is." The old man cast his gaze to the floor. "I'm not certain myself. Indeed, I'm not sure I could tell you what I know without taking up more time than we've got at present." Wilum paused a moment, lost in thought, then regained himself. "The important thing is that not too long ago he sent me some startling, although welcome, news. He's found the emblem and feels he's close to finding the Prince."

"Emblem?"

"The device that puzzled me, the emblem that the cottar's children saw, the emblem of Prince Starigan's abductors. Aelward has tracked it down to somewhere near the twilit shadowedland beyond the Alnod River in the East. That's all he told me. That's all I know. It was last autumn that he sent me his short message by pigeon from his place up in the hills many miles north of the Holding. It was the first time in almost twenty years I had heard from him, the first time since Prince Starigan's abduction. He said he had another long journey to make, more information to gather, and that he would be in touch with me again sometime during the month of May, before the end of the Octave of the Candle Festival. Well, the Octave has come and gone, and I'm beginning to feel somewhat fearful, since I've had no word from him. All the same, I'll give him another day or two before I worry overmuch. But it's enough talking we've done, lads. Hurry along now, Kal, and tell your father to blow the summons, the sooner the better. You'd best go together, though."

"What about the work that needs to be done here?"

"Since when do you worry about work that needs to be done, Galligaskin Clout? No, move along. The work will wait."

Kal wore a look of concern. "We can't just leave you here alone. What if there's somebody still out there?"

"Not to worry about old Wilum. You fellows routed them so handily they're hardly likely to come back."

"I have an idea," Galli said. "Why don't Kal and I swing around to his place by a side journey through the woods. That way I can check for trail sign just to make sure they're not still in the neighbourhood, and then, when we've given Kal's father the message at Mantling Moss, we can come right back and keep you company until the folkmoot this evening."

"All right. But I want you just to check for sign. You leave them alone if you get anywhere within sight or sound of them. They can be dealt with later at the folkmoot. We'll get some of the men to take them in hand. And if the need arises, you have my longbow. Now off with you," he said, ushering them to the door, "and mind you use the bow only if you've no other choice."

THREE

They had been scared, the two lowlanders, like frightened rabbits bolting for their burrow. Even Kal could read their sign. Clearly they were trying to put as much distance as possible between themselves and their now-discovered spy post above the Shaad.

"We're safe for now. But let that shorter fellow get his hands on a crossbow, then watch out," Galli said, halting for a moment. "I bet he's the brains of the outfit too. It must have been hard going for him here, more than it was for his partner. The short one carries more lard on him."

Heading east, they resumed their tracking, threading their way through a little-trodden path that was thickly overgrown. It took them through a steep hardwood forest high up into the coniferous reaches of the glencelands. There the air was brisk and cool, and the bulking massifs of the Radolans seemed like stark immobile giants with their heads lifted boldly to the azure dome of the sky.

When they reached a windswept copse of stunted pines, it became apparent that the two lowlanders had taken a branching trail that led them straight northwards, gradually descending towards the area where the glencelands ended along a steep-sided ridge, which merged farther down with the gaping pit of the Delf. At a break in the ridge they crossed over into the expansive upland shielings where many of the farmer herdsmen of the Holding had their summer pastures. The land they had now entered belonged to the Clouts of the Burrows. It actually formed part of their farm, although its abundance of large game animals and its difference in altitude and

79

vegetation from the more sedate pastoral landscape closer to their house made it seem alien and exotic.

In a sheltered dingle, well out of sight and protected from cruel mountain winds, they found the remains of a settled camp. Kal kicked at the still glowing embers of a fire, while Galli busied himself examining a patch of flattened grass, marked at its corners by empty tent-peg holes.

"Must be some kind of field camp," remarked Kal.

"For what reason?"

"They needed a place that was within easy scouting distance of the Howe, somewhere they could have a fire and make a meal. That way they wouldn't have to travel the length of the valley every time they were engaged in one of their spying missions. It would be too long a trip back and forth."

"You know, I did hear old Sarmel mention to Uncle Diggory just yesterday how strange he found Kenulf's new friends, that they seem to disappear and not a soul sees them for days on end, and then they're back poking around for another day or two at the Bottle or at Broadmeadows and then gone again."

"And it can't be they go far, certainly not out of the Holding. The gatewardens—not a field mouse could get by them without the whole valley knowing."

"There wasn't much chance of someone stumbling onto them here. Most folk don't start moving their livestock up to summer pasture until mid-month."

"Even then I'm not sure anybody would be apt to find them up here. Come on, let's get moving. We'll follow them as far as Mantling Moss, then swing down and tell my father what's hap-pened."

A couple of times along the trail, when Kal and Galli reached a fork in the path, Galli could tell from a confusing clutter of footprints that their quarry was uncertain which way they should turn. Evidently they had not come this way often enough to recognize the landmarks. The sign showed that they were forced to slow their pace, so as to take their bearings once more from the sun.

The two followed the lowlanders' halting tracks to a place where four paths intersected one another. Kal recognized the spot—part of Mantling Moss, his own family's homestead. Not too far off, lower down, lay Browside, the pasture where, only just the day before, Kal had folded their prize flock of Blackface Mereton sheep. Much to their surprise the tracks bore no mark of hesitation, but turned right, straight onto the path which led farther into the higher places nestled in the mountains.

"Will you look at this? There's so many footprints here, really unusual ones, like I've never seen before. And different footgear from anything we use in the highlands. Re'm ena, but where did they come from!" Galli crouched, fingering the ground in wide-eyed disbelief.

"There must be at least a score of men," he thought aloud, "then the two we're following came right on their heels." He paused and pointed, his attention drawn to the right edge of the footpath where a footprint was impressed clearly over the others. "What's this now? At least one Holdsman in with the lot, although he came a bit later. Not too long ago." Galli glanced up, catching his friend's eye.

"We'd better be careful. I can't say I like the look of this. It's strange, too strange."

"I agree, something's really out of kilter here."

"Don't you think we'd better leave? Tell your father? Get help?" Galli said, casting a squint-eyed look all around him, half-expecting the woods to disgorge a troop of strange, unbenign figures.

"And miss our chance to be the big topic of discussion at the Bottle for days and nights on end? Having people stop and point us out any time we step foot in Wrenhaven? We'll be the talk of the town. Why, old Sarmel—well, he'd keep the pot boiling for the next ten years, if he lives that long."

"If we live that long, you mean."

"We're not going to fight anybody. Come on, Galli, we're just going to sneak up on them and do a bit of spying, just like they did."

"They got caught, remember?"

"They don't know this land like we do. Besides, we'll be careful. For one thing, we won't stay on this path. Here, look, we'll follow Plunge Brook. It meets up again with the path about a mile up. That way, if these are foemen, and we know that two of them have no reason to love us, we're more apt to stay out of harm's way."

"Foemen, Kal? How do you mean foemen? Can't be! Where would they all have come from? Not Broadmeadows, do you think?"

"I don't know. Even if they are from Broadmeadows, how did they get past the gatewardens without every living soul in the Holding knowing about it? But it's no use worrying about that now. I feel exposed and out in the open here. We'd better search out some cover fast. Come on, this way." Kal dashed off the path into the underbrush. "I'd rather find whoever it is that made these tracks before they find us."

Galli paused a moment then fell in behind his friend.

The two of them were soon tramping alongside a small clear stream that gurgled across the face of the hill in a sunken ravine that was broad enough to contain a much larger river, as it did in the spring thaw. Deep moss covered the rocky banks, and the sun, where it slipped through the green canopy above them, was caught sparkling on the brook's surface. Its rose-moles flashing, a trout darted from a riffle. They scanned the forested sides of the ravine for any flicker of movement. It felt odd for them to be on the lookout for the presence of outlanders in these familiar woods.

"Will you look at this? We're not the first ones to have passed this way."

"What do you mean?" asked Kal, stiffening.

"A lone sheep. There's a lone sheep blazing a trail for us. A ewe, a couple of years old, by the looks of it. How did she get here? I didn't think you'd brought any of your sheep up from the lower pastures yet."

"We haven't. It must be a stray that's wiggled its way out of Browside. I'd bet you a small fortune it's Gardy-Good, the most unsheeplike sheep that ever was. Dumb animal's always finding a way to break through the hurdles, wandering where none of the others'll think of going. More trouble than all the rest of the flock put together. Plunge Brook flows into a pool just inside the fold. It's the weak spot in the fence. That's where she must've gotten out and then climbed along the streambed up here."

Kal and Galli talked no more. Their breathing became more laboured, for it was mucky uphill going along the soft-shouldered strand, especially when they had to tramp through water meadows. The banks of Plunge Brook became steeper and covered with a thickly matted undergrowth of laurel, its course taking several snake-like twists and turns. Galli had taken the lead and was skirting an outcrop of rock that was forcing the stream into another of its curling turns when he froze stock-still. He drew back to the cover of the rock.

"Men," he whispered, his eyes bulging, "around the corner, they look like—you'll never believe it—like soldiers."

Ever so slowly, Kal peered around the edge of the rock, hiding his face behind a screen of ivy creepers. There were two of them, each wearing a chain-mail hauberk and pointed steel cap, with their broadswords in scabbards hung on their backs. One of them was busy cleaning off an arrow and examining it with a view to using it again, while the other was hunched over something that lay on the ground. The latter man moved.

It was Gardy-Good. He had been right. The poor creature was as dead as a door-tree, the hoofs of her carcass having been tied to a pole. The two soldiers stood on a small expanse of pebbled shingle which lay submerged when the stream ran in full spate during the early spring. Above them rose the packed earthen path they had used to come down from the meadow that overlooked the gully of the stream.

They were deep in conversation. Strange guttural sounds, a different language, it was clearly not Arvonian of any dialect or description. Kal strained his ears to listen to them, wrestling with the shapes and texture of the sound. There was no mistaking the accents, the wharling which Landros the schoolmaster imitated so humorously when he gave the boys of the Holding their lesson in Gharssûlian.

"'Pir-r-rian D'Ar-rba'! Now tell me, Kalaquinn Wright, what do these words mean?" he would ask, spewing out the "r"s with enormous gusto.

"'Battle of the Trees,' sir. It's also the name of the capital city of the Autarchy of Gharssûl, where this ancient battle is supposed to have taken place," Kal would answer.

"R-r-right you ar-re, lad. You'r-re ver-ry lucky, most extr-remely for-rtunate to be learrning Ghar-r-rssûlian, ver-ry lucky, indeed, boys. Mind the sound of the Ghar-rssûlian 'r-r-r.' Not trilled like a highland 'r' but drawn out and growled, like a dog choking on a bone. Ther-r-re's no mistaking it. Pir-r-rian D'Ar-rba! Aye, boys, 'battle,' they'r-re mighty adept at that," he would say and wink.

Their talk was fast-spoken and colloquial. Nonetheless, Kal must have learned his lessons better than he thought, for he found himself able to make out snatches of their conversation. It seemed they were talking about roasting a spit of mutton for supper, how they were mightily sick of "dur-rabor"—Kal remembered their word for hardtack. Then the Holdsman saw other armed figures on the edge of the meadow above looking down at the two men below and gesticulating.

Putting an end to their talk, the two men grabbed opposite ends of the pole and ascended the path out of the gully. Kal paused in disbelief. Gharssûlian soldiers in the Holding, on his own homestead, no less. He turned and in a hoarse whisper gave Galli a quick account of the situation. They were reasonably well-hidden, much to their relief, by a thick tangle of bushes and thorny briars that rose to a close-growing coppice on the lip of the gully.

"What are we going to do?"

"We have to go, see what's happening. Whatever these men are here for, they're up to no good."

"Are you sure we shouldn't go back and get some help?" Galli urged under his breath. "There's no telling how many of these fellows there are, and they're probably armed to the teeth."

"Stop griping, Galli," Kal hissed. "Let's just scout out the situation a bit more before we head back. We need to see how many of them there are so we can make a proper report of it. I know this mountain like the back of my hand, every nook and cranny, and you're not exactly a stranger to it either. I could find my way around it in my sleep. There's a meadow above us to the left. I'm sure you remember it." Kal motioned, pointing with his chin above and beyond Galli's shoulder. "I'll bet they're camped out on that meadow. I'll tell you what: There's a perfect spot about fifty paces upstream, just past a narrow gap, where we could creep up to the meadow for a peek."

"And how do you propose we get from here to there without being seen?"

"Just a small chance we'll have to take. Only a short sprint and we're there. We can't go back and approach them from below . . . Can't you feel the wind? We'd be upwind of them, if we came at them that way. What if they've got dogs? And we can't circle round this gully and come at them downwind by meeting up again with Plunge Brook and crossing it. There are some steep bluffs blocking off that approach, except for a narrow sort of causeway which that path we left crosses over. And odds are it's under guard. The only way for us is to stay in this streambed and go straight ahead. Look," Kal peered around the corner, "we'd have made it already, if we'd cut all this talk and gone right away. They're too busy getting their meal ready, that's my bet, and a very tough stringy meal they're bound to get out of that sheep."

"All right, then, what are we waiting for?"

"You go first," insisted Kal, "and I'll cover you with Wilum's bow. I hope it's properly strung."

"What about you? Who'll cover you? All I have is my short-sword."

"You can watch from the other side and warn me if you see anyone coming. Make that cooing sound, the wood-dove sound, and I'll try to slip behind that rock."

"That rock won't give you much cover."

"It'll be enough, if I'm still. So don't worry. If we time it right and run like the blazes, we'll make it fine. Go on," urged Kal. "The coast seems clear. I'll watch for you and give you the same signal, if you need it."

Kal pulled the longbow off his shoulder and nocked an arrow, making ready to shoot a perfect stranger. Before he could entertain the thought for more than a fleeting moment, Galli, who seemed to glide along the ground like a disembodied wraith, had passed without mishap through the little valley, which was pinched almost closed by a narrow, neck-like opening upstream. That Galli—he had a born woodsman's way of crouching cat-like into a stealthy walk that Kal could not match, try as he might.

Now came Kal's turn. He slung the longbow back across his shoulder and ran. He had all but reached the spot where they had trussed up Gardy-Good when his ears caught the wood dove's coo and the sound of nearby voices—a thick, menacing blend of Gharssûlian syllables, drifting down from the brow of the ravine, not thirty paces above him.

"You'd best be quicker than quick about getting that water. We don't have all day. See that you make yourself useful for once," barked a gruff voice.

The warning came too late, leaving Kal no place to hide, only gorse and bracken all around him. The rock he'd staked his hopes on lay well behind him now, beyond easy reach. In a moment the Gharssûlian would turn down the path and see him, raising a cry when he did. Kal stopped himself in mid-career, like a hare frozen at the sight of a fox. In that moment there came to his ears a series of insistent bleats, the sound drifting from where Galli waited beyond the gap.

"What do you know! Another bit of mutton for the spit!" Bucket in hand, the Gharssûlian soldier descended, intent on locating the source of the sound, regarding it with curiosity instead of alarm. Rather than coming down the main path, he turned down a smaller side path in Galli's direction. A thick lug of a man, he did not spare so much as a glance Kal's way. Still clutching his bucket, the soldier waded into Plunge Brook in order to get through to the other side of the bottleneck, which was choked with purling water. A moment later and he disappeared out of sight. The bleating ceased and all fell quiet again. Kal rushed forward.

"Give me a hand, will you? Help me get his muzzle out of the water before he drowns, if he isn't dead already. I hope I didn't do him in . . . just wanted to draw him away from you."

"The sheep, that was you?"

"Aye, a fair imitation, I'd say."

"Not bad for a beekeeper."

"I gave him a couple of drubs with the pommel of my sword. Didn't know what hit him. I think he's still breathing," said Galli in a low voice, as he lifted the limp, sodden form from a turbid eddy of the stream, trying to pull him up onto the shore.

"I don't know that you should be so concerned about him," returned Kal, who had taken one of the soldier's arms. "Look at the insignia on his surcoat." A cold chill ran right through him.

"A black scorpion! Don't tell me—a dragoon! A Black Scorpion Dragoon!"

"And a heavy mean-looking piece of work, too," said Kal, straining at the dead weight of the man's thick muscular body, which seemed as heavy as an oak log. "One of Ferabek's fiercest troops. Landros says they're ruthless, utterly without pity. Just a handful of them are enough to keep things under control in Dinas Antrum. Re'm ena! The Holding's in danger, great danger. Here, give me that bucket and I'll take it quickly back to the bank of the stream. They'll be starting to wonder soon what happened."

"As long as they don't think he's run into any foul play."

"If we fill the bucket with water and leave it there, I think we'll be safe for a while. It'll look like their man went loafing somewhere. I'd better be quick. Here's the bow. Cover me, Galli."

Kal returned in a moment. They were right in the middle of

dragging the immobile body of the hapless soldier up the bank to the leafy underside of a lilac bush, when the quiet of the river bottom was broken by a lone loud voice.

"Where are you, you moron? Estvor, where have you gone to? Come on, man! Out with you. Where are you? . . ." The man's comrade swore, lowered his voice and said, "So you're playing games with me, are you? You think you're getting back at me for that little episode in Pirrian D'Arba? Well, we'll see who's the gull when you're in the stocks."

Kal and Galli crouched over Estvor as his comrade-in-arms stepped through the gap below them, had a perfunctory look around, issued a guttural curse, and then retraced his steps. A few more grumbling imprecations—which grew more faint and then receded—drifted down to the cowering Holdsmen, and after that silence fell once more. Kal scrambled back down to the gap and saw that the bucket was gone, taken back to camp by Estvor's disgruntled companion. With relief he surmised that it would be a while now before they realized their man had gone missing and was not truant.

Having taken care of the soldier, they crept through a densely twisted thicket of alder trees that covered the gradient of the hill to the left as they moved farther up from the streambed. At the top the ground levelled off into a tableland with close ranks of linden and beech trees. This tableland clung to the mountainside like a bracket fungus fixed onto the bole of a tree. Its lower lip was the sprawling meadow from which Kal and Galli had seen the Gharssûlian soldiers come down into the ravine after Gardy-Good.

The two stole like shadows through the burgeoning green of the woods that Kal knew so well. They stayed close to the sloping hanger of brush and tangled briar they had just climbed, moving along the edge of the woods, avoiding its further depths, which were broken by the main path that gave onto the tableland, a path sure to be well-travelled.

Not too far ahead of them the trees ended at an open field. They stopped, amazed at the number of human figures that could be seen milling about, limned against a backdrop of open sky. They decided in a huddle of furtive whispers that it would double the danger of discovery for both of them to continue. Although Galli was by far the more expert and silent stalker, Kal insisted he should be the one to go on ahead while Galli stayed back, since he had a far abler grasp of the Gharssûlian language. Besides, the woods were so close-woven in their spring array that it would be child's play to creep to the forest's edge and scout things out. Galli protested that with his sharper senses he would see more than his companion. Finally they compromised by agreeing to approach the Gharssûlian camp by short stages. One of them would go on ahead and wait for the other to catch up and so on, like two wrens flitting across a lawn.

This way they were able to reach the overgrown skirts of the clearing without being detected. Here Kal, peeping out from behind a gorse bush, counted a dozen pyramidal canvas tents arranged in the shape of a horseshoe, the open end of which they were facing. There must have been at least two score men, probably more, as some of them were in their tents. Many of them were dressed in chain mail with a surcoat bearing the dreaded figure of the black scorpion. Most were swarthy in complexion and tended to be short and stout with heavy jowls that made them look like dour-faced bulldogs. Indeed, story had it that Black Scorpion Dragoons did possess the tenacity of bulldogs, indomitable in the service of their lord and master Ferabek. One or two of them carried short stubby bows, while others were armed with thick-shafted spears—the weapons like the men.

A couple of the men were taller and fairer and dressed in simpler garb. Telessarians, no doubt—full-blooded ones, not half-breeds like Galli—the eyes and ears of the Black Scorpions, their master trackers and advance scouts. As one of them turned, Kal could discern the browmark. His mouth grew dry, his heart pounded.

At one of the farther tents, just above the ravine of Plunge Brook, a roasting spit had been set up. Close beside it a small knot of soldiers played at dice. One of them languidly turned the spit now and again. A pack of wolfhounds and surly-looking mastiffs were quartered in a makeshift kennel. Kal rubbed his eyes in disbelief. What were all these outlanders doing here in the Holding, the back of beyond? How did they evade the gatewardens at the Aerie—and them ready at the slightest sign of danger to blow a warning blast?

There arose a stir of excitement in the clearing. Someone important, it was clear, had arrived in the camp area enclosed by the semicircle of canvas. Kal and Galli exchanged puzzled looks, for there entering the encampment were none other than Kenulf and Enbarr dressed in huntsmen's garb.

The flap of one of the tents was flung open, revealing the strangest-looking character that either had ever seen. The man was short, short enough to make the other Gharssûlians look like giants beside him, yet there was a marked, almost palpable, air of authority that radiated from him, charging the air around his person. He had a full fleshy face with a bearded chin and thick protuberant lips beneath an upturned nose suggesting the snout of a boar. His flowing mane of coal-black hair cascaded down to his shoulders, which were covered by a richly embroidered saffron tunic with wide sleeves, pouched at the waist, reaching down to the tops of his high leather boots.

The Boar of Gharssûl—Ferabek himself. Looking wide-eyed at each other and pointing, they read each other's silent lips forming the dread name "Ferabek"—Ferabek, the undisputed master of the Autarchy of Gharssûl, and as such the liege lord of Arvon's usurper-king Gawmage, for he was the supreme leader of the Gharssûlian League, which grew stronger with every passing day.

From the tent behind Ferabek emerged two other men, one tall and sinewy, dressed in slate grey, the other short and stout, clad in green. Galli pointed in their direction and then to the wound on his arm. Kal nodded. Ferabek dismissed them and his subalterns with a peremptory wave of his hand and turned his attention to Enbarr and Kenulf, the latter looking very uncomfortable as he played with the fringe of his cloak.

Enbarr paid the Boar an obeisance with a quick bow, followed immediately by Kenulf, who did the same, but more diffidently, crowding his cousin like a child clutching its mother's skirts. Both of them were motioned briskly to stand aside even as Kenulf began to say something but was cut off, left to swallow his words, for Ferabek had turned to instruct his page boy, who had remained to attend him.

A slender oddly dressed figure emerged from another of the tents. He wore a distinctive black leather cap with flaps that were tied neatly with thongs beneath his clean-shaven chin, while cradled against his body, held fast in the crook of his right arm, was a common yard fowl, squawking as it struggled to break free. The man had a curious raptorial nose, with deep-set hooded eyes that scanned the scene with beady stealth, grudging only the merest telltale flicker to show that something had caught his interest. The page boy had scurried to one of the tents and come back carrying a tripod, which he unfolded, placing a large oval-shaped salver on top of it. The man holding the chicken wore a long white beltless robe that fell in billowing folds to the ground, covering his feet. The robe itself was decorated with odd intricacies in bright blue and gold embroidery.

Taking the knife that was proffered to him by the page boy, the man laid the fowl on the salver and held it steady with his free hand. Then deftly, with a slight effortless flick of his wrist, he drove the knife up through the gullet, releasing a gush of blood that dripped down onto the salver. Once the bird had ceased struggling, the man, who was being watched no less keenly by Ferabek, Enbarr, and Kenulf than by Kal and Galli from their hiding place, slit open its tail end and, reaching into the body cavity, pulled out the entrails, which he strewed across the salver. The carcass itself he handed to the page boy, who by now had brought a ewer of water with a towel and a basin, which allowed the white-robed figure to wash his hands. Having cleansed his hands of blood, he reached through a slit into the wide folds of his robe. He pulled out a small pouch and extracted something from it, which he placed in his mouth and began to chew. Similarly he procured himself a thin long-handled spoon, using it to turn and poke at the viscera of the fowl he had just gutted. With this his whole demeanour changed. His head rocked back. He began to chant in low sonorous tones that rose and fell with a hypnotic languor, all in some nameless language, entirely unfamiliar and utterly unlike either Arvonian or Gharssûlian.

The two young men were held spellbound as they watched. Kal surmised from his studies that this must be the bizarre ritual of augury, where the future was read by the unique colouring and configuration of an animal's entrails. It was Ardiel who had done away with the practice in Arvon and much of Ahn Norvys. The man wore a Thrygian cap, and what he was chewing had to be laurel leaves to aid him in the process of divination—a real-life Thrygian magician. Neither Kal nor Galli had ever seen such a creature, although many a highland tale was woven around these mysterious adepts from Thrygia, far to the east of Gharssûl.

The magician's trance did not last long, for he had stopped chanting in those strange rhythmic tones and had laid aside his spoon to let it be washed by the ever-attentive page boy. Then he turned to Ferabek and spoke, shaking his head as if in disappointment. Ferabek, not to be outfaced by the magician, glowered, barking some kind of order to him. The Thrygian remained cool, his air of calm unruffled. Then, ever dignified, he turned away and reentered his tent. A moment later he was slowly making his way back, carrying another bewildered chicken.

Again the ritual was enacted. Again it seemed unsatisfactory, for Ferabek nodded in the direction of the magician's tent, as if bidding him to fetch another fowl and try again. This the magician did, changing the colour of his cap to a blue of the same light aquamarine hue as the intricate designs adorning his robe. Once more Ferabek, now even more visibly angry and upset, sent the magician back. This time he returned with a much larger bird, a cock, as black as obsidian, its bright red comb and wattle dyed a deeper ruby red by the fountain of blood that spurted out from its severed neck. The cock's blood was everywhere. There seemed no end of it. The magician's own robe, until now unsullied, was spattered by jets of it. Turning up his aquiline nose with sniffing disapproval, he probed the inner organs with his spoon, all else hushed to silence by the lugubrious rise and fall of his chanting, which had now become a kind of ominous wail.

Once more the auguries proved unsatisfactory. Clearly there was a problem. Ferabek's face had grown flushed with anger. Thwarted thrice and again—not a good omen. But then the magician spat the laurel leaves discreetly into the closed palm of his hand and started to explain some point in earnest to his lord, who nodded in agreement and tugged pensively at his jutting chin, much mollified, it seemed.

Ferabek dismissed the bowing magician with a languid sweep of his hand and took notice again of the two Holdsmen in attendance. Kenulf appeared taken aback by the gruesome course of the rituals, while his cousin's eyes lit up at the prospect of obtaining a hearing at last. The three of them began strolling leisurely together and conferring. At least Ferabek and Enbarr were. Kenulf fumbled in their wake, ignored for the moment.

The three drew closer to Kal and Galli. Ferabek was heading right for where they lay hidden. Icy fingers of panic closed around Kal's chest. His first instinct was to run all out like the wind, in order to put as much distance as possible between himself and the Boar.

And Enbarr. There was something hardly less unsettling about him too. Enbarr had always seemed possessed of a sixth sense as far as Kal was concerned, as if he could read Kal's thoughts, feel his aversion. Whenever chance happened to throw them together, Kal would stand off, repelled by the man, and Enbarr would turn and pierce him with those fathomless blue eyes of his. Whatever it was about Enbarr—the sly knowingness, the cunning—the Boar exuded it too, except even more powerfully and malignantly. Kal shivered, sure that Ferabek had seen him or sensed his presence somehow. It was those eyes, even at this distance, their dark pupils sparked with a burning fire, sinister, grotesquely unnatural.

His voice, now within Kal's hearing, reinforced his naked terror, for it had a bestial quality, untouched by emotion. Not that it sounded gruff or unpleasant to the ear. Not at all. Rather it had a certain suavity to it, but with an underlying savage edge that seemed to spring from the darkness of the underworld itself, from which the Boar was reputed to draw much of his strength.

Somehow Galli was held less mesmerized, managing to keep his wits about him. He gripped Kal by the shoulder, which seemed to break his spellbound state.

"They're just following the path, that's all, don't worry." His voice had fallen to a whisper of a whisper in Kal's ear, for with his keener eyes he could make out the little game trail, overgrown with a lattice of leaves, that wound past their hiding place. Ferabek was merely wandering at leisure down this trail with Enbarr in tow, Kenulf being a few strides behind the two of them. In a moment they could hear Ferabek clearly, turning to speak to Enbarr in slow, measured Gharssûlian.

". . . The sun, Enbarr, I have to get myself out of the sun to consider the situation and away from the confounded odour of those chicken guts. It seems that they're no longer adequate for Cromus. The dream paths are blocked, he says. What do you say, Enbarr, about how he proposed to unblock them? A pretty idea, don't you think, with only one catch, as you well know. If I didn't value my Thrygian magician as highly as I do, I'd almost say he was mocking me. But we won't talk of Cromus now. Ah, this is much better . . . the shade and coolness of these trees after the stuffy air of the tent and having to listen to the bumbling apologies of those hotspur fools from Dinas Antrum sent by Gawmage. I should have sent a couple of Scorpions to do the job. I have half a mind to send the two clowns hopping headless back to that pigsty Gawmage calls his capital, but probably they're useless even as crow bait."

Enbarr knit his brows.

"What's that? You mean you haven't heard?" Ferabek stopped in his tracks and faced the Holdsman. "This morning they attacked the two men that help the bard, meant to do them in, if they hadn't proved unequal to the task and bungled it. Now the old man will surely have his back up, won't trust his own woods to be safe, with good reason, mind you. And he as full of tricks as Lostek the Fox by all accounts, knowing full well that someone will be watching his every move to try to discover where he has that brat of Colurian's hidden. Why, the Prince's blood would have dyed the ground red two decades ago if Gawmage hadn't been such a blundering fool right from the start.

"But now, to make matters worse, my trap is sprung, and I'm afraid the old man will find some way to spirit the lad, wherever he is, from out of harm's way, for the time being at any rate, so long as the lad's not here in this valley. For if he's here, and Cromus has a feeling he is, there's not a thing the old man can do to save him.

"On the other hand, if he's not hidden hereabouts, it makes the job of capturing him more complicated. Curse the whole business! Take the old man's pigeons, for example. There's no telling what messages he's sending out to those in league with him . . . but never mind. Whatever way he manoeuvres, in the end I'll not be flouted. Sooner or later, with my men watching the approaches to the Balk Pit and in control of this valley, we'll take the royal fire-bearer, since it's him and no other that'll rekindle the fire and carry it back to its sanctuary in the woods. Tradition won't have it any other way, will it, Enbarr? Still, I'm in no humour to wait. I want him now!" Ferabek growled with sudden ferocity, striking the palm of his hand with his fist.

"May it please Your Imperial Excellency, but I believe I've solved your problem, for I think I've hit on your royal pain in the neck at long last and he's not far off, not very far off at all, I can assure you. It was a marvellous stroke of luck and my own keen eye for detail, Your Excellency. I've kept my eyes and ears open for you, always vigilant on your behalf."

"But Enbarr, it was I who discovered it," ventured Kenulf, coming closer.

"Fool, you didn't know what you'd discovered until I rowed

out to the Castle last night in dead darkness to have a look for myself . . . even brought the blasted painting back to Broadmeadows with me. If it hadn't been for your dithering, we'd have had our bird in hand days ago."

"But I needed to think about it."

"You'd have been thinking 'til doomsday, if I hadn't wrung your secret out of you."

"It wasn't a secret. I just wanted to make sure, that's all."

"Aye, great way to make sure, sitting on your tail gnawing on your morsel of a clue, keeping it to yourself—"

"Stop, stop!" Ferabek flung forth his hand, palm outwards, in impatience. "What are you two jabbering about?"

"About our lost prince, Your Excellency. I think I've found him."

"Out with it then, man!"

"Well, it all came to pass because Kenulf's father found himself too ill with dropsy to make the trip himself to Raven's Crag Island this year. You've probably heard how the tradition hereabouts works, Your Excellency, that it is the Thane of the Stoneholding who every seventh year, within the Octave of the Candle Festival, makes the trip from Broadmeadows to the Castle to deposit an updated version of the manor rolls, a list that gives the names and ages of every living man, woman, and child in this whole backward clanholding and the names of all those who have died as well."

"Aye, we need that list."

"Not anymore we don't, at least not the way we needed it before. All the same, we should look it over. Just to double-check things, make sure all the Holdsmen of Starigan's age are accounted for when you sweep this valley with your Broom—"

"Aye, they're important rolls," Kenulf launched himself into the conversation again.

"That's not what you thought the other day." Enbarr rounded on him. "It was like pulling teeth to get you to make that trip to the Island."

"It was you who urged me to stand up to my father."

"Stop bickering. Get on with what you've got to tell me," demanded Ferabek.

"As long as I can remember and even before that, it's been my father who has undertaken the task of depositing the manor rolls," Kenulf piped up again. Enbarr let him continue with the thread of the story, while he himself kept silent, a smirk on his face.

"Well this year, imagine my surprise, my father bade me go in his stead. He was too ill. I thought it an infernal nuisance. You thought so too, Enbarr. Don't deny it. The whole idea of having to deposit the rolls in the Castle is sheer nonsense, no basis in reason, a worn-out tradition. Why not keep them at Broadmeadows? You said it was a stupid custom that allowed only the Thane to deposit the rolls in that old bat-infested stonepile! What difference does it make, really? It was only to keep him from nagging me to death that I finally relented and went. He said he'd dispossess me if I didn't go. I was forced to make the trip three days ago on an absolutely terrible, storm-tossed day. The sort of weather you wouldn't send a dog out into, least of all your only son."

Ferabek shuffled his feet impatiently, hands clasped behind his back. Kenulf rambled on with an increasing confidence, for he was showing himself to be a surprisingly fluent speaker of Gharssûlian, more so than his cousin.

"But no, he had to have it done that day, wouldn't hear any more of my excuses, as he put it, and before I can say jack-in-the-green there I am being rowed out by our head steward to the Castle with the wind blowing right through me and coming near to capsizing the boat, I should tell you, Your Excellency—"

"You should tell me indeed! What is it that you're driving at?" Ferabek spoke with brutal impatience. "I don't have the stomach today to listen to a braggart's tale of derring-do on that accursed pond you have the brass to call a lake."

"Yes, Your Excellency, by all means, if it please Your Imperial Excellency, I-I w-was only trying to fill in some of the d-details," stammered Kenulf, recoiling from Ferabek's affront.

"Spare me the details. Get to your point. Out with it quickly. There's much that needs doing, and I must be about my business."

Discomposed by Kenulf's tedious wordiness, Ferabek had stopped almost directly before the place where Kal and Galli lay hidden, scarcely daring to breathe, perhaps a good five paces away. He stood sideways to them in striking profile. A magnetic, compelling aura radiated from the Boar at this close distance. Kal thought he smelled a heady musk-laden odour, wafted to him by a downwind draft. The atmosphere was charged with a creeping menace, mysteriously compelling. Kal felt himself caught up and absorbed in it against his will, so that he had to make a great mental effort not to fall thrall to the spell of the Boar—a charm woven not merely out of the dulcet tones of Ferabek's suavely contemptuous voice, but more deeply from the very bones and sinews that netted together his flesh.

"Of course, Your Excellency—if it please Your Excellency, I mean to tell you directly that while I was making for the oaken chest in the Overlord's Chamber to deposit the manor rolls I chanced to be poking around in one of the side rooms, the scullery, I think, filled with all manner of odds and ends. Well, hanging all dusty with cobwebs on the wall was a huge portrait. It was labelled with an etched gold plate in Old Arvonian saying that this was a portrait of the High King Colurian in his twentieth year, the year he acceded to the throne of Arvon. Well, the portrait . . . the surprise of it, you understand, Your Excellency. There was something familiar about it that I couldn't place. But I searched and searched my memory—"

"And found nothing, a gaping void!" sneered Enbarr. "It was I who made the connection and I could have made it days earlier if you hadn't been so tight-lipped about your side jaunt through the scullery."

"But you know it's considered bad luck if you step foot outside the Overlord's Chamber. I didn't want anybody knowing—"

"Wait! There's a disturbance back in the camp. I must see what it is. Come along with me," grunted Ferabek, whose attention had suddenly been captured by a flurry of excitement in the clearing where the tents of his Scorpions stood pitched. Kal and Galli were puzzled too, until they saw with grim amusement that one of the chickens had escaped from Cromus's tent, a spry one, for several men, including two Telessarian trackers, were trying to catch it without success. Galli pinched Kal and whispered cautiously in his ear, urging that they should turn back, now that they had been given a natural diversion to cover their escape.

"No, no, Galli," Kal said, "we'll miss the most important part." At first Galli failed to follow Kal's meaning, for he had understood only a smattering of the overheard conversation. Hurriedly Kal related what he had learned.

In a short while Ferabek, discounting the cause of the commotion, turned back towards the shaded side path, deep in conversation with Enbarr. He had taken a friendly hold of Enbarr's arm, his face a glowing picture of pleasure. Meanwhile Kenulf trailed farther behind the two of them than ever, like a chastened puppy. It seemed to take forever for Ferabek and Enbarr to approach within earshot of Kal and Galli again.

"... is very good, my dear Enbarr. You've certainly earned a king's ransom, a king's ransom, with this bit of news, for my plans have been much skewed, thwarted you might say, by this youth who carries the weight of Arvon's faded glory in his veins. And now he's within my reach, aye, finally, within my very reach ..." Ferabek rubbed his hands together, and his voice trailed off into an awkward, reflective silence.

"Do you know, Enbarr, about the dream that's plagued me?" asked Ferabek suddenly, leaving Enbarr bewildered.

"No, Your Excellency."

"A plague, yes, a plague ... Night after night, shadows and voices ... Always the same, Enbarr, I awake with the words before my mind ... The words. Cromus says it's prophetic, but offers no answer to the riddling lines."

Ferabek paused, turned and looked up at the taller man, holding him captive in his steely gaze. " 'Beware the seed of Ardiel yet, else never shalt thou Arvon get.' Such is the prophecy, Enbarr. A prophecy against me! Me, the Overlord of the Gharssûlian League, Overlord of a dozen vassal kingdoms and more, a mighty empire. Aye, and Overlord too of this ancient folkdom of Arvon, the jewel of Ahn Norvys, excepting these bullheaded highland folk and their kindred in the Arvonian Isles. But now—now, Enbarr, you've brought me news that will put to rest this irksome fancy, this dream shadow. And there's more I need to ask of you yet." The tone of Ferabek's voice had changed yet again, becoming arch and smug.

"What is it you want me to do, Your Excellency?"

"I want you to return to Broadmeadows, you and your cousin. Keep your eyes and ears open. I don't trust this self-styled Hordanu, this holdout."

"Aye, Your Excellency," Enbarr said.

"He's a fox, sly and crafty. He knows that the Sacred Fire has been quenched in order to force his hand. Before the break of a new day, once we have the prince, this wretched Wilum shall vex me no more. He and the boy, both of them will be in my grasp this very night." The Boar clenched his fist. "Oh, how pleased Cromus will be to read the boy's intestinal fortitude!" He laughed, his throaty guffaw ringing through the open spaces of the upland forest.

The two young men felt themselves chilled to the bone. Even Kal could no longer bear the tension and longed for the chance now to flee. Every moment they stayed was fraught with danger.

How long would Ferabek and Enbarr linger here, shackling them to this perilous hiding place, a mere stone's throw away from the Black Scorpion encampment? How long would he and Galli be kept from making good their escape?

"And then the Talamadh shall be mine, and all of Ahn Norvys will step to a mighty Gharssûlian march." Redirecting his attention to the matter at hand, he sighed. "I digress here, Enbarr. My words are untimely and tempting of fate. First this night must bear its fruits. Go now. You know the plan. Tonight, in the smallest hours of the morning, when all save me and my men are asleep, we shall strike. Which means that at dusk you must make your way back to our encampment here."

"With Kenulf?"

"Aye, with him. He may be useful yet, as may those two thugs of Gawmage's, although I have my doubts." Ferabek had resumed his casual walking pace, and for the first time Kal and Galli dared to hope that he would move out of range soon and give them the chance to slip away. "Yes, my dear Enbarr," said Ferabek, warming to his subject, "we're going to put paid to the old man at long last. But him I want alive. I'll make a public spectacle of him in Dinas Antrum—hanged, drawn, and quartered to provide a meal for the carrion crows, a poor meal, all bones and gristle. High Bard, Guardian of Wuldor's Howe. Scum of Wuldor's Howe! Miserable pretender of a bard, who dares to try and stem the tide of change from this backward hilltop sanctuary, who dares to defy the martial might of Gharssûl on the strength of a few oafish highland archers and an ancient sham-king's timeworn grandeur. So much for the legend of Ardiel, the noble ploughman king. The whole world will see that it's no more than a hollow tale that's had its day. This Wilum, he's going to die a traitor's death, no need to tell you, Enbarr. We'll set fire to the Great Glence. That will be the signal to the squadrons I have posted at the Wyrdlaugh Pass, which, thanks to you, is now bereft of its wardens. Before morning they will have put to the sword every man, woman, and child in this clanholding, all of them save Wilum and our princeling.

"I'll have my men land on Raven's Crag Island and take the manor rolls in Owlpen Castle, so that we can make certain that no one is missing when our Broom makes its sweep. Cromus tells me they're important, that he's seen scrolls filled with list upon list of names in two of his dream trances and he's not sure but that these manor rolls may be the ones he's dreamt of. Whatever the case, I want every one of the oafish lot accounted for, every last one of them matched against the rolls. And I want the rolls themselves. It's not often Cromus misdirects me. Hah! Am I not clement, Kenulf? The very picture of benevolence? To grant them the mercy of dying in their beloved clanholding when I could have made a spectacle of them in Dinas Antrum or Pirrian D'Arba. The yokels will be surprised in their beds. And those who awaken to the danger will have no place to go, for we hold the Wyrdlaugh Pass. This wretched little place will no longer ignore the League. Hard to do when it no longer exists, eh, Enbarr? When their homes and farmsteads are razed to the ground, when their one little town is transformed into a charred ruin. There'll be no more High Bards arising from this fastness to challenge my might, to pretend that their power can equal mine. The old cult of Wuldor will die amid the rubble of the Great Glence," he spat out. "So much for the navel of Ahn Norvys—"

At that moment a gust of wind swept up from behind Kal and Galli. The breeze had changed direction, casting their scent full into the Gharssûlian camp. The dogs in the makeshift kennels, catching the smell of them, began barking and lunging at the ashwood palings that penned them in. A choking flash of raw panic overwhelmed Kal. He broke cover to escape, but froze in his tracks. With an animal quickness, Ferabek had spun around and locked eyes with him. The searing glare of the Boar's eyes was so intense, that Kal felt stripped of his very self. There occurred an eerie moment of calm, like the heavy stillness before the onset of a savage thunderstorm. It was as if Ferabek had had some sense all along that he was being watched from the shadows. In a timeless instant, Kal knew the chill terror the fox feels when beset by hunter and hounds.

"He's seen us! Run!" A limbering surge of adrenaline unfroze Kal's limbs. Galli had already sprung to his feet.

"Spies! Spies! To arms! Let loose the dogs! They must not escape! To arms!" Kal could almost hear the furious gnashing of the Boar's teeth.

With his barked orders ringing in their ears, they sped back through the forest at a furious pace, retracing their steps. They could hear the baying of dogs approaching closer and closer behind them, the lead they enjoyed over the dogs a slender one.

"We'll never make it if we go back . . . the way we came," said Kal, winded.

"What else can we do?" gasped Galli.

"Follow me . . . our only chance . . . jump across the brook . . . almost there . . . get ready to jump." Kal, who was in the lead, cast a quick look back over his shoulder and flinched to find that the hounds, with the heavy-jowled mastiffs in tow, were bearing down on them, no more than a bowshot away. The two had left the trees, headed for a great shelf of rock, the leading edge of which ended over a gorge, which dropped sheer. At the bottom of it gurgled Plunge Brook.

"All right," said Kal, pausing for a brief moment to collect his breath. "The other side. That rowan tree. It's a jump. Just have to hit full stride, throw your body into it. You ready? Let's go. I'll go left, you go right. Hurry . . . the dogs," he added, glancing back. "They're almost on us."

Running full tilt to the brink of the precipice, they lunged forward, hurtling their bodies through the air. It was Galli who, with arms flailing, landed safely on the crest of the earthen bank on the other side. Laying hold of the matted grass and hardy weeds, he pulled himself up. Kal had landed short and was clinging desperately to a confusion of roots dangling from the rowan tree perched on the very lip of the ridge. He felt a nip at his heel and wrenched away his flailing leg, leaving one of the pursuing dogs to slither yelping down the steep bank. He dropped Wilum's bow. Galli turned and, seeing Kal, knelt by the trunk of the rowan. He grasped Kal's outstretched arm and pulled him up. From the corner of his eye he could make out massed ranks of soldiers and hounds flooding towards the gap that separated them. Galli had rescued Kal not a moment too soon, for a spear kicked up the dust at the very spot where Kal had hung. The two of them scrambled to the top of the embankment. A spear whistled past, inches above Kal's head, grazed Galli's shoulder, and thudded into the ground before them. Galli swung his head around and lifted his hand, fingering the torn fabric of his tunic. It was fortunate the enemy bowmen had needed a few moments to gather and prepare their weapons, or Kal and Galli would have been picked off as easily as newly fledged ducklings in a small pond.

Now they ran.

FOUR

Kal and Galli thrashed farther into the forest, desperate to put as much ground as possible between them and their pursuers. Broken-winded, they stopped for a moment to take stock of the situation.

"What now?" said Galli between deep draughts of the mountain air. "We haven't gained much on them . . . It won't take them long to find a way across the gorge . . . pick up our trail . . . What do we do now?"

"The stitch in my side . . . a minute . . . give me a minute." Kal stretched, lifting his arm over his head. "There, it's better now . . . Got to think. We have to find a way to throw them off. It's our only hope. And we've got to warn the others. We have to get away from here, tell Wilum and father, and get the men together. I guess I have no use for these now." Kal slid Wilum's quiver, full of arrows, from his shoulder. "A pity I lost the bow—"

"Quiet! Listen, listen."

"Why, I can't hear anything but my own breathing."

"Exactly. There should be more bird song and other chatter. Did you hear that screaming jay? . . . There it goes again. Something's not right. We're being followed, I think. No, I'm certain we are."

"How did they get across the gorge so quickly?"

"Probably the same way we did."

"I didn't think of that. You'd think those short stubby fellows would never make it, all weighted down with their chain mail and armour."

"You'd be surprised. The weight they pack isn't all flab. But I don't

think it's them. I bet it's my blood countrymen. I don't know how
we're going to shake them. But we do have one advantage."

"What's that?"

"We know the terrain far better than they do. Let's go."

Even as he said it, Galli was off, leading Kal back and forth
up the mountainside. It was difficult going, for they did not linger on any of the travel-worn paths. Once they doubled back in
a loop and found solid evidence that they were being followed
by three men who wore the soft leather footgear of trackers.
Whenever they came to a stream, they waded in it for some
distance, usually as long as their feet and legs could take the
chilling stricture of the cold. This bought them a bit of time at
least, for the Telessarians would have to cast upstream and down
to rediscover their trail.

But, how to shake them? Kal racked his brain for possibilities.
Never before in the Holding had he had to deal with woodsmen who were Galli's equals or, as in this case, superior to him.
These were men of Telessar, born and bred in a wilderness land,
preternaturally keen at sensing every shifting nuance of the fields
and forests, their skills having been honed to exquisite sharpness
from boyhood by the elders of their race.

"What if we made a stand somewhere and fought it out with
them?" suggested Kal, as they plodded through a mire that oozed
around their ankles.

"These men are trained, battle-hardened killers, the absolute
cream of the Gharssûlian army. Did you see them in the camp?
As lean and muscular as whippets. And three of them, mind you,
to our two. We wouldn't stand a chance . . . That Ferabek, though,
he gives me the shivers right down to my very bones. So does his
magician friend. If he had come any closer, I think I would have
jumped out of my skin. There's some deep evil there. I thought
for a while there that Ferabek was weaving a spell around me,
drawing me into his web like a spider. Then I found that, every
time my mind turned to the Great Glence and the orrthon, the
power emanating from him waned. I could feel my own mind
coming back to me. Scary. I don't wonder he's Overlord of so
much of Ahn Norvys and that he had even Enbarr eating out of
his hand like a simpering half-man."

"What I felt exactly," Kal said.

They fell to thinking for several paces.

"But these trackers . . ." Kal broke the silence. "If we can't fight them, why don't we try to stay one step ahead of them and go back down the mountain for help? We could sound the alarm along the Edgemere Road and raise a clutch of Holdsmen with their longbows in no time. They would be more than a match for them."

"I don't know . . . If we can stay ahead of them—I'm afraid my delaying tactics are just child's play to them and that they're taking our measure and slowly gaining on us. All told, I'd say we're in a tight fix."

They trudged on for a spell through the woods, which would normally have lifted their hearts with gladness after the rigours of winter. But instead every shadow and rustle of leaves served as an unsettling reminder that they were being stalked. The sun had already surpassed its midday mark, and both were weary, hungry, and footsore.

"Wait . . . I have an idea."

"What?"

"Do you know Scathe Fell?"

"Of course I do. You know I do," Galli snapped.

"You know the talus slope on Scathe Fell? The rockslides?"

"Sure, it's dangerous and it can't be climbed. What possible good is that to us?"

"Easy, Galli, easy. Listen. Here's a thought. Why don't we lead them on right to Scathe Fell? We'd take the path under the talus slope and the trackers would be sure to follow. If we could time it so we climb around it and get to the top of the scarp when they're right down below, we could set a few tons of rocks rolling down on them. It would be impossible for them to get away in time. I've seen what a rock avalanche can do. It was on Rocky Scaur one time. What a sight! Set off by one of the rams in our flock. Ended up killing about half a dozen of our ewes. If we could get them where we want them, they wouldn't know what hit them."

"Well, it's not far from here. It's worth a try. A long shot, but it might work."

With a lighter step the two turned their feet higher up into the mountains, heading directly for the leeward face of Scathe Fell, which was situated on the lower hillsides that stood guard, like pickets, before the steep pinnacles beyond. Unmantled by snow, the Fell itself resembled a squat craggy troll compared with the alpine giants that towered over it. Crowning its expansive girth lay a flat top strewn with rock amid gnarled oaks and pines.

As they passed higher into the glencelands, the trees became more sparse, small and twisted, stark against painted floral meadows already blooming with the quick-growing grasses on which the Holdsmen pastured their summer flocks. Sometimes the shriek of a lammervulture broke the stillness over the dwarf pine and wolfwillow. Now they were able to trace the outline of Deepmere, a deeply tinted patch of cerulean blue far below them. Once Galli detected a flicker of movement not much below them at a place they had passed just a short while ago.

"There they are. Did you see them?" Galli pointed. "I'd say we have about half an hour on them at most. We're almost at Scathe Fell, though. I'd be surprised if this works. They're not stupid."

"Timing, this calls for good timing. We have to make it to the top of the Fell before they reach the bottom of that scree."

"Then we'd better pick up our heels."

The two broke into a laboured jog against the grade. Their path neared the lower base of the Fell, then climbed steeply, staying close to the sprawling granite mass that rose on a shallow but still forbidding slope to its slanting pate.

"Can they still read our sign on all this rock? Now we don't want to lose them."

"Don't you worry about that. It would take more than this mess of rocks to test their skill. Cast an eye behind you," replied Galli, pointing again. Outlined on the horizon strode the three Telessarian scouts. They made their way at a pace that seemed effortless, as if they could smell blood and were closing in for the kill. It did not seem to matter to them that they could be seen by their quarry. Then, as they turned a corner, the threesome disappeared from sight. For a bit, their way narrowed to a grassy path that clung to the bulking mass of Scathe Fell, its outer rim dropping off sharply to a foaming alpine stream. Following its bends and turns, they reached a rocky terrace, hardly broader than a ledge and tinted a brilliant pink by thousands upon thousands of flowers.

Kal and Galli picked their way along the path, crossing the course of loose stone, heedful of the tons of rock that could come sliding down on them. Galli spotted a mountain goat that peered down on them from the top of the Fell, perched on the very edge of the escarpment.

"I hope that billy's not thinking about leaping down," said Kal.

"Probably not. It's a long jump onto the scree from where he is. Not too many animals would care to make it, except if they're forced."

Clearing the threat of rockslide, they came to a natural archway, just barely passable. They ducked through and picked their way for several steps over a pile of rubble that littered the path. On the other side of the debris they quickened their pace, aiming to reach the prospect overlooking the scree as fast as possible. It remained their only chance to turn the tables on their hunters. They were disturbed to find that the trail did not ascend directly to the flat area atop the Fell, which became too steep here for any animal to scale. Precious time was lost as they followed the leisurely ascent of the path diagonally across the stout ramparts of the Fell, calling on strength and endurance they scarcely realized they still possessed.

Winded and gasping for breath, they reached the top. Galli lurched on ahead, startling the goat. The animal bolted by him towards the far end of the hilltop. Kal threw himself down doubled, heaving to catch his wind, then struggled up and staggered to where he could look out over the slope. Galli was already busy searching for the right kind of rocks for them to roll over and trigger their avalanche. One fair-sized rock lay poised on the edge already. The Telessarians were still nowhere in sight.

"After all this effort, I hope they show up for the party," gasped Kal with a lightheaded humour that arose from sheer exhaustion.

"They will. They most certainly will, or I'm not Galligaskin Clout."

"Whatever you are, Galli, you've got the strength and spit of one of your uncle's workhorses."

Galli smiled at his friend. "Here, give me a hand with this stone. The other one may not be enough. Let's get it as close to the edge as possible."

They had only just finished cradling the thing neatly on the very edge when Galli dropped to the ground, as if he had been poleaxed.

"Get down! Quick! . . . That was close. There's the first one. He hasn't seen us. They're coming. Don't want them getting suspicious. We have to give them enough time to get midway along the path."

Kal's heart pounded madly as they crouched together out of sight, shouldering the heavy rock, preparing to flip it over onto the nether slope. Neither of them dared to peek over the side. A minute rolled by and it seemed an eternity. Galli ventured a look.

"Come on!" he whispered. "Before they get too far along. Quick now. That smaller rock first."

The rock fell onto the slope and tumbled ponderously end over end, dislodging only a scattering of debris, until its momentum carried it over the edge of the terrace below. The Telessarians looked up in short-lived surprise, then one of them began immediately to nock an arrow to his bowstring.

"That one was too small!" screamed Galli. "We need the big one! Come on!"

Galli put his shoulder into it, and the great lichen-covered boulder keeled over on its side. With one last push they launched it over the edge just as an arrow whistled past Kal's cheek. They dropped to the ground and lay waiting in an agony of expectation. A low rumble like a rolling peal of thunder grew louder and louder. As the ground beneath them quaked, they were afraid they would be swept down in an awful jumble of crushing stone and earth. From below came the muffled shouts of the trackers. The clatter of falling rock subsided, and there ensued an eerie calm. They became aware of a staccato chorus of cheeps. A boulder near the top of the scree, displaced by the rockslide, had hidden a tiny bird's nest, now upended and exposed to the bitter mercy of the world at large.

It was Galli who was the first to slowly lift his head. "Re'm ena!" he exclaimed, a quaver in his voice. Kal looked now too. From the confused mass of rubble that littered the slope below there protruded the edge of a sword scabbard and a couple of grotesquely misshapen limbs—an arm and a leg that looked so rigid and lifeless they might have been petrified by some wicked spirit of the Fell. There was no sign of the other two bodies. Perhaps they had been swept off the terrace, which now lay submerged under rocky debris.

Galli whistled long and low. He turned to Kal. "Well, now," he said, "we've gotten rid of them, but how are the two of us going to get back down?"

"What do you mean?" asked Kal, who had turned to help the chicks, lifting their nest into a protected crevice in the rocks just as the alarmed mother bird alighted, scolding him.

"Look over there, towards that arched opening we had to duck through to get up here."

"Why, I can't even see it. It's full of rocks and rubble."

"Right."

"You mean we have to find another way down off the Fell?"

"Right again."

"But I've never heard of another way, have you?"

"No."

They sat for a moment, surveying the changed terrain.

"I'm so hungry," Kal said, "I could eat a horse. I need some food or I'll drop. Maybe we could find something before we worry about getting down."

They sat in silence, savouring the peace-filled quiet, as moments passed, until Galli, hugging his knees, rocked forward onto his feet and stood.

"You're probably right. Where we came up I thought I saw a damp area, probably a little spring or stream. Maybe there's something there."

"What wouldn't I give for a cool drink of water too. Come on, let's have a look."

Sure enough, there was the most delightfully cool spring percolating like a little fountain out of a dimpled fissure in a boulder stained purplish black by cushion moss. Once they had slaked their thirst, they gathered up handfuls of watercress and cuckoo-flower and munched, like rabbits, on the tender young leaves, washing them down with further draughts of chill clear water.

Refreshed somewhat, they turned their attention to their descent.

"I think that maybe it would be better if we split up for now. We haven't much time." Kal looked up with a frown at the sun, already declining from its midday strength. "Tell you what. I'll cast around on this side of the Fell, while you go up towards the other end to have a look. Maybe we'll find a halfways climbable route down. One thing's sure, we'll have to get going soon, even if we have to take a chance on that scree slope."

"If that wouldn't be near suicidal! There must be a better way."

"Find it fast then. We'll meet back here at the spring as soon as possible. I'm going to poke around the path we took to reach the top here. Briacoil."

"Be careful, Kal," Galli said, as he turned on his way. "Briacoil."

Kal descended slowly onto the track that ran slantwise across the face of the Fell towards the plugged archway farther down. He got down on his hands and knees and peered over the side, on the lookout for any hint of a spot that might give them purchase for a return to the terrain below. Here he saw a way. It was close to the rock-plugged archway and marked a break in the forbidding sheerness of the rock, for it was buttressed by a series of outthrust skirting ledges that might allow for a precarious descent without the benefit of ropes and grappling hooks.

Down on all fours, engrossed in making rough mental measurement of the distances, Kal glanced at the ground near his hands as he pushed away a rock, sending it dropping over the edge. He shivered. A long shadow had fallen across his arm—the unmistakable silhouette of a figure gripping an upraised sword, creeping up from behind. During that first instant of recognition, an instant that seemed to stand out from measured time, he remained frozen, paralysed by fear, his heart thumping in his chest like a drumming partridge. Almost immediately, his numbed senses recovered, so that, hackles rising, he lunged to his right and let loose with a terrific yell, the battle cry of the Holdsmen.

"Haree-hoo-sai!" Kal roared, letting the rounded syllables drain away some of the tension and fear. Scrambling to his feet even as he turned around to meet the adversary coming at him with a shortsword, he demanded in a raised voice that was almost calm, "What do you want?" Trembling, he fumbled to draw his own sword.

It was one of the trackers, dishevelled and limping, but deadly earnest nonetheless, a queer, murderous glint in his green eyes. Kal lifted his sword to defend himself, and the Telessarian grinned. With a quick flick of his wrist, the man struck the shank of Kal's sword with his own, deftly knocking it out of his grip and onto the grass. Kal blinked at the sword where it lay. The man's eyes gleamed with amusement. Kal took a step back, and reached for the small hunting knife he had sheathed at his belt. Brandishing the puny blade, Kal stood facing the man, whose livid face, framed by his garland browmark, had twisted in contempt. Kal fought down the sour choking taste of fear. Here was a dangerous adversary, better armed, better trained, and as lissome as a hazel wand, even in his haggard condition. Advancing a short step, the wounded tracker began hissing out steely cold-blooded curses in some strange language.

They squared off, the Telessarian's shortsword weaving a languid sinuous pattern in the air. The man's long fingers, white-knuckled, gripped the hilt of the sword. His other hand, fingers splayed, was held out to the side. The eyes blazed with malice. The lips twitched over bared clenched teeth. Then came one—two probing feints. Kal had scarcely enough room to turn, let alone react to these thrusts. Another jab tested Kal's defences. For a split second he slipped and lost his balance, teetering on the steeply dropping edge of the path. Yet his adversary was only toying with him, deriving a grim enjoyment from drawing out his advantage, or else he would have seized this opportunity to press home a lethal thrust. In a moment would come the kill. There was bloodlust on the man's face as he forced Kal into a clumsy shuffle backwards up the path towards the top of the Fell.

Down fell the shortsword at Kal's shoulder—a great, unflinching blow. On instinct he brought up his hunting knife to parry the cutting edge. The shortsword glanced off the knife, knocking it from Kal's hand, so that it clattered to the path. In that instant, when the Telessarian's shoulders and body were being pulled by the arcing momentum of his sword, Kal saw his sole remaining chance.

Kal lunged at the attacker's chest with outstretched arms and drove him back. The tracker staggered off balance. Kal closed with the man, and the two fell to the ground locked together, grappling in the dust and stones of the pathway. The Telessarian let go of his shortsword, now useless at close quarters in a contest of sheer body strength. Kal could feel the lean wiry sinew of the tracker's arms and legs squeezing him like constricting bands of iron. He found himself no match for this seasoned veteran of Ferabek's campaigns of conquest.

Kal squirmed in a vain attempt to escape the man's strength. They had rolled very near to the outward edge of the path, lying parallel to it. He pulled towards the drop with all his waning might. A dire fall, it seemed the only way to break the tracker's heavy grip. Kal found himself pinioned now beneath the man, who struggled to sit up on Kal's torso in a bid to pin down his arms with splayed legs. Kal was past caring. He needed air. He longed for a place light and free. Kal teetered on the very brink, one of his shoulders already in midair. The tracker had merely to spring to his feet and kick him over the edge. But he did not. It would make the killing too easy.

Kal's mind sharpened in this last moment of life. In the space of a heartbeat his distorted thoughts were brought to a focus. Already the tracker's strong fingers were clamping down over his windpipe. Once more, with his dying breath, he let loose the Holdsman's war cry, breaking for the briefest of moments the vise-like grip of the tracker's hands. With a mighty wrench of his shoulders, quivering with the strain, Kal lifted his own torso and the tracker's, turning himself over and heaving the two of them in a grim embrace out into the open space beyond the edge.

They dropped, but not far—perhaps five paces, to a rock-littered outcrop. Kal's twisting throw had spun their locked bodies over in the space of air. There was an abrupt thud and the sickening crack of shattered bone as a skull hit the solid rock that protruded jaggedly from the hillside. Kal's fall was cushioned by the broken body that underlay him. Shaken and winded, but unharmed, he wrestled himself free from the dead man's clasp, pushed himself away, and sat there in a huddle, collecting his breath, his wits, averting his eyes from the battered and lifeless heap beside him.

Minutes passed before he realized that he was stranded. He could not climb back up to the path from which he had fallen. The place was too steep, lacking holds for hand or foot. Galli was probably already waiting for him back at the spring. He couldn't be so far away that he was out of earshot.

"Galli, help me! I'm trapped here! Help!" He yelled again and again, pacing the ledge like a caged animal.

A head appeared over the brink of the path above.

"Kal! You all right? . . . Now how did you manage to get down there?" Galli looked down first at him and then the corpse.

A flood of relief washed over Kal which left him feeling weak, heavy-limbed, and slightly nauseous. He nodded in response to his friend's concern. A moment passed as he regained himself, lifting his eyes to meet those of his comrade.

"It's never been so good to see you, Galli. He took me by

surprise. Somehow he managed to get clear of the rockslide and make it through the arch. Must have been hiding, waiting for us. He nearly did me in. We fell. He's dead."

They both stared at the broken body of the scout, the gore from his cloven skull staining the stones that broke his fall. Kal shuddered as the adrenal rush subsided and the grip of the suppressed and now pointless fear rose cold and acid in his gullet.

"We've got to get off this rock, Galli. We have to get down."

"Right . . . the trouble is I couldn't find anything at the top of the Fell. Nothing but steep-sided cliffs and awful traverses that even a mountain goat couldn't travel."

Kal shook himself, looking up to the face above him. "Well, then. Jump down, Galli—but fetch my shortsword first." Kal glanced over the edge of the rock shelf. "I think I've found us a way. I figure we might just be able to drop from ledge to ledge and make it down from here. Take a look yourself. What do you think?" asked Kal, a slight tremor still in his voice.

"It doesn't seem impossible," Galli said after considering for a moment the succession of outspreading ridges fanning out below Kal's feet. "Well, we don't have much of a choice, do we? You can't come up, so we go down." He turned to collect Kal's shortsword on the ground at his feet.

"Throw me down that hunting knife of mine, too. Up on the path. It should be there somewhere. I owe my life to it," called Kal, when Galli reappeared looking over the edge above him.

Galli got down on all fours and lowered his legs down over the lip of stone, until, facing the smooth rock, he was hanging only by his hands. Then, letting go, he slid and touched down on the ledge beside Kal.

"Well, we're in this together now, win or lose. What should we do about him?" asked Galli, nodding at the corpse, its eyes grotesquely bulged in a face distorted by the sardonic rictus of death.

"Nothing. Unless . . ." Kal paused, eyeing the body. "If we strip him of his clothes, we could use them tied together for a makeshift rope. Or maybe he has something on him that we could use?"

Galli shook his head, flexing the muscle in his jaw, his fists at his hips. "No," he said, "no, Kal, let him be. We can't dishonour the body, enemy or not. He's Telessarian. Let these stones be his funeral cairn."

"So be it, then, Galli," Kal said, shaking his head. "Either way, we've got to move down from here, and fast." He peered over the side to the next ledge below.

Galli paused a moment, looking around the barren ledge, then approached the body and, stooping over it, placed the dead tracker's hands on his chest. "Thy browmark be thy warrant," he intoned and quickly turned away.

The next half-dozen drops proved easy and straightforward for them, shorter and less precipitous than the very first stage of their descent. But then they reached an impasse. The next two ledges beneath them were so narrow that they could not possibly drop down onto either of them without losing their footing and falling backwards. What made the manoeuvre doubly unthinkable and dangerous was a pile of rocks on the first ledge, the ledge immediately below them, which would make their footing even more treacherous. They examined the problem from every conceivable angle for some sort of solution.

"What do we do now, Master Kalaquinn? We can't go back up and there doesn't seem to be a way down. In short, it looks like we're right royally crag-fast. Might as well be in some deep dar-rk dungeon in Pir-rian D'Ar-rba," he growled, "for all the good we're going to do anybody way up here watching cloud shapes and counting the lammervultures."

"Aye, and the sun. We can't see it now for the clouds, but the day's wearing on. There must be some way down. There has to be. And with the Scorpions fixing to slaughter us all—"

"What do you mean?" asked Galli.

"Didn't you hear Enbarr and Ferabek?"

"Hear them I did, but as to understanding, that's a different story. I'm afraid that Landros's lessons in Gharssûlian never really took with me like they did with you. It's a good thing you were there to catch what they were saying, or we wouldn't be much the wiser about what they're up to. You understood what they were talking about, didn't you?"

"I suppose I did, most of it."

"Well, I'll tell you, as far as I'm concerned, they were talking so fast I could hardly catch a word. And then there was that powerful spell that Ferabek seemed to cast with his voice, like being hypnotized. It was all I could do to keep my mind from slipping out of its moorings and floating away, let alone trying to understand what he was saying. I caught a phrase here and there though . . . Wilum . . . Wyrdlaugh Pass . . . King Colurian . . . the words for kill and slaughter, but I couldn't for the life of me make out much more than that."

"Well, in short, their plan is to kill every last person in the Holding. The two of us may be the only ones left, when everybody else has fallen to spear and sword."

"They want to kill everybody?"

"There were snippets of the conversation that weren't clear. But I'm sure about that part. It seems, as well, that Enbarr has given Ferabek reason to believe that Prince Starigan is still alive. He's desperate to get his hands on him so he can get rid of him and end the line of Ardiel forever. From what I could tell, Enbarr has somehow discovered where he is. He and Ferabek were about to talk about it some more, but then that chicken caused the ruckus in their camp. Anyhow, the main point is that they want to wipe out every last living soul in the Holding, and they want to do it this very night. And Wilum too. Ferabek wants him really badly, him and the Talamadh. But parts of what they were saying were quite puzzling. Wilum, he might have an idea of what to make of it, if we don't end up spending the rest of our days stranded here on this vulture's stoop."

Kal stared off into the middle distance, his eyes blank and unfocused.

"Oh, but I'm so tired . . ." He yawned. "Just a short rest. Maybe if we rest a bit we'll have a better idea what we should do next."

They both leaned back against the cliff face on the broad shoulder of the crag, while the stark rock walls towering over them echoed to the screeching of the birds. Kal closed his eyes and let his mind drift away, dismissing thoughts about how terribly long the odds against them seemed, even if they did finally find their way off Scathe Fell, an outcome that looked exceedingly unlikely at the moment. Time slipped as he fought exhaustion's sweet temptation to sleep and to forget—the Holding, the peril, Black Scorpions, and slaughter.

Kal could feel the radiant warmth of sunshine spreading over his closed eyelids and face. He swept away the cobweb shrouds of doziness from his mind and, looking up, saw that the sun had drifted from its screening banks of clouds. Slowly he got up. Galli lay huddled under his cloak fast asleep. The sullen greyness of the

crags had given way to the sun's genial embrace, bathing everything in light. He gazed around him. All the rock had assumed
different, clearer outlines. At the far end of the ledge, just past the
point where it met the face of the scarp, there lingered a curious
space of shadow. Kal crept closer and discovered a cleft, a fairly
large one, somewhat wider than a chimney hole. Lying prone to
inspect it, he found it ran diagonally underneath their ledge and
met the narrow stone-strewn shelf below them at a place where
it was obscured by an overhanging cusp of granite. The cleft was
wide enough, he could tell, to fit a man and also, happily, narrow
enough for a man to straddle with his body without falling.

He left the firm ground of the ledge and sidled slowly into the
open recess. Down he slid by fits and starts, propping himself up
with his arms and legs and the small of his back. The scabbard
of his sword rattled against the rocks as he proceeded. Following the line of the shaft, he found he had passed the first of the
close little ledges that had daunted them and was not far from
the second when his way ended in a solid bottom of rock. Here
he sat down and paused, with both his feet dangling out over
the edge. Here he had a simple jump of perhaps a man's height
to reach the narrow but firm ground of the second ledge. Turning around so that he faced Scathe Fell again, he slowly lowered
himself down and almost stepped on the drooping crimson bells
of a columbine that had nestled itself hardily into a crack. This
was Ruah's flower, and Kal took it for a good omen. He could
now see that with three or four more easy drops they would be
down from Scathe Fell on more easily negotiated terrain.

Shouting louder and louder, he succeeded in wakening his
friend. Galli shook off the drowsiness and rubbed his eyes to make
certain it was truly Kal that he saw on the ledge below him.

"You're always turning up in the strangest places. How did you
manage it?" he asked groggily.

"I was lifted down on a fellhawk's wings, while you were busy
snoring. Look!" He pointed to a distant lammervulture riding a
thermal high in the sky. "Make sure you're ready. All you have
to do is hop on its back."

Galli started, glancing up at the sky, warily. Kal chuckled.
No doubt, his friend's sleep-worn mind, susceptible to suggestion, was conjuring up images of the huge terrible birds that
inhabited islands in the Cerulean Ocean, but only rarely ranged

as far as the Holding. The only one he had ever seen was the fledgling Kal had found by chance on one of his rambles about the mountainsides.

"Wake up, Galli, really! I'm just joking. Just sit down and relax for a minute. The last thing I want to do is bring another Telessarian, even a half-blooded one, crashing down on me." Slowly Galli returned to his waking senses as Kal outlined his discovery. While Galli scrambled down, Kal poked around and found the remains, long picked clean, of what appeared to be a mountain goat that had met its death on the ledge. Kal was kicking at one of its horns just as Galli reached the end of the cleft and was making ready to jump down and join him.

"Whatever dreams you were just having must have passed through a Gate of Horn, not Ivory. You remember, don't you, how the old saying goes, 'False dreams of deceit are through Ivory borne, but dreams truthful and right pass through Gates of Horn.' Presuming, of course, you were dreaming of a way down this Fellside."

"Odd that you should say that. As a matter of fact I was."

"Mind you don't crush the columbine there at your feet. Though it's probably survived much worse treatment than a clumsy-footed Clout," cautioned Kal. "You'd think a beekeeper would mind flowers better. You know, Galli, I'm beginning to think you could sleep through just about anything. Must have been some dream you were having." Galli now stood safely beside him.

"You know, in my dream I pictured that we were safely down from here." Galli's enthusiasm kindled as he recalled the details of his dream. "But then we were running and we had a far way to go through forests and fields and all kinds of strange places I've never seen. We weren't in the Holding. I could tell. Then came nightfall. There was this most fantastic display of the Boreal Lights, flaming red, like long fingers of fire reaching up into the heavens. I've never seen anything like it, even the other night when they seemed so spectacular. And then we were separated somehow and you called out for me."

"And then what happened?"

"That's when I awoke and heard you shouting fit to wake the dead."

FIVE

Kal clutched Star Thistle's mane and pressed his knees into the mare's flanks, urging her to a more rapid gallop against the stiff north wind that soughed through the restless trees. More than once he had nearly slipped from the saddle in a stupor of exhaustion. He had now alerted three of the homesteads that clung to the Edgemere Road and was fast approaching the outskirts of Wrenhaven. Already he could already see the lights of the Sunken Bottle looming like a beacon in the darkness.

He had lost altogether too much precious time at the Fletcher place. Old Thurfar Fletcher would not at first be persuaded that Kal was not playing a young man's mad prank. It was Thurfar's wife, Fionna, who had finally convinced him that Kal must be in earnest, but not before Kal found himself offering to swear solemnly by the sacred warrant of the orrthon and the Great Glence. At length Thurfar promised to spread the alarm to his immediate neighbours, who lived on the steadings flung out along the eastern margins of Deepmere.

Kal began to pull in the reins of the dark chestnut mare and sprang off her back before she had even halted. He had to find Tudno, the Town Warden, and explain the situation to him in person, his father had emphasized. Tudno was a man of parts, a man you could depend on. He needed to be alerted as soon as possible. His father had added too that Tudno might be found at the alehouse, where he was wont to catch up on the latest news in the valley and, occasionally, the wider world outside. On top of all that, he was an excellent longbowman, one of the best in the Holding.

The Sunken Bottle was a low-slung limestone building in the shape of a carpenter's square, its inside elbow looking onto a paved cobblestone courtyard. Closing the courtyard was a line of stables, fronted by some hitching posts and lit by an outdoor lantern. The only other illumination that spilled out into the courtyard came from the great bow window of the taproom.

Kal had only ever set foot in the Bottle twice before, and that with his father on business. Not that Kal was opposed to a pint or two, it was just that life had not yet afforded him the need to frequent such an establishment. From the stables he could hear the whinnying of another horse. He tethered Star Thistle to a post and rushed to the taproom door, above which hung the weathered device of an uncorked bottle being visited by a disinterested school of fish below the whitecaps of storm-tossed waves.

For a moment, he checked his haste and peered through the bow window, catching his breath. Just the other side of the glass, a large barrel-chested man with an apron stood peering out into the night. A fire burned briskly in the hearth. Someone seated at the inglenook moved away. Two fellows just on the edge of Kal's line of sight rose from their seats as well, leaving two other men in animated conversation over their cups at one of the scrubbed deal tables that were a hallmark of the Sunken Bottle. One of the men looked like Landros.

"And what brings you here to the Sunken Bottle this fine spring evening? You're Frysan Wright's lad, ain't you?" The man with the black tavern-keeper's apron accosted Kal almost as soon as he set foot inside the almost empty taproom. There was no mistaking his distinctive features. Old Golls, the boys of the Holding called him, poking fun of his meaty face and pendulous chops.

"Aye, Master Persamus, that I am. But I need to find Master Tudno. Is he here? I must see him." The words spilled out of Kal's mouth, his chest still heaving.

"Indeed he is. He's but stepped out to the privy. He'll be back in a moment to wet his lips again, I can assure you, young sir, or my name ain't Persamus Meade."

"But, I must tell him now. The Holding . . . Ferabek's—the Holding's been invaded. We're all in danger!"

"Invaded?" The tavern-keeper was taken aback, his face incredulous. He placed his fists on his hips. "What do you mean, 'invaded'?"

"We're all in grave danger. Ferabek himself has come, with his Black Scorpions. To kill us all. We must flee."

"Surely you can't be serious, lad."

"You must believe me. I must speak to Master Tudno."

"Calm yourself, young Master Wright. I told you, Tudno's about his business. He'll be back directly."

"But—but Master Meade . . ." Exasperation and panic coloured Kal's words. He could hear it in his own voice, and it made him feel embarrassed, juvenile and inept.

The tavern-keeper laid a thick hand on Kal's shoulder. "My friends call me Persy," he said, "and I count you among my friends. Come sit down here, while Tudno finishes what he's about. He won't be long. Kalaquinn, isn't it?"

"Aye, Kalaquinn."

"Come then, Kalaquinn, you look right worn and 'wildered, and perhaps a touch chilled. This way, my man, sit yourself down by the chimney," urged Persamus, taking Kal in hand and leading him to the wooden settle at the chimney corner. "Here we are, Persy'll take good care of you, while you wait a moment for the Warden," promised the tavern-keeper as he lifted a pewter tankard off one of the hooks that lined the beam above the flaming warmth of the great fireplace. "I'll be back as soon as a horse'll lick his ear, Kalaquinn."

The edge of dark urgency which had driven Kal to the Sunken Bottle was blunted by the warmth and cheer of the place. He sat on the settle, casting a glance about, while behind him he thought he heard the voice of Landros.

". . . and I say now's the time for weeding your cornfield. There's an old saying I just found in *Twelve Score Points of Good Husbandry*—"

"What's that you're talking about, Lan?" Kal recognized old Sarmel's familiar inflection and tone.

"*Twelve Score Points of Good Husbandry*. It's a manuscript I received just the other day all the way from Dinas Antrum, and I was reading in it just this morning that, 'In spring's third month get weed hook, crotch, and glove, and weed out such ones as the corn doth not love'—"

"But what do you know about husbandry, Lan," Sarmel said, setting his ale mug on the table with a thump, nipping the old teacher's dissertation in the bud. "You who've had your nose in dusty parchments when you're not drilling the lads in their letters? And what would you want with a lowland rag? Tell me, what do they know about corn and weeding?"

Sarmel and Landros fell into the banter of jocund argument, a place they had clearly visited many times. His attention wandering from one to the other, Kal listened to their voices blend with the other sounds of the public house—the crackle and spit of pine on the hearth, the hiss of a kettle, the mournful moan of the wind outside as it played with the pub sign creaking in its wrought iron hanger. Beneath this all now ran some kind of whispering talk behind his back that he could not catch. Again he shot a glance about the room.

After what seemed a touch longer than the time it would take for a horse to lick its ear, the ebullient alehouse keeper waddled back with a tankard full of mulled wine that he thumped down on the table before the young man. Kal hesitated. The stout man, smiling, nodded at the full cup and held out an open hand in a gesture of amicable hospitality.

"On the house, Kalaquinn."

Chilled and parched from his hard ride and the dust of the Edgemere Road, Kal acquiesced, seized the mug, and quaffed it to the dregs. It was a strong draught with an oddly bitter edge, and Kal sputtered a cough.

"Oh-ho, there's a thirsty fellow! I've never seen a body down one of old Persy's willy-waughts of mulled wine so speedily in all my days. Why, you must have a stomach like an ale vat, lad!" Persamus lowered his portly frame down beside Kal, straddling a bench, his jowls aquiver with amusement.

"Where's Master Tudno? Surely he must be back from the privy, Master Persamus. I must find him." Kal made to get up. "The news, he must have the news. We're all in grave peril—"

"Now, what might this grave peril be?" pressed the ruddy-faced Persamus.

"I told you, I must find Master Tudno. Please, I must sound the alarm to him and be on my way."

"Well, you'll have a bonny time finding Master Tudno tonight, I can tell you that, lad."

"How do you mean?"

"Well, I'm sorry to say, it appears he did his business and gave us the slip, you and me, although it seems he mentioned that he meant to go up to the Pass to talk to the gatewardens about something or other, and that he'd be back in the morning."

"He's gone where?"

"Why, up to the Pass, lad, checking up on them lads that are supposed to guard us all from evil hosting."

"He's in danger. The whole Holding's—"

"Howgates in danger? Are you certain Persy's wine's not addled your head a wee bit? Aye, sure you must be sore tired from your riding this night!"

"I tell you, Master Persamus, we're in danger. I'm going after Tudno. I'll catch up to him right enough, if I leave now."

Again Kal made to stand, staggering off balance, but the pub-keeper's great hand patted his forearm, encouraging him to remain seated.

"Persy, call me Persy. We don't stand on ceremony here at the Bottle."

"I have—I have to go," stammered Kal as if to himself. "Not a word of a lie . . . no . . . I saw it with my own two eyes—"

"Now, what did you see with your own two eyes, son? Sit you down. You may tell me then, and I may be able to lend you a helping hand. There ain't nobody more helpful to a fellow in distress than Persy Meade," Persamus said in low tones soothingly—an understanding uncle colluding with a favourite nephew. He seemed all at once so very friendly and wise and trustworthy. Kal sank back to the bench. Given the circumstances, he seemed the best person in Wrenhaven to pass on the alarm to—right at the hub of things here at the tavern, seeing as Tudno had eluded him.

Kal ventured a hasty look around him to see who else was within earshot. There were the two harmless drinkers he had noticed on coming into the taproom. And yet they seemed somehow changed. Perhaps it was the quality of the light that had changed. Someone must have extinguished some of the torches that were set in spaces between the oaken timbers that ran across the ceiling. The taproom seemed much dimmer and more cavernous than when he had come in, except for the crackling fire that blazed up before him in the hearth, the warm dance of its flames infecting him with a hypnotic languor, fixing him to the spot. The stout tavern-keeper rose from the settle to throw another log on it from the well-stocked woodbox.

"Come, Kalaquinn, out with it. I'm certain it would take more than a pull of Persy's mulled wine to jerrycummumble the tongue of one of Frysan Wright's sons. If there's danger, old Persy should know about it. The better to apply some proper physic to the problem, that's what old Persy says."

The story tumbled out from Kal's mouth in broken whispers as fast as his wine-fuddled lips could frame it, how he and Galli had been viciously attacked by the lowland spies, how the two of them had trailed these men and had discovered Ferabek's camp in an upland meadow on the Wrights' own homestead, and how they had overheard the Boar himself talking about an invasion of the Holding and slaughter, sharing his plans with Enbarr—a traitor, like Kenulf. Kal's mind grew more and more clotted and sluggish and he found himself struggling to follow the thread of his own tale. Even so, in halting phrases he managed to tell Persy of the strange, undigested bits of information he had somehow gleaned from his eavesdropping.

"You don't say, lad. Howshe, son, what happened after that?" encouraged Persy every now and again, whenever Kal's energies seemed to flag or his tongue got twisted. At last, Kal explained how his father had settled on Tarlynn's Coomb as the best meeting point, a place where all the Holdsfolk could regroup once they were alerted.

"And Galli, he's supposed to go to the Great Glence to tell Wilum and then I'm to meet them all at the Coomb as soon as I find Tudno and give him the news. But how can I do that when he's on his way up to the Pass and may be captured or dead already for all I know? Perhaps I can catch up to him still?" Kal wanted to rise from the settle but his body resisted. He found a strange lethargic heaviness had overtaken him. "What shall I do now, Persy?" asked Kal as his drooping eyes wandered from the fire towards his companion.

Like the thinning of a fog, the young man realized that something was amiss, for Persy had turned his head to the open doorway that led from the taproom to the scullery beyond. There were no lights there. Nor outside now at the stables. It was as if he had stumbled into the alehouse after hours. A figure was emerging from the shadowed entrance to the scullery. Persy nodded in that direction, beckoning on the newcomer, ignoring Kal, whom events had suddenly prodded into a new and frightened alertness. Who was this? There was something familiar in the profile and the gait.

"You've played me the jack, Meade!" cried Kal. "This is a trap! You've laid a trap for me!" Clumsily he lurched up from the settle, knocking it over, and turned to run for the door. He had scarcely stirred when two strong sets of arms stopped him dead in his tracks.

"Ho there, boy, now where's your manners to be getting up and going without so much as offering a by-your-leave to your gracious host, our dear Persy?" asked the shorter of his two captors. "We'd think it was downright unfriendly if you was to drink and run, and us wanting to get to know you better. Why, we hardly had a chance to exchange two words this morning. We was in such a hurry."

"Help! Someone help—" Kal tried to shout at the top of his lungs, but his cry came out feeble and strengthless.

"Shut him up!" barked Enbarr, who had slipped clear of the darkness and was now drawing near the alehouse keeper. Close on his heels came Kenulf. Skrobb clapped the palm of his hand over Kal's mouth.

"Shall I put him out of service for you, Enbarr?"

"No, no, you fool! Be gentle with him, gentle, or you'll pay for your roughness with your neck. I want to keep my prize intact 'til my lord the Boar has had his chance to look him over. Stuff a rag in his mouth. You've done me yeoman service, Persy, to clear out the Bottle on such short notice, allowing us to bag this fine young gentleman. And to learn his plans, which he has been so very liberal in providing us. A talkative lad, aren't you, when your father's not 'round about to hold your tongue? Other lads need their fathers to hold their hands. But you're the only pup I know who needs his daddy to hold his tongue," Enbarr said, a cold sneer playing across his face. Kal's stomach churned. How could he have been so naive and foolish? To have been fished in by old Golls of all people? "Here's a little something for your efforts, Persy," continued Enbarr, counting out four silver crowns and handing them to the innkeeper.

"My deepest thanks to you, Master Enbarr. That's right generous of you, right generous of you indeed," Persamus said, eyeing the money as he fondled it in his meaty hands. "I'm more than glad to oblige you, especially when there was so few as were here tonight anyhow, just Landros and old Sarmel, talking about them old days like they always do, the doddering fools. As much chance of bringing back the good old days, as they call them, as Deepmere freezing over in midsummer," he chattered on, greedily rubbing the silver coins in his palm.

"Oh, before I forget, there's something else I'd dearly like to give you for your efforts," added Enbarr, nodding to Grumm, who brought up his dagger from behind the tavern-keeper, swung it around, and drew it back across his throat in one swift movement. "Why, he's speechless with gratitude. You know, I think this is the first time I've ever seen Persy with nothing to say."

Enbarr stepped casually out of the way of the spurting blood as Persy slumped woodenly to the floor, spilling the crowns, so that they rolled to Kenulf's feet. Kal looked on aghast, his horror muffled by the gag, while Skrobb held him immobile.

"You . . . You killed him!" gasped Kenulf, shuffling away from the coins as if they bore contagion.

"Come now, coz, you mustn't be so squeamish!"

"I didn't know!"

"You didn't know what?" roared Enbarr, rounding on him. "That my lord Ferabek hasn't invaded this clanholding to play skittles with the local tavern-keeper? Tell me, what don't you know? What daydream country have you been living in, man?"

"Um . . . I'm just not used to this sort of thing," replied Kenulf, cringing at this new savagery.

"Well, you'd better get used to 'this sort of thing' and fast, now that the Boar is on the brink of his sweep. Just remember that it's you that helped to pave the way for him, dear cousin! Now, Grumm," continued Enbarr, turning aside to look at the tavern-keeper's inert body, "let the grubbing swine lie—"

"What about them . . . them silver crowns?"

"Go ahead." Enbarr flicked one of the coins with the toe of his boot. "But mind you look after this fellow as if your life depended on it. I want you to truss him up nice and tight and take him to Broadmeadows. Use Persy's horse and wagon. They're no good to him now, are they? And bring along the Wright boy's horse. We'd better stable it at Broadmeadows, in case someone comes looking for him and gets suspicious at seeing it. Put him in the Locker. You know where I keep the key. And then—I have an idea . . . aye, an excellent idea," mused Enbarr.

"What is it you want us to be doing after we've done that, Master Enbarr?" Grumm said.

"I want you and Skrobb to make sure Wright is safely tucked away in the Locker, and then you are to take to the Westwynd Way with all the speed your sluggish bodies can muster. There's too much danger along the Edgemere Road, too many homesteads thereabouts. He's given folk the alarm. You may take Strawboy and Windstorm. They're the two finest mounts in the old Thane's stables. I want you to fly as if you had the Greymalkin at your heels. Go to the Great Glence and capture the old man, before he has a chance to scurry up into Tarlynn's Coomb. That's not too far away from the Hordanu's Enclosure, and the hiding holes he may have up in the mountain heights . . . ? Even with their expert trackers it could take the Scorpions days, if not weeks, to ferret around and dig the old fox out of those wild upland places. You'll have to watch for the other fellow, the Clout lad. He may reach the old man before you do. But you can handle him alone. It'll be the two of you against one of him."

"What do you mean two against one? What about the Hordanu?"

"Oh, Grumm," Enbarr shook his head. "Do you need to ask? If you're worried about a sorry old bag of bones . . . Really! Though I don't dare say his mind is gone. Aye, it's his mind that makes him a force still to be reckoned with . . . but not for two fine footland-rakers from Dinas Antrum like you. His mind lacks your exquisite refinement," remarked Enbarr with a burst of harsh laughter. "Anyway," he went on, stopping before the hearthfire to look into the flames, "here's your chance to redeem not only yourselves but me too with my lord Ferabek. He's none too happy with your antics this morning. But mind that the old man and Clout come to no harm at your hands or you'll end up providing a feed for the Boar's dogs. We'll leave it to him to decide the fate of the old man and his boy."

"What shall we do when we've got them?"

"Just guard them well 'til the Scorpions come. If this one spoke truth over that mulled concoction of Persy's, there'll be only his friend helping the old man make the trek to the Coomb. So you should be snug and safe just waiting for the rest of us to relieve you. It's a good thing Wright stumbled into our hands here or we'd never know what plans these clanfellows of mine have hatched."

Enbarr wheeled about from the fire.

"Now get to your business. Bundle him into Persy's wagon, cover him well. The last thing we want is any curious townsfolk asking questions. Make sure you take his horse. Go now. Kenulf, you and I had better make haste to the Boar and tell him of these newest events."

"Aren't you afeared to be on the Edgemere Road with the alarm being raised and all?" asked Grumm.

"You may spare yourself the anxiety. There's no one that'll see us but foxes and night owls. You don't think I've spent so long in this wretched highland backwater without learning my way around a bit along the bypaths and side trails? More than cousin Kenulf here, and he's been a Holdsman all his life, eh Kenulf?"

"No, not likely," sniggered Grumm, "when he don't hardly stir from Broadmeadows or Wrenhaven except to journey out to Dinas Antrum? He can't tell a tree from a turtle nor one end of a longbow from the other. But one thing's sure, he knows his way around the gaming tables, don't he?"

"W-well, I . . . I . . ." stammered Kenulf.

Enbarr ignored him.

The two thugs seized Kal, shoving him through the door into the courtyard. Moments later he was being trundled through the cobbled streets of Wrenhaven in the cart of Persy's wagon. The effects of the drink that the innkeeper had given him were beginning to wear off. In the stuffy black air underneath a great canvas tarpaulin he squirmed against the stout hempen rope that bound his hands and feet together, and him to the cart itself. He could hear the steady clop of Star Thistle following the wagon and a couple of times the hoofbeats of other riders passing by heedless in the night. Once a townsman on foot exchanged coolly distant greetings with Grumm and went on.

The wagon slowed and its wheels rang out a different duller sound on the pavement. They must be at Broadmeadows. Kal strove to remember the manor's architectural layout. He had only been at the place on a handful of occasions, mostly when Wilum had sent him on errands there. Kal could smell fresh manure. The stables. The wagon came to an abrupt halt. Kal heard the sound of tack and harness being loosened.

"Skrobb, you stay here, and I'll go fetch the key to the Locker and have the horses stabled. That one's a fine-looking animal, ain't she? I'll be back in a minute. You start getting him untied from

the cart, and when I get back, we'll heave him into the Locker."
Grumm and the horses moved away.

The wagon rocked as Skrobb climbed into the back. He drew
up the tarpaulin and snorted in contempt as he stooped over,
squinting into the darkened corner, to untie Kal from the paling
of the cart.

"So you've been trying hard to wiggle out of my nicely knotted
handiwork, have you? This might discourage you right enough,"
he said with a brutish laugh as he straightened and gave Kal a
painful kick in the ribs. Kal doubled and heaved against the gag
in his mouth.

When Grumm reappeared, they each took one of Kal's shoulders
and dragged him off the bed of the cart. The quarter-moon had
drifted behind a bank of clouds. All around them it had turned
dark, except for the occasional twinkle of light from the main
buildings of the manor and the lamp that shed a murky pool of
light on the stableyard at the far side of the stalls. Skrobb cursed
Grumm for not bringing a torch, until Grumm reminded him
that, if they were carrying a light, they might readily be marked
by anybody who happened to look out a window towards the old
abandoned wing of Broadmeadows.

"Tell me now who'd come out to have a look, if they sees a
light. Might be one of the stableboys for all they knows or cares,"
Skrobb scoffed.

"Better not to take any chances with this here cargo, Skrobb,
or our heads is forfeit. Anyways, here we are," Grumm said, panting, and let go his grip of Kal's shoulder at a break in the stretch
of crumbling ivy-clad stonework where they stopped before a
thick oak door banded with iron and fitted with a small keyhole.
Reaching into a leather pouch that he carried slung by his side,
he produced a metal key, which he fitted into the lock. The door
swung open into a dank musty cellar that had once served as a
jail in the early days of the Thane's Assizes. It was shrouded in
a thick darkness, as heavy and oppressive as a set of shackles.
Grumm brushed away the cobwebs and felt his way down the
short steep flight of stone stairs that led from the door, fumbling
to get his bearings.

"Very well, then," he said, when he remounted the steps, "we'll
commit him to the nether depths of the Locker. The stairs is
right in front of you. Let me lead the way. Grab hold of one

of his shoulders again. Mind your step. It's a bit of a fall if you miss your footing. Don't be hurrisome or you'll pay for it with a broken head. Have you got him?"

"Aye . . . Easy does it—"

"There we are, Skrobb. Let's lie him right here. Here's the whipping post. We'll fix him fast to it. Have you got some more rope?"

"Here."

"Good, we'll just make certain the rat don't get no notion of turning down our hospitality. There we are. What's there to tie him to?"

"Don't know . . . Oh . . . Here's an iron ring. Near the top."

"Pass the rope through it. Got it?"

"There it is, Grumm, old stick. I'll have him fixed as good as if he was in leg irons directly."

"Right cozy you'll be in this snuggery, boy-o, 'til our night's work is done," exclaimed Grumm, after they had laid Kal on a heap of mouldering rags and then tied him securely to the whipping post. He and his partner then remounted the stairs. Grumm bade Skrobb fetch Kal's longbow and quiver together with his shortsword and knife from the cart and tuck them into the Locker for safekeeping. Kal's weapons were thrown into a corner far from his reach, and the thick oaken door was shut fast, leaving Kal in the darkness of the Locker, tethered to a stout wooden post at which prisoners had once been flogged for their misdemeanours.

Kal lay there for what seemed an eternity.

He felt the scurry of mice—at least, it seemed like mice—clambering all over him. It proved almost impossible to chase them off, with his hands firmly bound behind his back and his feet tightly secure. All he could do was helplessly rock from side to side or move his head. But this became tiring after a while, for he was limited as well by the scant three or four feet of play that his tether afforded him. There would be rats down in this hole as well. He shuddered at the mere thought. After a bit he became indifferent to the creatures, seeing them as no more than what he deserved for his folly. He cursed himself for having put into deeper danger his own family and Galli's and Wilum, not to mention the other folk that had received the first alarm along the Edgemere Road or the rest of the people in the Holding. It was not as if things weren't desperate to begin with—but here he had succeeded in making matters even worse. In the midst of his thoughts he drifted off into a troubled sleep, his body racked by the day's exhausting events.

The Locker remained cloaked in pitch blackness. He had no idea how long he had slumbered. The left side of his body, on which he had slept, felt sore and full of cramps. He ached to be free of his bonds. He could not even cry out to ease his frustration, although it would probably do him precious little good at this hour of the night, in an unkempt overgrown part of the grounds of Broadmeadows, where nobody wandered even during the daylight hours. They had ensured he would not work loose the gag stuffed in his mouth by wrapping yet another one across his lips. And like all his other restraints they had tied it as tight as possible.

Now that Kal had rested, the weary self-pity that had taxed him earlier yielded to a growing determination to find some way out of this predicament. He wriggled his hands and his feet until his skin was chafed raw. There was no give. Grumm and Skrobb had done their job well. In desperation, he began to test the tethering rope that led from the iron ring on the whipping post to the cords that bound his hands behind his back. Pulling with all his might, his feet against the post, he tried to draw the ring out of the ancient wood. The rope bit into his wrists under the strain and his shoulders ached, yet the ring remained fast. But the old, dry post itself—it seemed to shift a bit. Kal let the tether go slack and explored the base of the post with his back to it. His bound hands clawed at the loose crumbling mortar and swept it aside. Leaning against the post for support, he pushed himself struggling to his feet and bumped the beam with his shoulder. It moved out of the vertical. Play—it definitely had some play. He hit against the thing once more. More movement. Again and again he threw his weight at the post, until at last it listed in its hole. Now he stepped away and pulled as hard as he could on the rope once again, until the circulation seemed gone in his hands. Not enough purchase that way. If somehow he could gain a solid handhold nearer the base of the post and lift it out. His back against it, he slid numbed fingers down the wooden beam, fumbling for a grip. He felt something solid, cold—fixed low to the post—a ring, a handhold. His fingers curled around it, and he pulled, straining every sinew with the effort. The post was coming free of its moorings. At last the base of it cleared the hole. His heart pounding, Kal let the post drop flat on the ground and fell to his knees to catch his breath.

Having recovered, he sought out his blade, which lay against a corner of the wall, dragging the uprooted post in his wake. Crouched over his hunting knife's upturned edge, he began cutting away at the ropes that bound his hands. It was slow going, even though the weapon had been honed to a fine cutting edge. Kal always kept his blades sharp. It was the awkward angle of his bound hands behind his back, and several times the blade slipped, nicking his wrists. All the same Kal knew he was making progress.

He froze. His heart jumped up into his craw. A voice drifted in to him from outside the Locker. Had his captors come back for him already? Had he slept that long? Feverishly he began to saw at the rope. He tore into his restraints until the blade had clumsily severed the last stubborn thread of hemp, allowing his hands to break free. He loosened his feet, expecting the door of the dungeon to swing open at any moment, although he could no longer hear voices. Stiff and sore, not stopping even to undo his gag, he groped for the stairs in the dark and climbed them, ready with his knife to lash out. At the top of the steps he paused, straining his ears. Then he heard it again, fainter now and touched with the native accents of the Holding.

"Kalaquinn, Kalaquinn Wright, are you there?"

At once, Kal recognized the voice. It was drawing farther away along the walls of the old manor. He ripped the muzzling band of cloth and spat out the rag balled up in his mouth.

"Master Landros, here I am, over here in the Locker!" he shouted. Again, he cried out, leaning his body towards a small window with thick iron bars that now let a touch of moonlight into the dingy jail from above him.

"Hello, lad! Where are you now?"

"Here in the Locker."

"How did you end up down there?" The Holding's schoolmaster stood now directly under the window, just above head height. A faint glow from the lantern he carried filtered into the musty chamber.

"It's a long story, Master Landros. Enbarr's Dungheap lackeys, they cooped me up in here. They're off to the Great Glence, wanting to capture Wilum. The Boar has broken through our defences. He's in the Holding. He's going to attack us and put us all to the sword. I was to tell Tudno, but they captured me and brought me here. How is it that you're here, Master Landros, and what time do you make it to be?"

"It's nigh on the midnight watch, lad. But never mind the time nor any more explanations. I'd rather talk with you face-to-face. We'd better get you out of there. Trouble is that we don't have a key and that's a thick door. It would take a giant to get you out."

"Or a Star Thistle."

"What's that, lad?"

"My father's horse, Master Landros. She's an Aenonian, light as the wind and strong as an oak. There isn't a horse anywhere in the Holding like Star Thistle. They've put her in one of the stables here. If you could find her, bring her to me."

"How would I recognize her, Kalaquinn?"

"As I said, there isn't a horse anywhere like Star Thistle, even at Broadmeadows. She's dark chestnut with a white star marking on her forehead. But wait now! She might just hear me if I whistle for her even from here, if I could raise myself and get closer to that window somehow. Let me see. I think I can do it."

At this Kal took a run at reaching the window ledge from the stone staircase, leaping towards it. He missed and slid down the wall of the Locker to the ground. The second time he found a handhold on the sill and pulled himself up, using the iron bars that were set into the crumbling mortar of the window frame. Holding on with one hand, he used the fingers of the other to whistle an ear-piercing call with all his breath. Three times he whistled his summons and then rested for a space by gripping the bars with both hands. As he got set to whistle again, his ears caught the powerful, earth-pounding thud of hooves and a scant moment later he saw that Star Thistle had broken free of the stable area and was drawing near in the moonlight, still saddled and dragging her lead rope. She must have left a sleepily confused groom or two in her wake. Now she stamped on the cobblestone outside the Locker with a restive tossing of her mane, while the schoolmaster retreated beside the trunk of a large beech.

"It's all right, Master Landros. She won't harm you. She's looking for me. Here I am, Star Thistle. Come, Star." Kal pulled himself up, and the chestnut mare drew near the window, nuzzling Kal's face through the bars with her soft nose. He dropped to the floor.

"Master Landros, she won't hurt you. Come toward her. Gently. Stroke her neck. Are you there?"

". . . good girl—yes, Kal. She's a beautiful horse—good girl . . ." The schoolmaster continued to soothe the animal.

"Master Landros, she has the lead rope. Is it long enough to tie from her saddle to the window?"

"Yes, I think so."

"Good. Listen now. Take the rope off her. Loop it over the pommel of the saddle—easy, Star, easy—it's all right, she'll let you do it."

A moment passed. Star Thistle nickered, and Kal could hear Landros cooing to her again.

"Good, Kal. That's done."

"Bring the other end to the window here. Tie it off to the bars."

The schoolmaster's hands appeared at the window.

"The bars, they're forged together, but the mortar's loose. It should pull out."

"Yes, I can see the stonework's crumbling in places. There, that should hold."

"All right, stand back. Keep an eye on the saddle. It may shift, but it should hold . . . Pull, Star Thistle, pull! 'Unsheathe your flashing hooves and bring them down with crashing fury.'" The line from *Hedric's Master Legendary* tumbled out from Kal's lips. Even as he finished the verse, Star Thistle leaned her mighty weight against the rope. The rope held. Iron grated against the ancient masonry, and the prison bars broke free amid a shower of dust and stone shard, clanking on the cobbled courtyard.

Before the dust had settled, Landros again appeared at the window with the rope, lowering it through the opening. Kal fumbled in the darkness for his sword, which he strapped to his hip. His bow and quiver Landros pulled up on the rope. Again the rope was lowered. Kal clambered quickly up the wall and through the opening, where Landros helped him regain his footing outside.

He breathed in the fresh night air, almost intoxicating after the stifling confinement of the Locker. Star Thistle neighed and pushed her muzzle affectionately into Kal's chest.

"Good girl, Star Thistle, good girl. Where would I be without you now?" He stroked the mare's nose and forehead. "Master Landros, I'm glad to see you. What are you doing here? I thought most sober-sided Holdsmen were asleep at this hour."

"I suppose I'm not always as sober-sided as I ought to be, lad. Now quick. To my place. With all this commotion we'd best make ourselves scarce. This way."

Landros led Kal and his horse away from the manor buildings. After skirting a paddock, they turned onto a footpath that soon disappeared into a grove of beech on the edge of Darran Wood, emerging again in a meadow overgrown with teasel and burdock. In a neatly mown clearing the other side of a split-rail fence stood a low stone cottage, its windows lit by a faint glow.

"Take a seat. Draw it closer to the fire," said the schoolmaster, ushering Kal to a chair, as soon as they entered the cottage. He bustled to light another candle, placing it on the rough-hewn table nearby.

"Let me get you something to unparch your lips." From a shelf behind him Landros handed Kal a tankard and then disappeared into a small larder. He reappeared carrying cheese and bread together with a pitcher, from which he filled Kal's tankard and another for himself with ale. The schoolmaster settled into his own chair and brought a taper to the bowl of his pipe. Kal raised his mug in thanks and took a long pull of the ale.

"I know that something's amiss. I could smell it at the Bottle." Landros sucked on his pipe—the taper's flame flared and subsided, then flared again. Smoke wreathed the old teacher's head as he restored the candle to the table. "I wouldn't trust that smooth-talking Persy as far as I could throw him. I saw how he glad-handed you, lad, when you stepped into the taproom, after young Enbarr and his cronies made themselves scarce. Something's brewing here, I thought to myself, even while I kept up my end of the conversation with old Sarmel, as if I hadn't noticed a blessed thing. And then Persy cleared us out extraordinarily politely, too politely by a half, mind you. I've never seen Persy so smooth . . . Very strange, when we'd hardly even begun the first watch of the night, and Sarmel and I, we'd scarcely had more than a couple of pints." Landros paused to pull on his pipe, then continued. "So, puzzled though I was, I made my way home here, and then, next thing I know, as I'm watching the stars and enjoying a pipe, I see those two shifty Dinasantrians riding Persy's wagon past my place, with a lone horse hitched to the wagon from behind and a tarp stretched over its box. I could tell they were bound for Broadmeadows. And then, no sooner had I seen them go to the manor than I see them tearing up the turf, each of them on a strong mount. By then I'm getting an odd feeling that you may be in trouble. So I walk to the stables and ask one of the grooms about Persy's wagon and he tells me that the two 'heapers had left it somewhere by the old manor buildings. And then, he mentioned the fine Aenonian mare they'd brought with them and that it looked like the horse he's seen young Kalaquinn Wright riding, the envy of all the folk who admire fine horseflesh." The lean man pushed himself back in his chair and ran his gnarled fingers through the wisps of white hair crowning his head.

"I started poking around the old pile, calling your name just for good measure. I had this strange idea that it was you they had carted away in Persy's wagon, for it was clear enough to me that it was Kalaquinn Wright they were after in the Bottle. They didn't do a very good job of hiding their intentions, I daresay. I suppose they thought we were just two old drones, Sarmel and me, an oldling and a schoolmaster, dullards deep in our cups, unaware of the things happening around us." His eyes sparkled over the rim of his tankard as he winked at Kal. "Well, the truth is," he said, setting down his ale, "I really don't know what's on here, lad. Tell me now what I'm missing. What's this about the Boar being in this valley of ours? How do you expect me to believe such a thing with hardly a word of explanation?"

"It's true, Landros. Let me tell you what's happened, but quickly. We don't have any time to spare. I have to be on my way to Wuldor's Howe. Perhaps I can save Galli and Wilum yet."

"Just a minute now, Kalaquinn Wright. Begin at the beginning, and then perhaps I can do something to help the situation out, even though I'm just a simple scribe. Don't you go underestimating me as well, for I tell you there's no quicker way to wrack and ruin than when you misjudge a man by underestimating him or worse still, giving him more trust than he deserves, as you well know."

"It all began this morning when I went to fetch Galli at the Burrows." Kal went on to explain to the schoolmaster all that had occurred. Landros pulled at his chin and twisted his face into a squint of deep concentration amid billows of pipe smoke.

"No doubt about it, lad. You'd better rush to Wuldor's Howe as fast as Star Thistle can take you, if you're fit to ride, that is." Kal was already headed towards the door of the cottage.

"I'm fine."

"Are you sure? They were none too gentle."

"Aye, I'm sure. Just chafed wrists, that's all."

"All right then, I'll sound the alert here in town, beginning with the Town Warden, for he certainly hasn't gone traipsing up to the Pass." The schoolmaster had risen from his chair, placing his hand on the young Holdsman's shoulder, as he ushered him outside. "If fate is kind to us, we'll meet at Tarlynn's Coomb. We'll tweak the Boar's snout with the stoutest longbowmen in all the highlands. I feel my blood rising, lad. There was a day when I could flourish a sword with the best of them, and I was a passable shot at the Holdsmeet, when all the bowmen of highland Arvon used to compete at the butts in this very town of Wrenhaven. Why, there was one year I was the only one to hit the mark at a hundred paces. A pity the Holdsmeet has been suspended, now that it's become a handy occasion for Gawmage to pack with his wheedling spies—but I'm babbling now. You're right. We must be quick. And may the spirit of Ardiel watch over you, young Kalaquinn Wright."

Outside Landros scanned the road that ran not a stone's throw from his cottage. Star Thistle grazed, screened from the thoroughfare by a hedge of flowering lilac. The horse whickered a greeting.

"There's not much time. Come, up you go. With a mount like this, you should be in Wuldor's Howe more quickly than a bird. Re'm ena, this beats anything that's ever happened in the Holding. Goodspeed to you, Kalaquinn. Briacoil."

"Briacoil, Landros."

SIX

"Blackthorn, blackthorn,
  Bar the Pass and sound the horn,
  The Fell One's come to Lammermorn!

  Blackthorn, blackthorn,
  Bar the Pass and sound the horn,
  The Fell One's come . . ."

The doggerel lines were battering Wilum's sleep with the rhythmic ebb and flow of waves, flooding his mind like a powerful tide
and then receding—again and again. In a sudden convulsion of
fear he jerked awake in the chair in which he had dozed off and
made as if to shield himself from a furious onrush of threshing
horns and gnashing teeth. Still beguiled by sleep, he recoiled,
convinced that he was sharing his chamber with the feral face
that glowered at him from the arras hanging on the wall over the
wooden chest. By degrees, he regained some of his waking senses,
enough of them to realize that he had been having a nightmare,
dreaming of a game he had played decades ago when he was just
a boy like any other in the Holding.

In the murky half-light his memories turned to "Horned One
in the Dark"—one of those magic boyhood games. It took place
in the woods at night only under the spectral illumination of a
moon at its full. The moment dusk began to shroud the valley,
all the boys would slip out of their homes. Most times, as they
assembled on the village green, Deepmere lay still and recumbent

before them, as if its waters had been hushed by the westering sun. There was a deep peace that fell on the valley with the coming of twilight. *Funny how when you're an old man it's the peace and the stillness you remember most, the aspect of the whole thing you cherish more than anything else.*

Wilum's thoughts turned now to that one night, decades ago, when the boys had gathered together and he had been chosen to play Hircomet, the horned he-goat. This unpleasant role was normally reserved for one of the older boys. The rest drew lots to decide who, on the other hand, would be awarded the brave heroic role of Tobar, chief and mightiest of the anagoroi, who were the scourge of the dreosan, the Fallen Ones.

Even now the old man winced, remembering his reluctance and dismay—the desertion he felt in being Hircomet, as all the boys scattered into Darran Wood, a small beechwood copse that adjoined the deerpark close by Broadmeadows Manor, while Tobar watched with diligence that all remained in bounds.

Wilum pictured the scene again in his mind's eye. After counting to a hundred, equipped with a willow switch and disguised in a black goat's-head mask with horns and a pelt that draped his back and trailed along the ground, he began to stalk the other boys. Tied to the belt around his waist he carried a pouch of red paint made so he could dip his switch into it with a minimum of fuss. One by one he caught the boys in hiding, tagging them with the stain, having each of his captives cry out:

> "Blackthorn, Blackthorn,
>   Bar the Pass and sound the horn,
>   The Fell One's come to Lammermorn!"

With this he touched the snout of his mask to his victim's throat, making the captured innocent the Horned One's thrall and duty-bound to help him run the others to ground. Once he had snared a couple of accomplices, it did not take very long to capture all of the boys in Darran Wood. This done, he trooped his conquered subjects to a meadow in the heart of the forest, where he ensconced himself in a chair hewn out of stone atop a hillock. Looking down on the boys he had captured, he demanded they prostrate themselves before him and shout, "Hail Hircomet," cuffing anyone who showed himself slow to render acclaim.

The sound of the acclaiming voices became the cue for Tobar, lingering watchfully just outside the wood. That night, Sarmel's younger brother, Hacnoris, had been chosen to be Tobar. Clad in a white tunic drawn together in the middle by a leather belt with a silver buckle, embossed with the figure of a great heron, Tobar strode into Darran Wood. Brandishing the wooden sword that he had pulled from a scabbard at his side, he skirted the prone bodies strewn along the moonlit sward. Wilum remembered rising from the stone chair and recoiling in a mock gesture of fear, letting Tobar cut him down with a furious volley of sword strokes, as he wailed miserably and slumped to the ground, feigning death. The wooden sword could be a bruising cudgel. Hacnoris had wielded it with great gusto and none too gently. Wilum felt sore for days, even with all the padding he had worn under his costume.

Having vanquished Hircomet, Tobar pulled out a rowan-wood sceptre, which he wore tucked into his belt. He stooped to touch each boy with it while intoning in the Old Tongue: "In the name of Wuldor, I free thee from thy bondage."

When all the prostrate figures had been revived and were standing upright again, Tobar himself occupied the stone chair amid a rousing chorus of lusty acclamation:

"Hail Tobar, Mighty One, be by our side!
  Scourge of Evil! Destroyer of Darkness!
  King of Freedom! Wuldor's Pride!"

How relieved Wilum had been that night at the third repetition of these words, which signalled the end of the game. The boys dispersed and trudged home, most of them reluctant to leave the ghostly spectacle of light and shadow that had fed their imaginations in the forest depths, where stock and stone were changed by a lunar alchemy into thrillingly sinister forms. In their hearts the boys knew that the game symbolized something that was as real as real could be, as real as anything else in their lives—an event of timeless significance, part of the ultimate victory of good over evil. A victory Wilum found it hard to appreciate at the moment, even now that he had wiped the veil of sleep from his eyes and had regained a measure of waking consciousness.

Nagging at him was a feeling of pervasive dread, all the more acute because neither Kal nor Galli had returned to his keeil that day. He had waited for them until even his anxiety was not enough to hold his drooping eyelids open a minute longer, and he had fallen asleep where he sat near the window waiting, watching. The folkmoot would have to wait a day. Strange, though, for the two not to have come back to the keeil with news. Perhaps they'd been sidetracked by other things. Wilum allowed himself a wry smile. They were young lads, after all. Who knew but that they had not been casting for trout on Deepmere, even as he cradled his reeling head, fighting sleep? It was doubtful the lowlanders could've caught them. Not only had Kal and Galli bested them when they'd had the aid of a Telessarian tracker, but a mountain goat would have a hard time keeping up with those two lads when they took to the wilds. Besides, he recognized with chill clarity, the men were here to watch his movements, hoping he'd lead them to the missing heir. The fact remained that the Sacred Fire had been snuffed out, and that there were strange and ominous things afoot—more than ominous. He could feel it in his heart—a deep unease.

Again the face leered at him from the tapestry with its predatory grin and distended features, all the more horrific for being part human and part animal. He rubbed his eyes and shook his head, trying to clear away the shrouds of sleep.

"There we are. It was all just a nightmare, thank goodness," he murmured to himself, looking again more closely at the moonlit wall hanging. Nothing now—only the scene that had always been depicted on it, a stirring episode in the tale of Ardiel's voyage from the court of Undenor, the forgeland king who had given him Vali's harp. Pursued by the raven-beaked longboats of Tardroch, Ardiel and his companions, the Seven Champions of Ruah, scuttled their vessel and hid for two days and two nights in the echoing chambers of Dorla's Cave, a sea cave set into the chalk cliffs of coastal Thrysvarshold. On the tapestry before him stood Ardiel locked in deadly combat with Dorla, the scaly many-tentacled monster who inhabited the cave. The goatish face of Wilum's dream had filled a space beside the flailing figure of Dorla, in one of the recesses of the cave. It had disappeared now, but its distorted malignity hung over him yet like a pollution.

He shuddered, his body still knotted with nervous tension. Some evil power loomed close at hand. He could feel it in the marrow of his weary bones with an intensity that he had never before experienced.

Heaving a deep sigh, he rose from the chair and reached for his staff. Clutching it, he stood by the window.

The pale light of the moon in its last quarter spilled through the window, broken by a crosshatched pattern of glazed lozenges, which were surmounted by the figure of a rampant white hind that was cut into the spandrel. Wilum stepped into the silver light. He lifted the latch and pulled the window open to let the night breeze cool his uneasy sweat-soaked body, half thinking that the gloom and oppression that hung over him like a poisonous vapour might be dissipated by an infusion of fresh air.

Scarcely had he breathed in one full draught of evening air before his nostrils curled back at the odour—the strong and unmistakable smell of blackthorn, the warm heavy scent of its blossoms as pungent as rotting meat, a harbinger of death. Wilum resisted the impulse to close the window. His squinting eyes swept the dimly lit landscape, framed in the distance by the silent mass of the Radolan Mountains. On the surface, the scene which he took in seemed wholesome and peaceful. In the middle distance, dominated by the Haltadans and Ram's Knap, everything appeared as calm and tranquil as always. The snowy peaks of the mountains, faint bands of white in the weak half-light, seemed as ethereal and insubstantial as the nimbus of misty clouds that enshrouded them. Wilum always found the scene to be hypnotically evocative. It made his spirit long to be liberated from its bonds of clay and to take flight on airy pinions to the heavens.

Tonight, however, no such idle musings distracted him into reverie. Not even the passionate liquid melodies of the nightingale perched on the oak tree outside his window could break the spell of nameless fear. Rather its soft tremolo "jug, jug, tereu" seemed desperately sad and poignant, full of tears and pain beyond words.

"Take hold of yourself, Wilum. Come now! You've only had a nightmare, for goodness' sake," the old man muttered, as he retreated into the room, shutting the windows against the night. "Enough of your petty fears. After all, you're the Hordanu, the High Bard, and this is Wuldor's Howe. Your predecessors all lived in peace and tranquillity in this valley and are buried right here in Stillfields. Come now, you're being ridiculous, like a rabbit afraid of its own shadow. Take hold of yourself, man."

All the same, Wilum tried not to dwell on the fact that never before since its kindling had the Sacred Fire been extinguished. And now its ashes lay cold. And try as he might, he could not help worrying about the young men. "I've been a silly doddering old fool," he chided himself. "I should have had the two young rascals promise they'd make straight for the nearest farmstead to get help. No detours through the woods. I should have been more careful . . . more careful . . ."

Wilum decided to get changed from his sweat-sodden clothing and ready himself for what would no doubt be a long day ahead. It would prove to be of small good to anyone, least of all himself, if he dozed in the chair again, or tossed and turned on his bed until morning. Better to get up. He left unlit the cresset torches that lined the room. Instead he turned to a panelled walnut chest carved with rosettes that lay by the wall beside the window. He laid down his staff and opened the chest. He lifted out a long brown robe and an undergarment and changed into these and then put on his sandals.

From the same chest he took out the Talamadh, the golden harp, the binder together of earth and sky, handed down through the ages from Hordanu to Hordanu. Intricately worked and fitted with an ornate leather strap, it was an object of exquisite craftsmanship and consummate grace, chased with patterns and runic inscriptions that a person could marvel at for hours on end. It was to the accompaniment of the Talamadh that Ardiel of the Long Arm sang "The Lay of the Velinthian Bridge" to reharmonize the discordant elements of Ahn Norvys after Tardroch's long convulsive reign of terror.

Wilum closed the chest and took up his staff again. Pushing aside a curtain, he left the modest bedchamber and entered his study and scriptorium, where a huge oaken door, set into a high arch, led to the Great Glence. Holding the harp, he slowly swung the door open, pushing it with his staff. He passed through a chamber beneath the bell tower and stepped into the half-darkness of the Great Glence itself, dappled with lunar shadows all along its windowed circumference. Here the Stones of the Four Seasons, each marking one of the four cardinal points of the compass, rose like ghostly ships from their plinths. At the centre of this circular building stood the Glence Stone, a massive rock fenced in with a screen, where the High Bard recited the orrthon on the great festival days of the year. The most important of these in the cult of Wuldor was the Candle Festival, the night of the second full moon after the vernal equinox, celebrating the cosmic victory won at the Battle of the Velinthian Bridge by Ardiel. In the silence the old stone walls seemed to resonate still with the ritual measures of the orrthon.

Wilum made for the Stone across a floor still strewn with rushes from the Candle Festival. Had his two attendants been with him today, he would have had them clean it. The latch on a door was scarcely distinguishable from the rest of the wrought-iron grillework that made up the glence screen. He lifted it and stepped with sandalled feet onto the mosaic stone floor of the temen. Within the sacred enclosure, the Glence Stone bulked large before him, its whiteness just barely visible in the gloom. A couple of the windows were thrown open, allowing for a cross-draught. Wilum noticed among the windows that the Aeolian Aperture stood open as well.

He leaned his staff against the inside of the glence screen and wearily mounted the flight of steps that had been chiselled into the Stone. At its top was a shallow flat depression on which was positioned a simple board stool from which the Hordanu would pluck the Talamadh and recite the orrthon. On the night of the Candle Festival the ritual called for him to place the Talamadh on the embrasure of the Aeolian Aperture and wait for a breath of wind to arouse the inborn melody of the Talamadh, turning it into a marvellous wind harp.

For scores of years now, extending back even to before Wilum's time, the Hordanu had waited in vain for the wind music. Even this year, despite the battering winds that had racked the whole valley that evening, there was not even the faintest stirring of a breeze that entered through the Aperture to caress the pliant strings of the golden harp. For some reason its powers as a wind harp lay dormant.

These days, as the water level of Deepmere had begun to decline, even the light of the sun and moon which streamed in through the Aperture seemed weak and pallid. With the inexplicable lowering of Deepmere's waters, the Great Glence itself had sunk. What light did shine through the Aperture was no longer able to touch any of the four Stones. Instead the light of sun and moon would miss the Stones altogether, causing yet another sundering of the link that bound the solid earth with the harmonies of the heavens. The visible sinking of the building had thrown the Aeolian Aperture off for the Loosening, the ceremony that ushered in each of the four seasons.

Wilum sat on the stool atop the Glence Stone and began to strum the golden harp, not having any particular lay or ballad in mind at first, but letting the dulcet sounds of the strings arise spontaneously, almost unbidden. At once his spirit was soothed. Rejoicing in the balm of the harp's voice, Wilum ceased his random thrumming and entered into the first notes of "The Lair of the Lyrebird," which described Ardiel's toilsome quest for the marvellous lyrebird amid the Ocean Isles of the West, the utmost boundaries of Ahn Norvys. The music of the ballad echoed through the empty glence, filling it with reflected tremulous sound that seemed at times to trail off, absorbed at length by the dark concavity of the timbered vault that held the roof above him. Wilum was immersed now in the ballad, surrendering himself to its re-created atmosphere of wind and wave and island promontories.

As he approached the end of a canto, Wilum could have sworn he heard his name being called. He paused, brushing back a stray strand of hair from his eyes, then launched himself into a fresh new canto. There it was again—a voice. No mistaking it. Unbowing his head and looking up from the Talamadh, he stopped his singing and squinted into the darkness. He was startled. At the door of the glence screen loomed a dim figure motioning frantically to him and calling.

"Master Wilum, Master Wilum!"

Slowly Wilum recognized a familiar voice and frame.

"Galli, is that you?"

"Aye, it's me, Master Wilum."

"What's the matter? Where have you been?"

"The Black Scorpions, they're here. They mean to kill everyone in the valley. And it's you Kal said they're really keen on getting their hands on. You can't stay here. We've got to leave right now. We're to meet at Tarlynn's Coomb. We have to get to Tarlynn's Coomb. Come now, please Master Wilum."

Galli, haggard and dishevelled, had a longbow slung around his shoulder and a scabbarded shortsword hanging from the belt at his hip. He had still not quieted his breathing and was plainly overcome by dread.

Wilum left his board stool and, still clutching the Talamadh, slowly descended the Stone. Galli stood just outside the temen, his eyes narrowed, his forehead creased. Meeting the younger man's gaze, Wilum ran a frail hand through his hoary mane and stroked his beard, as white as the wood doves nesting in the cupola of the Great Glence. He retrieved his staff and opened the door to the glence screen. Leaving the temen, the Hordanu rested a paternal arm on Galli's shoulder. Together they made their way toward the keeil.

"It's all right Galli, everything's fine," he said. "Just tell me what's happening. From the beginning. Wait a moment, though!" Wilum commanded, turning to face Galli with a rising tremor in his voice that resonated through the bell tower. "Where's Kalaquinn? Tell me, is he safe?"

"He's fine. He rode into Wrenhaven to tell the Warden and then he's to meet us at the Coomb. Somehow the Black Scorpions got past our guards at the Pass. Kal's father would have gone himself, but his ankle was really acting up again. So he sent Kal." They passed from the bell tower back into the keeil.

"Wait a moment while I light a torch . . . Here we are . . . What are these Black Scorpions you speak of? It seems to me Frysan mentioned something about them to me just the other day. I'm old and tired. I've been Hordanu for over half a century, nearly sixty long years, lad, and things have been going from bad to worse. Malignant forces hold the upper hand now in Ahn Norvys. The reign of evil waxes with every passing moment. I'm past worrying how Ferabek is dotting his 'i's and crossing his 't's and getting his minions to do his evil work. But tonight there's something in the air that has my blood running cold . . . But I'm sorry, lad, I'm maundering now. Carry on." Wilum sensed Galli's restiveness.

"The Black Scorpions are Ferabek's crack troops, a new-formed cohort, his most disciplined soldiers. And he's brought them into the valley and he's come here himself too," Galli said in a breathless cascade of words. "They mean to kill everybody in the Holding. But he wants to take you alive. And he wants to get his hands on the Talamadh and on all the manor rolls so he can make sure all of us are dead and accounted for. Kal and I overheard him ourselves talking to Enbarr and to Kenulf too, but he's just a lapdog. Enbarr is his spy. We were up in the hills and then they spotted us and tried to kill us, and we ran for our lives. We just barely escaped them. I didn't think we were going to make it,

Master Wilum, nor did Kal. One of their spears almost laid me out. Look at this hole in my jerkin." Galli lifted up the torn cloth of his jacket with a finger. "And then we were followed by his trackers, Telessarians. We couldn't shake them, so we lured them all the way up Scathe Fell. We led them right into a rockslide on the scree. But one of them survived and he came within an inch of snuffing Kal out. Well, after that we tried to get down from Scathe Fell and were crag-fast for a while. Finally, by late afternoon we managed to make our way back to raise the alarm. But we were held up by a couple of Black Scorpion patrols that were combing the mountainside for us. When we finally struggled into Mantling Moss, it was just after nightfall. There's no telling when the Boar will make his move and strike."

"And then what, lad?"

"Then Master Frysan, he decided Kal should go on up Edgemere Road, alerting the farmsteads on the way, telling everyone to meet at Tarlynn's Coomb. Then he was to go into Wrenhaven to the Warden's house and then straight on to the Coomb along the Westwynd Way. The Edgemere Road is probably none too safe anymore. For all we know it's already crawling with Black Scorpions. I was to go home to the Burrows, alert my folk, which I did, and after that come warn you, Master Wilum, sir, and then help you get on up to the Coomb yourself."

Wilum placed the Talamadh on a writing table. Closing his eyes, he leaned against his staff, his aged face creased with thought. Riddling lines from *Hedric's Master Legendary* sprung to his faltering lips, words which he knew by heart and had recited countless times before.

"When Wuldor's Howe is worsted by the brazen foe
    And the Great Glence in utter ashbound ruin lies razed,
    When the dark host of dreosan doth stain the Vale—"

"Can it be? In my time? Has the moment come . . . ?" Wilum muttered to himself, shaking his head slowly.

"What . . . What do you . . . What do you think? Master Wilum?"

The candle sputtered on the table. An awkward and discomfiting silence had cast a pall on the deeply shadowed room.

"How's that? What did you say? Oh, yes . . . They're coming for me. I must collect my things." Wilum stirred from his musings.

"Aye, Master Wilum, with all speed!"

An evening breeze came wafting into the keeil from the Great Glence. It was heavy-laden with the fragrance of herbs. At once, the pair realized that the great doors which gave onto the entrance of the Great Glence had been opened, for the portico was strewn yet with marjoram, southernwood, and thyme from the Candle Festival.

"Someone's here. Quick, bar the door," urged Galli in a hoarse whisper, stepping forward to close the big oak door, while Wilum made to snatch up the Talamadh.

"Hold it, right there, both of you, unless you want to be gracing one of my trim little bolts. There's nothing I'd like better than some real live target practice. It would do my heart good, Skrobb, it would, to fine-tune the sights on this new twanger. Can't say what it would do for his heart, though," joked the shorter of the two men who had stepped into the faltering torchlight. The speaker, dark-haired and heavy-browed, had his crossbow trained right on Galli's chest. There was no mistaking him, nor his partner, the large-boned florid-faced man who had stepped up beside him.

"Now you, old man, you come here—while you, you lay that bow down. Nicely now. Yes, very nicely and you'll keep your skin for a while at least," ordered the man with the crossbow, bobbing the end of his weapon at Galli. "And your sword as well. This time we won't let him get away, will we, Skrobb? There'll be no mistakes this time. We'll make sure this hayseed don't escape us, won't we, Skrobb?" There was a deadly glint in the short man's dull eyes, as he spat out the words through clenched teeth.

"All right, all right! See?" Galli said, crouching, seeking the floor with his hands, his bow in one, the sword in his other. He kept his eyes locked warily on Grumm.

Wilum sidled towards the Talamadh.

"Oh, no you don't. No, you long-haired old billy goat, we want you to leave that right there. Yes, indeed we do. We wouldn't hear of it any other way, would we Skrobb?" He laughed a mirthless laugh. "What a fine reward we're sure to get for it, aren't we, Skrobb? A country estate on the Lake of the Swallows. Doesn't that just steady my aim."

"Aye, Grumm," said the taller man, brandishing a crude dirk that he had pulled from a sheath at his side.

"Do you see that, young sir?" His partner turned to Galli. "Do you think Skrobb wouldn't use it on your old friend? What a nice red gash it would make across his throat!"

"Aye, it would give him some colour, Grumm," Skrobb said, turning the blade in his hand. "The old man could use some colour."

"Come now, oldling, come gently now, and there'll be no harm done. Not by us anyhow. Now Skrobb," Grumm said, when Wilum had stepped forward. "Use that rope you brought to tie the young knave up—now all you need to do is just nice and gently give Skrobb your hands to tie. Place them behind your back and Skrobb'll take good care of them. There's a good fellow."

Galli had no choice. He did as he was bidden and grimaced as the coarse rope chafed and dug into his wrists.

"That's it. My knot'll hold him fast, as good as gyves." The big lowlander tied Wilum's hands as well.

"Now what shall we do with the two of them?"

"We'll keep them here. One of us'll sit and wait with them, while the other goes to fetch the Boar."

"But Enbarr said we should stay and wait."

"He didn't say we both ought to stay and wait. I don't see how it is we need both of us to guard them, not if we wrap them up really tight. It's dankish here, downright creepy somehow too. Let's shut the door." Grumm went to the door that opened into the bell tower and began to pull on the latch, swinging it shut, while Skrobb hovered near Galli with knife in hand.

Galli eyed the nearest window.

"If you're thinking of making a dash for it, you're sore mistaken, my young fitchew. You don't know Grumm. Why, he'd drop you before you got halfway, and then I'd make short work of you, believe me," warned Skrobb, as if reading his thoughts. Skrobb moved closer and jabbed the point of his knife into the small of Galli's back. He pulled a truncheon from his belt and hit him a vicious whack on the head. Galli slumped and fell with a thud onto the floor.

"There we are. We won't have to worry about that one for a while."

"You fatheaded idiot! What did you go and do that for? How do we know he ain't wanted by the Boar?" barked Grumm, who had bolted the door leading to the Great Glence and stood close on Skrobb's heels with Wilum now.

Wilum shoved Skrobb aside and stooped over the fallen figure of Galli.

"Oh, don't get yourself all riled," Skrobb said, ignoring Wilum. "I just gave him a love tap, just a touch with me trusty little wooden protector here. Tell me now, old man, didn't I?"

Wilum remained silent, cradling the limp body of his young friend, his fingers gently exploring the back of Galli's head, where grew a goose-egg bump.

"A mild knock on the cap, just as I planned it. I've always told you I've got it down to a fine art. I know just how much a man's noggin'll take." Skrobb looked down his nose and nodded. "The tenderest, kindest cutpurse in Dinas Antrum. Relieving folks of their valuables without relieving them of their lives. The 'Caring Cutpurse' they calls me."

"You lying gallows-bird. We'll leave matters be now that they're done. Luck I call it, damnfool luck. One of these days you'll prove your own undoing, Skrobb, if not mine as well. Planned it indeed," snorted Grumm. "Here, let's have some light in this place." He took the solitary candle that burned on Wilum's writing desk to light the cresset torches fixed in brackets along the wall. "But first you tie up the old man to the chair there, nice and tight. And don't hit him."

After they had finished securing Wilum, they dragged Galli, bound and gagged, into a closet in the keeil. Wilum remained silent and self-possessed, lost in stupefied reverie, entirely absorbed in sifting through his memory reams upon reams of lines from *Hedric's Master Legendary*. His mind's eye shifted from phrases of prophetic word to scrap of legend, from ancient auguries to odd lines of bardic lore and ballads. As hard as he might, he tried somehow to find the larger meaning in the dramatic events that seemed now at long last to be overtaking the Holding, as Ferabek threatened to cast out the last traces of light and harmony that had clung to Wuldor's Howe—the last bastion of light in all Ahn Norvys.

"Snap out of it, you old goat!" Grumm gave Wilum the back of his hand across the mouth, drawing blood. Wilum's head bowed again to his chest. "I'm no fool. I don't believe them old wives' tales about this heap of stone. Wuldor's Howe? Wuldor's Hole! I hate this place."

"What if we leave these two here. They ain't going nowheres.

We could go tell the Boar we bagged them. We can take the harp with us," suggested Skrobb.

"Don't be stupid! Not both of us. He'd have our heads. You stay back. It's for me to go. You know you can never explain things right. You're always getting the story wrong. Why, it was you as got the notion that Enbarr wanted us to jump the lad that helps the old man here. And you saw what a pile of trouble that got us into." Grumm laid his crossbow down on the writing table beside the Talamadh. "It was a good thing we had Enbarr pleading for us, begging for a second chance, or we'd be swinging from some makeshift gallows up in these forsaken hills a thousand leagues from home!" Grumm's voice had risen, as he paced about the room.

"What's more, are you certain you even know the way back through the forest up to the camp? What if you get lost? Do you know the forest hereabouts well enough to go rambling into it at night alone?" Grumm strode to the window of the keeil and stared outside, rubbing his empty hands together. "All alone, mind you, Skrobb, all alone with all them bears and boars and wild beasts. Nor much of a moon to see by neither, and you daren't take the high road along the lake." Grumm turned to face Skrobb again. "There's no telling how many of these here loutish snipes are on their mettle. Enough of them, I'll wager."

Skrobb's huge frame slumped in resignation to a chair by the door. He cast a defeated glance at his mate and said, "You go then, Grumm. I'll wait here for you."

At first, Grumm maintained he should take the Talamadh with him to present to Ferabek as the triumphant spoils of their capture of Wuldor's Howe. Skrobb would have none of this. What, he had said, and let Grumm get all the credit! So when Grumm took his leave, the golden harp remained on Wilum's writing table, its burnished yellow frame reflecting the shimmering flicker of the candle which played on the golden strings amid the sullen torch-limned shadows of the keeil.

SEVEN

The Westwynd Way was treacherous going, making for painfully slow progress, even though the north wind now blew at Kal's back. A severe windstorm a few nights earlier had left limbs and trees strewn across the way. To make matters worse, desultory banks of clouds would waft like billows of smoke across the sky, casting the Holding into a sombre darkness each time they hid the slender crescent of the moon. Even so, Kal made better time on Star Thistle than he would have on any other mount, for the chestnut mare had an almost supernaturally keen sense and slowed to sidestep every windfallen obstacle that she could not overleap.

It was a lonely road, little used by folk of the Holding, for the whole western side of Deepmere remained unsettled, a wild tangle of thickly wooded swales and ridges rifted with gloomy hollows. Unlike its counterpart, the Edgemere Road, which ran along the other side of the lake, the Westwynd Way followed a winding career, broken often by steep ascents and sharp down-turns. Once, when Kal swung down into a low-lying little valley, still soft and marshy from the spring thaw, he noticed, amid a deafening chorus of spring peepers, fresh hoofprints where the lowlanders had gone before him.

At the top of a rise Star Thistle clopped into a rocky clearing. Kal stopped for a moment and looked back in the direction of Wrenhaven. For the first time since he had left Broadmeadows he gained a clear line of sight allowing him to make out the ancient town seat of the Holding, once a settlement of echobards, which fringed the northern shores of Deepmere just below the Wyrdlaugh

Pass. Kal sat up in the saddle. Where he had been expecting to see only a few pinpoints of lamplight, there seemed to be many. Landros must have found the Warden and managed to have the alarm raised, rousing the sleepy residents of Wrenhaven from their beds. But there were now larger baleful fires springing up, reddening the far horizon of the night sky, and there were many specks of light that formed a serpentine pattern up beyond Wrenhaven in the direction of the Pass. Kal now stood in his stirrups.

The main body of Ferabek's Scorpions, positioned up at the Pass, had received the signal to begin their attack earlier than planned. The element of surprise was lost. The blaze of firelight in the distance waxed more luminous, engulfing the horizon in its kindled glow.

Reckless and desperate, knowing that his own indiscretion at the Sunken Bottle had not helped matters at all, Kal dug his heels into Star Thistle's sides, urging her on through the twisting, overgrown bridle path that now sloped down softly to a long stretch of level ground very close to the edge of Deepmere. Here on a broader straightaway Kal goaded the mare to a canter and then a gallop. Not far off, in the dark undergrowth of the forest, he heard the yip of foxes on the hunt, while to his left he felt reassured by the familiar lapping of waves that washed up against the shores of the lake. Kal came to an old stone bridge that spanned the channel of a wider stream, the Lower Skell, at the very spot where it flowed into Deepmere, broadening there into an inlet that was called Riven Oak Cove—a ghost-ridden spot, haunted by the spirit of an ancient echobard king who had here met a violent death.

Kal paused again on the bridge, listening to the rushing water that frothed and coiled around the stone piers below. He strained his ears and thought he heard the creak of oarlocks. Friend or foe? It could be either. "If only I'd kept my mouth shut at the Bottle," he chided himself under his breath.

As things stood, Enbarr and Kenulf would have explained to Ferabek that any Holdsmen escaping by boat and heading for Tarlynn's Coomb would be making for the mouth of the Skell, since the Coomb was to be found behind the bulwarks of a sheltered dingle midway up the mountainside in the valley of this same Skell. Kal could only hope that Ferabek would be too preoccupied with storming Wrenhaven to worry overmuch for the moment about any straggling survivors that might plod their way up to the Coomb. Or was it perhaps possible that Ferabek had already turned his attention to the Coomb? How long would it have taken Enbarr and Kenulf to reach Ferabek's camp from Wrenhaven? And how long had he lain bound up in the Locker? Star Thistle stamped restlessly beneath him.

It was impossible to say and idle to speculate. Wilum and Galli remained in terrible straits. Every moment counted, since any way the situation fell, Wuldor's Howe was bound to be a pressing priority with Ferabek's troops. And if the Scorpions reached the Howe first, on his own Kal did not stand a ghost of a chance of rescuing Wilum and Galli.

Kal leaned forward and stroked the neck of his mount. With a word from her master the great chestnut mare flew off again at a gallop. On the young Holdsman pressed, south along the broken road which traced the lakeshore as the miles before him dissolved beneath the horse's thundering hooves.

It was not far now, for the Westwynd Way began to curve eastwards, following the taper of the southern shores of the lake. Kal could just dimly make out the dark mass of battlements on Raven's Crag Island and then, when there came a sudden break in the drifting night clouds, the magnificent dome of the Great Glence itself, overtopped by the star-studded figure of the Shepherd in the windswept and sparkling canopy of the southern sky.

Kal passed the broad, pebbled sidepath that sloped down to Ardiel's Well. He was drawing near to the Great Glence. He reined in Star Thistle and wheeled her around, bringing her back to the lane which fell on a grade into a deep, secluded hollow thickly wooded with elm, oak, and hornbeam. In the bottom of the hollow was the Well itself, a spring of mountain water that gushed forth from the sheer rock face that bounded the northern side of the dell. He slowed his horse to a stand and dismounted. This had always been a place of peace.

How often had he walked down from the Great Glence and stood at the top of this path, watching folk come on pilgrimage to the restorative waters of the Well. But Wilum had told him of a time when this lane and the Westwynd Way all the way to the Great Glence itself had seen a solid press of people from all over Arvon and even from beyond. As the years passed, like a ground spring in the heat of summer, the flood of visitors had ebbed, dwindling to the mere trickle Kal knew. Wilum had said that the world of men had grown forgetful—forgetful of their past, forgetful of their story, forgetful of themselves. And these—a people and their history—were at the heart of this place, for legend had it that Ardiel, wasted and worn, had travelled here after the Battle of the Velinthian Bridge to lave his severely wounded shoulder with the water. The waters had cured him. From then on it had been known as Ardiel's Well.

How often had he walked down this lane! Kal sighed. He took Star Thistle, spent and wet with sweat, by her bridle and guided her along the grassy verge beside the path. Every footfall, every movement was guarded, for he could not afford to stumble once more into the hands of Grumm and Skrobb. He left Star Thistle ground-hitched down by the stone hut which enclosed the Well, its walls thickly covered by ivy-leaved toadflax, and its slate roof leaning back into the rock face. He would approach the Great Glence on foot. Kal whispered an endearment to his mare and left her chomping on the strip of lush grass that carpeted the very bottom of the quiet glade, taking with him his bow and a quiver full of arrows.

Kal began to climb the steep ridge which closed the southern end of the hollow, threading his way through the dense undergrowth. Well before he reached the brow of the ridge, he heard a horse neighing. It might be Galli's, but more likely one of the mounts of the two lowlanders. Crawling to the top, Kal could see a lone horse. It capered skittishly close by the woods that descended to Ardiel's Well, spooked by some animal or perhaps by the bodeful unease that seemed to charge the air. Kal sensed it too as he sniffed the mingled odours of honeysuckle and blackthorn which spiced the breeze—cloying and overripe. A second horse could not be seen. Kal scanned every inch of the darkened landscape for any sign of movement.

Crouched on the edge of Stillfields, he could see the Haltadans—towering forms that seemed to sway and touch the sky like dancers. Beyond the Haltadans on a prominent knoll stood the Great Glence and the Hordanu's keeil, still overlooking the level expanse of the Howe with regal haughtiness, even though in recent years they had sunk into the ground. Kal could have almost sworn that the Haltadans hovered on the brink of movement, so suggestive of life were the monoliths tonight under a star-bright canvas and the wind-driven clouds.

His mind hearkened to the legend of these large standing stones, which were purported to be the petrified shapes of the Hidden Folk, who had, in the primordial mists of time, even before the dawn of the Age of Echoes, run afoul of Wuldor's power in the First Undoing. It was in the *Master Legendary* that he had read that once in a century these frozen forms were allowed one night's freedom from moonrise to moonset. On these occasions they would dance and make merry and fill the Howe with their song and laughter, rejoicing in Wuldor's promise that at the end of the Ages they would be liberated from their immurement in these monoliths that dwarfed Kal now as he drew nearer to them through the grave markers and tombstones of Stillfields. He had never, however, heard tell of anyone who had actually witnessed the Freeing, though old Sarmel made his claims.

Kal nearly jumped out of his skin, his senses jarred by a deep wail which filled the darkness of the night sky beyond the apple orchard behind Ram's Knap. His heart drummed. His pace quickened to a jog. Skirting Ram's Knap, which formed an embankment at the funnelled end of the Haltadans, where the space between the two rows of standing stones narrowed, he drew closer to the Great Glence, mantled with darkness, its long perpendicular windows like the gaunt eyeless cavities of a corpse. At right angles to it slanted the keeil, whose sole window on this side was pouring out light onto a flowerbed. Very slowly, with his eye cocked for any sign of danger, Kal made for the window, using the Haltadans for cover, running from one stone figure to the next.

There was no clamour of sound nor evident sign of movement. The Black Scorpions had not yet arrived here. That much was sure. There was no telling where they were, though. If it were not for the soaring cliffs of Raven's Crag Island, with its castle sitting plumb in the middle of Deepmere, he might be able to see something, even if it were just the firefly specks of distant fires. How much more he would be able to see from the belfry that overtopped the dome of the Great Glence. No doubt, his family would be a good way towards the Coomb by now.

For himself, he had only the two lowlanders to worry about, and he stood a fair chance against them. Their eyes would be trained on the Eastmarsh Causeway, a broad avenue of cobbles which led from the Edgemere Road, forming the main approach to the Great Glence. There would be no good reason for them to be watching the rear of the Glence—not if they were not expecting to be attacked.

Kal stole up to the rounded stone slabs that rose massively to the domed pinnacle of the Great Glence, around which bats dipped and darted. Peering in through one of the darkened windows, he saw nothing to give him pause, only the bulking outline of the Glence Stone, topped by the Hordanu's stool, and the Stones of the Four Seasons. Around the exterior wall of the Great Glence he crept, passing a stout wooden door that led to an antechamber which connected the Glence to the keeil and from which there were stairs leading up into the belfry.

Kal slipped beneath the light-filled window. Laying down his longbow, he warily edged an eye past the trim of the bay window and peeked into the torchlit shadows of the keeil. Nothing to see at first except for Wilum's writing desk and on it the gilded frame of the Talamadh, catching the sputtering light of the candle that burned in a holder atop the desk and cast gloomy silhouettes onto the dark-grained oak of the wainscotting. On the top panel of the wall there loomed dusky carven figures, part of a continuous frieze that circled the keeil, illustrating in intricate detail the epic events that had ushered in the reign of Ardiel and with it the Great Harmonic Age.

Like a shadow, Kal slid towards the centre of the window, which afforded him a larger view of the inside of the keeil. There sat Wilum tied to one of his high-backed chairs, inert, his head bowed down to his chest. Moving over a little and shifting his position, he caught sight of Skrobb sitting slouched at the open front door of the keeil, casting nervous glances out into the night, a broadsword drawn. The horse neighed again. Hearing it, Skrobb straightened in the chair and looked back askance towards Wilum. Kal ducked away from the windowpane. The stillness was again broken by the insistent neighing of a horse in fright.

"Now you stay here nice and quiet like the good little Hordanu I knows you are, whiles I has a little look around." Kal heard Skrobb through the glass. "Ain't nothing but some animal giving old Strawboy the jitters. I'll just go and tie him up with the lad's horse here in front, wheres I can see them both 'til Grumm comes back with some help. He's been a long time coming." A growl rose in his throat. "I knew I oughtn't to have let him go on his own. I knew it." There was no doubting the fear in his voice.

Kal hazarded another glance. His back turned to the window, the big man brought his broadsword down on the chair he had been sitting on, reducing it to splintered boards. He stomped out and slammed the door of the keeil behind him. Grumm must have gone to fetch reinforcements, leaving his partner alone. Galli was nowhere to be seen. What had they done with him? A surge of choking anger came welling up inside him.

Reaching for his longbow, he felt for an arrow in his quiver, driven now by an awful desire for vengeance. Running back along the wall of the keeil, he nocked his arrow to the bowstring, ready to draw and let fly. When he reached the curving wall of the Glence, he saw Skrobb, stalking, with broadsword held before him, towards the horse. The animal remained skittish, pawing the ground around the maple trunk to which it stood tethered. The hulking lowlander's back was turned to Kal. It presented an ample target—an easy shot at twenty paces, like putting meat on a skewer. Kal drew back his bowstring, sighting the shaft on the small of Skrobb's back.

"Skrobb! Hold!" barked Kal.

For the briefest of moments Skrobb hesitated, casting a glance back over his shoulder. Then he broke into a loping run towards the forested slope that dipped down to Ardiel's Well. There was a crisp twang, and Kal's shaft, meant to hobble now rather than kill, sped to its mark. Skrobb groaned and kept on running even with the arrow shank sticking from the back of his thigh. There was not enough time to hail the lowlander again. If he made it to the woods, precious moments would be lost looking for him. And in the closeness of the trees, where the fighting would come to swordplay, Skrobb, aroused to a fury by his injury, would have a dangerous advantage. With the practised ease that was second nature to a Holdsman, Kal, with one quick seamless motion, picked another arrow from the quiver at his back, nocked it, drew, and released. He had aimed high—at Skrobb's right shoulder. Still not a death-dealing shot, but enough to drop the big man.

The Dinasantrian stumbled, falling near the restless horse, within a mere stone's throw of the shelter of the woods. From somewhere farther up the valley there came a steeply pitched howl, chilling Kal to the marrow of his bones. Looking up, Kal saw the thing, whatever it was, still far off in the sky, winging now this way, now that, in quick jagged movements, caught in the pale moonlight. It looked to Kal, from the cut and shape of its pinions, like a monstrous bat.

The horse, maddened to a frenzy, strained against its tether and reared up, raising its churning forelegs high into the air. Before Skrobb could move his injured body, the horse brought its hooves pummelling down upon him. Kal ran to grab the reins, trying to calm the horse. Still talking to the riled beast, he edged away from it and dragged the bleeding body of Skrobb out of harm's way, laying him on his side. Sickened by the blood and fighting his revulsion, Kal pushed each of the arrows gently through Skrobb's wounds, until the barbed head broke free of the flesh. As he drew each arrow out, the fletching emerged slick and rumpled. But it was too late. There was no breath, no pulse left in the big man, who lay bleeding in the grass, his eyes already starting to glaze over in death.

Kal's stomach churned. He turned away and retched into the grass. He fought against tears. He fought down the notion that Galli had died at the hands of Grumm and Skrobb. He fought the growing sense of despair. Again there came the fiendish, drawn-out shriek. Even the shrill sounds of the spring peepers were stilled by it, silenced by a power stronger than their seasonal instincts. Here was a creature unknown. Down in the hollow below at Ardiel's Well, Kal heard Star Thistle nickering. He pushed himself off the ground and sped back up the slope.

As Kal entered the keeil, Wilum moved his head in a listless acknowledgement of another person's presence in the room. The young man moved towards him. Wilum's eyes flashed in recognition.

"Kal? . . . Kal, lad! You're truly a sight—but how on earth did you get here? But nevermind, untie me here quickly. Hurry, lad, before Skrobb returns."

"Briacoil, Master Wilum. Not to worry. That one won't ever be coming back, not in this life. Where's Galli? What have they done with Galli? Is he dead? Where is he?" Kal's blue eyes blazed.

"Now, now, rest easy. He's alive and safe. Just finish untying me here, and we'll see about him. We'll have to act fast before the other one brings Ferabek's troops down on us."

As Kal undid the knotted coils of rope to free Wilum, he heard muffled groans coming from a closet set into the wainscotting.

"There we are," said Wilum, rising stiffly from his chair. "Don't mind that racket. It's only Galli waking from a nasty crack on the crown. Come, let's set him free." Wilum slid open the closet, revealing the crumpled figure of Galli, in a daze, but conscious.

"He'll be fine. Thick-skinned Galligaskin. I put a salve on the bump before he was stuffed in the closet. The two oafs were too busy arguing to notice. Untie him. I'll gather up the things that we must rescue. Any minute now and Wuldor's Howe will be swarming with the enemy."

From the closet in which Galli still lay, Wilum extracted a large oiled canvas sack. He strode to his writing desk and took up the Talamadh, slinging it around his shoulder by its leather strap. Shaking the sack open, he hurried back to a darkened recess of the keeil, close to the fireplace.

Kal helped Galli, still rubbing his head and groaning, to his feet. Together they tottered to where Wilum was shovelling all manner of leather-bound manuscript volumes into his satchel from a large oaken chest that lay draped in shadows.

Kal knew these volumes. They formed the most precious record of Ahn Norvys's history and lore. The bundle of parchment seized now by Wilum, Kal saw, was *Hedric's Master Legendary*, the great compilation, mostly in verse, of ballads, lays, formularies, and laws that had been brought together by the very first Hordanu. The rest of the hoard that Wilum pulled out of the chest consisted of the *Chronicles of the Harmonic Age*, a hodgepodge of writings authored by each Hordanu in succession over the centuries.

Once more a hollow wail raked the night air.

"What is that?" demanded Kal. "I saw it outside. Like a huge bat cutting through the air. And that howl . . . it gives you the chills to hear it."

"It's Ferabek unleashing yet another weapon from his armoury. A night-bred beast that defies the conventions of flesh and blood," Wilum said, pausing at his task.

"What do you mean?" asked Galli, still nursing his head.

Wilum regarded Galli, smiling. "Ah, Galli, you've weathered your blow well."

"That's because it's not just his skin that's thick. There's that dense Telessarian skull he's inherited, too."

Another low wail rose. Louder. Closer.

"There it goes again!" Kal cried. "I heard the night sounds of preying fellhawks once, when Father and I travelled one autumn to Thrysvarshold. I remember stopping on the roadside while Father drew his sword, and I was so afraid I clutched at his tunic. But this beats it all."

"There's good reason why this creature is beyond your ken. The Great Harmony has grown weak. There are many things that Ferabek may hazard, many powers of the night that fall under his sway, many creatures, for long centuries unknown within the bounds of Ahn Norvys, that he can summon forth from the underworld to do his bidding. I'll tell you later about thraganux, the night drake. For now we'd better make shift to escape its talons," said Wilum, even as he stuffed the last of the manuscripts from the chest into his sack. Reaching down into the chest once more, he grabbed hold of a small box of green stone shaped like a half-moon, which hung from a short gold chain, and then attached the end of the chain with a clasp to the Talamadh.

"Is that the Pyx of—"

"Yes. The Pyx of Roncador. And there's an end of answers to your questions. We've got to go now and fly as fast as we can. Come, Galli, you'll carry the satchel. I'll carry the Talamadh. But first I must pen a note."

Kal and Galli exchanged puzzled glances while Wilum opened his writing desk and took out a small piece of parchment, as thin as onionskin. Dipping a quill in the inkwell, he scribbled furiously.

"Wait here a moment," he bade them, as he rolled up the parchment into a tiny scroll, bound it tight with a thin golden thread, and then hurried out the front door of the keeil. Almost immediately he returned to them empty-handed.

"May the hawks and owls and all birds of prey lose their taste for my doves tonight," he half-intoned, eyes raised. "Come, lads, we've lingered here too long. Time to be off before we have unwelcome company. Kal, take the candle on the desk there and place it in that lantern . . . over there, by the door. And here's a tinderbox. Whatever you do, make sure nothing happens to the lantern. Keep it burning. We'll need light where we're going."

"Look, Master Wilum, the winding sheet." Kal pointed to the candle that flickered atop the writing desk. A thick gobbet of tallow had risen up against the wick of the candle, casting a white shroud over it. To the Holdsmen this was a sure sign of impending death.

"Aye, lad. I noted that. It does nothing to rest my heart, but let it pass for now. For some time the highlands have been dogged by uncertain foretokens of death. This is simply one more portent. Come now, hurry, lads. We hardly need dwell on omens when the events themselves stand ready to overtake us. Now we—"

"Wait! Listen! I hear hoofbeats on the Eastmarsh Causeway," said Galli, who had stepped to the door, cocking an ear to catch the whisperings of the north wind. "Aye . . . There it is. Many horses. Not far off."

"Come. This way. Out the window to the Well," said Wilum.

"But where—"

"Hush, Kal. No time for questions. Just follow me, the both of you, to Ardiel's Well."

Wilum stepped to the bay window through which Kal had earlier peered. He flung open the hinged panes, drew up the hem of his cloak, and stepped over the sill onto the soft soil of a flower bed. Kal and Galli followed, Kal guarding the light of the lantern beneath his cloak, shielding it from view, and they descended the long grassy slope. The cries of men and the clatter of hooves on the flagstone pavement of the concourse in front of the Great Glence reached them, hastening their flight. On each side loomed the towering Haltadans. Past Ram's Knap they fled, through the solemn grave markers of Stillfields, until they came to the lip of the ridge that fell off sharply towards Ardiel's Well. There were further cries, and a cohort of mounted horsemen carrying torches began to circle the Great Glence and the keeil, anxious to cut off all avenues of escape.

"Mind that lantern, Kal!" admonished Wilum, as the lamp beneath Kal's cloak clanged mutely against one of the gravestones. "If you break it . . . Take my word for it, lad."

Slipping down the incline, the three of them remained unseen. It was a close thing, too. If but one of those Black Scorpion troopers had caught a hint of the fleeing Holdsmen, it would have drawn the lot of them in hot pursuit, with nowhere to run except Ardiel's Well. Kal pushed his way through weeds and brambles and low-hanging branches, careful to keep the lantern out of harm's way. When he heard the spirited neighing of horses in the distance, his thoughts went to Star Thistle. He was glad he had left the mare ground-hitched and free to run. "Into the woods with you, girl," he whispered into the night.

Another dreadful howl, almost above them, spurred them on through the wooded thicket with its awkward footing. Though Kal held the lantern, Wilum led the way, while in the rear Galli hoisted the weighty sack around the obstacles.

They reached the bottom of the hollow. Wilum turned on the pebbled path, heading for Ardiel's Well. Opening the door, which was overhung with toadflax that had crept across it from the thickly festooned stone walls, he gestured to Kal and Galli, bidding them come down the steps behind him. Closing the door, they began to descend a short flight of stairs hewn out of rock that gave onto the floor of the Well. In the murky gloom, Kal's lantern cast fantastic flickering shadows on the walls. Here the waters of the Well cascaded out of the mouth of an ancient stone gargoyle into a square pool set into the ground. The grotesque figure, with its water-stained grimace, seemed so quaint and ornamental in daytime, when light from the door provided some illumination to the inside of the Well. Now it had taken on a leering malevolent cast. The sonorous flow of water being disgorged from its mouth made the atmosphere seem even more baleful. It masked a person's sense of hearing and rendered the ear incapable of distinguishing other sounds, making the darkness even more disconcerting.

"Here, Kal, shine your lantern here. I need to see." Wilum had stepped up onto the far side of the water pool. Adjusting the Talamadh on his shoulder, he stretched his hands out towards the gargoyle's head, standing just below its jet of water.

Kal thought he heard the baying of hounds above the sound of the water.

"But—what are you doing? We've got to get out of here. We're stuck like rats in a trap if they find us like this."

"Hush, Kal, have a little more trust in old Cloudbeard. Just give me a moment to box this dour fellow's ears." Wilum turned to the grim stone face and reached up to its jug-ears with both hands. He began twisting the head to left and right, pivoting it on its axis with a disarming boldness. Then he let go of the gargoyle's ears and stepped back. "Well now, what have I done wrong?" Wilum frowned at length. "I must be losing my memory in my old age. I'll have to try again. How does it go now? Let me think . . . What a time to forget!" He stepped again towards the fountain. "Right, right, left. I'll try that. I'm sure that's it," he muttered as he reached once more for the gargoyle's jeering face. This time, no sooner had he taken down his hands from the stone head, now restored to its original position, than there arose a low rumble above the sound of the splashing waters.

"What's that? What's happening?" cried Galli, laying down the sack and drawing his sword.

"I don't know. It's coming from inside, from over there!" shouted Kal, who had also pulled his own shortsword out of its scabbard and in doing so almost fumbled the lantern.

"The wall! It's opening!"

"Easy now," Wilum said. "Put away your weapons. Nothing to worry about. Here, Kal, give me the lantern and follow me. Quickly now, both of you."

Wide-eyed with amazement, Kal and Galli trailed Wilum's cloak-draped figure, stooping below the lintel of the secret doorway to enter a small antechamber. Its walls were of the same mortared stonework as the inside of the Well, a ceiling of huge transverse wooden beams spanning its width. Kal could see that when the door was closed the joints of mortar that separated the hidden door from the rest of the wall would look completely unobtrusive, so well had the mechanism been engineered. Once they all stood inside, Wilum reached for the handle that was fitted into the wall on his left and twisted it two full turns. The hidden door swung ponderously back into its normal place to the accompanying reverberation of hidden wheels and pulleys. With a thud they were enveloped by dead silence. For a moment Kal was choked by a surge of claustrophobic fear at their unexpected entombment. He felt the warmth of Galli's body draw closer to him. They stood, teeth chattering from chill and overwrought emotion in the penumbra of the lantern's quavering light. The two let Wilum take his bearings.

"Absolutely incredible, isn't it?" whispered Kal, heartened by the sound of his own voice.

"Who would have thought all these years that the old Well . . . ?" said Galli in awe. "Do you remember how as children we always thought there was something mysterious about the Well and made up stories about secret passageways guarded by the Hidden Folk?"

"Aye, it's a strange place, always sparked imagination—"

"Look, you'd never be able to find the seam of the door."

"It's kind of eerie. Not a place I'd come to if I didn't need to."

"No, certainly not my idea of cozy, but Cloudbeard's brought us here. So here we are—"

"Look, what's he doing there?"

Ignoring their exchange, Wilum was busy at the far end of the chamber, hunched over and peering down. Kal and Galli approached the stooped figure. He was looking down a square hole that dropped flush against the wall, with a ladder hanging down one of its sides. On a shelf close to the hole there lay a box of candles alongside some candleholders.

"You'd better equip yourself with a light as well, Kal, just in case," Wilum said as he snatched up a candle from the box and lit it from the flame ensconced in the lantern. Attaching it to a holder, he pressed the thing into Kal's hands. "Now let's get going down this ladder. It'll take us down this hole a good forty paces to a passageway that goes under Deepmere to Raven's Crag Island and ends up right in Owlpen Castle. When we get there, we'll see what we can do to salvage the manor rolls, before the Boar gets his trotters on them. There are a couple of old coracles in the castle. With any luck, they're still water-worthy enough. If we use them, we can row out to the other side of the Mere and then hike up to Tarlynn's Coomb. Come, Galli, I'll go first with the lantern, and you follow. Kal, you go last with your candle. Now let's move. Those soldiers and their hounds'll be at the Well here any moment, tearing it apart stone by stone, if needs be, trying to make out where we've disappeared to. So disappear we must."

EIGHT

For a man in his eighty-fourth year Wilum proved surprisingly nimble. The golden harp, slung like a bow across his back, did not seem to impede his ease of movement, nor did his long cloak. Indeed, Kal and Galli found themselves hard-pressed to keep up with him, as he clambered down the ladder ahead of them. They touched bottom, which lay submerged under half a foot of turbid water. Off to one side of the small chamber in which they now stood branched a narrow gap down which the water underfoot plunged noisily. Ahead, the passageway that led to Owlpen Castle opened before them. Squared off with large timbers, it stood only shoulder-high.

"Come, lads." Wilum motioned with his lantern. Stooping, he entered the shaft and was swallowed by the enveloping gloom. Kal and Galli looked to one another, then fell in behind him. The wooden supports above them dripped down large beads of cold lake water.

"Just a moment, Master Wilum," said Kal, "we'd better unspan our bows. All we need is waterlogged bowstrings, and they'll end up worse than useless to us in a pinch."

"Very well, quickly then."

"What about the harp?"

"No need to worry about that, lad. It would take considerably more than some stagnant old water to damage it."

Kal passed his candle ahead to Galli, then unstrung both their longbows and stuffed the strings in a leather pouch attached to his belt. Galli returned the candle to Kal and gathered both bows in his free hand, allowing Kal to nurse the uncertain flame of his candle, as they hurried on. They were soon drenched to the skin. Once Kal's light spluttered and died, extinguished by a drop from the roof beams. At this he had to squeeze past Galli in order to allow Wilum to relight the candle from his own lantern.

"You'll have to be more careful, lad. This isn't the best place in the world to fiddle about with a tinderbox," said Wilum, a brusque edge to his voice, as he deftly lowered the wick end of Kal's candle down through the unshuttered top of the lantern to the exposed flame of the candle fixed within.

It did not help that Kal was incessantly being speared by the rearward tips of the bowstaves held by Galli. All three kept stumbling and losing their balance on the slick rocks and debris submerged in the sluice-run at their feet. Kal found the tunnel suffocating. The space was so narrow, the candlelight so weak, and the oozing moisture so unchecked that he expected at any moment to have the life squeezed out of him by tons of overlying lake water, sweeping them all to an awful death. Kal again glanced at the roof of the shaft ahead of him, caught in the undulation of Wilum's lamplight. It was as if only a flimsy shell of wood separated them from the crushing weight of Deepmere.

Kal saw Galli's stooped frame ahead of him, struggling with Wilum's precious satchel, trying to keep it dry even as he slipped once and fell. How far was it from Ardiel's Well to Raven's Crag Island? A good half-league, no doubt. But to the young Holdsman, cramped, chilled and wet through, it felt as if they were slogging all the way to Dinas Antrum.

Kal marvelled at the dogged determination that had gone into the building of the tunnel. Where had they gotten the labour to carry through this daunting project—those enigmatic figures who had lived during the Age of Echoes? It was speculated that the echobards were responsible for Ram's Knap and Ardiel's Well, in addition to all the most ancient sections of Owlpen Castle and the settlement of what was now Wrenhaven. With the coming of Ardiel, the echobards had disappeared from Ahn Norvys without a trace, save only the allusive glory of their monuments and some few faint but evocative shreds of legend. It was said by some that they could not abide the Great Harmony inaugurated by Ardiel. So they left their haunts and took up their abode in remote woodland glades and oakwood coppices, far away from the prying eyes of men, on the unmapped fringes of the world, like the Hidden Folk, as evanescent as a morning mist on a bright summer's day.

On they plodded. It seemed that the tunnel would never come to an end. Above the din of the rushing water Wilum raised his voice, and they came to a halt.

"Let's stop for a moment, lads. I need to catch my breath. It isn't far now."

"Where do we get out of this place?" asked Galli, wrestling with the shifting sack on his shoulder.

"Just up ahead, we're almost there. You'll see soon enough."

After a moment's rest, Wilum pressed on again in the lead, steadying himself, his unencumbered hand moving in steps along the stone wall of the passage. About a hundred paces farther, the tunnel broadened and opened onto a large chamber.

"Watch it, be very careful now. Stay close by the wall to the left here," warned Wilum. They were standing side by side now on a narrow ledge that gave onto a murky pool. The dark lambent waters threw back an oily reflection of wavering light and spilled past their feet with a burbling echo down the floor of the tunnel from which they had just emerged.

In the wan light of the two candle flames, Kal could make out the rough contours of the chamber. Directly ahead of them the pool was met by a wall of massive cut-stone blocks that rose straight to the ceiling of vaulted natural rock above their heads. On a large stone in the centre of this wall was carved an inscription in spindly runic characters, flanked on either side by the figure of a rampant wolf. Where they faced it, the pool described a gradual half-circle that was bordered by the mortared rocks of the ledge on which they stood.

"Look, there's something in the water!"

"How's that, Kal? What do you see?" demanded Wilum, who was already halfway up a flight of rough-hewn stairs that ascended from the ledge.

"You're right," said Galli. "It looks like a body. With coiling grey things wrapped around it . . . like vines. And look, on the ledge here. Blood, and a fair bit of it at that. There's been some kind of struggle here."

"A body? How?" Wilum had retreated down the steps to peer into the depths of the pool. He then lifted his gaze. "And what's that? An opening of some kind? At the far end of the pool there. In all the times I've been here I've never seen anything . . ." He was pointing to a dark gap in the solid granite of the cavern's face which marked the beginning of some other passageway that he obviously did not recognize. "There's danger here without a doubt. Come, follow me quickly. But be very careful and watch your footing, lads. To slip into the water here means certain death." He had raised his forefinger in admonition, then let it fall, pointing to the waters. "This is what the echobards called the Pool of Retribution. It's deep, fed by icy springs that percolate up from the netherworld. You can see the long tendrils of yffarnian water ivy just below the surface. Let only one of them fasten onto your arm or leg and there would be no escape, just as there wasn't for this poor wretch. It's said that the echobards meted out punishment to evildoers and criminals here."

"What is that inscription, Master Wilum?" asked Galli.

"It's written in runes that date back to the Age of Echoes, and neither Ardiel nor Hedric nor any Hordanu since has been able to unlock their mystery. In the Great Flight of the Echobards their meaning was lost. Even the runes on the Great Harp have refused to yield their secret. Let's move on. We can't afford to linger." He turned back to the stairs.

The hazards of the Pool of Retribution did nothing to slow Wilum's sure-footed progress along the ledge to the base of the steps. Kal and Galli, however, clung to the wall of the cavern and moved ahead by fits and starts, testing every footfall, lest any slip or loss of balance send them tumbling into the choking clutches of the ivy. They safely reached the foot of the stone stairs. Wilum stood waiting for them.

"Well, I'm quite glad to see you survived that ordeal," he quipped.

Wilum looked considerably less solemn and stately than he had looked some nine days ago on the evening of the Candle Festival or even than he had as recently as yesterday morning. His venerable white hair was a jumbled mess of sodden wisps, while his thick woollen cloak, drenched as it was, looked as heavy and cumbersome as a suit of armour. He turned, and up the stairs they continued, following what had become a continuous trail of blood.

The stairway curled up sharply to meet the stone wall which

bounded the Pool of Retribution and ended in a landing which was recessed into the cavity of the wall itself. Wilum stopped and turned to face the two young men, who had reached the landing now themselves and stood before another set of stairs that rose from it.

"More blood." Galli pointed to the floor.

"Hush. Speak only in whispers and sparingly at that. I'm at a loss as to how to explain the blood, lad. It unsettles me. But there's precious little we can do about it anyway but be cautious, and quiet. The stairs before you are cut into the width of the wall of Owlpen Castle. The walls are thin, so we'll have to tread carefully. For all we know, the Castle may already be overrun by the Boar's troops. I hope not."

Straining their ears to catch the sound of intruders, they began to climb the stairs, their way a steep diagonal hollowed out from the core of the wall. Soon the quiet was broken by Wilum breathing heavily from the physical exertion. The flight of stairs turned and gave onto a small rounded alcove. Wilum whispered for them to remain at the top of the staircase for a moment. Then he crawled forward and pressed his face into a nook in the wall. Kal heard the faintest of clicks as of a latch being lifted and in a moment another click.

"A peephole," he said by way of explanation as he turned back to them. "It looks all clear to me down in the Great Hall." He crouched on hands and knees to examine a wooden trapdoor set into the space of floor at their feet. The pool of candlelight from the lantern he had placed on the floor glowed a ruddy hue on the boards, bloodstained where someone else had strained to lift it.

"Here, lift this up for me, Galli. Careful now," Wilum whispered, pointing to the two rings attached to the trapdoor. Wilum stood above the opening with his lantern and motioned silently to Kal, bidding him go down the ladder which was fixed to the wall below the trapdoor. After a short awkward descent, Kal, still nursing his candle, touched ground and was followed by Galli, burdened with longbows and satchel. Wilum, guarding the lantern and shifting the weight of the Talamadh on his shoulder, came last. They found themselves in a square niche, scarcely large enough to hold the three of them. But now for the first time since they had descended into the darkness of Ardiel's Well, they encountered natural light. The light of day streamed into the close space from a strange opening in the farther wall.

"Look at all the blood," whispered Kal.

"Quiet, Kal," mouthed Wilum. Before them, a whole section of the facade across from the ladder yawned open—a door set on a pivoting hinge at its centre. There were bloodstains all over the floor of the tiny room, as well as the walls themselves. Whoever had come here ahead of them had felt his bleeding hand along the wall looking for the doorway and for what controlled its mechanism. He had found it, for the small knob mortised into the stonework of the wall just beside the hidden door was covered with blood as well. Wilum pushed Kal aside, cocked his ears, and peered through the nearer of the two openings that had been formed by the crosswise slab of moving wall. Wilum signalled to Galli, bidding him listen. The young Holdsman motioned that he heard nothing.

The area beyond seemed safe and clear. Wilum lifted the glass shutter of his lantern and blew out the flame. Then, bidding the two young men to stay silent by drawing his finger up to his lips, he gestured for them to follow. With this he stepped through the slantwise gap.

Kal knew now where they were. He had visited Owlpen Castle once with Wilum. This was part of the gallery that girdled the Great Hall and the Overlord's Chamber on the main floor. From it a company of archers could defend the castle, for the walls of the gallery were liberally punctuated with arrow slits. A series of long thin clerestory windows provided illumination for the entire main floor of the keep. The hidden chamber behind them was built into a column that abutted the interior cross-wall which separated the Great Hall from the Overlord's Chamber. Diagonally across from them were the turreted winding stairs that formed the main entrance to the keep. There was not a sign of another soul in the castle.

Once they had all come clear, Wilum swung shut the door, which closed with a dull thud. Again the fine workmanship made it almost impossible to distinguish the seam between the secret door and the adjacent wall, except for a bloody handprint which ended mid-palm in a straight line.

Kal made his way to the nearest window. He beckoned to Wilum and Galli, while cautioning them to keep their bodies clear of the opening. From there, landing on a jetty on the island's eastern approach, limned by the weak half-light of the rising sun, they saw a company of five swart figures—Black Scorpions clad stoutly in chain mail. They watched the men moor the shallop and now turn in ones and twos to look up at the Castle.

"Come on, Kal, let's have those bowstrings," said Galli, breaking the spell of silent apprehension.

"Let me dig them up here," said Kal, fumbling for his pouch. "They'll be making their way to the main gate. We should be able to pick off at least two of them, if not more. After that they'll scatter like rabbits. Too bad they've got so much in the way of cover between here and the jetty. What do you think, Master Wilum? Don't you think we'd better go on the attack ourselves before they make the entrance of the keep?"

"Aye, Kal. You and Galli had better give them something to think about. It'll afford us some breathing space, a chance to fetch what we've come for and get out."

The soldiers were roughly two bowshots distant and appeared almost casual in their actions, unconcerned about any possible danger on the island. Kal and Galli had strung their yew-wood bows and had each extracted a water-soaked shaft from the quivers slung over their shoulders. Nocking their arrows in readiness, each of them took up his station at an arrow slit and waited until their quarry moved closer into range.

"When shall we let loose, Kal?" breathed Galli.

"Hold 'til they're just within comfortable range. What after that, Master Wilum?"

"We can't waste time. I'll get the rolls and the map while you two finish your business here." Wilum pointed to an opening in the cross-wall that divided the castle keep in two. "I'll meet you at the staircase in the corner of the Chamber. You'll see it readily enough when you cross over there. Then we'll go fetch those coracles from the castle cellars and remove ourselves from this island. I'll see you both soon. Just take your time and make sure those grey-goose feathers of yours fly true and find their mark. Briacoil, Kalaquinn. Briacoil, Galligaskin."

Wilum clutched his staff and strode to the steps that led from the gallery down into the Great Hall, which lay bare of all furnishings save for a great oak table and some benches. These had once seen much merriment and feasting, but now stood bedecked with only dust and cobwebs.

Wilum disappeared from sight into the adjoining room, leaving Kal and Galli at their perch in the gallery, tense and expectant, peering out onto the path below. The air was heavy-laden with the fresh sweet smell of primroses. A great yellow tide of them grew in wild profusion under emerald larches on the gentle slope by the ramparts of the Castle. Golden daisy buds lifted their white petals to a brightening sky, while linnets flew around the bushes and trees, swelling now with leaves in the springtide.

The shrill cries of a kestrel on the wing sent a shiver of apprehension into Kal. It was not so much fear as a feeling of revulsion at the slaughter their fearsome longbows were about to unleash. Skrobb had been different. Kal had shot him only to wound and to slow him down. He and Galli had only ever hunted game animals in the Holding, and here for the first time they were peering down on a human quarry.

"I can't say I like this," whispered Galli from his point of vantage, hardly daring to speak louder than a whisper. "Are we really going to shoot them down? I suppose it's still hard to believe all this murder and mayhem is really happening in our own peaceful Holding. Here we are about to actually kill a person, I mean, with an arrow that we've sped on its way, you know, not like that landslide we started. Somebody living and breathing with families and loved ones probably. I mean they must have families, mustn't they, Kal? Just like us? Even though they're ugly and humourless? How can we just pick them off from up here?"

Kal turned from Galli to watch the soldiers tramping along the overgrown flagstone footpath up from the landing.

"I can't say I care for this any more than you do. But look what they've done, how close they came to doing us in, and what they plan to do. They're the Boar's trained killers. Trained killers. Think of that. Think of your cousins in Wrenhaven, all put to the sword, any of them that couldn't escape. And I can't help but think that some of them didn't, seeing as how the Boar attacked without them getting much of a warning. There wasn't enough time for that. When I left him, I reckon Landros couldn't have had the time to raise the alarm for all that many townsfolk before they fired the place. And your cousins, hardly more than babes . . . Picture those men as ruthless beasts. Beasts hunting us down without mercy. It's up to us. We've got to fight back. We've got to try to stop them or they'll slaughter us all." Kal's body stiffened, his head raised, his fingers flexing around the grip of his bow and the nocked arrow. "Look sharp, Galli. They're coming closer . . . Another few seconds and they'll be within range. Let's choose our targets. I'll take the fellow with the scorpion standard." Kal looked to Galli and saw the questioning look on his friend's face. "And you, you get the man just behind him on your left. Don't let loose, though, 'til I give the word. Get on your mark now. Don't worry, it'll be fine. You trust Cloudbeard, don't you?"

"I do, Kal. But there's more than one of the folk that's beginning to wonder if he's not a throwback, clinging to the old things and the old ways when it's clear there's a new era dawning, a new order of things. They say it's his arrogance and pride that sets him at odds with Gawmage and the Mindal."

"Have you ever looked to the source of all that poison talk?"

"Aye, it's mostly Enbarr and Kenulf and a couple of their cronies stirring things up against him."

"There you are. Wilum is to be trusted. If all else fails, he will not. Hush now. Let's look to those Scorpions. We'll give them a sting— Get down! One of them's looking up towards us." Kal slid away from the slit. He had seen the Scorpion with the standard stop and point up at the Castle. The murmur of quarrelling voices drew ever nearer, yet he dared not peer around the edge. The voices of the soldiers now grew silent, as if they had composed their differences. This was discomfiting. Knowing now that they must have come within range, he ventured the slightest peek and realized that they were walking more slowly, looking up and around them, their swords extended and their shield arms raised.

Kal laid his longbow down and crawled under the threshold of his slit to whisper into Galli's ear.

"We'll have to make it a good shot. They've seen something and they're on their guard. Aim for the sword side. I'll give the word." He scrambled back to his post and took up his bow.

The moments passed with charged stillness, their bodies poised.

"All right, Galli, now! Let fly right now!" The tension was broken like a thunderclap by Kal's whispered command, as he moved himself into view at the arrow slit, his bow bent into its full arc.

The two shafts flew loose with a thwack of unclinched bowstrings. One of them, Kal's, sped with unerring marksmanship to its target, piercing cleanly the chain-mail hauberk of the hapless soldier. Driven off target by a vagrant downdraft, Galli's arrow caught its intended victim in the thigh. Almost before the first had met their mark, a second flight was cutting through the air. Another man fell, clutching at the arrow in his chest—Galli's mark. This time it was Kal who missed. Amid shouts of surprise, the three survivors scattered for cover. The standard lay beneath its mortally stricken bearer, its gilt-edged purple streamers entangled in the thistle that had overgrown the footpath.

"Come, let's find Wilum," Kal sputtered. "The rest of them will be skulking through the underbrush up to the Castle. Gives us a bit of time to make good our escape, I hope." Kal did not wait for Galli to answer, but slung his longbow over his shoulder and ran down the gallery stairs, heading straight for the Overlord's Chamber with Galli close on his heels.

The two fled into the Chamber, awash now with beams of morning sunlight that came pouring in through the high thin windows just above the gallery on the east side of the Castle. The Chamber, once the sleeping quarters of an Overlord and his family in the Age of Echoes, was even emptier and more desolate than the Great Hall. In one corner, beside a large open hearth, lay a wooden chest from which Wilum had clearly already taken the contents, for he stood waiting for them on the other side of the Great Chamber in a recessed nook that was cloaked in the coolness of still lingering night shadows, his arms overflowing with the thin parchments on which the manor records were kept.

"W-well, Master Wilum, two of them are out of action and now we have only three of them to deal with. And one of them's wounded," said Kal. For the second time in the mere space of hours he had dealt out death even as it stalked him.

"Three left . . . Well, let that be as it is. You've trimmed the odds. Now we must fly again." He turned to Galli to hand him the parchment rolls. "Take these. Put them in the satchel. Now let's go down below. We'll need a light—oh, where was my head when I blew out the lantern and candle? Where are they?"

"I've got them here in the sack— Listen," cried Galli. "It's a hunting horn being winded somewhere in the distance. But it's not one of our horns, the note's too harsh."

"Here, as you value your life, let's get them relit." Wilum took out a small tinderbox from beneath the folds of his cloak. It took no more than one strike of flint on steel to ignite a small pile of tinder shavings, from which they took a fresh light for the two candles. Wilum took one of them and closed it behind panes of lantern glazing while giving the other to Kal to tend.

He turned and hastened down a narrow spiral staircase—the Overlord's private entrance to his castle. Enclosed by a small circular stone tower, it felt more like the shaft of a well. Down one flight of stairs they reached a landing with a small but sturdy wooden door.

"This is the postern gate, our way out," whispered Wilum. "But first we have to go down into the cellars and procure ourselves a boat or two."

Following one another down a farther short stretch of stairs in single file, they reached a musty place where, from out of the earthen floor, rose huge stonework piers that undergirded the building above. These used to be the Castle's storerooms, now littered with earthenware jars and several piles of odd planks and worm-eaten bits of wood—the decrepit remains of the Castle's furniture—bedsteads, chests of drawers, sideboards, and chairs, along with ancient suits of armour, rusting in the dampness.

Wilum stepped around a solid rectangular abutment that flanked a portion of the outer foundation from floor to ceiling, housing the well of Owlpen Castle. He held his lantern over a dark bowl-shaped hump.

"There's one of our coracles. But where's the other?" Wilum poked about here and there through the cellar looking for the other boat, but was brought up short.

"No wonder you can't find it," Galli said. "Whoever it was that left his blood all over the place made his way down here too and took it. It was a smaller boat. And look at his tracks here, small ones. And did you see the flecks of dried blood on the stairs coming down?"

Wilum returned to where the young men stood. He wore an expression of growing consternation.

"Fine. We'll have to make do with one, then, and hope we're given the chance to make two trips. Blow out your candle, Kal. Mine should be enough to light our way to the door. I shudder to think what's happening out there. The valley's probably swarming with Ferabek's minions." Wilum grimaced. "Here, turn the coracle around. I think you'll have to carry it sideways to get it up the stairs. There you go." Wilum helped Kal tilt the coracle up on its plaited hazel gunwale. The young man grasped it with two hands by its side and began lugging it along the dirt floor to the steps leading up to the door. Wilum returned to the stone wall and picked up two paddles that hung there. Darting ahead of Kal, he lit the way for him up the steps. Galli followed behind with the bows and the overstuffed satchel. At the top of the stairs by a thick oak door bound to the jamb with broad hinges, he bade them stop. The door stood ajar.

"Lean the coracle against the wall," he ordered Kal in an undertone. "There you are. It should stay like that. You too, Galli. Leave off your load for a moment. Both of you, nock an arrow. I need you here."

Hurrying up the steps, Galli joined Wilum and Kal, pulling an arrow from his quiver.

"Keep your silence now, and unplug your ears—especially you, Galli—our lives depend on it."

By slow degrees Wilum widened the opening of the doorway. On the other side of it, from a recess above their heads, there hung suspended the iron fretwork of a small portcullis that had barred the way to the outside. For several moments they stood under the portcullis, but heard nothing beyond the tangy chirp of sparrows and a cliff swallow, perched on the upper branches of a tall silver birch, its urgent "kwik, kwik" impelling them to make a run for it.

"The way looks clear. Put away your bows for a moment. Grab hold of our baggage, both of you. Step smartly. We've got to reach Deepmere before they can overtake us."

Wilum stepped out into the fresh spring air, which carried a strong pleasant scent of lavender from the profusion of bluish flowers spread out along the earthworks of the Castle's northern face. A startled honeybee came buzzing past him towards its nest in a hollow willow pollard, draped by sprays of wild gooseberry that grew out of the decayed touchwood on its ancient crown. Close by the pollard stretched a little pond, white with water-crowfoot, entirely covered from bank to bank, not a tiny section of it ungraced with a blanket of silver cups. Some greenfinches had alighted for a drink at its shallow edge. Wilum waded knee-deep into the meadow grass of what was once the pleasance of Owlpen Castle.

After squeezing the coracle through the portal, Kal laid it down

in the grass. He pulled the bow off his shoulder again and reached
for an arrow. Galli, who had left the doorway open behind him,
placed the sack down beside Kal and readied his bow as well. In
silence all three of them craned their necks, surveying the scene
around them and letting their clammy water-laden bodies absorb
the warming rays of the eastern sun.

"So far so good," whispered Kal. "Let's get away from here.
Which way should we be going, Master Wilum? You know the
island— What's that?" he exclaimed, for a sudden rustling sound
came from the woods by the pond. "Here, let's take cover. No,
not back in the Castle. We haven't a hope in there. Quick, behind
this hedge."

Leaving the boat in the grass, they ran towards the uncertain
cover of the hawthorn hedge. Setting up, the two young Holdsmen pulled back on the arrows they had nocked.

"There's our enemy. She doesn't look very fearsome to me,"
Wilum said, as he pointed to a deer and her capering fawn who
browsed on some thick hazel bushes on the meadow's edge,
unaware that they were being observed. "Kal, go fetch the coracle
again," continued Wilum, as Kal and Galli returned their shafts to
their quivers. "We'll take that path through the woods there"—he
pointed—"to the Hollow of the Eagles by the Raven's Crag. We
can launch the coracle there and quit this island."

Traversing a small orchard of apple, plum, and quince trees,
their twisted limbs hoary with lichen, they entered the forest
which had once been the Overlord's deer chase. It was a hand-
some stand that had remained unmolested by the woodsman's
axe. As they approached it, the doe lifted her head and vanished,
leaping with her fawn into the sheltering depths.

To make the coracle easier to carry, Kal had passed his longbow
to Galli and hoisted the thing onto his back, so that he looked
like a gigantic black beetle. Keeping silence, they listened intently
to all the forest sounds around them as they trod. For the first
while the path took the form of an ancient flagstone walk closely
overarched with flowering bushes. Walking through it, Kal was
forced into a stoop. To his great relief, they emerged from this
bower into the higher canopy of unmanicured hardwood forest. Once or twice they were startled to attention by a rustle of
bushes or ferns—a rabbit or a stoat peering out at them with
alarm through the filtered sunlight of the forest.

Farther into the heart of the deer chase they stole, driven by their need to escape. Kal slouched under his burden and was forced to take his bearings from Wilum's sandalled feet and the rustling hem of his cloak. It was he who caught the reflected glint of something metallic on the forest floor amid a tangle of decaying leaf litter.

"Master Wilum, there's something on the ground here just off the path." Kal gestured from under the coracle to where a fragile shard of sunlight had managed to penetrate the cool dimness of the woodland shadows.

"It's a coin," said Galli. He had come to Kal's side and stooped to pick up the shining bit of silver, which he now held up to view with a puzzled look. "Here, Master Wilum, what do you make of it?" Galli handed the piece to Wilum, who took the coin and turned it in his fingers, running his thumbnail along its edge.

"This is coinage of very recent minting. The date . . . 3012 H.R. And the inscription too . . . Quite interesting. It's in Gharssûlian and reads, 'His Illustrious Majesty Ferabek IV, Firstborn Scion of the Mighty House of Soluda, Beneficent Wielder of the Sceptre of Keftiu.' Goodness." The old man chuckled. "It's so long-winded that Ferabek has hardly left room for his own scowling ill-favoured countenance. This is a Gharssûlian Crosskeele Groat." He sent the coin spinning into the air with a flick of his thumb and caught it. "And it certainly hasn't lain in this spot for years."

"This seems to be another path," Galli said, scrutinizing the forest floor around them. "Look, it cuts across ours and continues in that direction towards the Castle."

Kal laid down the coracle and began kicking aside the leaves and humus that littered the spot, revealing a beaten trail. "Doesn't this path come up from the beach by the Lochar Rock?"

"The Egrets' Cove, yes, a fine little cove, a superb landing place. I'm afraid that there are more enemy soldiers here than the ones we first saw. These aren't the Scorpions you fired on . . . No, these are others—"

"That's it!" said Kal, "The horn. They were summoning their comrades, who'd landed at the Egrets' Cove to avoid being spotted from the Castle's turrets. They must think the Castle's held by Holdsmen."

"Quite so. It's fortunate we didn't cross paths with the soldier who lost this Groat and his fellows. What I'm afraid of now is that there may be more Black Scorpions on their way up this path from the Egrets' Cove. Come, we'd better push on. This is definitely not a good place to hold conference."

Wilum pocketed the Groat and turned with a quick step back to the trail they had been following, so that Kal, having taken up the coracle once again, found himself hard put not to lose sight of his receding figure. Along a gently ascending grade the three of them trod, scanning all around them for sign of ambush. Once their hearts leapt to their throats as the air around them was pummelled by the drumming wings of a partridge they had flushed from its roost. Another time Galli called them to a halt when he spotted, about a hundred paces away on a ridge above them, a glittering pinpoint of light like the sun off the boss of a shield. Wilum had Galli test the curious gleam with a well-aimed bowshot. When the shaft had sped to its mark and there was no stir of movement, they decided it was just a vagrant trick of the eye—light caught reflecting on stone. Even so, for a while they kept casting sidelong glances back, half-expecting the suspect ridge to disgorge an attacking company of Black Scorpions from its sun-dappled mask of trees.

They stepped over a shallow rill that purled past them, stained brown by peat, and veered to the right along the rising slope. The path began to twist this way and that, sinuously avoiding the gulleys and the brambles, the streams and lichened rocks, following the way of least effort along the contours of the hill, which was studded with willows and ancient oaks. The path left the woods and was swallowed by a sheltered cusp of open heath that led to a promontory jutting into the lake, framed against the vaulted azure of the sky. The cries of nesting waterfowl filled the air, drowning out all other sounds. The path made an arching turn to the right through a carpet of heather back into the woodland.

"Let's stop here for a moment," bade Wilum, looking out along the promontory. "There's the top of Raven's Crag. From there we'll be able to see the beach. Come, both of you. Let's have a look. Three pairs of eyes work much better than one weary old pair. Let's take cover close to the ground under those bushes by the edge of the cliff."

They left their baggage hidden from the path and traversed the shoulder of the Crag, stooping down as they neared its edge. Lying prone under a flowering currant, they peered over the side.

All around them rose a din of screeching birds, swarming over the jagged niches and clefts on the face of the Crag below. Kal tugged on the sleeve of Wilum's cloak.

"Look." He pointed. "Down there on the beach. Look how many boats there are!"

"Keep your head down."

"You were right," continued Kal. "More Scorpions have landed. Eight boats of them. They must have gone to the Castle. Must be thinking they'll have to storm it."

"Aye. We were indeed fortunate not to have stumbled into them. Even so, we still may before this day is out. Let's draw back now and take stock of our situation."

They eased themselves away from the cliff top and walked back to where the hidebound boat lay propped up by a spongy bed of heather.

"No, Kal, leave it where it is. Galli, give those longbows to Kal. There, that should make your load a bit easier. My lads, we shall avail ourselves of Ferabek's much too ample bounty."

"Steal a boat?"

"Exactly," continued Wilum. "It's a lucky thing too, since that little basket couldn't possibly carry the three of us. Nor would these soldiers have given us the opportunity to make two trips. So while the hounds are on a bad scent, we'll make a run for it and turn this invasion of theirs to our advantage. Here, let's continue along this path to the Hollow of the Eagles and from there along the shore to the boats. We'd better be quick about it."

As they pressed on along the path, they could hear high above them the honking chatter of geese coming home to nest in the coves and reedy inlets of Deepmere, its age-old quietness riven by the fell clash of arms. Their progress was much faster now, as they struck back into the arcading deepness of the woods without the awkward weight of the coracle to impede them. The trail plunged into the narrow trough of a steep ravine that rent the eastern flank of Raven's Crag. The ground underfoot was strewn with the musty remains of last autumn's leaves. Here and there stood small pools of water that had collected on the floor of the ravine from runnels scored into the sides by melting snow and spring rains. Kal felt exposed and vulnerable and hoped that Wilum had calculated things right. Then, as if to jar him from his self-pitying reverie, he heard in the hush of that solitary place the lovely flute-like warble of a hermit thrush, which had alighted on a bare larch root a mere stone's throw away. One little creature, at least, who cared little that there were Black Scorpions abroad.

For several hundred yards, they followed the ravine in its sharply falling course against the bulk of the Crag until it flattened out and gave onto an apron of rock set flush against the adamantine walls of the Crag itself. Spreading its talons on a cornice of stone that overhung the three companions was a large eagle, which eyed them disdainfully from its perch. The three paused, struck with amazement, for over time the name of the place—Hollow of the Eagles—had become ironic, a mere throwback to the Age of Echoes, when eagles still soared majestically on the currents of air that blew through the valley. Kal looked out to the lake. From the open side of the Hollow he could see the surface of Deepmere, its opalescent ripples spreading in the morning breeze. Striding up from its shores were the snow-crested summits of the Radolan Mountains, aflame with the burning of a spring sun. There was a rush that parted the air above them. They spun around and saw the eagle rising slowly from its coign of vantage, a mighty sweep of pinions propelling it through the rift before them. Catching an upcurrent of air, the bird began to circle and glide, needing only an occasional stroke of its wings to remain airborne.

Breaching the Hollow was a set of wide rough-hewn stone steps that led down to a ribbon of sandy beach behind a veil of maidenhair ferns that covered the scree under red ash and mountain hemlock trees.

"We've got to be even more careful now," advised Wilum as they descended the steps, "for we don't dare meet up with the enemy along the shoreline. We'd be helpless and with no place to escape. Galli, we're in dire need of your talents at this point."

"Aye, Master Wilum. I don't see anything strange at the moment. Nor hear anything. The birds are too loud. I sense that they're in a fright. This island hasn't seen so many men in quite some time."

They reached the shelving stretch of sand beneath the over-hanging mass of rock that made the shape of a raven's head. All around them the air resounded with the raucous cries of water-birds. Deepmere, bounded on the horizon by its eastern shoreline, lay sparkling before them.

"Wait," said Galli, who held up his hand to shield his eyes from the sun and peered out across the waters of the lake. "I see some movement in the distance. On Edgemere Road. The speed—some of them are on horseback . . . Fire . . . They're fighting! There's the flash of arms and armour—"

"Come, men." Wilum regained their attention. "We've an escape to make. We can't be of help to them with a lake between us."

They scanned the area around them. The eight boats of the Scorpions farther down the beach at the Lochar Rock lay hidden from their sight by a curving elbow of land that enclosed the reedy shallows below the Hollow of the Eagles, making a little inlet.

Wary of discovery, the three Holdsmen rounded the corner beyond which, about three hundred paces distant, the Egrets' Cove cut abruptly into the regular sweep of the foreshore. On the fringe of the bight carved out of the island by the Cove they descried the indistinct shapes of the boats they had seen earlier from the headland which dominated the skyline at their backs. Galli jostled the heavy sack of Wilum's papers on his shoulder while his hand rested on the hilt of his shortsword. Kal fitted an arrow to his bow.

By the time they reached the Cove the tension had abated somewhat. In his vigilance Galli had seen and heard nothing to cause them alarm. It seemed that the Black Scorpion Dragoons in their haste to answer the horn's summons, or their enthusiasm to join in combat, or simply their raw excess of self-confidence, had chosen not to place a sentinel at the boats. It was no small blessing, and for this the three Holdsmen were grateful. Kal had put away his longbow, his attention taken up by the flat-bottomed fishing boats that now lay at hand. Wilum gestured to Galli, ordering him to put the satchel in the stern of the first boat they came to.

"This way, lad. We'll take this one and scuttle the rest."

"It's a shame. These belong to the men of Wrenhaven. I recognize Sendar's mark on this one," said Galli, setting his foot on the gunwale of another of the boats.

It took only one or two solid thrusts of the sword to tear a gaping hole in the planks of each of the hulls. Then, while Wilum took a seat in the stern, Kal and Galli pushed the one undamaged boat off the beach. They ran alongside it in the water until it floated free of the shingle, then clambered aboard.

"Galli," said Kal, "it's better if I row alone. Here, let me get by and I'll sit there between the oarlocks. You can kneel in front of me here and keep a lookout."

"Very well, steersman. Set a course for Riven Oak Cove," instructed Wilum. "But give the island a wide berth."

Galli scanned the shore. "It looks all clear. The only sign of movement I can see is an egret rising out of the marsh in the Cove."

Soon they were skirting the Lochar Rock, an islet of moss-encrusted weathered stone that broke the water level of the lake just beyond the Cove. Waving in the breeze on a tiny patch of earth at the very crest of the Lochar Rock stood a lone beech tree. Beneath its stunted limbs teemed a colony of cormorants. Some of them were nesting and some stolidly stretching out their wings to dry in the sun. Just a short way past the Rock, when they were well outside the range of bowshot, Kal began to steer them north. Raven's Crag loomed above the waterline to their left, and from this distance the large rocky outcrop did indeed bear the shape of a raven. It was said that this was the reason the echobards had chosen to build Owlpen Castle on the island, since for them Corvus, the Raven, was a talisman to ward off evil. Looking back to the Island, Kal hoped this talisman still retained some of its former potency.

All they could hear beyond the splashing of oars was the background din of nesting fowl. Kal was working hard at the oars, his face now covered with dripping beads of sweat. Once they began to pass the northern extremity of Raven's Crag Island, they could no longer discern in profile the outline of the raven. The Crag looked like just a shapeless mass that, knife-like, cleaved the strong north winds which so often came funnelling down the valley. That morning, however, there were merely soft-blowing airs that teased out gentle ripples and cat's-paw on the surface of the water, as pure and clean as crystal. Above them, far over the shining lake, lay fantastic carven billows of cloud, spreading rank beyond rank to the horizon of mighty peaks ringing the valley in every direction.

Kal broke the monotonous plash and creak of the oars. "Master Wilum, I'm going to head due north towards Wrenhaven for a stretch. We should try not to give them any idea where we're headed. They'd probably see us from the Castle if we turned the corner and changed direction here . . . Although it doesn't much matter, I suppose."

"Why do you say that?"

"They know where we're headed anyway. Like a fool I told them everything at the Sunken Bottle. And it's not as if they had to torture me to wring the information out of me either. Old Golls fished me in, played me for a simpleton. It was my own stupidity."

"I'm certain, lad, that it would not have taken them long to find us at the Coomb in any case. I can see that you're worrying at this like a dog over an old bone. We all make mistakes, Kal. Why, I should have been wise enough to take the measure of that sneaky messenger of Gawmage's. And there's more, so much more I should have done before things came to this pass. It's what we learn from our errors that makes all the difference. Aye, therein lies the gift of wisdom. The main thing is to make good on our mistakes, and you have most of a lifetime to do that. You've learned a lesson in human trust, Kal, and I daresay that it could have been much more costly." Wilum put a hand on Kal's shoulder and smiled reassuringly.

"Can you see anybody up on the Crag, Galli?" asked Wilum, changing the subject.

"Nobody at all. My bet is that they're much too busy ransacking the Castle trying to find us, not to mention these manor rolls."

"Give them time," Kal said, "and they'll be combing the island from stem to stern."

"No boats, no manor rolls, and no prisoners to show for their trouble. They'll be as angry as hornets." Galli said.

"Here, Galli, you switch places with Kal and take over at the oars for a while. As for you, Kal, come, sit here and tell me how you happened to meet up with Ferabek, and what exactly you overheard him saying to Enbarr. If we're to counter his latest move, I've got to know everything you can tell me. And on the run as we are, this may be my last chance to speak with you for some while. Better start at the beginning. What happened after you left the keeil yesterday morning?"

NINE

Seated beside Wilum, Kal gave a brief account yet again of all that had happened to him and Galli the day before. When he reached the point of telling about their ill-fated venture on the edge of Ferabek's camp, Wilum lifted his head and regarded Kal with a quizzical squint.

"Go on, lad. Surely you can remember more of their conversation than that. Come now. What exactly did they say? Every word, I must have every last word you can remember. Go over it again from beginning to end," he urged with kindled animation.

Knitting his brows, Kal searched his memory, struggling to recollect the conversation. The harsh Gharssûlian accents came flooding into his mind. To his own surprise he was able to piece things together again and recount almost word for word what he had overheard high up in the clearing. When, in the middle of this effort, Kal tried in turn to question Wilum about some of the more puzzling aspects of what had been said, the old man demurred.

"We'll talk about that presently. First carry on—I must say, though, what a bold masterstroke, to track the Boar to his lair. I commend you both. Dangerous and ill-advised, but well done all the same. Go on. What did they talk about next, after he and Enbarr started walking back towards you?"

"What was it now? Let me think . . ." Kal frowned. "Now I remember. Yes, it was a dream, a recurring dream, and riddling lines, he said."

"Go on."

"Well Ferabek, he didn't mention what the dream was about. Just that he always woke up with the same words in his head. He said his magus—Cromus was his name—he said Cromus said the words were prophetic, but that he couldn't explain them. He was angry, very angry. You could sense it in his voice."

"Can you remember the lines?"

Kal racked his brain, trying to recall the exact words of the prophecy, straining to re-create in his mind the rhythm and wording of the exchange between Ferabek and Enbarr in the growling gutturals of the stark foreign tongue. The doors of his memory seemed slowly to come unbolted once more. He managed to reproduce the dream-spun couplet and then, stammering and uncertain, Ferabek's bitter outpouring of hatred for the Holding and all it stood for.

Wilum thought for a moment, and then, at his behest, Kal related the story of their discovery and their hair-raising escape, followed by their hurried council of war last night at Mantling Moss under the leadership of his father, and how it had been settled that Tarlynn's Coomb would be the marshalling point for the escaping folk of the Holding. He spoke of his ride to Wrenhaven, his indiscretion and subsequent capture at the Sunken Bottle, and his escape from the Locker at Broadmeadows.

"But what is it that Ferabek is after?" asked Kal, giving voice to his bewilderment, when Wilum had again sat in pensive silence for a moment. "Master Wilum? . . . Wilum?" But the old man had slipped from the realm of the waking world and seemed lost in the depths of his inner being. "A queer old bird when he goes into that thoughtful pose," Kal pondered aloud, "like one of the doves he raises in the cote. Gentle, brooding creatures, but largely at the mercy of the bigger more savage birds that roam the skies."

Now, however, something had changed, touching Kal with a hint of respectful awe. There seemed a fiercer cast to Cloudbeard's features. "Re'm ena, but today he looks more like the gyrfalcon than the dove." Kal looked to Galli. Still plying the oars in the broad sweep of their stroke, Galli met his gaze with a look of equal bemusement under raised eyebrows.

"Master Wilum . . . ?" Kal's voice seemed now to break the trance. "What is it Ferabek wants so desperately in the Holding?"

"Ah, yes . . . yes . . . Well, lad," Wilum said, recovering himself, "first of all, he wants to get hold of me, true Hordanu of Ahn Norvys. He's keen to put paid to me and Wuldor's Howe once and for all in favour of Gawmage's pliant toady, Messaan, who styles himself the rightful Hordanu. I've been a thorn in Gawmage's side for some time.

"Ferabek finds the very fact of my existence an affront, for Gawmage's inability to bring all of Arvon under his control weakens the whole Gharssûlian League. It means that here and there, especially in our highland redoubts, there remain pockets of resistance. I've heard from Tudno that there are rumours drifting up from Dinas Antrum that even in Gharssûl, even in Pirrian D'Arba of all places, the old ways still have their loyal adherents. But much fiercer than Ferabek's desire to stamp me out is his desire to obtain the Talamadh here. This, the masterpiece of Vali's goldsmithing art," Wilum said, caressing the harp, which he held cradled now on his lap.

The famous harp with which Ardiel had tamed the disordered elements—never before in his life had Kal seen it in the clear bright light of day. He found himself squinting at the light-laden halo that radiated from the harp's surface of gold. The proud curve of its frame was slender and graceful, like a water-borne cygnet—a conscious effect of Vali's craft, for adorning the widening top of the harp's neck, where it arched haughtily above the taut strings, lifted the regal head and bill of a swan.

"Master Wilum, never have I seen the Talamadh like this. So beautiful . . . You know how keenly everybody in the Holding looks forward to the Candle Festival for weeks beforehand, just aching to listen to its music. Listening to it takes you out of yourself somehow. It's as if it helps you see deep down into things. Do you know what I mean?"

"Indeed I do." Wilum smiled.

"And its wind music, too. I've never heard it, but the old folks say its wind music used to bring a bit of heaven down into the Glence. You can tell old Sarmel is brokenhearted about the failure of the wind music. And he only heard it once, as a little boy, and Sarmel's grandfather told him that what he had heard on that occasion was like tuneless noise, a shadow of what had raptured him in his own distant youth. Sarmel says he can't bear to think about the wind music without the tears welling up in his eyes."

Kal paused a moment, lulled by the shimmer of sun on the water and the gentle lake breeze which pulled a stray lock of hair across his face, lulled by the movement of the boat and the rhythmic dip and swing of the oars groaning in the oarlocks. After the anxious vigilance of the past several hours, Kal now felt exhaustion beginning to overtake him. Yet stronger than the weariness was a deep sense of well-being, a sense of focus, almost of purpose. This overwhelming peace did not come from within himself but washed over him, flooded him, consumed him, from . . . the harp . . . the Talamadh . . . just its presence, like its music. Its presence sings a tune, a tune unfashioned by sound, unheard by the ear. It is strength— Kal's reverie was cut short by the knock of an oar on the gunwale, a slipped stroke of his friend, the oarsman. He turned back to meet Wilum's gentle gaze.

"Why? Why has there never been a breeze to charm the strings of the Talamadh for all these many years?"

"You know that's a mystery, Kal, something to do with the slow weakening of the Great Harmony. You know that we wait and we wait, none more anxiously than I." Wilum turned his gaze over the water, his blue eyes moist. "The Great Harmonic Age is drawing to its dire close, lad. The sad mystery of endings now enfolds Wuldor's Howe and the Stoneholding. Hedric descried its shadowings in his *Criochoran*. It may be that others did too, the writers of the unintelligible runes that have teased my tired brain during many a candlelit night. I've always sensed that there are some awful secrets in them, waiting for the time to be ripe for them to be discovered." Wilum turned from the sparkling waters of Deepmere, his face burdened with a strange fey smile. The thin shoulders beneath the coarse cloak were hunched, and Kal could see that exhaustion was taking its toll of the old bard. His body heaved a whispered groan.

"I'm a Hordanu of sere tattered endings. Endings call for resignation and submission, qualities that I've always possessed in ample abundance, sitting patiently in my Glence-shadowed keeil, the dwelling of my slow-footed dull-witted dotage, waiting . . . Always waiting . . ."

"But don't endings usually foretoken beginnings as well?"

"The beginnings of what, lad? Of chaos and misrule, of treachery and injustice? How do you turn back years and years of decline, the gathered weight of a world in headlong descent, like a great stone sent hurtling down the side of a steep mountain? Waiting . . . Always in a state of waiting . . . Until now. Now, finally, the sovereign force of events has overtaken us, you and me and all of Ahn Norvys to its very bounds and farther, beyond the fields we know, even as far as the realms that have never felt the caress of the sun's sure light."

Kal caught a flash from the fine-wrought gold of the harp. "But what about Hedric? Doesn't he say that, at the end, 'girded with might the good shall rise to take up arms against the gathered dark'? Surely that means there's hope?"

"Without a doubt." Wilum met the young man's eyes. "There's always hope. Forgive me for croodling mournfully like some old dove shrivelled in its cote, starved for sunlight and free air. Sometimes I'm overwhelmed by the darkness, jaded by age and time, and I forget to be mindful of hope. Yes, Kal, even in the end there remains hope. Listen." Sitting on the thwart, Wilum began to strum the harp's supple strings and chant softly.

"When Wuldor's Howe is worsted by the brazen foe
And the Great Glence in utter ashbound ruin lies razed,
When the dark host of dreosan doth stain the Vale
And the Hordanu leaves the harrow of the Howe,
Shall rise a second foe upon whom few have gazed
From half-lit shadowed land of ancient dormant tale.
The royal one shall then rebel against the gloom,
His rank new-marked by crown and arms, by sword and belt,
Shall he seek out amid the isles shrouded by thick sea mist
The wondermaking goldsmith's well-hid island tomb.
In ocean lands where sea folk oft leave off their pelt
To take on human form by curlew-haunted cliffs."

It was a melancholy air. Kal did not recognize the ballad, but was smitten by its brooding melody. Even Galli paused for a moment, lifting his wet oars streaming into the air.

"That's an old song, lad, called 'The Unquiet Grave,' part of Hedric's *Criochoran*. It's about Vali's burial place and isn't often sung. An oddly turned out ballad. That's why you probably don't recognize it. Another of Hedric's prophecies."

"And it's now come to pass?"

"Aye, indeed it has. At least the first part of it has. The rest of it remains quite unclear. It has something to do with the saving and restoration of the Harmony, linked somehow with the finding of Vali's grave, somewhere among the Ocean Isles."

"That's one big swath of territory," commented Kal.

"That it is, and much of it unexplored and uninhabited."

"And what does he mean by the royal one who's to seek the grave?"

"In truth I don't know, Kal. It may be one of Ardiel's royal lineage that is meant, the lost Prince Starigan perhaps, or it may be the scion of some other royal house in Ahn Norvys. Hard to say. That part's certainly not as clear as the lines that refer to the Sacred Fire and the Balk Pit of Uäm. Alas, we're not about to solve the mystery of its meaning, so we'd better let the question pass for now."

Wilum fell to tracing the flowing lines of the harp with his fingers. "Did you know, Kal, that there was once a time, early in the Great Harmonic Age, when, if the Hordanu sang such a lay on the Talamadh, the sun would have beamed brighter in the sky and dispelled storm clouds, the flowers and trees of forest and field would have swayed with joy to its measure. All the folk to the furthest reaches of Ahn Norvys would have felt it in their bones that in Wuldor's Howe the Talamadh was being played. Their spirits would have resonated to its harmonious strains. Sitting beside me like this, you would have had to stop your ears for the sheer ecstasy of it. Alas, the Great Harmony is muted to a mere whisper of what it once was . . . But all the same, lad, take the harp and play me a tune."

"What do you mean? I touch the Talamadh? How could I, Master Wilum? It's forbidden. I'm just another farmboy, tending a few sheep in the Holding."

"Very good, lad. Keep your humility intact always. A true Hordanu should always have before his eyes that he is the servant of all that is holy and that he has no power but what comes from above in sacred trust."

"What do you mean, Master Wilum? What are you saying?"

"I mean, Kal, that as of this moment you have a special warrant to touch the Talamadh, for I'm invoking the ancient Right of Appointment, even though it's never before been invoked."

"What? I don't understand—Master Wilum?" quailed Kal.

"I can tell that your heart is all aquiver like a hen in thunder, lad, but don't be afraid. It's the power the Hordanu has in extreme danger or time of dire upheaval and war to appoint his own successor, somebody to share the office of Hordanu with him and to take over when he dies. All the normal rites of election are thereby superseded, making you, Kalaquinn, the Master of the Talamadh, with no less title than myself. Here, Kalaquinn, put your hand on the Talamadh and swear allegiance to Wuldor and all the sacred ceremonies of the orrthon."

"But I'm too young. How in the world could I be made Hordanu?" Even Galli had stopped rowing.

"Get back to those oars of yours, Galli!" ordered Wilum. "Here we are running for our lives, and you're gawking like a mooncalf."

Quick with the oars, Galli fumblingly obeyed.

"I was only slightly older than you, Kal, when I was elected Hordanu by the folk of the Holding. That was nearly sixty years ago, and I remember it as if it were just yesterday. I was every bit as bewildered as you are now. But it was meant to be and I couldn't fight it. It would be easier to fight one of the mighty anagoroi, as Hedric did, to his cost, and to his benefit. I've long had it in mind that you would make a fine successor to me, Kalaquinn, and I've hoped that the folk of the Holding would show enough sense to elect you when the time came for my spirit to take its final leave. You've got a certain wisdom that sets you apart and belies your years. So come now, and place your hand on the Talamadh. Repeat after me. 'Arim cot adamrugud . . .'"

Too dumbfounded to offer further resistance, Kal stretched out his hand and hesitantly touched the harp. He had resigned himself in the matter and knew full well he would not refuse. He was overcome, like an innocent shepherd boy out to pasture with his flock who is stunned by a side branch of errant summer lightning fingering down on him from a cloudless sky. It would be pointless, even impious, to offer resistance. All the same, he could hardly bring himself to stumble through the solemn oath that Wilum administered by having Kal repeat after him the ancient ceremonial words of investiture.

"Take now the Talamadh and set your fingers to its strings to seal and make fast the Debrad you have just spoken," bade Wilum, when they had finished.

"What should I play?" asked Kal, as, with some uncertainty, he accepted the golden frame of the harp, holding it as if it were a searing hoop of fire.

"Any of the turusorans I've taught you in the past little while."

"And this, the Pyx of Roncador . . ." Kal held the half-round emerald vessel in his palm, still attached by its golden chain to the Talamadh.

"Indeed. It's of capital importance for our mission. But first, play. Let us finish the rite. Play, Kalaquinn."

Kal deftly positioned the sacred harp on his knee and began to pluck at the strings.

"Very good, a turusoran in the mode of the Southern clanholdings. Wonderfully appropriate."

Kal chanted "The Horn of Lynd," one of the many journey songs from *Hedric's Master Legendary* that he had learned in the course of his studies. Kal felt the Talamadh respond to his touch, and then he lost all sense of the golden harp as an instrument over which he could impose his will. It was as if it had taken control of his hands and was sweeping his fingers in sure mellifluent movement along its corded filaments. His heart overflowed with an even deeper sense of peace as the words of "The Horn of Lynd" sprang unbidden to his lips. He had only chanted a score of verses when Wilum asked him to stop. It cost Kal an effort of the will, however, to disengage himself from the seductive melody. Wilum placed his hand on Kal's brow.

"Hordanu, sealed in song, thine office beckons. How great thy power, no mortal reckons." Wilum withdrew his hand.

"It's absolutely amazing. Why, it's as if the harp itself took over and guided my fingers and my lips while I sang."

"Such is Vali's craftsmanship, it doesn't matter how talented or worthy the harpist is. Given the right conditions, the Talamadh has its own power. That's why the Boar would not hesitate to comb all of Arvon with a fine-meshed net in his search for it."

"To do what with it?"

"To suborn it, if he can, to deflect it from its long service of light and remake it into an instrument of his darkness."

"But how? How can he do that? I thought that the Talamadh would not lend itself to the performance of any evil."

"True enough in the past. Of course, you remember the evil-hearted Sandron, who succeeded Metan as Hordanu in the year 565. Believing he could use the Talamadh to further his own unsavoury ambitions and designs, he found the harp itself chafed under his crooked fingers and would not let him. But that was centuries upon centuries ago, when the Great Harmony was still young and vibrant. From all accounts it was a world infinitely different from our own.

I fear now what Ferabek may attempt to do with the Talamadh, if it falls into his possession. At the very least he could simply hide it away from us so that its power could not be used against him."

"What about destroying it?"

"Never. He could never destroy it. Never can it perish utterly, for it is not just ordinary gold that Vali wrought it from, not gold that the fire of merely human forges can undo. No, Kalaquinn." Wilum fixed the young Hordanu with a piercing gaze from eyes that flashed like liquid blue flame. "It is human heartstrings, the mortal flesh of man that is much more easily severed and undone than Ardiel's Talamadh. That's why I'm filled with dread that his search for King Colurian's son may somehow stand on the brink of bearing fruit, that he may be ready to pounce on the lad. And he would be much more easily undone than Vali's harp."

"Now, Enbarr's told him some vital piece of news about the lost Prince." Kal pondered aloud, still half-embracing the harp. "He knows something, something he's only just discovered. If only that infernal fowl hadn't gotten free to distract the two of them, I could have heard that crucial part of his conversation with the Boar."

"Aye, in some way that old portrait of Colurian gave him the clue. How, I wonder, and what . . . If I had known . . . But in some way it has allowed the Boar to move against us, putting all within striking distance of his tusks. Ah well, perhaps the Boar would not have waited too long in any case," Wilum mused, his tone now darkening. "Perhaps he was intending with a bold stroke to capture me and extort the information from me. He's a fearful adversary, with a host of the black arts and arcane powers at his disposal. They were powerful forces that let that messenger broach the sacred barrier of Oakenvalley Bottom."

Wilum let his gaze now wander across the water to the eastern shore—deep forest rimmed by jagged heights surmounted by banks of clouds. In the sky gulls wheeled, calling mournfully.

"But for all that, my guess is that he still fears the tattered shreds of harmony that cleave yet to the Talamadh and to the Great Glence. He doesn't know how little or how much remains. For that matter neither do I, or we might have stood our ground at the Great Glence. But in my heart I'm certain it would have only been a holding action. Alas, too much of the ancient power and glory of the Great Harmony lies wasted and sapped of its strength. To think that the night drake now overflies the sheltered woodland paths of Wuldor's Howe. Unbelievable, that I should live to see the harrowing of the glencelands, what was once a mere dream vision, a veiled prophecy in the mind's eye of Hedric long ago, an event in the far-off distant future . . . I'm sorry, but there you have it." The old man's shoulders heaved in a deep sigh. "The Balk Pit can only be broached by one of Ardielid stock, and you can be sure that as long as Prince Starigan, wherever he is and whoever he is, eludes capture, the approaches to the Balk Pit will be closely watched. Aye, Kal, to recover Prince Starigan and then the Sacred Fire. Therein now lies our main task."

"But how can we even . . ." began Kal. "I mean to say, what chance do we have to get out of the Holding alive, let alone find Prince Starigan and journey to the Balk Pit?"

"Do you know what would happen to Ahn Norvys if there were no Candle Festival?" Wilum let his gaze turn back to the raven-haired young man beside him. "What small measure of harmony there remains would rapidly turn to discord, and there would be precious little to stop Ferabek and those to whom he pledges liege from enslaving all the known regions of Ahn Norvys. There would be imposed a new dispensation, grim beyond all words and conceiving, one shorn of all truth and wisdom and beauty, sundered from the sublime music of the spheres and filled with malignant chaos and blackness."

"But Wilum, even supposing we are able to get out of the Holding, and supposing we are able to obtain the Sacred Fire once again, even then where would the Candle Festival be held? Mustn't it take place in Wuldor's Howe, or not at all?"

"There are other places where the Candle Festival may be celebrated, at least in extreme times like this. Hedric explains it in his little-known *Book of Festivals*. I'll show you in due course. We have almost a year of grace in which to regain the Sacred Fire. And, most important of all to us at this moment of headlong flight, there exists another way out of this circling shield of mountains that only the Hordanu has ever been privy to. If we can meet the others at Tarlynn's Coomb, all may yet not be lost, Kal. Thank goodness Frysan seized on Tarlynn's Coomb as our meeting point. I couldn't have chosen a better spot myself. Here, let me show you what I'm talking about," said Wilum, who now began riffling through the oiled canvas satchel that lay at his feet.

He found what he was looking for and pulled out a small scroll of parchment held neatly rolled by a carmine leather band, which he now slipped off and placed beside him. "It's an awkward spot for us to be unrolling this map. But in the hours to come there will be no more private spot for us in all the Holding. As soon as we make land, there will be danger of hidden eyes and ears, if not open attack, and no time either to malinger over maps and strategies. And you, Galligaskin Clout—don't stop rowing—you must swear by all the sacred mysteries of the orrthon that you will not reveal any part of what you now hear or have heard. Swear it. We must trust no one, even our kinsfolk here in this valley, for what they do not know, they cannot chance to let slip, or, perish the thought, be forced to divulge."

Galli nodded his assent to the oath, still plying the oars. "That I swear, Master Wilum, by all that's sacred in the orrthon. Have no fear. I'll keep my lips firmly sealed— Look up there, back towards the Island." Galli pointed with his head.

"They've set fire to Owlpen Castle!" cried Kal. "And to the Great Glence and keeil too! There's more smoke curling up over the trees farther back towards the Howe—"

"Come, Kal . . . Come have a look at this," bade Wilum, who had averted his eyes from the distant plume of smoke and busied himself unfurling the small parchment scroll whose ends he weighed down with an old pair of otterskin boots left lying on the bottom of the boat.

The map looked quite ancient and seemed to be a detailed representation of the Holding, with its place names given in the antique cursive script favoured by most Old Arvonian manuscripts. Kal noticed a red cross that marked a spot just above Skell Force high up amid the western peaks of the Radolans. At the base of the map there was listed a legend.

"Do you see the red cross? Do you know what it signifies?"

"In the legend here it says 'path' or 'way' in Old Arvonian. What does that mean?"

"It means there exists a hidden passage out of the Holding. Hedric learned it from the echobards. Not that they told him willingly, of course. He was a young man, long before the Battle of the Velinthian Bridge, when he dared to explore our isolated little valley, a spot sacred to the echobards. One day Hedric slipped into this valley and tracked an echobard to the headwaters of the

Skell, where he discovered another way past the impenetrable barrier of the Radolans besides the Wyrdlaugh Pass. This is the map he drew as a permanent record. Apart from Hedric, only Ardiel knew of it. And it was decided by them that the map would stay in the safekeeping of the Hordanu, and that its secret should be guarded by him as one of the mysteries of Wuldor's Howe. I make it known to you now, Kal, because our need is great and you share now in the solemn office of Hordanu."

"There is a pass through the mountains! In our rambles we've often mused about finding a hidden path to the other side of the Radolans. Many a time we've lain awake by the smouldering coals of a campfire looking up at the stars, excited by the thought of all the adventures that must lie beyond the mountains."

"Just like proper young men you are, aching for life on a grander stage. Well, now you've got your path to the outside and you're bound to get your bellyful of adventures, if, that is, we can reach it safely. You know what I'm asking of you, Kal, what you must help me do, once we reach the other side of the mountains. Something that must be done, desperate work, and with me too old to do it alone?"

Kal nodded slowly. "But where do we even start? It'll be like trying to find a needle in a haystack. And how can we even be sure he's still alive? And if he is, it looks more than likely now that Ferabek will reach him before we do. And if he does—"

"That Thrygian sorcerer of his will no doubt have royal human entrails for his augury."

"Is that what you think Cromus meant? I wasn't sure about the man's sneering hints, and part of me feared to ask you."

"I think so."

"I should have known. He made my flesh crawl. Almost worse than Ferabek."

"Your instincts are probably right. There's no such thing as a good Thrygian magus. It's not yardfowl whose entrails they usually examine these days."

Wilum placed a hand on the young man's shoulder. "What a mission. I've hardly got the heart to ask you to undertake it. Such danger, such need. But whichever way I examine the problem, I see no other alternative. Somehow it's meant that you should share my burden, but I don't want to force you."

"I hardly know what to say. From farmboy to Hordanu all

within the space of hours . . . But I will go and help you find Prince Starigan, whatever we have to do," affirmed Kal, even though formless fears clutched at his throat, and his lips trembled as he spoke.

"You must have no illusions, Kalaquinn. It will be a dangerous journey, fraught with uncertainties and perils you can scarcely conceive of, especially now that even the highlands are falling to the dominion of the Boar. Who knows how many troops he has ranging the hillsides on the other side of this valley? More than enough to overwhelm our highland men, I'm sure, doughty warriors though they be. I'm asking you to help me beard the lion, Kalaquinn, for even if you find Prince Starigan and return with the Sacred Fire, we'll be no stronger than we are now. And we must remember that though we have nearly a year to accomplish this task, the Balk Pit is two hundred leagues distant as the crow flies. The Boar, meanwhile, has one whole year to lay his traps for our capture, for he'll have at least two good tries at us, both going out and coming back. And beyond the borders of Arvon you'll be hunted by mightier and more malignant forces, seeing as the Boar has had longer to establish himself in the regions that lie beyond the Coolcower Alps. Even in Arvon, he's Gawmage's master, and this is one task he'll want to supervise closely himself. No doubt that's why he's come here to the Holding in person. His grand design depends on it. The dangers are more than great, Kalaquinn. But failure would mean the end of all mortal hopes."

"Put a Holdsman to his mettle and he'll storm the underworld itself," boasted Kal, his mood shifting, like an untested youth boldly brandishing his newly tempered sword in the safety of the village smithy. His blood rose at the thought of an adventure beyond the confines of the Holding.

"Rashly spoken words, Kalaquinn. You will want to be a little bit wiser than that and not let enthusiasm get the better of you. Nonetheless, I sense an underlying leaven of fear, and that's healthy."

"I won't deny it, Master Wilum. Here I am the wheelwright's son and now the Hordanu, I suppose, of all Arvon and Ahn Norvys. It's a lot to absorb," answered Kal, who was thinking with rue how jauntily he had tramped the Edgemere Road only yesterday morning, how eager he had been to come into his own. And now here he was. His own was a bardic title that linked him

down the ages with Arvon's first and greatest Hordanu, whom
Ardiel himself had invested. And with the title came a mission
that seemed to defy all reasonable odds of success.

"I wouldn't dwell on the honour and glory of it if I were you,
Kal. As matters stand, your being the Hordanu doesn't amount to
a molehill, and you're sure to have, together with my own aged
carcass, such a bounty on your head as would knot the insides
of the stoutest highlander with fear. It's not just any ordinary
adversary we're facing. The yoke ordained for you to shoulder is
heavily laden with wrath and strife. But now, let us to the immediate task that faces us, and it's a daunting one, I must say. We
and all the survivors we can muster are going to have to make
our way over the Radolan Mountains down into the windward
clanholdings of the coast. If we get that far, it's my hope we can
find some sheltered spot to regroup."

"Where do you think we could flee?" asked Kal.

"I was thinking that the place that once harboured Ardiel long
ago might give shelter to whatever remains of our Holdsfolk."

"The Marshes of Atramar?"

Wilum nodded, returning to the chart, smoothing it. "But as
for you, Kal, it's important for me to acquaint you with a rough
sketch of your mission in the event something happens to me.
I'm an old man, after all. You'll need some knowledge of the tasks
you're being called to undertake, for everything may well depend
on you." Wilum placed a reassuring hand on Kal's shoulder. "And
fortunately you won't have much time to fret and worry about
things. The urgency is too pressing. In the end we might neither
one of us survive." Wilum cut short the melancholy reflection and
turned to stare over the side of the boat at the bubbling wavelets
in its wake, rapt suddenly in his own train of thought.

Raven's Crag had become an ever more indistinct landmark in
the offing behind them and Galli, confident now that they had
not been spotted, swung the boat around and started to make a
course westward towards Riven Oak Cove, the place where the
waters of the Skell tumbled into Deepmere.

"Hedric's *Criochoran* is full of riddles and dark sayings," Wilum
spoke again as if to the rippling lakewater over the gunwales of
the boat. "Perhaps now they'll become clearer and free-flowing,
as these waters of Deepmere used to be. How fervently I always
hoped for some great burst of light to free us from the toils of

darkness and uncertainty in this beleaguered tag end of Arvon. It seems for years I lived in waiting and apprehension of our adversary, wondering what sly manoeuvre he would hatch to outflank and enslave us. Alas, I had become weary, Kal, worn and weary. But now, even though Ferabek's move against us has been by far bolder than ever I thought, I feel more youthful than I've ever felt, strangely quickened by these sad events. I suppose it's because, for good or ill, they bring to a close the long plodding years of mouldering decay.

"But enough, let's sketch out a rough plan of our journey. We scarcely have time for an old man's pitiful musings." Wilum caught himself. "Here, we'll make a deeper study of the map. You'll soon see what I mean. We'll trace our best route to the Marshes of Atramar. I told Aelward as indirectly as I could that we should aim to meet at his Cot. That's all I dared say in my message, for fear my feathered messenger might get plucked from the air by an arrow or something even worse."

"Who is Aelward? You mentioned him yesterday. But it seems so long ago, doesn't it?"

"Indeed. I'm not certain I could answer that question. You'll make his acquaintance in due time, I hope. If he's back from his wanderings, he'll make shift to find us.

"Look here," said Wilum, tapping a spot on the map. "Here's where, if we can manage to stay ahead of the Black Scorpions, we'll be coming out on the other side of the Radolans. There's a big meadow there. If we bear to our left, southwards here, we'll come to a rocky outcrop of slate. From its base cascades a spout of spring water that pours itself in a little rivulet down the mountainside. The gully of that hidden little stream will bring us to the level of the Eyke Sarn and keep us from being seen. We'll have to take care, as we descend farther down the mountain, that we keep quiet, for there's no telling who or what may lurk by that old pathway. After that, we'll have to follow it south a ways 'til we reach the Old High Road. The groomed part of the Eyke Sarn ends there, but its overgrown cobblestones continue on to Hoël's Dyke, which is itself seldom used, derelict and unbrushed, a fit place for those who are hunted, the likes of ourselves. I think it would be best if we made for Hoël's Dyke.

"Time to change maps," Wilum continued, gently rolling the stiff parchment. "Every minute's precious now, if I'm to tell you at least the bare essentials before landfall." He replaced the band around the scroll of the map that showed the Holding and its immediate surroundings. In its place he brought out a much ampler, more cumbersome map, one laid out on a larger scale, including all of Arvon and the many lands that lay east of Arvon on the other side of the Coolcower Alps and Lake Lavengro and the watchtowers of the southeast.

"Now, let's quickly chart our most likely way to the Marshes of Atramar and Aelward's Cot nearby, and then I can show you where the Balk Pit of Uäm is situated."

"But what I don't understand is how can you be so certain we'll even find young Prince Starigan to begin with?"

"I'm not certain at all. That's a goodly part of the problem. The wellsprings of hope have dwindled in me. But then there's Hedric's prophetic lines that as Hordanu I can scarcely ignore, timeworn, but true. They must be. Aye, they must. Murky as they are, they bear hope for me and for Arvon. And then, more strangely, I've had the same recurring dream the past few nights running, even while the Holding has been racked by wind and storm."

"What dream is that?" queried Kal.

"I've seen old King Colurian sitting on the Coronation Stone. At least I thought it was him. Perhaps it was Ardiel himself. Who knows? I couldn't see his face. But on the frontal of his tunic were depicted a hart and hind, both milk white, facing each other rampant. In his right hand he held the royal sceptre, wielding it with firmness and authority. And hovering above him was some sort of bird, a beautiful one, with spread fantail of many colours. I've taken the dream to be a good omen. It has reassured me.

"For these reasons I feel it's somehow right and even necessary for me to speak to you about reaching the Balk Pit of Uäm. That way, if Aelward's found the Prince, you too can serve as guide to him. It will be essential for you to have some knowledge of the Balk Pit and how to get there, although circumstances may be such that you'll have to make your approach to it in a roundabout fashion from way over here by the Alnod River rather than from the direction of Arvon." Wilum pointed with his bony index finger. "From here in the highlands it would be an arduous trip of several months there and back again, mostly on foot. Whereas if you approach the Balk Pit from the east, where it seems, according to Aelward, that Starigan may well be found, it would be much closer. But even in that case you'd need to spend several months travelling in order to reach the lands of the East in the first place. Mind you listen keenly, for the fate of many will depend on what I'm telling you, and I doubt even Aelward for all his cleverness could tell you what I can." Wilum's voice had grown insistent.

Kal swallowed hard against the lump in his throat. His mouth was dry. This was all too much—the breadth of the task being laid before him, the hard-edged urgency of the old man's words, and the glancing references to Aelward, whoever he was. A weight was being shifted ever more steadily onto him, a burden that he was scarcely prepared to take on. Kal felt very alone.

"Well, at least it won't be just the two of us . . ." He hesitated. "I mean just you and I, Wilum. Of course, Galli will be coming along too."

"It would be—"

"Why sure, I'll be going wherever you're going, Kal," cut in Galli.

"Aye, Galli, but you have your own job to do right now. Keep those oars of yours moving. As I was starting to say, Kal, it would be a great blessing to have Galli come along with us, given the desperate nature of our mission. Here, let me show you what some of the ground is like that lies between us and the Balk Pit of Uäm. On the windward side of the Radolans and to the south all around us here, lies some of the wildest and most mysterious country in the highlands," continued Wilum with a descriptive sweep of his fingers across the map spread out before them. "As I mentioned before, it would be best for you on this first portion of your journey if you were to hug the Eyke Sarn all the way to Hoël's Dyke. Then turn north along the Dyke. Keep in mind that, overgrown though it is, it may play host to any number of Gawmage's spies, especially since there live few loyal highlanders in that area to put the enemy's back up."

"What about the Thane of South Wold, Nuath? Doesn't he do anything to establish order in his own clanholding?" asked Kal, shifting uneasily on the thick plank thwart.

"Alas, Kal, no. He's much to be feared and little to be trusted. The rumour is that he's made a pact with Gawmage and traffics with the fell spirits. Indeed more than once he's come to the Holding with weasel words. Silvermouth they call him and with good reason, for he's sowing doubt and confusion in all the highland clanholdings. It makes me thankful that in our little valley clanholding we're liege to Thane Strongbow, although clearly I can't say as much about either his son or nephew. So here we are," continued Wilum, tracing his finger along the creased surface of the map. "As you follow Hoël's Dyke northwards, you'll be encountering the wilder regions of South Wold. You had best avoid the coast as well. It's bound to be heavily patrolled. Hoël's Dyke passes through the Woods of Tircoil. They're thickly forested, and even Thane Nuath's clansmen are afraid of the place, not daring to venture too far into them."

"What's in the forest that a body has to be so fearful of?" asked Kal, even though he suspected he already knew the answer from a score of childhood stories.

"The waldscathes. They thrive in the dense, ancient woodlands of the Tircoil. The clansmen call this peninsula the Black Cape because its woods are so dark and close. The valleys are deep and the hillsides steep with caves and embankments all mantled with a rich cover of forest. They're fearsome creatures, the waldscathes are. Cruel and dangerous, and they don't care much for other folk in Arvon. But they're night prowlers and won't go near a burning fire. So you'll need to get a strong fire going well before nightfall. The problem is that your fire will be like a beacon to anybody else who wishes you harm."

"You mean Thane Nuath and his clansmen?"

"Yes, I suppose so, if not Ferabek's scoundrels as well. But, as if this weren't enough, there are other evils to be found in the Black Cape."

"Such as?"

"I don't properly know. There's always been much whispering talk but few hard facts. Shades and shadows of things unnatural. The folk of South Wold alone have sure knowledge of the dangers in their clanholding. But for the most part they've kept to themselves even from the time of Ardiel. A tight-lipped, stiff-necked lot, but harmless up until now, although it's anybody's guess what they're about in our day. All I know is that Nuath cannot be trusted. Nor can his bard, Swaran. I should say especially not Swaran. In any case, I'd far sooner waldscathes and rumours of the wild, Kal, than Gawmage's scoundrels and Ferabek's iron-shod cohort," growled Wilum, frustrated at being saddled with these dire options. "Besides, there's a most important meeting we must attend at Aelward's Cot, and that's over here," he tapped the parchment, "just above what's called the Llanigon Mark Stone, this side of the Black Rock Gap . . . That is, if Aelward makes it back, and my message has gotten through."

"And that's just the first part of the quest? I was brought up a simple Holdsman, Wilum. How can I be of help to you? I feel like I'm being led on a thread." It was becoming clear this was not going to be just a merry walking tour through the banks and braes of highland Arvon—something he and Galli had often mused about on drowsy summer days while they lay nestled against a hayrick and boldy considered how exciting such a foray, even into the sinister clanholding of South Wold, would be. When it came down to it, however, the tales he overheard in his childhood of waldscathes and the thick trackless forests that lay on the farther side of the Old High Road loomed larger and more immediate in his imagination than the lure of adventure. Doubts came crowding into Kal's mind thick and fast. How could he ever be equal to all this, he, Kalaquinn, born and bred the simple wheelwright's son, who had only once in his living memory stepped outside of the Holding?

"Don't lose heart, lad," advised Wilum, a soothing hand on Kal's shoulder. "You're forgetting that Ardiel himself began as a simple ploughboy and Hedric the son of a forester. And remember that you may be led by a thread as readily as by a thickly braided rope, so long as you remain steady and refrain from pulling on it with your own strength. Stand firm and straight, Kal, and let yourself be led by the thread. You're not going defenceless. Why do you think you're taking the Talamadh with you?"

"How will it help us in all these dangers?"

"Didn't you feel the power of its music, Kalaquinn, even though it's merely a darkling spark of what it once was? Much of the harmony has been lost, but much remains, and even the little that is left may ravish a soul or repel an enemy. Yes, Kal, repel an enemy," reiterated Wilum, who noted Kal's look of astonishment. "Or, most importantly, perhaps, show you the way to certain places, if you're attentive."

"I don't understand. What do you mean, 'show me the way to certain places'?"

"Look at the map here again. Do you see the lines radiating out from the Great Glence?"

"Yes, they're like spokes of a wheel. A bit faint and hard to make out in spots."

"The map is faded. It's a copy I made of the original some while ago. But the lines are still discernible, if you look closely. There are sixteen of them. They're songlines, one for each of the turusorans. A turusoran, as you well know, has much minute description of landscape as well as telling a story. Well, in this case the turusoran describes the scenery of its particular songline, so that one who knows the turusoran and follows the songline can never be lost. He will be led from landmark to landmark with unerring accuracy."

"Look, this songline goes right through the Balk Pit of Uäm and then on through this island off the coast of Zacorlon, not too far from Telessar," commented Kal, who had noticed the red-inked letters marking the Balk Pit in the lands beyond Arvon to the northeast.

"Yes, Kal, these are all guiding lines for us as we journey. You will notice too, for example, how this other line runs through Wardwyst Castle, the seat of Thane Nuath's clanholding, which we will have at all costs to avoid. In the olden days it would have been unthinkable for evil in any form to be found on a songline. Not so now, so we'll follow Hoël's Dyke in order to avoid the Old High Road and Wardwyst Castle and meet with the Horn of Lynd somewhere around here, where it passes through the northeastern edge of the Woods of Tircoil and strikes a useful northwestern bearing toward the Calathros Peninsula."

"Horn of Lynd?"

"Each of the songlines is named after its turusoran. The journey song you chose to sing to seal the Debrad is the one we'll try to follow first as we put as much distance as possible between us and the Holding."

"What a coincidence!" exclaimed Kal.

"I would not be overly quick to ascribe to coincidence anything that happens in connection with the Talamadh."

"Still, how does the Talamadh show us the way?"

"If you reach a songline and pick at the strings of the Talamadh, it will cause you to enter into a recitation of the songline's turusoran at whatever point it describes the landscape you have reached, while, if you leave the songline ever so slightly, it will not respond in this way. So you see how it will help keep us oriented on our way to the Balk Pit. And its virtue is such that it can turn away much evil, especially on one of the songlines, and even then it's not certain what lies within its power still."

"Why's that?"

"Because the Great Harmony is so weak in all of Ahn Norvys that, besides the Great Glence itself, only the songlines yet hold a portion of its strength. How great this portion still is I don't know. If I had been surer, as I said, we might have made a stand at the Great Glence itself. What is clear is that the harmony is slowly, ceaselessly waning in vigour even as we speak, like a cask of choice wine that has had one of its staves pierced by a nail. Even the Candle Festival cannot forestall the steady unremitting outflow of the Harmony."

"But, where will the next Candle Festival be held, if the Boar still has the Holding in his grip this time next year?"

"In a time like this, says Hedric in his *Book of Festivals*, it may be celebrated along any one of the songlines, since each of the songlines is like an extension, as it were, of the power of the Glence Stone. But even so, a celebration of the Candle Festival on a songline would scarcely be the same as its celebration at the centre."

"But, it would be adequate?"

"You've hit on the right word. Yes, I think adequate is the word. Adequate, indeed, but hardly more than that . . . I'm not sure what this bodes for Arvon, Kal, or how the harmony may be restored to our world. It's not easy to understand parts of *Hedric's Master Legendary*. But I have a feeling that these parts of the *Legendary* will become clearer with time and that the extinction of the Sacred Fire is the first act in a larger drama in which you and perhaps I are destined to play a role."

"What do you mean by 'perhaps'? Surely it's you that will play the largest role."

"I don't know, Kal. I'm an old man, a Holdsman born and bred, as are you. My two journeys to Dinas Antrum have been the closest I've come to venturing forth into the wider world. I don't know that I'll have the strength to fulfil this quest of ours. I'm too old, much too old, to be dodging soldiers and scaling mountains and braving who knows what kind of hardships. My service as Hordanu is almost done. I feel it in my heart. My work as Hordanu has been one of preparing you for your work as Hordanu. You must carry on in my stead."

"It seems so futile," said Kal, absorbed in the palpable air of despondence that seemed for a moment to settle over the old man, "to make a long and dangerous search for Prince Starigan and then make a long and dangerous trek to the Balk Pit to fetch the Sacred Fire, then a long and dangerous journey back to the Holding, when it's clear that the restoration of the Harmony is the chief problem. I mean, what good is the Sacred Fire in a world that has lost its moorings in the Harmony?"

"Aye, but the one cannot happen without the groundwork of the other. First things first, as they say, even though it may be very hard sometimes to see at the beginning of an enterprise how the end is served. You'll find, too, Kal, as you journey through life, that much will happen that will appear at the time to be blind and fickle chance, but will later be shown to fit into a larger more patterned scheme of things. That is how our lives are ordained, from the greatest to the smallest amongst us, king and thane, bard and yeoman alike. We accept the task of the moment without knowing or worrying whether it's taking us backwards or forwards. It's like an intricate dance, a cosmic dance, in which we are asked to play our part, so long as we don't stand by our own wisdom and insist on dancing a haydigee when a jig is what's called for."

"And our jig now is a trip to the Balk Pit."

"Precisely my point. Although, I'd be the first one to admit I'm all but overwhelmed by the blackness that compasses us all around."

Wilum then led Kal quickly into some more of the immediately relevant details of the map and projected journey, explaining how they would make for Tarlynn's Coomb and from there continue following the valley of the Skell up to the river's source high in the Radolan Mountains above Skell Force, the mist-wrapped waterfall just below the Seven Springs. Wilum explained to him exactly where the secret passageway to the western slopes of the encircling peaks was to be found. And then Kal was admonished again as to the importance of avoiding Wardwyst Castle by following Hoël's Dyke, traversing the bottom of the Black Cape. Kal bristled at the prospect of the much-dreaded forest.

"But what about the songlines? Couldn't we use one of them to protect ourselves from the dangers that lurk in the Woods?" Kal asked.

"How would you do that? Examine the map more closely and you'll see the problem. Look, here's the Black Cape," said Wilum, pointing a finger at the spot.

"All right, I see," conceded Kal, noting that the two songlines that cleanly bisected the Black Cape would veer them off course to the western shore of the peninsula, offering no advantage. "Besides which, it doesn't seem like such a terribly long stretch of the Dyke that passes through the Woods," he observed with resignation.

"Come now, let's trace out the rest of the route to the Marshes of Atramar," urged the old man. "Mark how Hoël's Dyke coincides with the Horn of Lynd much of the way here, after it leaves the Woods of Tircoil and fords the Wellbeck River. The river forms the boundary between South Wold and Thrysvarshold. Here, see? Keep following Hoël's Dyke almost right to where it ends here at the Black Rock Gap in the upper marches of the Westland clan-holdings. The Gap is one of many passes through the Sheerness Spur, but is little used, for obvious reasons."

"The Marshes of Atramar straddle the Gap on either side," remarked Kal.

"Precisely. That's why the Gap is not a normal way to cross the Sheerness Spur."

"And here's the Llanigon Mark Stone."

"Aye, Kal. It skirts the marsh area on a rise of land, very close to where Aelward has his Cot, our meeting place. You'll have to decide from there how to slip into the lowlands. Anyway, lad, this is as far as my advice about the particulars of your choice of route can take you," pronounced Wilum abruptly, lifting his hand from the map. "And I'd be less than honest if I said I didn't have doubts about this advice of mine, since Arvon, even here in our highland retreats, is in the throes of unpredictable change. As for the lowlands, I can best offer you only a pennyworth of my wisdom. Keep as much away as possible from villages and towns and roads and waterways. Keep to the byways and the forests. Look closely at the map, Kal, whenever you have a chance. You can keep this copy. I've got the original in the sack here. Take note of the rivers and roads, towns and cities, forests and marshes, mountains and plains. Examine it. See where all the songlines run. Try as much as you can to stay on one of them. Avoid the northern coast here along the Dumoric Sea and head towards the

Coolcower Alps somewhere around here," he said, circling a piece of the map with his finger, "many leagues from Dinas Antrum and the Boar's head legions quartered there.

"I need not tell you how wary we'll have to be, for there will be much evil abroad in the lowland counties, some of it of Gawmage's merely human making and some of it more wicked still, for it germinates anew from the black depths of Ahn Norvys's Age of Echoes, like a patch of weeds that has overgrown the untended wheat. I shall try, lad, as far as I can, while fate keeps me at your side, to outline some of the dangers and pitfalls that await us there in the lowlands. Much of the information I can give you about lowland Arvon and about the transalpine regions of Ahn Norvys beyond the Coolcower Alps is old lore from the *Legendary*. Of which there's a great deal that you already know from your six years of service to me here in Wuldor's Howe. I'll make it my job to tell you as much as I can whenever we have a chance, so as to refresh your memory and so that you may learn other things as well that I've hidden from you in your youth. But the main strategy that I counsel is for you to take the songlines as your guide, travelling from the safety of one songline to that of the next, in order to reach whatever place you are bound for.

"Notice, Kal, how this songline that goes through Dinas Antrum comes closest to the Balk Pit itself. That's why, if you are bound for the Balk Pit, you can't follow its line of approach until you're past the Coolcower Alps."

"I don't understand, Wilum. Why?"

"For the same reason that you must avoid going anywhere near Wardwyst Castle. Dinas Antrum will be crawling with troops and spies and unconscionable dangers. It would be far better, I think, to skulk by night in the woods and fields around it. And notice too, quite obviously, how much greater the distance is between songlines the farther removed you are from the Great Glence. So that when you leave the safety of one of them, the security of the next will take that much longer to reach. So you see there's no easy road for us on this mission."

"That's for certain," affirmed Kal. "So . . . We're not to go alone, then?" he asked.

"No, you won't be going alone. Unwrinkle your brow. I wouldn't lay such a heavy burden on you as to saddle you with only a doddering old man as your helpmate. It's good to have company in trouble, since evil shared is more easily borne, and, more importantly for us, more easily overcome."

"Who is coming with me then?"

"Patience, Kal. How can I tell you when I don't know myself for certain? The matter bears more thought, and we've hardly had time to sit down and consider our situation. Events have happened so quickly. Galli, for one, at least, can come with you, if he wants, and if you're willing to share the dangers with him." Hearing this, Galli looked up from his rowing with a beaming smile and said nothing.

"Now that you put it that way, in terms of danger, maybe Galli shouldn't come along."

"Really, what do you think I am, Kal? Some wasted half-man? Any danger you face I will face too," asserted Galli, unable to contain himself.

Wilum nodded gently, amused.

"As I was about to say to you, Kal, before Galli let his eagerness get the better of him again, it would on the contrary be exceedingly prudent of you to have Galli come along with you. He's shown himself to be a true friend in the tried and longer way of your lives together in the Holding. I can see the deeper bond of friendship that lies between you. He's a true and trusty fellow, your friend Galligaskin Clout. A body may search high and low for such a one and never find him in this life. Yes, you would be wise to ask him to come along."

"Ask me? Who needs to ask me? Diggory's team couldn't keep me from coming along with you, Kal," blurted Galli, his face flushed with shame at Wilum's unstinted praise.

"There you are, Kal. You're stuck with him," humoured Wilum, a smile breaking the worry on his face.

"Re'm ena, but that he is, Master Wilum, begging your pardon."

"Don't worry, Galli. You're coming with me all right. I wouldn't have it any other way. There's no arguing with a Clout," returned Kal.

"It won't be long now. I can see the shoreline," Galli said, turning back to the oars.

"Here, Kal, fold the map and keep it with you," counselled Wilum. "As I said, you can look at it more closely later."

All talking ceased now, and, while Galli rowed, Wilum and Kal looked westwards towards the little inlet of Riven Oak Cove. Slowly the rugged western shore of Deepmere, brimming with a multitude of brooks and torrents, took shape. Everywhere there were heaped huge piles of rock that looked like they had been cast down from the heights by wanton giants in their sport. Some took the aspect of jutting piers, others of small peninsulas crested with tufts of dwarf oak and clinging ash. In places, rivulets cascaded in waterfalls over low-slung terraces and rocky outcrops which embossed a gradually sloping landscape of flowery meadows and deep-wooded glades.

As their boat turned into Riven Oak Cove, they heard the faint melodious tinkling of cowbells.

"Look, there's Master Tudno's animals," said Kal.

A small herd of cattle browsed beside a ruined stone bothy on a flat area of open grassland. As they drew up the long narrow arm of the Cove and the clink of the cowbells receded, a pregnant calm, framed by the trumpeting of a pair of swans, descended on them. Sweeping right down to the shore on either side of them were wych elms and maples. As well, there were wild cherry and pear trees pricked out with spring blossoms as white as the cloak of Tobar. Already the ground was carpeted with wood violet and cinquefoil. An air of mystery and awful stillness hung over the place. Small wonder that few ever ventured into this Cove. Even Warden Tudno rarely frequented this spot. Kal recalled that his practice was merely to bring his cattle up in the spring and, leaving them to fend for themselves, return to drive them up in midsummer to the higher pastures in the steeper lee of the mountains. Certainly Tudno would never have dared sleep in the decrepit old stone bothy round which his cattle grazed contentedly.

Both Wilum and Kal, who sat facing the rowing figure of Galli, looked out onto a gently sloping meadow flat at the farthest end of the Cove, where they made out the outline of King Herne's Oak, the great misshapen tree from which the Cove derived its name. Close by it, the Skell added its waters to those of Deepmere in a rock-strewn stretch of whitewater that churned and eddied under the graceful arches linking together the stout piers of the bridge over which ran the Westwynd Way.

Moments later Galli was scraping the shallow bed of the lake with his oars.

TEN

Galli shipped his oars and leaped over the side knee-deep into the frigid spring waters flowing out of the Skell into Deepmere. Kal helped him haul the boat up onto the pebbled southern shore just below the stone bridge which crossed the narrow span of the Cove. There was every chance the enemy might be lurking in the area. Their nerves were stretched taut, and they started at the slightest rustle of leaf or branch or any sudden trill of birdsong.

Kal was struck by the overpowering feeling that they were all being watched, but he in particular. He could sense the tragic presence of the echobard king who lay long-buried in this spot—not a presence he could pinpoint, but one diffused through the air itself, affecting him as a barely perceptible tingling along the nape of his neck.

The boat well on shore, he and Galli let Wilum climb out. Talamadh slung over his shoulder again, Wilum clambered up to the site of the Riven Oak, onto a small lift of land that overlooked the stone bridge and the beaten earth of the Westwynd Way. It seemed an age ago that Kal had paused, listening on the bridge atop Star Thistle. Galli had taken the satchel of irreplaceable books and manuscripts out of the boat and laid it aside. They hid the boat behind a boulder in a thorny brake beside one of the solid stone piers of the bridge and turned to join Wilum. Up beyond the bridge they found him staring with glazed eyes at the broken stem of King Herne's Oak, chanting verse of some kind, his tone grave and prophetic.

"When royal oak is cleft from root to crown,
Fell ruin shall fall upon Wrenhaven town.
If this betide, let wise folk bring to mind,
That Arvon's fall be not too far behind."

Kal and Galli regarded the ancient oak where it stood broken on the grassy hillock. Its trunk was rent completely asunder, as neatly as if it had been split in two by a gigantic axe. The fissure that had formed a hollow crook on the bole of the tree, where the two parts of trunk had once been knit together as one, was gone. The once solid base of the tree was entirely ripped open, its wood scored and charred black. It was a wonder that the tree remained standing at all, for only the stubborn tangle of bedded roots served to keep the two halves upright. Close to the splintered tree, oddly untouched, sprang a solitary oak sapling in the full vigour of its springtime growth. Kal called to mind the thunderstorm that had filled the valley with its sound and fury two nights after the Candle Festival. It had been the worst storm in living memory and had, besides blowing off more than one roof of thatch, laid low many a stout tree of ancient dimensions.

Wilum turned to his two companions, his face serious. Ignoring the snowy wisps of hair that an offshore breeze kept blowing across his face, he fixed a look on Kal. "There you go, lad, yet one more indication that the dire times foretold by Hedric have come upon us. Hardly allows for any doubt that the Great Harmonic Age is coming to an end. But there's hope here all the same," he continued, gesturing towards the sapling and frowning with an effort of concentration. "That's it, I remember the couplet now. 'When Lammermorn feels sharp death's dreadful sting, Shall Arvon once more gain her rightful king.' There's the bright day that shall surely follow this storm. Where one king fell, another is destined to take his rise. It was here on this nuddick of ground that the last of the echobard kings met his end—betrayed. His body was stuffed unwept and unsung into the hollow of this tree. King Herne's spirit rests uneasy here and will never find peace while the Great Harmony lies shattered and unstrung. But make no mistake, lads. Herne was the gentlest and noblest of the echobard kings.

"But we'd better go. We're in uncommon danger so close to the Westwynd Way. No point in lingering here any longer than we have to." Wilum turned heel from the oak and made for the path. "All right then, the two of you, follow me."

Wilum set the pace, threading his way through the rising tumble of boulders which girdled the Lower Skell, a wild foaming stretch of water. For a long while it was difficult going on the rocks, made slippery by a ceaseless spray of cold river water that soon had them soaked to the skin once more—the second time that morning.

The Lower Skell made a slight bend, and the three of them were forced to clamber up a steep ridge of rocks which ended in a flat bank of smooth pebbles. Here the Skell gathered itself into a broad sequestered pool, a quiet break in its headlong flow called Hart's Leap Pool. Ahead of them cascaded a small waterfall by which the water that Hart's Leap Pool lost by spillover was replenished.

Many a drowsy summer afternoon of herding on the shielings was spent by the pool's refreshing edge, a safe peaceful interruption of the Skell, untouched by King Herne's restless spirit. While the sheep grazed, the young herdsmen would languidly watch the dragonflies darting in and out of the tall grass on its fringes and give ear to the song of the linnet and the thrush vying with the sound of the water.

"Not much left of Thane Hector's cairn . . ." Wilum stopped to catch his breath, gazing at a formless pile of rocks beside the pool. "That animal . . . worn-out and wounded . . . now I know what it must have felt . . . driven by the huntsman."

"Just like us," Kal said.

"Like us . . . like the Stoneholding . . . like Arvon . . . in its death throes." Wilum grew sombre.

It was here several centuries earlier, Kal recalled from the lore of the Holding, that Thane Hector Strongbow witnessed the death agonies of a great stag, a quarry that he had pursued in a desperate chase down the entire length of the Holding. In the last stages of exhaustion from its wounds, it had leaped down from the crest of the waterfall into the Pool and then dragged its battered body onto shore. His heart cut to the quick by the creature's grace and nobility, Thane Hector had it buried there, erecting a cairn over its grave.

There existed no path up the mountain on the cairn side of the Pool, where the three now stood, so close to the Hart's Leap that they were caught in its cascading mist. Here, however, lay the Tahr Steps, a natural causeway of level rocks that ran below the waterfall and reached the other side of the water. Beyond the stepping stones lay the path up which they would continue their journey along the purling course of what had now become the Middle Skell.

Kal bounded with sure foot across the Tahr Steps, which lay hidden on the far side of the pool in a tussock of dark flowered sedge, dusted with light yellow pollen. Wilum and Galli followed and came to a halt for a moment beside the young Hordanu amid the fragrant scent of elder-bushes in full white bloom. There were crab apple and wild plum beside the footpath that climbed to meet the level of the Hart's Leap and then settled into a more gradual ascent beside the winding bed of the stream. They scrambled up and, with the tumbling waters of the Hart's Leap now at their feet, looked down on Riven Oak Cove. They could discern no sign of pursuit. Yet it remained impossible for them to gain a notion of what armed intruders might be creeping their way through the wooded mountainside all around them or along the Westwynd Way, which hugged the forest-shrouded shores of Deepmere.

At either end of the lake hung a pall of grey-black smoke marring the pristine beauty of the mountains that ranged the Holding. The three men stood in silence. The fires still burned. How few souls had survived the ravages of the Boar and had escaped the charred wreckage of Wrenhaven and the scattered homesteads along the Edgemere Road? How many lay slain under the hot ashes of their own homes?

Galli was the first to turn away. "It's all gone. There's nothing left." He choked on the words.

Wilum and Kal now turned as well from the outlook above the Pool and joined him at the stream's edge where it slipped over the cliffside.

"Never nothing," Kal said, "There's never nothing left. There's always hope." He tried to look into his friend's face.

"Aye, Kal," said Wilum behind them, "but that's a saying that is both true . . . and cold comfort. Particularly at a time like this when, despite the sun, all seems darkness. But now come, we must go."

The three fell silent again, despondent and sorrowing for their fallen clanfellows as they trudged along the path. Kal looked

about him. The sheer beauty of the highlands and the memories
it evoked only sharpened his grief. Here the boys of the valley
used to come in the gathering dusk to "burn the Skell." Bearing
torches, they would light up the shallows of the river and impale
the startled trout with three-pronged spears. Then in the evening
they would feast on fish roasted over their campfire, singing and
carousing until it was almost dawn. Which of these fellow revellers
might be numbered among those who felt the Scorpions' sting,
their spirits now swirling like curls of smoke skyward from the
white spire of Mount Thyus, which cleaved the distant horizon?
And what of his family, Uncle Lentum and Aunt Halimede and
their children who lived in Wrenhaven? What had happened
to them? Had they escaped or been crushed by the scourge of
Ferabek's sword?

By slow ascent they continued up the wide foothill glades of
Mount Thyus. The mountain reared its unbowed head with indomitable pride from its sun-mottled fundament of meadows and forest.
The unique way in which Mount Thyus was configured—a spire
rising from a gentle grade called the Saddle through which they
now trekked along the Skell—afforded its lower slopes the richest
source of summer pasturage in the western end of the Holding.
The flanking shoulders of Mount Hecla and Stonehead, whose
snowcapped peaks towered over Thyus, gave the area the aspect
of a valley by protecting it from the stormy blasts that swept in
from the north, rendering it more temperate than normal.

To their left, the brimming waters of the Middle Skell wound
through a meadow and seemed to tremble on the verge of overflowing, like wine that crowns a glass. Level with the lush grass edging
the path, the river water gleamed in the sunlight, as if burnished
by spring's warm touch. Here and there the dark shadows of a
stately oak or a stooping willow covered the stream. Elsewhere,
the braided stream slipped into a peaceful side hatch dressed in
watercress and toothwort.

In places their path was broken by tiny gurgling becks which
they overstepped with ease. In another spot the way would turn
soft and spongy underfoot, as it skirted a boggy tarn of rifted
peat that sprouted hart's tongue fern and bog asphodel. The moist
earth was strongly redolent of spring. The sweet smell of new
growth pushing through the mat of decaying grasses and ferns
brought back to Kal's mind his first journeys as a boy to these

verdant haunts of the Middle Skell. This place...it gave him a love for the soil of the Holding, made it seem a privileged land set apart.

He glanced back and noticed that Galli had paused to rest with Wilum, who seemed unusually stiff and withdrawn ever since they had drawn up the boat in Riven Oak Cove.

"How are you feeling, Wilum? Getting tired now? I hope I haven't been setting too brisk a pace for you."

"If you want to know the honest truth, you're walking just a touch too fast for me, Kal," replied Wilum, seated on the trunk of a maple tree that lay levelled by the high wind of the storm that had felled King Herne's Oak. "My years betray me. I felt the urge to stop here for a short bit to drink in this wonderful smell. The Saddle here around the Middle Skell has always struck me as such a beautiful spot, the most beautiful, perhaps, in all the highlands, if not Arvon, or indeed all of Ahn Norvys for that matter."

"It's funny, I was thinking the very same thing."

"I know, Kal. You're one in spirit with the soil of this highland valley of ours, rooted in it, as am I. Many's the time on my way up to my Enclosure I've skirted your campsite, while coming near enough to hear the merry voices of you lads—"

"Will you look at that brazen little thing?" interrupted Galli, pointing to a brown water rat perched on a dead branch that had become lodged in an eddying elbow of the river. The little creature was bent over the surface of the water, picking with its paw at the plants and rushes that had drifted downstream and had become entangled in the obstructing branch. Holding the stem of an uprooted marsh marigold exactly as with hands, it drew one of the leaves to its mouth and nibbled it, feeding without fear, even though Kal stood only a few paces away. In a flash it let the plant drop and darted its paw down into a clump of wood poppies that the stream had whirled into a sodden yellow mass. In the same instant as the water rat held up its wriggling prey—a newt—the fronds of fern behind him parted, to reveal the lustrous form of a river otter. Oblivious of the rat, the otter lunged muzzle-first at the struggling newt. The rat, refusing to be done out of its tasty morsel, pulled the newt out of harm's way and rounded on the trespasser with its teeth bared. A savage tussle ensued. The water rat was forced to drop the newt to take up a fight for its life. The struggle was unequal. But chance was with the doughty water rat, who happened to find the soft underside of the sleek river otter, just below the throat. Once the water rat's stubborn little jaws had clamped onto this soft spot, it was not long before the body of its opponent fell limp.

"Well done, water rat!" exclaimed Kal.

The animal spun, startled by the acclamation of the three laughing men. Its nose twitched once, and it shot off into the long grass, leaving the lifeless otter floating at the river's edge.

"Aye, that he should stand up to the otter! Usually he would have just dropped his prey and bolted for his tunnel," Galli said.

"A dauntless little creature." Wilum grew still again. "We'll take a lesson from him and make our stand against the mighty Ferabek, as slight as the odds appear to be. But only if we're forced to. First we run, not from cowardice, but as part of a wiser strategy, in order to marshal our strength and find the Boar's soft underbelly."

"Aye, Wilum, if we could only find some tunnel we could burrow into, some way we could just hole up, 'til we sort things out and devise a way to fight back."

"There are many places in the coastal clanholdings and even amid the Arvonian Isles that would serve our purpose well. And both South Wold and Thrysvarshold are honeycombed with caves and hidden dells. But the best spot of all, I still think, is the Marshes of Atramar."

"And all we have to do is get from here to there," moaned Kal.

"Don't fret. Getting to the Marshes is the least of your worries. You have a very much longer journey than that to make," Wilum replied. "Truly, Kal, our worst misfortunes are often those which never befall us."

Kal started as if Wilum had read his thoughts.

"Take what's happened up until now for instance. I'm overjoyed that neither you nor I nor Galli nor the Talamadh has yet fallen into the Boar's hands, and that we've managed, so far, at least, to escape his attack on the Howe. Besides which, we've salvaged all those key manuscripts that Galli's carried so patiently all morning."

"Seems a small victory."

"A very mistaken assumption, my young Hordanu. As long

as the seed of Ardiel remains alive somewhere, and this holy harp remains intact, we have hope of restoring the Harmony. No, Kalaquinn, a great good is being accomplished here merely by virtue of the fact that you and I are hale and hearty, and the Talamadh remains safely in our hands, even though we do have a horde of Black Scorpions in hot pursuit of us, and even though we'll have to skulk our way by stealth through Arvon's hidden hills and valleys, and we may all be forced to live in some cave like rabbits in a warren."

"I understand. I'm sorry for sounding so defeatist, especially after all you've told me and the confidence you've placed in me," said Kal, abashed, gazing on the Talamadh, which Wilum had held on his lap.

"I'm glad about that. If only I could put my own preachments into practice. There's not a more sorrowful doom-saying bard in all of Ahn Norvys than am I. Well, I think my old bones have had enough rest," Wilum said, rising with a sigh from his make-shift seat. "We'd better carry on. You first. But, please remember that I'm not young, and Galli here is laden down with a fair bit of parchment."

"Oh, you needn't worry about Galli. He's as strong and sturdy as a workhorse, eh Galli?"

"Aye, Kal, but even a workhorse needs his victuals. What I wouldn't give for some sausage and cheese and a nice big tankard of Gammer's nut-brown ale."

"And you sure keep Gammer and your fair cousins hopping, don't you? It's a wonder they have any time at all to spare for your dear uncle Diggory."

"Never mind, anything I eat I more than make up for in the work I do around the farmstead. I'd like to know if you do as much!" Galli had grown surly, nettled now by Kal's banter.

"Ah, that's what I was looking for." Kal broke out in a smile. "There's the old Galli that I know and love, grumpy when he's hungry and letting me know what's what. For a while there you were treating me with kid gloves, like I was a stranger or some-thing."

"Well, I suppose I'm just getting used to the idea of you being 'Great High Hordanu.'" Galli pulled a look of haughty disdain, and rolled his eyes.

"Aye, sure, all dressed in state and giving wise and august

counsel to all comers here on the Saddle. Next thing you know you'll be addressing me as Master Kalaquinn."

Wilum stepped up and placed a hand on Kal's arm.

"Nevertheless, you are indeed Hordanu, not publicly invested, that's true, and leagues yet from being in secure possession of your office, without a doubt, but all the same, you are now Hordanu with me. Nothing, not even the meanness of your station in life, can change that. Your office makes you a direct and living link with Ahn Norvys's first Hordanu as well as with Ardiel. One day, when things are put to rights, many will pay you the deference and honour due your high station, and it will be your part to accept it without balking or else betray the trust of your people and so risk again the unravelling of the order of things. But all of this you have yet to learn.

"Still, given our present circumstances," Wilum continued, turning to Galli, "it would be prudent for you to treat Kal no differently than before. You're hearth brothers. Any awkwardness and unwonted respect you show to Kal will tend to draw suspicion down on us while we're on our journey. Very well." Wilum smiled at the two, ushering them with his arms up the path. "It would be a good idea for the two of you to take the lead now. I can trail along in your wake. I think, though, we should keep a vigilant silence."

The Middle Skell gleamed like silver foil as the sun approached its meridian. It flowed bright and clear over a sculpted bed of milky white pebbles that imparted a murmuring voice to the passing waters. Here and there the stream darkened into a deep pool, overhung with birch and willow bowing to their reflection over the watery depths beneath them. The path was bordered much of the way by a flowering hedge of hawthorn, coiled with climbing honeysuckle. Under the hedge, wildflowers abounded in profusion, swaying in the lucid spring air. Broom, full-flowered and visible at every step, ran along the coppiced stands of forest in veins of gold.

A quick-darting squirrel would occasionally clamber along the upper reaches of a leafy grove nearby, scolding the passersby. The bright melodious outpourings of finches and song sparrows were interrupted sporadically by the impertinent chatter of jays. Two ravens, in their ebony plumage, croaked in a beech tree by the meadow's edge. On the other side of the Skell a sleek red fox skulked down the sloping brae beside an oak pollarded by time that sprouted leafy antlers from its broken brow. Nestled in the crown of the oak was a wren's moss-built nest partly veiled by a growing tuft of primrose. When the fox caught sight of the three wayfarers, it took fright and disappeared into the seclusion of the woods above the brae. On either side of them, the Saddle had gathered itself into sloping folds of forest and meadow, broken here and there by rocky battlements.

For a time, Kal and Galli walked several steps ahead of Wilum, sharing the unspoken feeling of deep friendship. Galli broke the silence. "You know, Kal, it's not easy to think there's apt to be real danger lurking in these hills around us. It's all so beautiful."

"Yes. I've always held a special place in my heart for this part of the Saddle. Maybe because it's so far away from the bustle around the Mere. It's so peaceful and secluded, unnaturally so, I mean in a good sense. Hallowed somehow. I don't know. I've always loved to come tramping up here from the time I was a boy. I'll never forget the day my father—I'm sure I can't have been more than about seven years old—'Son,' he said, 'I'd like to teach you a special song that goes with this place. Always has, as far as I know. One day it'll be your turn to pass it on to your own son, as my own father passed it on to me.'"

Galli nodded, smiling and thoughtful. Then he began, and the two friends sang in a whisper, like the breath of a breeze, the lines as familiar to them as their own childhood.

> "From King Herne's cloven oak,
>   Where the waters churn broke,
>   'Neath the Westwynd Way bridge to the Mere.
>   Hie thy feet! Hie thy feet!
>   Else that restive wraith meet
>   By the Lower Skell's banks, rough and sheer.
>
>   Climb higher! Climb higher!
>   Through bramble and briar,
>   Up stony slope dire.
>   Climb higher!
>
>   To Hart's Leap and cool peace
>   By the clear Pool's green crease,

Deep in bloom spread beneath shading tree.
Soft! Here linger the strains
Of cheer's wistful refrains,
Here where once the greenwood rang with glee.

Climb higher! Climb higher!
O'er stag's final byre,
Where falls yet aspire.
Climb higher!

Here herdsman and drover
Drive for the sweet clover
Spring flocks o'er the green upland brae,
Up on to the Saddle,
Where rich meadows straddle,
The Middle Skell's wandering way.

Climb higher! Climb higher!
Amid the sweet briar,
And song sparrow choir.
Climb higher!

And along each deep bank,
Willows grow rank on rank,
Where the trail from Llyn Idwal descends.
Higher pressed to the base
Of dark Stonehead's grave face,
Bleak the Stonefoot Path wearily wends.

Climb higher! Climb higher!
Past Perch to admire
The falcon's wide gyre.
Climb higher!

Then upon Saddle Horn,
Where Skell waters are borne
From a mouth in the face of its wall,
To Tarlynn's green hollow,
Where few men dare follow,
The way 'neath mystic Fearney's pall.

Climb higher! Climb higher!
Towards the steep spire,
Where burns day's death-fire.
Climb higher!

Behold—climb no more,
None on this mortal shore,
Save one, shall trespass the Tarn's edge,
And to then mount the course
Of long-plunging Skell Force,
To stand on Skell's seven-source ledge.

But look ever higher,
Look higher! Look higher!
But look ever higher,
Look higher!"

A hush ensued as the sweet savour of the words lingered on the
tongue and in the ear of the young Holdsmen. A few sparrows
twittered, preening amid the silver spray of waters tossed from
their wings along the shallow edge of the Middle Skell. The river
gurgled and burbled between its banks over mossy stones. The
breeze whispered through the tremulous leaves of a small aspen
grove rustling above them. It seemed to Kal that the Skellside
had taken up the song's quiet strains.

"Will the Song outlive us, Kal? I mean— Well, just think of
it. Will we ever get the chance to pass it on? We've been all but
wiped out. Who is there to remember? I guess it was just that
one line . . . 'Here where once the greenwood rang with glee'—"

"Yes, that struck me too. I thought of all the fallen folk of
the Holding. But know this, Galli, their spirits are immortal, as
is their remembrance. The strains of our song, even as a spark
of the Great Harmony, strained and fading though it be, are a
warrant of their immortality. They are, even in their destruction,
held in Wuldor's eye. And their memory will remain green for
generations unending in ballads and songs sung by Arvon's finest bards."

Galli smiled to himself. Kal caught his eye and the two friends
burst into laughter. Their mirth rang off the cliff face that had
risen over them.

"How's that for sounding the part of 'Great High Hordanu'? I suppose there is something to it."

"That's all right, Kal. I like you all the same."

Wilum had closed the gap behind the two of them, for they had slackened their pace.

"I really don't think it's a good idea to break silence, lads. We don't enjoy the luxury of knowing the Boar's movements. For all we know his men are scouring the hillsides close by even as we speak," whispered Wilum at their backs.

"May I make a suggestion?" asked Kal, turning to Wilum. "We're only a few minutes from the Perch. We just passed by the path leading to it. Galli could have a good look around from it."

"An excellent idea. Let's make use of Galli's keen eyes. Lead the way," Wilum said with a wide sweep of his arm, letting Kal and Galli turn around and step past him. Just a few score paces down to their left was the path that branched off from the Skellside Path, climbing up to the Perch, a tongue of rock which, running out at right angles from a sheer precipice, overhung a yawning abyss. The Perch was only a bowshot's distance away from the Skellside Path, but was not visible from it through the thick cover of forest. The path took a sharp turn and ended on the top of a broad escarpment shaded by maples and oaks all the way to its very edge. They stopped beside an ancient moss-bound oak of enormous girth, half of whose huge limbs hung suspended over the chasm. From where they stood, they had a spectacular view of the whole southern end of the Holding.

"On second thought, I think it would be better if we didn't venture out onto the Perch," advised Wilum. "We'd be much too easily seen from there."

"But it gives us a much better point of vantage," Kal said.

"What about this old tree? If we climbed up on it, we'd get a view that's as good or even better than we would from the Perch?" Galli looked up into the spreading canopy of the oak.

"Here, I'll boost you up first. You've got a hold there? Good. Now give me a hand up."

"Sorry, Kal. I can't reach down that far."

"We need a bit of rope."

"Here, would this be long enough?" asked Wilum, who had loosened the braided rope by which he girded up his cloak in ample coils around his waist.

"That'll do fine," replied Kal, throwing the belt up to Galli, who in turn lowered one end and helped pull Kal up to the stout branch on which he was crouched. Kal followed Galli to the middle height of the tree, just below the crotch of two thick limbs that provided shelter for a pair of nestlings chirping shrilly in their bower.

Galli became less sure of his movements and more deliberate in assuring himself handholds. Kal climbed no higher, but guided Galli with words of encouragement and caution as he skirted the small unfledged birds clamouring for food. He straddled his legs across the branch curving into the vacant air beyond the edge of the precipice. By cocking his head to one side Galli said he could make out the whole lower part of the Saddle and Deepmere beyond, a patchwork pattern of pasture and wood furrowed by a network of streams and pathways.

"Can you see anything there, Galli?"

"Give me half a minute, while I get my bearings . . . That must be the Old Drove Road. Are those soldiers I see on it? Yes, I think so, must be. They're all marching in formation. The sun's shining off their helmets."

"How many of them, do you think?"

"Hold it. Let me make a rough count . . . Must be about a hundred, I wouldn't be surprised."

"Which way do you think they're headed?"

"They're making for the Skellside Path. At the rate they're going, they have about an hour's marching yet to reach Hart's Leap. Wait a moment now, I can see some more figures . . . maybe seven or eight people. They're farther up on the Saddle on one of the other paths leading to the Path."

"Soldiers too?"

"No, it doesn't look like it," said Galli, peering intently at the scene beneath him. "Why, if it isn't Gwyn. There's no mistaking that walk of his even at this distance. I think I can almost make out that thatch of red hair. Aye, it's him. And the others around him. Must be the rest of the Fletchers. Judging from their pace, they stand a good chance of stumbling right into the path of those soldiers once they reach the Skellside Path."

"Can you make out anything else?"

"Let me see." Galli's eyes scanned the heights. "Yes, over there . . . I see some folk coming up the path by Stonehead. It looks like they're on their way to the Coomb as well. Must be our own people, Kal. But they're not in any pressing danger. In fact, they'll probably make the Coomb ahead of us."

"Do you have an idea where exactly the Fletchers are?"

"On the edge of Llyn Idwal at the moment. If there were only some way of signalling them, of letting them know the danger they're in!"

"Is that all, Galli? What about back towards the Great Glence? Do you see anything on Deepmere?"

"There's nothing on Deepmere. I suppose we wrecked most of their boats. But wait. I can make out more men. I think there are soldiers, on the Westwynd Way, coming from the Great Glence, or what's left of it. I don't see anything but smoke coming up from the Howe and from Raven's Crag Island too—"

"Where are the soldiers headed?"

"Towards the Skell, on their way up to the Coomb, no doubt. But it'll be a while before they reach it, although some of them are mounted."

"It'll be a tough time for them on the Lower Skell with horses. They'll have to dismount and go on foot," Kal said.

"Aye. But I'd worry more about the ones on the Old Drove Road. They're much closer, more of a threat, certainly to the Fletchers."

"Do you see anything else?" asked Kal.

"No, that's all. There's nothing else that I can make out. We'd best get up to the Coomb."

When they had both swung down to the ground from the lowest limb, they girt themselves with their sword belts, which, together with their longbows, they had laid on the ground by the trunk of the oak. Wilum was looping and rearranging his belt.

"You two carry on to Tarlynn's Coomb," Kal said. "I'm going back down to warn the Fletchers and try to lead them out of harm's way. I wonder what held them up. They were one of the first to get my warning last evening."

"What on earth are you talking about, Kal? What did you see?" asked Wilum, glancing up sharply at his two young companions.

"There are soldiers coming up to the Skellside Path, hundreds of them. And Galli saw some of our folk on their way up. But the Fletchers, they're near Llyn Idwal, and it looks like they might run right into a mess of those Black Scorpions if someone doesn't warn them, and soon."

"Aye, the Fletchers must be warned. Every life we save from the Boar's clutches is precious," Wilum said despite the misgiving evident in his tone. "But, Kalaquinn, I don't know if—"

"Then I should go with you, Kal," said Galli, "in case there's trouble."

"No. You'd better stay with Wilum and guard him against danger. We can't leave him on his own."

"But what about you? If you run into those soldiers . . ."

" Aye, Kal," said Wilum, "there's danger in—"

"—and what if there's more trackers skulking in the woods? Arvon can't afford to lose you, now that you've been made Hordanu. Master Wilum's given us a job to do, remember."

"Ahn Norvys can't afford to lose its older and wiser Hordanu either, Galli, not to mention the Talamadh and the writings you've been lugging around. Besides, I don't intend to encounter any soldiers or trackers or anybody but the Fletchers. And even if I did, two would scarcely be better than one against— No, it makes more sense for me to go alone. No one knows this country better than you and me, and with your eyes and ears, you're better able to protect Wilum than me. We've scouted the path from the Perch, Galli, and the way is clear to Llyn Idwal. I can nip down and guide the Fletchers up by a different path to the Coomb. No, I'll go, and I'll go alone. Besides, I'm the one that had to convince Thurfar Fletcher in the first place. I have to go. I can see no immediate danger, so I'll just run down and back." Kal looked to his mentor. "Wilum?" he asked.

Wilum nodded and said, "Very good then, Kal, you go, but mind, Galli's correct in saying that we cannot afford to lose you, so be careful, be very careful. It would serve no good purpose if you went with him, Galli. I need you here by my side, and to help with the others when we reach the Coomb."

"We have a further problem, though. It looks as though the Black Scorpions are headed towards the Skellside Path, and if so, then they're bound for Tarlynn's Coomb. It's a sure thing that's the place they're headed for. Thanks to my loose tongue. That means the Coomb's no longer a safe spot. We have to find another place. We'll have to take another route. The Fletchers and I should meet the rest of you somewhere else. But . . ."

"I know your thoughts, Kalaquinn. The Hordanu's Enclosure is forbidden ground." Wilum's gentle gaze met Kal's own. "But don't forget that you have every right to enter the Enclosure yourself now, Kal. As for the others, yes, I see your concern." Wilum paused. "However, there comes a time when you have to bend the rules to serve the common good. So when you reach the Fletchers, take them directly to the Seven Springs."

"But I don't know the way."

"Just get to Tarn Cromar. You know the way there readily enough, don't you?"

Kal nodded.

"Good. Once you reach Skell Force, go up to the waterfall. You can walk to it. There's a path beside the Tarn. You cannot miss it. It will lead you past the waterfall to a landing tucked in behind it. There you'll find stairs of stone that will take you right up to the Seven Springs. Remember, just follow the path beside the Tarn and you won't get lost. If all goes well, we will all come together there, I mean Galli and I and any of the others who manage to make it to the Coomb. We'll drink together from the waters of the Springs. Now go quickly, Kalaquinn, and safely. Briacoil."

"Briacoil, Wilum!" Kal turned and broke into a headlong run as he retraced his steps to the Skellside Path, following it downhill as fast as he could towards Llyn Idwal.

Wilum and Galli wasted no time either in returning to the Skellside Path, where once again they set their bearings uphill. They came to a lookout that afforded them a partial view of the ground below. From it even Wilum could spot the tiny figure of Kal wending his way ant-like along the course of the Skell.

Their path now took a steeper aspect and became more rocky and wild, less given to the amenity of lush glades and cool virescent woodlands. The Middle Skell was now a roiling flux thrown from a cave-like mouth worn smooth by the waters that had cut through the face of the Saddlebow, a high ridge of rock bounding the upper limits of the Saddle. On the other side of this barrier lay Tarlynn's Coomb, a broad meadow nestled in a hollow below the sheer face of Thyus.

Wilum and Galli struggled up the sloping approach to the Saddlebow. Above them, the cliffs spewed forth the churning waters of the Skell. When they drew nearer to the Saddlebow itself, their path veered away from the river, following a narrow walkway along the base of the escarpment.

The two trudged along until they came to an opening, where the stern ramparts of the Saddlebow fell sharply, becoming no more than a shallow breastwork footed by a tumble of broken rock. Clambering over the breach in the solid face of stone, they entered a small lea of tall grass spotted with buttercups. They had hardly set foot in this meadow when three figures emerged from behind a large boulder at the bottom of the ridge.

"Hold, Master Wilum," warned Galli. His first instinct was to shrink back the way they had just come, but he recognized the figures of Narasin, a farmer, and his two sons, who lived at Thornycroft Pools, a farmstead lying close to Wrenhaven.

"Not to worry, Master Wilum. It's Narasin, Garis, and Artun." Galli stepped forward, waving to the three men. A few quick strides closed the gap between them.

"Briacoil, Master Wilum, and you too Galli," hailed Narasin, his sons at his heels.

"Briacoil, Narasin. What's happening here? Where is everybody? Tell me now, how many of you have managed to slip the Boar's net?"

"Few, Master Wilum, too few. I'd say there must be only thirty of us so far—"

"What? Only thirty? So few . . ."

"We've posted sentries here and on the other path that leads into the Coomb."

"And Thane Strongbow? Is he here?"

"No, he's not. Must be dead, I reckon. Can't be alive, that's my feeling. Broadmeadows and all of Wrenhaven's been levelled. We saw its fires filling all the night sky, and what a sight it was, by the welkin, to see them flames lighting up the darkness. No, Master Wilum, afraid to say. There's next to no one from Wrenhaven that's survived, excepting for Devved the blacksmith and his son, sore wounded, and that fellow Relzor, the cobbler. Aye, and the Thane's two retainers, Dellis and Nechtan." The farmer shot a glance at Galli. "It seems they was doing some courting at the Burrows last night, interested in a couple of the Clout girls. That's howcome they happened to get the alarm in time. They crossed the Mere with the Clouts. That's not counting that traitor

son of the Thane's, Kenulf, and his kinsman Enbarr—now, there's
a starved snake so poisonous mean he lives on venom."

"What! Both Kenulf and Enbarr here?"

"Aye, Master Wilum, sure enough they are. And you'll find
that Enbarr's using that artful tongue of his to stir the people
against you. You may find a few wavering in their loyalty, even
though Frysan's doing his level best to tell them all about Enbarr's
treacherous dealings with Ferabek."

"And what does Enbarr say to that?"

"He says Kenulf can back him up. He says he was only trying
to come to terms with the Boar, in order to save the Holding
before it was too late, so he claims, and he's a persuasive fellow,
though for my money it's all smoothly turned lies he's giving
out. I don't believe a word of it. It may be his mother was a
Strongbow, but a more black-souled ill-fared token of the old
Strongbow line than her son I've yet to see. And what's almost
worse, he's got Kenulf eating out of his hand and trailing him
like a new-weaned calf."

"What else?"

"He's been uncommon concerned about young Kal Wright and
even asked Frysan all kinds of queer questions about his son. I
shouldn't say asked. Commanded rather, fretting and strutting
like he'd got all the right of the old Thane himself, telling Kenulf
to shut his mouth and keep out of it. But Frysan, he stood up
to him, wouldn't tell him a thing. It did my heart good. By the
Great Glence—beg pardon, Master Wilum—but Frysan is like
to myself. Doesn't trust Enbarr a whit and was all for binding
and trussing him up and waiting, 'til you come up, but then it
looked like there might be a right bloody fight develop if he tried.
Anyhow, Enbarr's told everyone to let him know instant his Kal
comes." Narasin fell silent, nodding respectfully to the Hordanu,
a thick calloused hand working the back of his neck.

"Thank you, Narasin, I appreciate the news, as bleak as it is. It
seems that Enbarr's playing for high stakes, perhaps his own skin,
I shouldn't be surprised. His master can be none too happy, seeing
as he's let me and the Talamadh escape from right under his nose.
In any case, I think it would be better if you came along with
me now. We'll let your two stout sons keep guard here, while you
and Galli and I continue on into the Coomb . . . Beware, Galli,"
he turned to the young Holdsman, speaking softly, "don't breathe

a word about Kal or where he is. There's no trusting Enbarr, or Kenulf. Why should he want Kal so badly? Granted, Kal's witnessed their treachery firsthand and knows much—"

"There's always been bad blood between Frysan and Enbarr," said Galli.

"That's part of it, no doubt, but there must be more to it than that. How did he discover that Kal had escaped the Locker? He must have doubled back to Broadmeadows after his late-night conference with the Boar. But why the interest in Kal? . . ." Wilum's muttered questions petered out into disquieted rumination. Then, as if continuing a train of thought unbroken by silence, he again addressed his companion. ". . . And not a word either of what we spoke about in the boat earlier. Do you understand, Galli?"

"Never fear, Master Wilum," Galli reassured him.

Wilum and Galli, accompanied now by Narasin, left the meadow and climbed the ridge of the Saddlebow, following a footpath that snaked through the sun-warmed rocks. Reaching the top, they cast their gaze down on Tarlynn's Coomb from the heights of the ridge. Through the sloping meadows of the Coomb wound the Middle Skell, closer to one side than the other. At their feet far below, the languid waters funnelled into a gaping pit and disappeared beneath the base of the Saddlebow. Gathered under a broad willow in the shadow of the ridge, close by the stream, a group of people milled about. Some of them looked up and pointed. Galli took a quick glance around before he and Wilum began their descent to meet them. Higher above, in the farther distance, now dimly visible was a cascading ribbon of water on the face of Mount Thyus.

"Skell Force . . ." he said aloud.

"Yes, I'm afraid we're going to have to make great haste to reach it. You can be sure that company of Black Scorpions will be moving much faster than we can. Well, let's find out who's managed to weather the storm," Wilum said, an edge of pain in his voice. Many familiar faces were bound to be missing.

When they reached the floor of the Coomb, they were met by a throng and plied with anxious questions—how had they escaped and what or whom had they encountered along the way? Some of the women were sobbing, too distraught even to talk. One of the first queries came from Marina, Kal's mother, flanked by her husband Frysan and their younger son, Brendith.

"What about my son? Where's Kal, Master Wilum? He is all right, isn't he?"

"Marina, don't worry. He's safe and sound," replied Wilum. "As for ourselves, I daresay we're in much greater peril than he is and can't linger here at length. There's danger close on our heels."

"But where is he, Master Wilum?"

"Hush, Marina, stop your fretting about Kal. Master Wilum has his reasons for not telling us, especially as we're within earshot of certain folk," said Frysan, now turning to Wilum. "How do you mean danger, Wilum?"

"There's a company of Black Scorpions making its way up the Saddle along the valley of the Skell. Unless we move quickly, they'll find us here and finish their misbegotten work."

"And why should we run again, Master Wilum?" demanded the valley blacksmith, folding his great arms across his chest. "Why not make a stand here? We have at least ten stout longbowmen, true sons of the Holding, and you can add one more to that number now with young Clout."

"No, Devved. The odds are much too steep against us. It would be far better if we made for the Seven Springs. Two men could hold an army there. We must garner our strength, while we hold council and decide what to do next." Wilum chose his words carefully, aware that hostile ears listened to him.

"I still say we hold our ground and fight. We're the finest archers in all of Ahn Norvys, and we're fighting on our own terrain. We can reduce the numbers of those crop-eared vermin by a hundred men."

"At what cost?" countered Narasin. "If it turns out that even one of our men is lost, that's one too many for us. For the Boar the loss of a hundred men is nothing. If he wants, he can fill this valley with men thick as the leaves in the forest. There's nought for us to gain by ridding the Saddle of but a handful of Black Scorpions. You're revenge-blind, Devved. You've lost wife and children, aye, but mind, your son Chandaris is alive still. Odds are he'll recover, so long as we keep from throwing our own lives away—"

"The words of a coward, Narasin, you toady of a bardic half-man!" The words cut through the air from a scowling figure raised as if on a dais above the startled company. Enbarr stood on a large stone. Galli had a much clearer view of him now than he'd had from the woods yesterday. He knew the man—a man of middling height with dark hair and protruding lips set in a bland oval face lightened by steel-grey eyes which flickered now with malice.

"What kind of highland men are you, to be browbeaten into flight by this pale shadow of a High Bard? He just wants to save his own stiff-necked stubborn hide. Ferabek isn't really after us. As far as he's concerned, he's only paying out a punishment to us for harbouring this villainous impostor, who, in his pride, opposes the Mindal and Ahn Norvys's sole true Hordanu, Messaan, in Dinas Antrum. I say we take a stand here and strike up talks with them. We have what they want and there's a chance yet for us to bargain for our safety. For too long we Holdsmen have flouted the might of the Mindal, making a mockery of the High Lord Ferabek and his Gharssûlian League. The time of choice is upon us, Holdsmen."

"Some choice!" grumbled one of the men above the restless murmurs of the scattered company.

Arms wide, Enbarr held out his hands in appeal.

"All around us everything lies in ruins. Yet we can still salvage some part of the sum of things. We can start by acknowledging, as all of Ahn Norvys does, that Messaan is the High Bard, the Hordanu, not this pathetic impostor!" Enbarr pointed to Wilum, his face twisted into a disparaging sneer. "Holdsmen, it's high time we stopped being obdurate, clinging wilfully to the old ways. We have a chance yet to save what little remains. What do you say, men and women of Lammermorn? The unthinkable has happened. You thought you could defy the might of the Mindal and rest secure in your highland sanctuary. Now, at last, justice has swooped down on us like a mighty bird of prey. How many years did you think we could beard the lion and escape unharmed, a small band of holdouts in the fastness of the highlands presuming to teach the rest of Arvon, let alone Ahn Norvys, about the sacred scheme of things? Our pride and folly have unleashed this scourge upon us. What do you say, fellow Lammermornians? Shall we bend to the reality of the situation, to the shape of things that be? Or shall we resist this new arrangement in our blind self-will, headstrong defenders of an idle dream, of an order of things that can no longer be defended? No, I say we must abide here and make terms with our liege lord. And it's not just me that's saying so. We've no choice but to heed our newly minted leader, the lord of our clanholding, seeing that the good Thane, his father, is no longer able to lead us. Ask Kenulf—rather my lord Strongbow here," Enbarr said as he cast an eye and deferential bow of his head to his cousin who stood to his left.

"I speak for you, do I not, my lord Strongbow?"

"Aye, you do, you do!" confirmed Kenulf, bobbing his head.

"Again I ask"—once more his arms, in open invitation, swept the breadth of the small crowd—"fellow Lammermornians, what do you say?" Enbarr stopped the wide gesture and pointed, hands open and palms up, to a withdrawn figure on the edge of the clutch of Holdsmen. "Relzor, you for one stand with the Lord Strongbow and me, surely?"

For a moment the cobbler scanned the faces of those around him, looking for a sign that there were others ready to cast their lot with Enbarr and Kenulf. Some nervous murmuring could be heard, and darting looks were cast in the direction of Wilum, who had stepped up before the rock. The Hordanu looked on his accuser face-to-face.

"Well spoken, Enbarr. You're a fine orator, but a very poor image of your illustrious uncle, who took you in as an orphan only, it's clear, to nourish a poisonous viper in his bosom. Now there was a lover of justice and truth—"

"Doddering old idiot, you mean," Enbarr mumbled under his breath, but loudly enough for Wilum to overhear.

"And a fine upstanding son you've turned out to be." Wilum turned on Kenulf. "Lackey to this vile foul-spoken cousin of yours. If it weren't for him and his base treachery, your father would still be alive!"

Whispers passed among the gathered Holdsmen.

"As would our kinfolk and neighbours," Galli called aloud.

"Kinfolk! What kinfolk are you talking about, you Telessarian mongrel!" snarled Enbarr.

"Nonsense and lies!" Kenulf cried. "It's all nonsense and lies! Enbarr'll tell you, won't you, Enbarr? Why, my father's just being detained by Ferabek, for his own good, to keep him out of mischief. Isn't that what you said, Enbarr?"

Wilum's eyes flashed. "And you would believe him, wouldn't you? Your father would have shuddered with shame to witness the disgraceful spectacle of his son under the thumb of this fiendish guttersnipe, betraying the hallowed trust vested for generation upon generation, even from the time of Ardiel, in the great family of Strongbow. You've spent too much of your time with him in Dinas Antrum currying favour with the Mindal and filling your head with their poison and treachery. What do you know of highland courage? You're a spineless coward, Kenulf, easily manipulated by your cousin there who's got you wrapped around his finger, so purblind you're taken in by his weasel words. His actions show him for what he is, a disgrace not merely to the mighty line of Strongbow, but to the highland honour of the Stoneholding." Wilum shook with rage. "Do you think that we Holdsmen are rank fools, ready to wait meekly for your precious Enbarr to deliver us up to the untender mercies of the Boar? Weren't he and you seen in his very camp dealing treasonously with him, thinking to ingratiate yourselves at the cost of our lives?"

The murmuring of the listeners grew louder.

"Lies, all lies, I tell you, made up by that stinking lowborn wheelwright and his dung-cart of a son." Enbarr was losing his temper and his audience. "I was risking my own skin to save you all, making peace terms with the Boar, but for your balking mulish presumption—"

"By surrendering all of us into the Boar's grasp. As if we would believe you! If you weren't such a ruthless two-faced rogue, I'd almost pity your blinkered folly. You think you're so clever to deal with a tyrant. You're caught up now in the glamour of his imperial power and his promise of reward. You suppose that you can save the sum of things for pay and that your paymaster is worthy of trust. What happens when he no longer has any use for you? Ah, I know what you're thinking, you're too clever to get caught flat-footed. But we'll see, won't we?"

"Aye, that we will," declared Enbarr, his eyes narrowed with amused disdain.

"Now let me tell you something, Enbarr, you too, Kenulf, and also you, men and women of the Clanholding of Lammermorn." Wilum turned his back on Enbarr and faced the remnant few of the Stoneholding. "You'd do well to heed me. There was a time when there was much sacred power here in our highland clanholding. But it has been entrusted, even in its waning, to the care of the Hordanu, one of an unbroken line from the time of Hedric to the tattered threads of my own day. Nevertheless, rest assured, there is power that resides here still, waiting for the moment of its revival. Never doubt it." He shot a glance over his shoulder. "It is a power that has always come from Wuldor through the harmonious measures of the orrthon, which in turn partake of the Great Harmony. And now that this Harmony is coming apart and is waning in its vigour, my voice is weak and quavering in Ahn Norvys and all that this office of Hordanu once was stands in the far-cast shadow of complete extinction at the hands of Ferabek. But while a germ remains of that great and glorious lay sung long ago upon the Mountain of the Quivering Cromlech by Ardiel of the Long Arm, Ferabek's conquest rests insecure, for, like a glowing ember, the cosmic harmony can be rekindled, fanned into a new and blazing fire, a fire that will cleanse and anneal our gloom-darkened world. Many prophecies in the *Master Legendary* speak of the desolation that will accompany the weakening of the Great Harmony. On the other hand, many prophetic texts also give us reassurance. They speak of the glorious renewal of harmony in the fullness of time.

"So stand with me, men and women of the Stoneholding. Our best hope lies in fidelity to the sacred music of the Talamadh and its keeper from time immemorial, the Hordanu, both of which Ferabek seeks with single-mindedness. My good people, it is not for nothing that we have survived thus far the ruthless might of Ferabek while our brothers and sisters lie smitten and unburied, though not unwept. Your role is to be the helpers of the true Hordanu, the true Guardian of the Talamadh. Your role is to keep safe the Hordanu and the Talamadh, no matter if all of Ahn Norvys yields to Ferabek and his usurping puppets Gawmage and Messaan. Will you play your part, men and women of Lammermorn? Holdsmen, do you stand by me, who am the true Hordanu, the Guardian of the Talamadh?" Wilum's blue eyes flashed like finely cut gems, while his arms and gesturing fingers, animated by his passion, drove home the points he made in reply to Enbarr.

Frysan was the first to shout out. "Hail, Lord Myghternos Hordanu, I acknowledge the true Hordanu and true Guardian of the Talamadh, as did our fathers and our fathers' fathers before them."

This provoked a clamorous repetition of "Hail, Lord Myghternos Hordanu."

Enbarr, realizing that the tide had turned against him, cried out crimsoned in a towering rage, "You have no right to opt for this . . . this washed-up old coot! You're my uncle's vassals! Tell them, Kenulf! Now that my uncle isn't around, Kenulf becomes the Thane Strongbow, Lord Protector of Lammermorn Valley and Wuldor's Howe. He commands you as your liege lord to stay here in Tarlynn's Coomb. Don't you, Strongbow? Don't you?"

"Why, yes, of course . . . I command you," Kenulf echoed, cringing beneath his cousin's fury.

"From here we will negotiate with Ferabek's soldiers and declare at long last our allegiance to Gawmage, the rightful High King of the folkdom of Arvon, and to Messaan, Ahn Norvys's High Bard, the rightful Hordanu, and, above these all, to the mighty Ferabek, Lord Protector of the Harmony, Emperor of the Free Peoples of East and West. You two there, Dellis and Nechtan, take hold of old Cloudbeard and bind him fast. Kenulf, tell them."

"Yes, do what he says. Take hold of him and bind him fast," parroted Kenulf.

"On pain of death," spat Enbarr.

"On pain of death, you heard," confirmed Kenulf.

Dellis hesitated, looking first at his companion, then towards Wilum. He began moving slowly through the crowd towards the Hordanu, followed by Nechtan.

"Stop, Dellis. One more step and you're a dead man." Galli had moved beside Wilum and drawn an arrow.

"Go on, you cowards. There are two of you. He won't dare shoot. Bind him as well, the insolent cur," bade Enbarr. But Dellis and Nechtan backed off. Reluctant and uncertain to begin with, this threat of force was all the persuasion they needed to side with their fellow Holdsmen for Wilum.

"I say 'yea' for Master Wilum," shouted Galli. "What do you say, my fellow Holdsmen?"

"Yea, yea, well said," resumed a loud and lusty chorus of voices, while Enbarr stood on his rock, livid and sputtering, unable to control his rage.

"Very well, have your way, the whole stinking lot of you! You'll see soon enough who was right. I leave you to your fate. Come, Kenulf! Dellis, Nechtan, come!" Leaping from his point of vantage, Enbarr shot a glance at Relzor, who made no move to leave. He then set his back to the survivors and, trailed by Kenulf, stalked off. The Thane's two retainers hung back for a moment, then shook themselves free of the group and broke into a quick stride to catch up with their master. There was the rattle of an arrow being drawn from its quiver.

"Let them pass," Wilum commanded softly. "There's nothing to be gained by shedding the blood of fellow Holdsmen, even the most false-hearted. Leave them to the mercy of the Boar."

"Where are they going, Master Wilum?" Galli said. "Shouldn't we keep them in sight? There's no telling what Enbarr'll do, now that he's got his back up."

"Aye," said Frysan, as he watched Enbarr and Kenulf climbing back up to where Garis and Artun guarded the lower approach to the Coomb. "Did you see him wink at Relzor? They were sore busy whispering and talking together before you came, Wilum. And now he and Kenulf are going off alone, leaving Relzor behind as their spy, no doubt. Perhaps we should stop the two of them, traitorous rascals."

"Leave them be for the time being, Frysan," answered Wilum. "There is little enough harm that they can do at the moment. I notice they're unarmed."

"Not that they could do very much, even if they were armed. Enbarr's always been a poor hand with bow and sword, and Kenulf's only slightly better."

"It's just as well they're moving down the Saddle," continued Wilum. "I think Enbarr expects to meet up with the Black Scorpions advancing on us from below."

"I wouldn't trust him, Master Wilum, not as far as I could spit. I've no doubt in my mind that he's seeking to sell us out," Galli said.

"That may be, but by that time we'll have made it to the Seven Springs, I trust." Wilum's mind turned to Kal with a silent supplication for his haste and safe passage there also.

"But the Boar will know where to find us. Enbarr knows where we're going."

"It hardly matters, Galli. Sooner or later Ferabek will scout out the Seven Springs on his own, since he's sure to know from sources other than Enbarr and Kenulf about the Hordanu's Enclosure. Besides, our trail to the Seven Springs will be easy enough to follow in any case. He won't need Telessarian trackers for that. No, Galli, you can let those two scoundrels be. The main thing is that they don't know where Kal is, or what our plans are once we reach the Seven Springs. If Enbarr had a clue, he'd be desperate to see that we're captured before it becomes too awkward and difficult for the Scorpions to close their trap. His own wounded pride and perhaps even his life depend on it. And if he had stayed with us, we'd always have to be on our guard, seeing as he's no fool and a man of murderous wiles who thinks that our cause is hopelessly doomed."

"I think we'll have to be very much on our guard anyway. What about Relzor?" said Frysan.

"We'll just have to keep an eye on him while we move out of here now as fast as we can," said Wilum.

Just then, Narasin disengaged himself from the buzzing throng of Holdsmen.

"What are we to do now?" he asked as he drew near to Wilum.

"We must move out of the Coomb and on up to the Hordanu's Enclosure, with all the speed we can possibly muster."

"The Enclosure?" Frysan's surprise was mirrored in Narasin's weathered face.

"Aye. Be at peace, men. It is our only haven, our only hope. How many of us are there?"

"Twenty-nine including yourself, Master Wilum. Eleven men, nine women, and nine children. One of the children, Devved's boy, is wounded quite badly. We've rigged up a stretcher for him."

"We'll have to travel quickly together. The smaller children will need to be carried by the adults."

"Which way do you think we should take, Wilum?" queried Frysan.

"We'll just plough on ahead, 'til we reach the path that leads to Fearney Hey. That's the shortest way to the Hordanu's Enclosure, and we've got to get to it before that company of soldiers catches up to us."

"Good," Frysan said, "Fearney Hey is about a mile off."

"And, I reckon it's not but two miles from Fearney Hey to Skell Force," added Narasin, a look of wonder still in his eyes.

"Which is in truth the entry point to the Hordanu's Enclosure," Wilum said. "To reach the Seven Springs we've got to make it to Skell Force, Narasin. Now quickly spread the word, you and Frysan, that we're headed for Fearney Hey. See that every child who can't keep up is carried by an adult. You, Galli, go on up to the ridge and call down Garis and Artun from their sentry posts. We'll need their strong young backs. Leave the sack here for the moment and collect it again when you come down. Be on your guard though. Enbarr and Kenulf may be lurking about still. Let's all of us meet at the Threadneedle Rock up there by the rapids. We don't have much time. Let us go."

ELEVEN

Wilum took a seat at the base of the Threadneedle Rock near the centre of the sheltered upland glen. Beside him, the Skell babbled cheerily to itself, sparkling in the bright spring sunlight as it ran the course of a gentle fall in the lie of the Coomb. Head bent, he pondered all that had happened, wondering how the whole group of them would ever be able to keep one step ahead of the Boar. His mind kept turning over and over, as it had done all morning, countless lines from *Hedric's Master Legendary* that seemed to presage this disastrous attack on Wuldor's Howe and the Stoneholding. Sullen survivors, shepherded by Narasin and Frysan, gathered around him. He broke from his reverie and exchanged light banter with the tired folk, spent from the dread flight up to the Coomb and the pervasive grief that held the remnant few in its grip.

"Briacoil, Master Hordanu," Rindamant greeted Wilum as she approached with her husband Athmas.

"Aye, briacoil," the man added. "Just wanted to let you know I'm glad you told them two rotters from Broadmeadows what's what."

"Briacoil to the both of you, and you too, Manaton, briacoil! Good to see you!"

"Briacoil, Master Wilum. Gara and I want you to know that we throw our lot in with you. We'll do whatever we can to help you."

"Yes, we stand behind you four-square," added Gara herself. On her shoulder lay a sleeping baby, while two older children, a brother and sister, clutched at her skirts. "Have you had anything to eat yet, Master Wilum? We've got oatcakes here and some elderberry wine, more than enough."

It was fortunate that, with the coming of unsettled times in Arvon, most Holdsmen kept a codynnos or night bag always ready and provisioned, in the event that the men were called out to waylay one of Gawmage's forays into the highlands. Even in their haste they had been able to bring a goodly stock of provisions.

Manaton rummaged through the haversack he had swung from his shoulder until he produced a biscuit which he proffered. "Here, have one."

At the sight of the cake, Wilum, who had not eaten since the previous evening, became conscious of a gnawing hunger. The urgency of their flight had, until now, made him unmindful of it. He took the oatcake with a bow of his head and did not demur when Manaton offered him another and handed him a flagon of wine.

"My deepest thanks to you both. You're most kind. Already my spirits feel restored. Narasin, are we all here now?"

"Aye, Master Wilum. Here comes Galli with those sons of mine. We'll need Artun for the stretcher."

"Who's the boy on the stretcher?"

"Devved's son, Chandaris, the only one left of his family, apart from Devved, of course. Riandra tells me the lad's no worse, which is a small comfort. On the run like this, it's not the time to be tending to him. We need a safe place, somewhere to rest and recover our strength."

"That's what I hope we'll attain by climbing to the Seven Springs. Here, let me take a closer look at the boy." Wilum walked to join Devved, who stared blindly at his unconscious child. Wilum stooped down to feel the boy's forehead with his hand and lifted the covers to look at the shoulder wound, which had been cleaned and dressed with a herbal poultice. Wilum covered the boy and tightened again the bonds which held him securely to the stretcher. He stood and placed a hand on the blacksmith's broad chest.

"Your son will recover, Devved. His wound has been well tended and doesn't seem to be festering. I'll look at it more closely myself, once we've reached safety."

"Thank you, Master Wilum. I'd give anything to get back at the dogs."

"Peace, Devved. Rest assured that in the end justice will be done. 'Til then it will serve neither you nor your boy nor any of the rest of us the tiniest bit of good to focus on revenge. Take courage, man. Tomorrow's another day. Things may seem dark now, but there's your son, wonderfully alive, and soon enough he'll thrive again."

"Words, words . . . Idle, empty words from an old fool." Wilum turned to see the diminutive form of the cobbler. Relzor glowered at the Hordanu and the clutch of folk around the injured child. He snorted derisively, drew his cape around himself and turned tail, slinking in the direction of the river's tumbling waters.

"Hold, Relzor! Come back and say what you've got to say to my face!" commanded Wilum, but Relzor ambled on.

"You'll never get him to come at your bidding, Master Wilum," said Devved. "He's an odd fish, that one is. Has no truck with anybody. You just leave your shoes as need mending under the ash tree in front of his cottage with a couple of coins and he'll fix them as good as new. It's amazing what he can do! There's some swear it's deviltry. Enbarr, now, Relzor's right friendly with him. Many a day I've seen Enbarr heading off to Relzor's place past my smithy. Passing odd it seemed to me. Queer cards, both of them, most 'specially Relzor, the way he creeps and slinks around. Won't go into the Glence for anything, keeps to the shadows in the forecourt, and he won't take part in the Candle Festival. Passing strange, I say, passing strange."

"Aye, Devved. He's an odd little man. Keep a close watch on him. I'm afraid there's a reason why he hasn't gone off with Enbarr and Kenulf," answered Wilum, turning now to meet Galli, returning from his errand.

"Briacoil," Galli hailed both Wilum and the group. "Everybody's here. We're ready to push on."

"Excellent. You've got our satchel. Good. We mustn't forget that. You did have a chance to see your family, I hope?"

"Yes. It's sad, Master Wilum. I had two sets of aunts and uncles in Wrenhaven. All sorts of cousins too, and friends. If they're not here, I suppose they're dead."

"Very likely, I'm afraid." Wilum's eyes lifted to meet Galli's. The young man broke the gaze, casting his to the ground, where he kicked at a half-buried pebble with his toe.

"As you'd expect, Gammer and Diggory are pretty shaken up

about it, especially Gammer. Kal's mother too. I tried to reassure her about Kal, told her he's safer than we are here in the Coomb. That was all I told her, of course."

"I do hope you're right about Kal being in less danger than we are," said Wilum. "And did you get to satisfy that hearty appetite of yours?"

"Yes, Gammer made sure I was well-fed."

"I'm quite certain you didn't shame her efforts. You don't look any the worse for wear. I want you to stay here with me. We'll lead the way together. Hello there, Frysan. Everybody's ready, don't you think? Let's be off then. Why don't you and Narasin bring up the rear and keep an eye out for stragglers?"

With an exuberance that was almost youthful, Wilum stepped through the scattered group of survivors, offering words of encouragement as he passed. One little boy was crying at his mother's side. The reassuring touch of Wilum's hand on his head and the soothing timbre of his voice served to calm him.

Galli followed close behind as the people made way for him and Wilum. They passed the Threadneedle Rock and set foot to a path that cut through a broad expanse of water meadow, aflame with orange hawkweed that grew in profusion right up to the steep wall of the escarpment that overhung the Coomb. As they proceeded upstream, the rapids at the Threadneedle Rock subsided again into a placid fillet of water that flowed from a ravine which broke the looming walls. They entered the gorge that steadily climbed the mountainside, but the path proved too narrow to allow more than three people to walk abreast. The survivors were strung out in a column, at the end of which lay Chandaris on a stretcher, carried by his father and Artun, who had fallen behind the group. Two children, both infants, were crying. There was little conversation. Everyone knew the pressing need to cover ground in spite of the encumbrances of baggage and wailing children. Still, their progress was painfully slow, and Wilum and Galli found they had to slacken their pace.

Ahead of them, the sheer bulk of Mount Thyus soared, near enough now for them to make out Skell Force, a ribbon scoring its leeward face. The early-afternoon sun shone bright in the heavens, bearded by tufts of cloud. Daylight, however, had abandoned the area around Thyus. Up the gorge, the narrow horizon, crowded by jagged mountains, was louring, sullen and black, emblazoned by blue-white forks of lightning that etched the sky like darting vipers' tongues. An eerie phosphorescent light suffused the darkened sky, imparting an unnatural clarity of line and feature to the peaks. Striving against the sun, darkling cloud banks now filled the firmament like islands in an inky blue sea. It was a beguiling display of darkness and light that for some moments had every eye fixed on it. Only Artun, carrying the upper end of Chandaris's stretcher, chanced to look back downstream once, as Devved stumbled over a rock.

"They've seen us, they're onto us! Look, there, back on the ridge!" he cried. Down the talus, where the Saddlebow towered over the lower end of Tarlynn's Coomb, marched a double line of Black Scorpions, headed by a soldier who bore the standard, its dread insignia drooping limply in the dead calm that had descended. On top of the ridge two men had stopped. Galli, peering into the distance, descried that one of the men was Enbarr shading his eyes with one hand and pointing with the other back up the slope to where the fleeing Holdsfolk were straggling in a line by the banks of the Skell. They were a mere bow's shot from the side path that rose to Fearney Hey across a heather-covered slope which broke the precipitous steepness of the escarpment. They could see the forested brow of the Hey, which overlooked the ravine of the Skell. As it was, the hapless group had been caught out in the open. They had been seen by Ferabek's own, a full company of them, now hard set on the scent of their struggling quarry.

"What should we do? We haven't got much leeway here," said Narasin, who had jostled his way up to Wilum's side. "I say we forge on ahead to Fearney Hey," he continued. "We're almost there anyway. That way we'll command the heights and can keep them pinned down in the Coomb with our bows. If we can stall them 'til sundown, we might still be able to slip away in the night and make it to Skell Force—"

A sudden shaft of lightning split the air above them, its crack booming up the walls of the gorge.

"A harbinger of destruction," thought Wilum aloud, gazing at the turbid sky looming over them. The farmer's frank clean-shaven face darkened into a frown. "Oh no, not our destruction, I trust, Narasin. We're close enough to safety, but I can't say as much for the horde below us. Look at the frogs. Do you see? They're leaving their streamside burrows. They're clambering up, trying to move higher above the river. It's strange how animals can sense things where we can't."

"What do you mean?"

"I mean a flood of rainwater's about to come rushing down this rift, sweeping away anything and everything in its path. In the many years that have flung their snows on my head, I haven't seen such a marvel of nature but once. Look, Narasin, look at the storm raging around the crest of Thyus. It's loosing a load of rain that's going to rid us of our pursuers. Those Black Scorpions don't have the slightest notion yet that the waters of the Skell are going to be their burial shroud and the river bottom their grave." Wilum tamped the ground with his staff. "Aye, your plan is excellent. We'd better be quick off the mark, though, since those floodwaters may come heaving down on us at any moment. Narasin, go spread the word. Tell our people they need not fear the Black Scorpions at their backs as much as the gathering head-waters of the Skell that lie before us. We've got to reach higher ground. Galli, you and I will set the pace."

Anxiety seemed to give wings to the feet of the fugitives, so that, with words of stern encouragement from Narasin and Frysan, they kept on the heels of Wilum and Galli. Soon they were climbing the last stretch of the sidepath leading to Fearney Hey.

"Skell Force has broadened out. Unbelievable!" exclaimed Galli, casting an eye upstream.

"That means we'll soon be in for it," added Galli's uncle, who had come up alongside. Diggory began to recite a thunderstorm rhyme that was a part of the weather lore of countless genera-tions of Holdsmen.

"If it sinks from the north, it will double its worth.
If it sinks from the south, it will open its mouth.
If it sinks from the west, it is never at rest.
If it sinks from the east, it will leave us in peace."

"One thing's for certain, Digg, this storm ain't sinking from the east," Narasin said with a wry chuckle.

"Least we know as much, which is miles more than I can say for those rug-headed kernes of Ferabek's," answered Diggory.

The sky above them blackened, as the storm moved down

the Saddle from the heights of the Seven Springs. Fat drops of rain began to fall, thudding into the ground around them, each kicking up a little cloud of dust where it hit. Another hundred paces or so and they would be out from the Skell's ravine. Behind them the dragoons had cleared the ridge and had filed into the bottom of the Coomb like a thick black snake winding its way up the Skellside.

A rumble filled the air, like a low unbroken peal of thunder, but deeper and earth-born, shaking the ground under their feet.

"It's coming. The waters are coming down on us!" shouted Galli, who had an unbroken line of sight a mile or so up the valley, which was shut in by sheer bluffs on either side, towering above the strip of marsh and green sward bordering the Skell. It was only the branching shoulder of ground on which they were standing that broke the canyon walls and offered them an avenue of escape from the mounting onrush of crushing water. In that moment, light was extinguished. A pall of darkness, as close as a night clouded and moonless, fell over the landscape. The sky opened. Rain, whipped by frenzied gusts of wind, slanted down on them in torrential sheets. The fugitives scrambled in the murk by touch as much as by sight along the rain-slick path, falling and stumbling over one another amid screams of horror and the wail of terrified children.

Encumbered as they were with Chandaris bound to the stretcher, Artun and Devved trailed behind the rest. In a moment it was too late. The wall of water had reached them, fierce and foaming. Almost all of them had climbed far enough along the path to Fearney Hey to be safe from the roiling flood. It was only Artun, last of the escaping Holdsfolk, who was given a swingeing blow by the swollen waters full on the chest. His legs swept out from under him, he cried for help and clung to one of the poles of the stretcher.

"Hold on, man, hold on tight. I've got it," Devved bellowed above the storm. "Help! Somebody! To Artun quickly!" His powerful arms, thick from years of toil in the smithy, anchored the upper end of the stretcher. Lashed to the stretcher, Chandaris groaned. It was Garis who raced first to his brother's aid. Leaping down to where Artun's hands kept a ferocious grip on the stretcher pole, Garis called out, appealing for more help, as he grabbed hold of his brother's wrist and wrestled him against the flood, leaving himself teetering over the turbid spate of waters. Devved could now pull his son on the stretcher up out of harm's way. Passing the makeshift litter on to the safety of others farther up the path, he sprang down to aid in the rescue. The great man seized Artun's other arm and pulled him out of the swirling torrent. The young man lay sodden on the path for a moment, heaving to catch his breath, then pushed himself to his knees. He sought out the blacksmith with his gaze and nodded his thanks.

"Are you all right, son?" asked Narasin.

"As right as rain, Father, you might say," Artun said, mustering a pained grin. "No more than a bruised ankle. I must have hit it against a rock."

"Can you walk?"

"Yes, I dare say I can." Artun stood up, favouring his injured ankle. "Here we are. Devved, I'm ready whenever you are."

"Let me take your end," Garis offered.

"No, I'll be fine. Devved? Shall we?"

The blacksmith nodded, looking back at the seething floodwaters that raced down the side of the mountain and pooled in the Coomb below.

"All right then," Narisin said, laying a hand on Artun's back, "we'd best get moving again."

"The waters . . ." Devved said as if to himself, still standing at the edge of the surge, staring down the ravine. "They've met the Saddlebow and are being pushed back. It's like a washtub. Can't empty fast enough. Look, the Coomb's filling." Like rag dolls discarded by some neglectful child, black bodies, small in the distance, surfaced, gyrated, and disappeared again in the churning water that filled the hollow. A muscle flexed in the blacksmith's jaw, and his eyes narrowed. "By the Stone, they got what was coming to them. May they rot, every one of them, unburied and unmourned."

"As cursed as they may have been in life, Devved, do not you curse them in death as well." Wilum drew near the blacksmith and placed a hand on his shoulder. "Be at peace with yourself. Come, we must move on."

The blacksmith turned away from Wilum's touch, stepped to his son's stretcher and seized the poles. "Let's be on with it then, Artun," he said, and lifted the stretcher.

The winds had died down and the rain had slackened off. The

storm's force was spent. A few feeble rays of sunlight had broken the tossed mantle of black overcast. Soon the whole group had reached the wooded area above the Coomb. Yet the waters in the hollow were still rising, and they could not rest, but continued to struggle, damp and tired, to the top of a grassy knoll. This was Fearney Hey, a round woodland clearing, banked along its sides by a majestic grove of hardwoods growing straight and true, like the fluted columns of some great castle. By now the day's light had vanquished the storm's cloud, filtering through the rain-glazed foliage above them. The men, women, and children sat and stood along the Hey's meadowed crest in the blissful light and warmth of the sun. Yet they whispered to one another, casting furtive glances about the stand of oak, ash, hornbeam, and maple surrounding them. It was believed that this was a fairy mound. Few had ever come this high up the Skell before. They were approaching the sacred ground of the Hordanu's Enclosure.

"Father, do you think they mind us being here?" asked a little girl above the hushed voices of the adults.

"Who do you mean, Laloke?"

"You know, the hudori and the dendrils. Don't they live here? I thought they didn't like us coming here. You said, 'How would you like it if someone just walked into our house without knocking?' That's what you said, just the other day, when we were riding in the wagon on the way to the Candle Festival. I asked you why we didn't go anywhere near some places in the Holding, places like Fearney Hey. Remember?"

Wilum, standing nearby, had overheard the question. "You may rest without fear, little one. There's nothing to harm you or your father or anyone else here. When danger threatens, we don't worry about things like knocking on doors. Besides, Fearney Hey is part of the glencelands, which the Hordanu oversees." Wilum cupped the back of her silken head with a gentle hand.

"And that's you!" cried Laloke.

"Aye, that's me," said Wilum, nipping off the conspiracy of whispers.

"Look, Laloke, look at the rainbow," exclaimed a relieved father to the daughter snuggled up against him, pointing up at the splendid arch that bridged the jagged peaks of the mountains above. In a moment everyone else was gazing up into the sky. Heartened by Wilum's words and by the rain-washed bands of brilliant colour that the sun had knit together out of the fragments of the storm, they all fell to their ease. Wilum sat down with Frysan and Narasin. They discussed the next portion of their journey up to the Seven Springs, while Galli sat nearby in silence.

"I think we've had a long enough rest," said Wilum presently.

"Aye," Frysan stood to stretch, faltering on his weak ankle, sore again from their scramble up the Skellside. "I don't expect we've seen our last of Black Scorpions."

"How's that ankle of yours, Frysan?" inquired Wilum.

"Just the old injury. I'll be fine."

"Right enough. Let's be off," Narasin said, pushing himself to his feet. He and Frysan began to rouse the people from their rest and soon had them moving again in the direction of Skell Force, which every eye could make out now above the curtaining trees of Fearney Hey. Wilum led the way, accompanied once again by Galli, while Narasin brought up the rear with Artun, guarding the group's flanks and shepherding stragglers. Garis had taken over his brother's stretcher duty just ahead of them. Even Devved, who held the other end of his son's stretcher as before, seemed to have a lighter air about him after their stop for rest.

Frysan watched over the middle of the column, where he bantered with Diggory Clout who, in good humour, whistled a tune that put all his hearers in good heart. There seemed nothing, thought Wilum, that could put the shadow of a frown on Diggory's broad-beamed and sunny countenance. The man seemed to be perpetually jocund. "Must be infectious," he murmured to himself, noting that Galli shared a good measure of the same disposition.

The path from Fearney Hey took a steep turn into a dell that looked as if it might have been scooped out of the mountain slopes by a giant spoon. The way was twined with the sombre shadow of birch and aspen, ash and oak, that crowded them in the wide-spanning depths of the hollow. The smell of sweetbriar perfumed the still air, although every now and again a tree bough quaked at the breath of a vagrant breeze that drifted down from the heights above. Here and there a hulking rock broke the seamless wicker weave of the forest, affording space for a tangled undergrowth of hazel and hawthorn at its base. It seemed such a forgotten out-of-the-way spot, the haunt of bear and wild boar and fox, that even in broad daylight Galli clutched at the hilt of his sword and marvelled at Wilum's fear-lessness in coming this way alone so many times on his way to the Enclosure.

They struggled up a thinly wooded ridge that enclosed the upper side of the hollow. The children became testy and petulant at the effort, and their whimpering broke the eerie calm. Above them on a too-narrow ledge stood a mountain sheep nibbling contentedly on some grass that had taken root in a bowered cleft of the rock face.

As the fugitives reached the top of the ridge, a view of the entire Holding opened up to them. Here there were few trees and these a pathetic collection of stunted pines on a thick purple carpet of freshly blooming heather, mingled with briars and thorns and hardy windswept wildflowers. They had climbed very high, close now to the towering bulk of the mountain, where Skell Force rushed headlong from the dusky mid-regions of Thyus. Below them lay Tarlynn's Coomb. The floodwaters had subsided, leaving a scattering of tiny figures, twisted and lifeless, on whom the carrion crows had already begun to feast. Closer to hand the Middle Skell babbled its way through a maze of rocks from the stony lip of Tarn Cromar, its clear alpine waters still too far above them to be visible. They were close enough, however, to hear the faint plash of Skell Force's leaping cataract resounding on the surface of the Tarn. Their pace had slackened.

"By my ten finger bones, lads, I must have a rest. 'Tis more walking and climbing than old Diggory has done in years. I'm fair near exhausted, I am."

"Ah, stop your carping, Digg. If it were off to the Bottle for a pot of ale you were going, you'd be spry as a gamecock. Of that I'm sure. You should be sore ashamed of yourself! Do you think it's easy for these here little ones? If we was all to stop for you, we'd all end up in the briars." Gammer Clout clucked at her husband as she bustled about, disentangling her skirt from a persistent patch of blackthorn.

"Ah, smash me, Gammer! You're pulling your old man about like fury. I ain't a young buck anymore. All this walking up hills—why, it'll shove me underground as sure as them Black Scorpions, that it will," replied Diggory, between wheezing breaths. This light banter provoked a laugh from the weary company gathered about.

"It's quite all right, Mother Clout," Wilum said. "We'll take a short break here. The little ones need it as much as Diggory, I'd wager, and the Hordanu's Enclosure is not that far—"

"Look, there's Kal and the Fletchers, up there, on that rise over there. He's waving, Master Wilum." It was young Garis who had spotted them.

"That's Headstone Edge. Not far," said Wilum. "I think we'd better move on. I'm truly sorry, my dear Diggory." Wilum nodded to the jolly Holdsman. "Don't worry. It's just a short hike to the Stairs of Tarn Cromar, about three middling bowshots by my reckoning. And it's best that we rejoin forces with Kal as soon as possible. I have a gut feeling there's more danger lurking for us in the shadows than we care to think." Wilum shook his head to quell Diggory's questioning look. "As I said, it's just a feeling. I don't rightly know myself. There's some evil brewing nearby, and we can't be too vigilant. I felt it on my last trip up to the Enclosure before the Candle Festival. Whatever it was, I felt its presence, but it kept a distance. We can rest for a bit by Tarn Cromar, although I won't feel safe 'til we've made it to the Seven Springs. We have been granted but a short respite in our flight. The Boar will be in a fury. He'll not be deprived of me and the Talamadh. He will bend his whole will on my capture, so we are none of us safe yet."

Wilum's words moved them with a new sense of urgency. Parents coaxed the last reserves of patience and obedience from their children and set off again. The river course rose out of its ravine, and soon they trudged again along its banks. Their path swung away from the Middle Skell to avoid a fetid peat bog and then veered back towards the stream right at the spot where it rushed headlong from Tarn Cromar down a boulder-strewn spillway.

In the throes of exhaustion, the few Holdsfolk laboured up the embankment that checked the flow of the Skell and emerged onto the grassy shores of a small lake which marked the boundary of the Hordanu's Enclosure. Here at Tarn Cromar, a clear mountain lake, long and narrow, the Middle Skell became the Upper Skell. To the rustle of astonished whisperings, the band waded into the lush alpine meadow, smitten by the beauty and stillness of Tarn Cromar and even more so by Skell Force, tumbling down from a lofty precipice. Fringing the Tarn was a wide walk of paved stone, laid out with intricate patterns—circles and whorls and labyrinthine mazes, woven together with cryptic skill. The grass on the verges of the path and lake lay flattened and still sodden from the floodwaters, now spent. Not far from the curtaining spray of Skell Force stood a huge oak tree, spread with countless branches reaching far over the surface of the water, rippled into cat's-paw by a freshening breeze. Against the background thrum of the cataract, a hush descended on the group, for they were well aware that, except for a succession of Hordanus down through the ages, they were the first since Ardiel's time to set foot in the Enclosure. Even the children sensed they were treading hallowed ground and fell silent.

"Step carefully, there's something amiss," admonished Wilum. "Yes, something quite out of the ordinary, though I can't say if it's for weal or woe, or both."

Wide-eyed and gazing about in bemused wonder, Laloke had let go of her father's hand and skipped ahead of the ragtag band of Holdsfolk, leading two or three other children in her wake down the flagged walk towards the towering Meeting Oak.

"Laloke! Stop, Laloke! Help, Manaton!" Gara's frenzied shriek broke the euphoric calm of the Enclosure. The little girl stood paralysed. A crouching sable wolf had appeared from nowhere and leaped onto a low stone along the sandy margin of the Tarn. Its teeth bared and hackles bristling, the wolf was poised to lunge. Even while the echo of her mother's cry yet resounded over the waters, and before any of the Holdsmen could draw an arrow, there came a sudden sweep of powerful wings. In that instant, the wolf was dashed to the ground, broken by the dagger talons of a great fellhawk, which wheeled up in a banking arc, weighed down by its limp prey.

"Well done, Dhu!" cried Kal, striding towards Wilum. Behind him, half a dozen figures had stepped into the meadow from a winding pathway not fifty paces distant.

"Briacoil, Kal. Aye, but you certainly have a gift of showing up at just the right time, lad!"

"Re'm ena, you saved our little Laloke. How can I ever thank you enough?" Manaton said, while Gara in tears clutched their daughter with joy and relief.

"It was Dhu's doing, not mine." Kal waved off the man's thanks. "He found it quite enjoyable too, I'm sure. Will you look at him." The great dark-plumed bird had settled on an outcrop of rock just clear of the spray of Skell Force to tear undisturbed at his prize.

"I don't understand," broke in Galli. "Isn't the valley supposed to be free of wolves? Since the time of Hedric?"

"Yes, quite so, Galli. Hedric drove them out of the Holding—"

"Many echobards kept them as familiars. Black wolves. Didn't they?" asked Kal.

"Aye, particularly some of the more unsavoury ones, as had haunted this area here." Wilum leaned on his staff. "Wolves in the Enclosure . . ." he muttered to himself, lost for a moment in thought. "But for Dhu—" Wilum broke off, straightened, and smiled at the little girl.

"Briacoil, Master Wilum!"

Wilum turned to see the small group that had arrived with Kal. "Briacoil, Thurfar, Fionna." Wilum greeted the armed Holdsman and his wife, who had drawn near with their three dark-haired daughters and a misshapen boy with a tousled thatch of fox-red hair. A clubfoot made him shamble, while his dangling arms gave him an awkward contorted look. Other children had called him Mommick—"scarecrow" in the dialect of the Holding. His face, however, was an open and unmarred page that revealed a depth of guilelessness. "I must say I'm glad you've managed to meet up with us all safe and sound. For a while there we were worried, seeing as you were headed right into the clutches of that company of Black Scorpions."

"Aye, thanks to Kal here we was saved from that fate," replied Thurfar, nodding towards Kal, who was too busy being embraced by his mother to take notice of anything else. "We'd have been at the Coomb with the rest of you if it hadn't been for Gwyn. We spent well nigh an hour looking for the lad. Found him at last out in the woods behind our barn. Pale as the moon the boy was, a flock of birds around him chirping away. There was squirrels, too, chattering and leaping from tree to tree. Looked like they was all busy telling him something. And there he is making a motion that we was to run away. I never seen the nipper so agitated. We was started up the trail towards the Saddle and we fair near had to drag him up, as if he knew we was headed into danger. I never seen the beat of it. And to cap it all, we was just about come level to the Tarn here, and he starts tugging at Kal, pulling him along, running, making mad with his arms. It must have been the wolf he was trying to let on about. Never been this way with him before. Sure he's always been a dreamy young lad living in a world all his own. I doubt me a little now if the boy be not somewhat more special than we thought he were," said Thurfar, running his fingers through Gwyn's hair and pulling the mute boy to himself.

"You may speak more true than you know, Thurfar," said Wilum. "It seems there's some flaming spark of the prophet's gift in him for all his misshapen speechlessness. We mustn't scorn the gift though it be belied by its wrappings. Every now and again in the history of the Holding the fey mark resurges, like a spluttering flame fanned into a great devouring fire, or a trickle of water swollen by rain into a mighty watercourse. Metan, the tenth Hordanu after Hedric, enjoyed this gift. His writings show it in their wisdom and beauty. So I bless and thank you, Gwyn. You're a token sent to us in our trials, a token that only the wise and the humble can perceive."

At that Gwyn, who wore a blank look of bewilderment, drifted towards Kal with his noggling walk and pulled some marbles from his pocket, which he began to play with on the flat of a rock.

"Aye, the lad's sure keen on Kal. Always has been. His face as good as beams every time Kal comes around," remarked his father, who now turned to look to his wife and daughters. "Can we rest here awhile, Master Wilum? I'm fair moithered and I know Fionna, the girls, and Gwyn are too."

"Just a moment to catch your breath. We've got no way of telling how close on our heels the enemy is. Far better to push on up the Stairs of Tarn Cromar here. With a few stout men we could hold out against an army from the top of the Stairs as long as our food lasts. Go, Thurfar, take your rest, but be ready to leave soon." The old man looked tired and leaned more heavily on his staff, while the Talamadh seemed to bend him down even further under its burden.

Galli had turned to seek out Kal and his family. He found Frysan explaining how the sudden spate had saved them after the tense encounter between Wilum and Enbarr. Kal, in his turn, gave an account of his own perils and adventures, interrupted by the restless questions of his young brother. It was Bren who had let Dhu free from the mew at Mantling Moss where Kal kept him.

Having gorged on the wolf's carcass, the fellhawk alighted on the grass beside his master, casting a fierce eye around him.

"Well done, Dhu. How did you find me up here on this mountain?" Kal spoke to the great bird that stood to shoulder height, stroking its glossy dark plumage. "What's that? You're not saying? Fickle bird. I'm proud of you all the same."

Kal had found Dhu as an unfledged nestling two years ago lodged high on a cliff shelf after his mother had been killed. The fellhawk was a bird rare to the Holding and dread to its folk for its size and nature. Against the better judgement of many of his elders, the young Holdsman nursed the fellhawk to maturity. And yet, Dhu in turn became Kal's constant attendant, so much so that Kal had to leave him locked up in the mew whenever he preferred not to be burdened by him. On the occasions when Kal took him out into the forest, Dhu would rise with easy quickness from tree or rock to take his prey. Kal needed only to nod or motion with his arm ever so slightly for Dhu to know his quarry. Holdsmen never ceased to be amazed that he did not need to restrain the fellhawk with hood or jesses, so docile and understanding was he of his master's subtlest promptings.

For now the great bird remained beside Kal, surveying under its louring brow the gathered remnant of the Holding's populace, scattered about the wet grass, fretfully taking what rest their haste would allow them.

"Attention, all. I know you're tired, but we've got to push on. Do you hear me? Everybody? Attention, Master Wilum's saying it's time we left. We've got to get up them Stairs. This way now. This way, we'll gather at the waterfall." Narasin spoke above the soft drone of conversation and turned to the flagstone walk. "I never thought I'd see the day as I'd be up in these parts of the Holding." He lowered his voice, shaking his head and musing aloud to himself. "No, not in a thousand years."

TWELVE

Unbidden, Kal and Galli took their places beside Wilum. Just a few steps behind them shuffled Gwyn, his marbles restored to a pocket. The rest of the Fletcher family had fallen in with Frysan and Marina towards the middle of the milling group of refugees gathered under the Meeting Oak. The intricately ornamented flagstone footpath led past the oak and ended beside the waterfall in a grotto that had been carved from the granite face of Thyus.

"Come along!" commanded Wilum. He walked along the path up to the grotto, where it appeared to reach an end. When he had gone as far as he could, Wilum turned left and stepped, it seemed, into the thundering spray of Skell Force, disappearing altogether from sight of the others, swallowed up by a spuming wall of water. Kal and Galli, treading close on his heels, also stepped behind the curtaining spray. Gwyn made expressive beckoning gestures to those who followed, urging them to make haste. The rest of the group entered the grotto, within which were set the broad stone stairs that rose behind the waterfall.

Manaton and Gara, with their children, were the first to follow, gaping and fearful, into the gloomy half-light of the Stairs of Tarn Cromar—stone steps that unknown hands in the Age of Echoes had hewn out of the side of this upper flank of Mount Thyus. They were cut on a diagonal across the very face of the mountain, incised into it like a groove. Here, at their base, the waters of the Force shielded the Stairs from view, while casting a damp mist of waters on the fugitives, who could almost reach out and touch the cascading stream. All talk was suspended and a baby, hanging on the back of its mother in a wicker basket, cried, unheard above the deafening roar of the waters. The older children clung to their parents in fear, while Diggory, flanked by Gammer and his daughters, sweated his way up the gradient, his puffing unnoticed, just as, for once, were his wife's good-natured gibes at his expense. Devved carried the lower end of his son's stretcher, while Garis and Artun took turns holding the other end. Behind Devved trudged Relzor with a scowl. Last came Narasin, throwing constant glances back across his shoulder to their rear.

Beyond the screening waterfall, the steps rose higher and became more steep. The Stairs were no longer a dark groove veiled by an oblique curtain of water. In a sunken trench, they lay open now to the sky, and, against the unclouded azure above them, Dhu cut arcs as he soared in lazy circles up the sharp face of Thyus. A wall of rock on either side kept them out of view to anyone who might be looking up from below. In the light Galli had seen faint splotches on the walls and in cracks at his feet. Again, the fading trail of blood, here staining the granite of the Stairs where it had not been washed away by the storm. He shot a puzzled look of concern to Kal and Wilum. The old Hordanu met his eyes and shook his head.

"Not a word," Wilum whispered. "I see it." Then lifting his voice and turning to look over his shoulder, he said, "Keep on, my good people, not much farther now and we may take our rest. Just to the top of the Stairs."

The intricate figures that graced the path alongside Tarn Cromar were resumed and became even more splendid. Every now and then, a small colony of yellow avalanche lilies bloomed in the gaps of the rocks—a welcome break of colour amid the drear stone. At one point, the Stairs doubled back upon themselves and then continued their steep ascent. As they neared the top, the grey of the rock gave way to a fascinating gallery of brightly painted pictures. Mostly they depicted the chase, full of oddly clad figures from long ago hunting deer, elk, and other game animals, some of them strange and unfamiliar.

At long last, a good half a mile from where they had started, high above Tarn Cromar, the Stairs gave onto an alpine meadow, an open stretch of ground boxed in on one side by the sheer wall of Mount Thyus and on the other three sides by a broad parapet of rocks, chest high, broken only by the outflowing headwaters of the Skell. In this lonely spot, the Skell took its rise from the Seven Springs, a small water pool of great depth, banked up by a low-slung half-circle of mortared stone. Out of the pool there issued a long triangular watercourse, similarly enclosed, which broadened out and slipped with deceptive languor over the edge of the meadow, the very crest of Skell Force.

When they had all finally emerged from the Stairs, the tension they had been under ebbed almost palpably, for at long last they had reached a place of relative safety. Before they could stretch themselves out in the meadow on a natural carpet of wildrye and anemones, secure in their aerie near the very roof-eaves of the Holding, Wilum bade the men collect stones in order to construct a breast-high barricade across the opening of the Stairs.

"There we are. That should do," he said as they finished the makeshift fortification. "Now we'll have to establish a rotation of watches. Three men on every watch of four hours. How does that sound, Frysan? What about you, Narasin? Are you happy with this arrangement? Good. All right, then. That's how we'll do it. Now on every watch, two of you need to stay at the barricade. As for the third man, step over here with me and I'll show you something." Wilum moved along the stone parapet a brief distance and came to a stop, gesturing. "Look, here's an opening that can be used as an observation post. It'll give you a good prospect of Tarn Cromar and all the approaches to it, which means you should have plenty of time to spot any sort of movement on the part of the Boar and then raise the alarm."

"Wilum, we'd do well to lay aside anything we have that's made of metal before we take up sentry duty," Frysan said. "The glint of sun on a brooch or a pendant or the hilt of a sword could give us all away. The sort of thing apt to be seen for miles around." He had slipped comfortably back into the role of soldier, though it had been years since he had served.

"Yes, good. The longer we can keep them off, the better our chances of working out some sort of strategy of escape. And it'll take a bit of serious thought, of that you can be sure. Now, let's all take a well-deserved rest before I show you any more of the Hordanu's Enclosure. In the meantime, Frysan—ah, is that ankle still bothering you? Are you all right? You and Artun together would make one sound man—perhaps you can devise a rotation of watches while we're catching our breath and giving our weary bodies a rest."

It was the first time Wilum admitted to being tired. Unslinging the Talamadh from his shoulder and putting aside his staff, he laid himself down in the sun-drenched hollow of a mossy boulder and closed his eyes. Reclining like this, he looked wan and haggard and desperately sad, a tattered manikin living on the shadowy margins of Arvon's long-fled glory. His hair and long white beard had become matted and unkempt. The gleaming Talamadh looked incongruous propped up against the bedraggled folds of his cloak. On the boulder above him, Dhu had perched. The fellhawk now stretched wide his pinions, flapped twice, folded his wings again, and resumed his vigilant contemplation of the alpine sanctuary.

While Wilum and the others rested, Galli and Kal explored the area of the Seven Springs—a small water-soaked meadow decked with a profusion of wildflowers. It was said that, before the springs had been dammed up with their stonewall rampart, all seven of them could be seen bubbling up from hidden pools in the mountain.

"Look here, Father. Look at these tracks. I've never seen anything like them, have you?" called Kal, standing with Galli beside the Well of the Seven Springs. Frysan walked over to investigate, frowned, and called for Wilum, rousing him to join them as well.

Wilum stared at the imprints in the clay. Some of the other men now began to move within earshot.

"Look," called Galli, who was crouched down on all fours. He had followed the clues like a bloodhound through the moist meadow, brushing aside thick cushions of moss campion and yellow clusters of fringe-leaf cinquefoil to reveal a trail. "The tracks lead to our lookout post here. It seems the creature has been keeping watch as well."

"What do you mean, 'keeping watch,' Galli?" Diggory said, walking to where his nephew knelt in the crushed grass. "It was probably just some brute beast cropping that nice patch of grass, not knowing or caring if the whole of Arvon was being slaughtered."

"Look at the tracks. It was no browsing mountain goat or errant bear, Uncle Digg. The way they're laid out—something two-legged. They look most like a man's bare footprint."

"What are you talking, Galli?" Narasin said, drawing toward Galli as well. "Men? Up here in the Enclosure? Could it be them Scorpions are up here already?"

"No, Nar, unshod, barefoot. And not a man's, like a man's. Look, come here by the Well." Galli rose and walked to where a group of men had gathered around Kal, Frysan, and Wilum. He stooped beside a clear impression in the clay. "You see." He traced the print with a finger. "It looks like a man's footprint—heel, ball, toes—but it's squat, and far too wide. And these here . . ." he said, pointing to the top of the impression, where tapering marks slightly scored the clay, "claws, or I'm a poor excuse for a tracker. And these are all fresh—these here and the ones by the lookout. All made since the rain." He rose again. An anxious murmur passed through the gathering of men. Among them, even the most experienced hunters and woodsmen could offer no opinion.

"Then what could this be, Wilum? What creature could it be, haunting the Hordanu's Enclosure? Could it be— Do you think?" asked Frysan.

Wilum looked at the men around him, his eyes moving from face to face. He spoke slowly, softly.

"'Haunt' . . . Funny you should use that word. I have a notion, as do you, I think. A creature that's been spoken of only in tales, a way to frighten children when they're naughty. Yet real enough, I daresay, real enough once . . . And now again."

"Bah, gathgour!" It was Devved, feet planted, arms crossed over his broad chest, shaking his head in disbelief. "Gathgour! Don't be talking nonsense, Master Wilum, not now, not here, not at a time like this." His jaw flexed. "Gathgour! Why, that's the stuff of fairy tale and child's play. For scared little boys in the moonlit woods." Devved glowered. "Gathgour!" he muttered again. His growing fear, mirrored in the eyes of his fellow Holdsmen, was masked by a very thin veneer of anger.

Wilum allowed the silence to settle a moment before he fixed the great man with a look both compassionate and authoritative. "Not child's play, Devved. Nor fairy tale, but the stuff of legend. And in legend there is often more truth than we would care to, or are able to, admit. The gathgour is as real as the danger we find ourselves in today. Unthinkable, unexpected, almost unbelievable, but real nonetheless."

There was a strength in Wilum, boiling up from his depths.

Kal, standing close by him, could feel it radiating from him like a warmth. It moved like a breath of breeze, sustaining his words, a gentle spirit of protector, defender, provider, teacher, leader and prophet—gentle, yet of immense power. It resonated in Kal's heart, leaving him in profound awe.

Wilum continued, leaning less heavily on his staff. "Aye, the gathgour is real. As is the night drake which Kal saw and whose baying howls you all, no doubt, heard last night. Real, as was the wolf by the Tarn. Real, as are the Black Scorpions that have desecrated and destroyed Wuldor's Howe. The balance has tipped, as the last strains of the Great Harmony fade. As order crumbles, misrule ensues, and the powers of chaos grow in strength. As day gives way to night, the creatures and events of darkness must increase. You will see stranger and more fearsome than this yet. But do not be afraid. The Talamadh survives, as does the Hordanu." He shifted his weight, moving, almost imperceptibly, towards Kal. "The Lay of Ardiel still reverberates in Ahn Norvys. And while it does, there is hope and power, and strength to go on. Do not be afraid. No, open your hearts to this hope and do not be afraid."

Wilum fell silent in the strange stillness that had descended on the small group of men standing in the near twilight. He traced the outline of the gross track with the end of his staff. He spoke again. "For the time being, I think it best if we don't speak of this in the presence of the children. They are quite frightened enough." Wilum looked up. "Save those on watch, we will gather and stay close to each other. See that no one strays."

The sun had sunk further behind Thyus, casting long cold shadows onto the lonely rim of the Radolan Mountains. The wind, too, had freshened into a chilling breeze and sent ripples scudding across the surface of the Well of the Seven Springs.

"Don't we have to start thinking about where we'll stay the night, Master Wilum?" queried Galli, wet from stalking through the soggy grass.

"Yes, indeed. Frysan, do you have your schedule of night watches settled?"

"Aye, Diggory and Galli and I, we'll take the first watch. Narasin, you and your sons will take the second. Athmas, Manaton, and Thurfar the third. Kal will stay with you, Wilum, to keep an eye out for anything suspicious." Frysan made a glancing gesture towards Relzor, who skulked close by the wall of the pool. "Devved, your boy will need you when he wakes."

"Very good," Wilum affirmed. "You three be as vigilant as possible. Keep your swords at the ready. The gathgour was said to be a sore powerful and crafty creature, and no lover of men. We'll send along the three men of the next watch with a fourth to show you the way back to the cave where we'll be spending the night. Don't go making any fire. There will be quite enough of the moon's light for you to see by, I expect."

"What if we spot something during the first watch? How would we know where the rest of you are?"

"Excellent point, Frysan. I'll take Galli with me now and send him back to you here for the first watch immediately, as soon as we reach the Cave of the Hourglass, which is about half a league from here farther up Mount Thyus a ways. You'd be hard put to find it if you didn't already know where it was."

"My hunting horn," Thurfar said, proffering Frysan a curled brass horn bound in leather hanging on a strap. "I'll leave it with you here. That way, you can blow a summons, if need be."

"Excellent," said Wilum. "But make sure you use it only in case of dire emergency, Frysan. Let it stay here with whoever is on guard."

"Good. Let the alarm signal be two short bursts, followed by one long winding. Understood?" Frysan said. The men all nodded.

"So be it," Wilum agreed.

In the gathering shadows of the late afternoon, after a last word from Gammer to her husband, the Holdsfolk took their leave of Frysan and Diggory. Passing the Well of the Seven Springs, they followed a path through the verdant highland, heading higher up the mountain. Soon the path veered off to the left into the rocks and boulders strewn everywhere along the edge of the open meadow. Here their course began to ascend and meander, threading its way back and forth across the rising ramparts of the mountain. In places, they were able to look down and see the two men on sentry duty on the edge of the grassy area. They entered a long gloomy gallery of rocks that hid them from sight. At a turn in the path, daylight spilled into the passageway. Wilum motioned for them to stop. Everyone halted, while he examined a large breach that opened full to the outside. Wilum sidled through the gap, followed by Kal, who was in turn followed by Gwyn and Galli.

"Hold it, Kal," he said, glancing as well towards Gwyn and Galli. "Everyone else too, get back for a moment while I have a closer look. Let me see what we're apt to face here. Better to do it now, while we've still got some light, and then we'll push on to the Cave of the Hourglass."

"It looks like these two big rocks were shunted aside to make the opening," Kal said, examining one of two large slabs.

"Aye, they were prised apart long ago, long before Hedric found this spot."

"Is this it then? Is this the secret pass?"

"Hush now, Kal. Let me have a look and gain some notion of the lie of the land. Believe it or not, in all the years I've been frequenting the Enclosure, I've never had cause to take much more than a brief peek at this spot before now," explained Wilum, creeping forward to explore the situation.

"May I see too?"

"Aye, come, but keep the others back." Wilum let Kal follow along behind him, as he ventured out onto a broad platform of granite set diagonally into a jagged bay of the mountain, its forward edge ending in a sheer drop to the crevasses below. Above them, the mountain reared itself in a series of spiking terraces to its snow-crested top. At first glance, there appeared to be nowhere to go from this place but up, a daunting, if not impossible, task even for a hardy climber. Wilum shuffled on to the far end of the ledge, where it angled towards the right, seeming to end there at an impassable pier of rock. He turned his body to the mountain and, hugging the rock face, all at once disappeared from sight. Curious, Kal pressed forward towards the same spot, while some of the others looked on, among them Relzor, crowding Galli and Gwyn at the opening to the ledge.

"So that's how he did it," Kal mumbled to himself, moving closer and seeing the narrow slab of rock that Wilum had used as a bridge to round the flank of the mountain. The windblown folds of Wilum's cloak billowed out from around the corner.

"Hold it, Kal! I'm coming back," Wilum called, working his way back across the gap.

"What did you find? What's there on the other side?"

"Windward, Kal, windward," Wilum said in a low voice beyond the hearing of the rest. "Go on, have a look yourself. But be careful."

Kal inched across the rocky bridge, trying not to look down and trying not think that a slip of the foot would mean a headlong fall to certain death on the rocks far below. Once he turned the corner, the flank of the mountain broadened. Kal stood at the head of a narrow rift etched into the westward side of Thyus. It fell precipitously, but not far, as it quickly lost a great deal of its steepness, sloping gradually to a trough of gently rounded foothills, nestled between the towering bulk of the neighbouring mountains.

Within the vista afforded him by the rift, there lay the coastal plain, a dim brown band. The horizon, suffused with the rosy glow of the sun as it dipped gently into the Cerulean Ocean, made him feel like he was standing on the roof of the world. He beheld a sight unlike any he had experienced in the Holding on the leeward side of the Radolan Mountains, where there was always the answering view of other alpine peaks to block his field of vision, limiting it to the confines of his own native clanholding. And now he and the Holdsfolk who remained were being thrust out into the wider world, provided, of course, they could escape the cordon of mountains, which served no longer as a protective palisade, but a prison.

In that moment, overlooking the greater world, his heart quickened, for it dawned on him that here lay their avenue of escape. Here, stretching out before him, was the way out of their prison. In the air below him, above the falling slopes of the alpine valley, Dhu wheeled, his feathers burnished in the fading rays of the setting sun.

Kal turned from the prospect to rejoin Wilum. He had failed to notice it before, but now he clearly saw that a shelf of unbroken ground lay under the narrow ledge like a safety net. It would make passage easier for the tired and burdened clanfolk—especially the children.

"Our way out of the clutches of the Boar, Wilum. Our way down! And then we'll have all the length and breadth of Arvon in which to hide ourselves from him."

"Keep your voice low, Kal. It does seem so, yet I fear we must not be overly confident of anything."

"What do you mean? The Boar has probably only just begun to suspect that we're even up here. And should he decide to do something about it, we could hold him off—"

"If we didn't have other enemies within our gates."

"Are you talking— Do you think Relz—".

"Kal! Above you!" Galli screamed. Beside him, Gwyn, terror-stricken, was flailing his arms, pointing at something above their heads. Kal's eyes shot up in time to see a huge stone hurtling down on them.

"Master Wilum!" Kal threw himself at the old man, pushing him into the dubious shelter of a long niche etched by time from the rock wall. There was only the hint of an overhang to shield them from the ponderous weight of granite that came crashing down with a shudder. Crouched on his knees, with one hand clutching his longbow and the other shielding his head, Kal felt the debris whizzing past himself and Wilum, who lay opposite him head to head. The ground beneath them shook from the force of the concussion, and it seemed a whole section of the mountain would give way and tumble with them into the chasm below. When the avalanche of stone had exhausted itself and passed, cascading down the side of Thyus to the echo of crashing rocks, it grew still. The dust settling, Kal ventured to crane his head out from his sheltering crevice, now so tilted and narrow that he felt a mere shift of his body would dislodge him. The place where they had stood just moments earlier was but vacant air. The whole area around them had yielded before the dreadful momentum of the rockfall, leaving Wilum and Kal stranded on the side of the mountain.

Kal, frightened and pale, turned to see the crumpled form of the old man. "Are you all right, Master Wilum?" he asked in a hoarse whisper. The form beneath the dishevelled cloak stirred, and Wilum shifted, lifting his head to look at the young Hordanu.

"I'm fine, lad, except for a little gash on my hand." He smiled thinly and brought his hand up for Kal to see. "It's nothing, really. It seems like I've been left with a bit more elbow room than you."

"Not much more. Talk about not having room enough to roll over." Kal made a light attempt at keeping up his courage.

"Are you two all right?" Manaton called from the opening.

"Aye . . . aye . . . seems we are," Kal said, looking across to the men gathered at the opening. A small shower of rock chips and dust spilled from the edge as Kal moved his foot.

"Careful there, Kal. Watch it! You don't have even an inch of firm ground left. How are we going to get you back? Rope—we need rope. Did any of you men bring rope?" There was a stir among the men who had clustered themselves at the lip of the steep drop that yawned open at their feet. Drifting down to them from somewhere above came the long screech of a fellhawk on the hunt.

A good fifteen paces of gaping chasm separated Wilum and Kal from their comrades. The sun had set even farther on the horizon, and the air had become more damp and chill. Athmas had handed Manaton a hempen rope with a grapnel tied to it. Manaton unfastened the grapnel, fixing a rock instead to the end of the rope. Kal lay nearer to Manaton than did Wilum. Still it took more than half a dozen throws for Kal, his hand outstretched, to catch the rock weight and with it the rope.

Leaving his son's stretcher aside, Devved prepared to bear the brunt of the job of pulling Wilum and Kal one by one to safety. Kal tried to lean forward into the slight rift in the rocks as much as possible and loop the rope around the old man in a sort of makeshift shoulder harness, making sure to attach the Talamadh securely.

"You're all set, Wilum. Just watch yourself, it's a long piece over. There's some jagged edges there under the opening. You may hit them hard. Throw out your arms and legs to catch yourself. The men will pull you up. All right, are you ready?"

"Aye, Kal, as ready as not," Wilum said and, whispering a prayer, cast himself into the air. Devved had laid his body down prone at the edge of the precipice, his muscular arms extended out over the deep canyon spread out beneath him. It was probably Wilum's tunic that helped to buffer him against a nasty gash on the leg as he hit the rock face. The blacksmith's legs and trunk were held pinned down by Galli and two others, while the rest anchored the rope in the passageway behind the big man. He wasted no time, but lifted Wilum straight up, keeping the rope clear of the sharp edges.

With Wilum back on solid ground, the rope was untied, and Manaton once again prepared to cast it across to Kal. Dhu's screams were closer, lower. Kal glanced up and saw his bird hovering off the rock face. Something had upset him. Kal tried to peer out farther. For one horrific moment he seemed to lose his balance.

On the second cast, Kal was able to grab the rope. He fashioned his own harness with its coils, careful of the bow and quiver he wore around his shoulder. When Devved lay in position once more, he made ready to leave the security of the ledge, fighting fear and nausea. Like an unfledged eaglet, he looked out uncertainly from his aerie and hesitated.

"You can do it, Kal. Just don't look down and you'll be fine." Galli encouraged him.

"All right, get ready for me. Here I go."

Kal braced himself to meet the impact of the angular granite on his shins. No sooner had he cast off, than he heard a coughing bark that sent wild spasms of panic through him. Kal screamed out in pain, as his right knee caught a sharp edge, and a rock the size of his head sailed past him.

"Kal!" Manaton yelled, catching sight of the strange creature poised to throw yet another stone. For a moment Manaton stared aghast, as another one of them appeared and hoisted a boulder. The two creatures were each no taller than a man, but huge, their thick, long-limbed bodies covered with a glistening grey coat. Their faces were broad and sharp-set, their large eyes slit-pupilled, their ears erect and tufted. They lifted their heads, fanged maws open, and sent forth guttural cries, part scream and part bark. The Holdsmen stood paralysed, as Kal dangled below the opening, his pleas for help resounding over the chasm. Then Manaton seized his bow, while Devved, in danger himself from being struck, strained to lift Kal. Screaming, Dhu swooped down on the closer of the gathgours, which dropped its rock and cowered before the fury of the fellhawk. Manaton found he could not draw a good line on the two monsters past the frenzied bird.

"No, Manaton. That won't do any good here," insisted Wilum, lifting the Talamadh from his shoulder. At once, with supple fingers, he began to pluck at its strings, while his lips burst into the rhythmic cadence of verse.

"Look, Master Wilum. They can't abide the sound. They're climbing away. Maybe I can prick them a bit from here, hurry them along," Manaton said, even while letting fly a shaft that struck stone, missing the trailing beast, as it bobbed and wove in its frenzied retreat. Dhu pursued the fleeing creatures. "Will you look at them make their way on that mountain! Re'm ena! This

is a sight I'd never thought to see. Incredible. In all my days!"
Manaton lost his chance to loose a second shot.

With muscles fashioned by years at the forge, Devved pulled
Kal up as if he were no more than a horseshoe being drawn from
the tempering fire.

"There we are. Move away. Let's get farther in," urged Manaton.

"Are you all right, Kal?" Galli laid his hand on his friend's
shoulder.

"What happened there? I couldn't see from where I was."
Marina pressed forward, joining her son. "What's that? Your leg
is all blood-soaked."

"It's all right, Mother. I'll be fine. It's nothing, just a bit of
blood, a scrape that's all."

"Don't worry, Marina. We'll look to him as soon as we get to
the Cave, and that's not far from here," Wilum said against the
rising sound of crying children. Wilum seemed undisturbed by
the encounter with the gathgours, while the rest of them slunk
through the narrow passage cowed and daunted, as if expecting
the creatures to leap down from the rocks and come bounding
into the passageway after them. Sensing their anxiety, Wilum took
the Talamadh in hand and began to strum it softly, chanting a
tune, this time from "The Lay of Gildasir."

"No need to be afraid. Just follow me," he said. "The gathgour
has no power to harm us so long as I'm singing,

> 'Wuldor, Wuldor plies his might,
> Lets the shadows with the light;
> Hope and fear and peace and strife,
> Twines he in the thread of life.
>
> Fate and fortune, fibres wound,
> From his distaff, by him bound;
> In the twist, in wonder spun,
> Coil our days unto their sum,
> From the infant's dawning breath,
> To its agèd twilight death.
>
> All life's joy and all life's grief,
> All are caught, without relief.

Pleasure's passions turn to pain,
Agony turns calm again—

In his spindle's twirling strand,
From his fingers, from his hand.
Steady spins he, steady still,
All is suffered by his will;
Steady spins he, twists he, twines,
Knowing thoughts and hearts and minds.

How he heeds our turning years,
Holds the burden of our tears,
Heaps man's ages, one on one,
Heals his body when he's done.

So, of hope left unbereft,
We, fine cords in hands so deft;
Patterned ends our lives bedight,
Though black shadows check the light,
'Til the Spinner's spinnings cease
And naught is left of Woe, save Peace.'"

THIRTEEN

Gwyn was the first to reach the Cave of the Hourglass, light-footed despite his limp, bobbing up and down as he kept time with the cadence of the verse. The others followed, equally charmed by the song's refrain, which Wilum had taken up again and again. Before long, many of them had begun to chant the words in unison with him.

They soon arrived at the broad mouth of the Cave, a hollow shell surrounded by the enormous bulk of the mountainside. With strong counsel to make haste, stay on the path, keep bow in hand, and to garner all vigilance of ear and eye lest the gathgour should choose to make more mischief, Wilum dispatched Galli back to the Holdsmen on guard at the Stairs. With the Hordanu's blessing, Galli took his leave.

The assembled Holdsfolk stood before the Cave, all eyes drawn to a squared column of rock that rose the height of five men and screened the entrance. Sculpted on it, separated by the stylized shapes of various heraldic animals, were a series of parallel friezes spread in bands across its face from its base to just below its helm-shaped top. Many of them showed scenes from the life of Ardiel, beginning with his early days in the remote reaches of the Calathros Peninsula and continuing on up the column with the memorable events in his struggle to overcome Tardroch.

Kal stepped toward the column and ran his fingers over the wind-polished stone relief. Here was Ardiel, the ploughboy, and his team. And here the white hind that led Ardiel deep into the Woods of Whorralsheaf, its forest of silver birch the abode of

Whÿlas, the mysterious hermit from beyond the seas who became Ardiel's tutor, here with harp in hand instructing the young king to be. As for the scenes sculpted higher on the pillar, Kal found them hard to discern.

Over the lintel of the door of the Cave, Kal examined the sculpted figure of a splendid bird, its tail spread out in a wide fan. Next to the bird were depicted several creatures that appeared to be seals riding the crests of billowing ocean waves opposite a heavily wooded island. The island was grazed by two tiny sheep, and emerging from the island, as if plunged into it, was the relief of a broadsword. Looking more closely, he made out two parallel lines of small runic characters etched into the blade. Clearly, this sculpted piece was more ancient than those on the stone column, perhaps dating back to the Age of Echoes. It even had the appearance of having been executed by a different hand.

Chiselled into the lintel as an epigraph to this strange seascape were carved verses in Old Arvonian which Kal read to himself under his breath.

> O Son of Prophecy, know surely that thy quest
> Shall not be satisfied nor brought to end
> When to the newfound place of Vali's final rest
> Thyself shall come and wearily attend.
> Ere gainest thou the covert of the Lyrebird,
> Ere e'en thy toil a mote of easement yields,
> Great woes by thine own kingly heart shall be endured,
> Amidst the time-lost realms, far from the fields
> Of 'pressed and joyless Arvon.

Kal stood fascinated by the puzzling beauty of the verse, struck at once by its gravity and its tenderness, its sense of the tears and restless striving that lay hidden in all man's mortal doings. The cleanly cut lines, moreover, the work of a master in stone, were inscribed so deep and sure that they seemed to set at naught the weathering winds and rain of countless centuries, as fresh and as immediate as the day the words were first framed.

Wilum placed a hand on Kal's shoulder, then left him staring at the stone and led the others into the Cave, where he found Gwyn gazing at the vivid murals which covered the circular wall in a riot of colour. It was plain to see why the Cave bore the name it did, for it was round and like an inverted bowl, with a large hole at its apex. The hole gave onto another chamber above. It too had an opening, through which they could just make out the purpling skies of the waning day. The fringe of the lower hole was darkly smudged, black from the smoke of many fires that had been lit in the very centre of the chamber, where a tripod for cooking hung suspended over a simple hearth of banked stones.

Wilum admonished the Holdsfolk not to venture beyond the main body of the Cave, its compass including the large chamber and two side chambers. To the huddled group, he pointed out that from the central chamber, as from the hub of a wheel, there branched out a labyrinthine maze of passageways that he himself had never explored. Nor had any other Hordanu down through the ages, since, from the beginning, it had been forbidden for even the High Bard to step past the main part of the Cave. The tangled web of passageways remained a veiled mystery linking the Cave of the Hourglass in some indefinable way with the subterranean roots of Mount Thyus.

Within the confines of the Cave of the Hourglass, they would remain quite safe, he assured them, leading them first to one and then to the other of the side chambers. In these, he had stored the peat he needed for his fires and other provisions for his sojourns in the Enclosure. Narasin and Manaton nodded to one another approvingly, for it was obvious that the old Hordanu, thinking ahead to the approaching feebleness of his declining years, had built up a stock of additional fuel and food. He told the men that in recent years, every time he came to the Cave, he would bring a little bit more than what he needed for his stay, building up a wealthy store of these necessities. One of the sidechambers enjoyed a constant stream of ice-cold mountain water that trickled down the wall into a little pool from which it could be scooped fresh and clear.

Thurfar had pulled out his tinder box and was fanning the sparks he had struck into curling tongues of flame. The women, meanwhile, having found Wilum's store of cured venison and his vegetables, were busy preparing a big cauldron of stew to hang from the tripod. Already, the aroma of herbs began to fill the Cave. Devved's son Chandaris was laid down on his stretcher near the bright warmth of the fire, while Wilum himself rummaged through his chest of simples.

"Ah, there we are, there's my groundsel and mouse-ear. And here's my whortleberry syrup. Let me see now, what else do I have here?" Wilum muttered to himself.

"Begging your pardon, Master Wilum, sir." Artun interrupted him. "But Garis and I have found more tracks. Right here in the Cave, on one of the dusty reed mats—"

"They're fresh ones too, with other tracks, more like a man's bare feet almost, but small and narrow. And there's blood," added Garis. Fear coloured the young man's voice.

"Here, put these over the lintel of the door and we'll be protected from them." Wilum handed Artun two sprays of dried rowan, the shrivelled berries still on the bough. "Then go and erase the tracks. We mustn't alarm anyone more than needs be."

"Yes, Master Wilum." The two departed, whispering to each other.

Wilum fell to pondering the strange trail of blood that had dogged them from the Pool of Retribution and through Owlpen Castle and Raven's Crag Island, even to here in the Cave. He thought about Frysan and his sentry detail. He shivered. A nagging sense of compunction crept over him. Now, after the vicious attack of the gathgours on himself and Kal, he realized with a start how bold and malevolent the creatures were. And there was no telling how many might be about. And Galli, he had sent Galli back with no more protection than a few idle words of caution! Oh, but he was tired . . . tired, sore pressed and growing careless—

"Wilum? Who's the Son of Prophecy?" Kal's voice nearby broke above the muted drone of voices echoing in the chamber and pulled Wilum, his brow furrowed, out of his thoughts.

"Wh-what? How's that, Kalaquinn? You startled me."

"The 'Son of Prophecy'? What does it mean?"

"Ah, you've read the verses on the lintel, I see. Good, good. I'm glad all those lessons in the Old Tongue have stood you in good stead."

"Who wrote those lines and cut all those other friezes on the big standing stone? Was it two different people?"

"I see I must commend you on your powers of observation too, Kal. It was Hedric who carved the stone pillar. He painted the murals here in the Cave as well. But nobody knows who sculpted the lintel. There's a legend, though, that says Whÿlas the Hermit, after he had sent Ardiel off to engage in his struggle against Tardroch, made his way to these parts and lived in this cave. Perhaps it was he who did it."

"And he had a knowledge of runes?"

"They say that he did, that he had been an echobard king from a far country beyond the sea before he became a hermit deep in the Woods of Whorralsheaf."

"Then, why didn't he share his knowledge of the runes?"

"I don't rightly know. Perhaps there's a reason for our ignorance of runes that will become clear one day. I must confess, though, that part of me rather hopes not. Where would the mystery be? Runes would not be runes somehow if shorn of their mystery. I'm of two minds about them, it has to be said."

Wilum returned to searching through his chest of herbs.

"Why did the gathgours make the attempt on us out on the ledge? A place outside the Enclosure really. There were better spots where they might have ambushed us. In the middle of some of those cramped twists and turns on the way up," Kal said.

"Because the ledge is, in truth, outside the Enclosure. Before that, while on the path to the Cave, we were still on safe ground. The creatures held back from their assault because an air of sacred inviolability still clings to the Enclosure itself. No doubt, they were loath to desecrate it with violence."

"But why were you as Hordanu not as inviolable as the ground of the Enclosure?" Kal queried once more.

Wilum paused again in his work and thought for a moment before he answered. "Because many things and places," he said at length, "though mutable, keep their identity more in time and space, whereas man is vested with a will, which, like a reed, may bend and even break with the winds of change. A will, vulnerable, caught in the shifting shroud of mortal clay, as fleeting as a morning dew on midsummer's day. A heart may despair." Wilum's mind wandered to the orrthon's Great Doxology, those piercing lines that Ardiel recited at the very climax of his "Lay of the Velinthian Bridge." His voice grew solemn as he continued, citing the age-old invocation:

"Thou, Wuldor, in the beginning hast laid the foundations of Ahn Norvys unto all its furthest marks. All within the compass of the rising and setting of the sun thou hast laid and even beyond these boundaries all is of thy founding might. When the sum of the ages shall be filled and century upon century shall lie in the procession of the years, these mighty works of thine shall march darkling into night, but thou shalt endure. All these shall wax old, like a garment, and, as a vesture, shalt thou change them, and they shall unto harmony be restored for the span of a Great Year, until chaos doth rise afresh from gloom-darkened fields. Though these works of thine wax old, thou art ever the same, and thy years shall not fail, from generation unto generation, though they be as countless as the leaves of spring."

Sighing, Wilum fell silent in thought again.

"How many years, do you think, make up the Great Year?" Kal broke the spell of Wilum's brooding reverie. The old Hordanu looked at him.

"Many Hordanus, and bards without number, have wondered how many years are destined to make up the Great Year—the length of an Age. Nobody knows." Wilum shrugged. "There have been all sorts of ingenious suggestions put forward by the learned and the humble alike, especially in recent years when the Great Harmony has seemed on almost every front to be suffering such tragic diminution. More than thirty centuries have passed since Ardiel sang his harmonizing lay. Are we now, at long last, approaching the endterm of the Great Year? I cannot tell you. The one thing I can say is that, in our day, truly, the darkness seems pervasive."

Kal frowned in puzzlement at these larger questions. Soon, however, his thoughts turned to his father and the other men on guard duty.

"If the gathgour treads wary on the sacred ground of the Enclosure, not daring to offer injury, why do we need worry that the Boar will ascend the Stairs to the Seven Springs and commit violence there?" he asked.

"Because Ferabek enjoys some deeper and more elemental power than the gathgour, some power that has risen anew in the sullen autumntide of Ardiel's Great Harmony. Witness the Boar's harrowing of the Great Glence and the extinction of the Sacred Fire.

"Even so, as outnumbered as we are, we must keep guard at the Stairs. It is the only way that we can maintain our food supply, once the provisions I have laid by have run out. There is a small peat bog, too, close to the Well of the Seven Springs, where we can cut our fuel."

"What about the long run? What can we do to escape this trap?"

Wilum sighed again. His voice grew low and doleful.

"Alas, I don't know, Kal. The pass to the other side of the Radolan Mountains is now destroyed and closed to us. The plans I laid so hopefully with you in the boat on Deepmere have gone awry, foiled almost at the outset." Wilum fell to staring absently at the flickering shadows on the wall, his words a low distracted mumble. "And what about Aelward? Where is he? What news does the man bear? But alas, no message has come from him yet. My pigeon cote is empty."

With a sudden start, old Cloudbeard returned his gaze to Kal, his attention restored.

"But what are we doing chattering away here? There'll be time for talk like this later. First, I must prepare some medicine for Chandaris, and for you and your knee. Here, let me see how bad it is." Wilum gestured for Kal to expose his wound. "Oh, it's hardly more than a scratch. If only all our hurts were so easily cured. He'll be none the worse for wear, will he, Gwyn?" The mute boy had trailed in behind Kal as silent as a cat. "You like those murals, don't you, lad? It's almost as if you were there, in the thronging ranks of battle, fighting at the Velinthian Bridge with Ardiel and Thrysvar, or in the Marshes of Atramar, with the Seven Champions of Ruah, witnessing a muster of the troops."

Gwyn smiled broadly.

"Aye, Gwyn has a quick imagination," Kal said. "For all that he can't speak, his eyes and ears drink everything in." He put an affectionate hand on Gwyn's shoulder, as Wilum passed by them into the main chamber, his hands full of herbal salves and preparations.

Kal decided to follow Gwyn's lead, feasting on the noble scenes that animated the walls with figures that were portrayed almost life-size. The murals were unlike any he had ever seen. Under the gathering cloak of evening, very little natural light came from the hole above. Besides the peat fire in the centre, the men had lit pine-pitch torches secured in brackets along the walls. A phantasmal play of light and tremulous shadows was cast on the murals. Kal stared at the images of Ardiel, stopping for a while in front of the scene showing the ancient king rapt in ecstasy while reciting "The Lay of the Velinthian Bridge" atop the Mountain of the Quivering

Cromlech in the highland Keverang of Orm. There was no mistaking Ardiel's regal face and carriage, even in the scenes from his early hidden life as a ploughboy in the remote Keverang of Tanobar. Ardiel's long flaxen hair fell down over his shoulders, a cascade of gold to match the sunlit gold of the Talamadh, which he played with head uplifted, staring into the eye of heaven. He wore a tunic of deep blue, emblazoned with his heraldic device of a white stag rampant. Such nobility, such splendour! To think that all his majesty and power had come to this—a broken, ragged clutch of Holdsfolk, huddled in a mountain cave.

"Come, Kal! Enough woolgathering. We have your knee to attend to, now that Chandaris is taken care of. Look, already the boy's on the mend. You'll make sure, won't you, Devved, that he's given a posset of this whortleberry syrup? There's a good man. Speaking of which, I have to thank you again for saving my weary old life."

"'Twas nothing, Master Wilum. You've repaid any small favour I've done you a hundredfold in bringing back my Chandaris from the shores of death," said Devved, his eyes glistening, as he beheld his son gaining awareness and stirring from unconsciousness. Wilum looked from father to son, then to father again, and, bowing his head, took his leave of the two.

"Come, Kal, follow me. We'll fix you up back at my infirmary, makeshift as it is."

Gwyn looked on while Wilum cleaned Kal's wound, ground hound's-tongue leaves with a small mortar and pestle, and applied a poultice to his knee.

"Ah! That stings!" yelped Kal to Gwyn's amusement.

"Give it a moment, and you'll feel it soothing your wound. Here, let me bind it up."

Wilum had just put everything away, when Marya came in. She glanced at Kal.

"Briacoil, Marya," he said, catching her eye. She blushed.

"Master Wilum, I'm sorry to interrupt, but I wanted to tell you that the food is ready."

"Thank you, Marya. It smells delicious," Wilum said.

She cast another glance at Kal with the hint of a smile and left the chamber.

"She's a lovely girl, Kal." The old man winked, as Kal reddened. "Come along, Gwyn, we'll put some meat on that thin frame of yours." Wilum rose and followed Marya into the main chamber.

The fragrance from the large cauldron filled the cavern. The others had already begun ladling out the stew, eating it with dumplings.

"You keep a well-stocked larder, Master Wilum," greeted Narasin with that air of contentment consequent to enjoying food and warmth after a period of cold and hunger.

"Not for much longer, not with a runaway group like this to feed, and all of them so hungry they could eat a horse behind the saddle!" Wilum said, as one of the women handed him a steaming bowl.

Kal joined his mother and his brother. Worry creased his mother's brow. Gwyn had gravitated to his own family. The children had been fed and most were well on the way to falling asleep. Somewhere on the firelight's fringe an infant suckled, grunting contentedly to itself, its mother humming a soft lullaby. Presently, the men, their stomachs full and pipes lit, drifted towards Wilum, eager to make plans and form strategies. Kal finished his meal and tried, in spite of his own misgivings, to reassure his mother. Then he and Brendith sought out Wilum as well.

"Master Wilum, is there any way for us to reach the other side of the mountains?" queried Thurfar Fletcher, glancing at his son, who had resumed his study of the murals surrounding them.

"You know as well as I do that the Radolan Mountains are impassable, particularly to a group with children and oldlings. That ledge, where Kal and I had our little adventure, was the only other way that I know of out of this valley except for the Wyrdlaugh Pass. No, Thurfar, there's now only one way in and one way out of the Holding. We'd have to be as stealthy as shadows to slip down from the Enclosure and get as far as just Wrenhaven, let alone to the Pass itself. And that will be held by the Boar's fiercest troops."

"Where does that leave us, then?" growled Narasin, removing the pipe from his mouth and knocking its ashes onto the ground with the heel of a callused hand. "Holed up here like cornered animals, 'til our food runs out, or 'til the Boar pokes his snout in the Enclosure? And him with the resources of a whole empire behind him."

"Resources, my dear Narasin, that run beyond abundance of

men and arms and that would curdle your blood to learn of. The rumour is, as you may know, that he has unlocked certain powers that have lain dormant since the Age of Echoes and before. The gathgours, too, we don't know when they might get bold enough to attack us here in the Enclosure itself. They haven't lacked the opportunity, that's for certain. Which is why all those on sentry duty must wear a spray of rowan around their necks. My heart misgives me about Frysan and Diggory and Galli. I hadn't realized what strength the gathgour possesses, and what a threat it may be. And then there's the night drake on top of that . . ." Wilum's expression grew dark and brooding. "Kalaquinn," he said in a tone of resolve, "I want you to leave immediately and take rowan branch talismans to them. If your knee is healed enough?"

"I'm fine, Wilum. You said it yourself. Hardly more than a scratch. I'll go."

"Then get moving quickly now. And stay with them, 'til the next men arrive. That'll be two hours from now. Don't take a torch. The light of the rising moon should be enough for you to see by. We'll have further council later, when your father arrives. I have to take some time to think. Perhaps there's some way over these mountains . . . But with the children? No . . . Yet there are many nooks and crannies here in the Enclosure that remain a mystery to me. It may be that, with some ingenuity, we'll find a way out of this trap. And of course there's Aelward too . . ." he added, glancing to the empty wicker pigeon cote that swung on a rope attached to the wall. "In the meantime, let's try to keep our hopes up. Just remember that in the coldest flint there's hot fire."

Wilum took Kal to his medicine chest and gave him a sheep-skin bag full of rowan branches for him to tie to his belt. Then he took a leather thong and tied a spray of rowan around the young man's neck.

"So you want to accompany your friend, do you?" Wilum turned to face Gwyn, who was trying to attract Wilum's atten-tion, pointing to his own neck. His eyes alight with eagerness, Gwyn nodded so fiercely that Wilum thought for a moment he might suffer some hurt.

"No, boy. You're too young. I could never forgive myself if you came to any harm. No, it's for the best if you stay here with the rest of us, lad, although I admire your enthusiasm."

Gwyn's face clouded in the most piteous frown, quivering on

the verge of tears. He slowly turned tail and shuffled out of the cavern.

"Perhaps I could take him along, Wilum. I don't think he'd be a hindrance, no, not at all. In fact, he might be a great help."

"Well, I don't know. That's all you need, to be caring for him when you're trying to survive yourself."

"But Wilum, it's clear you don't know Gwyn. You'd be absolutely amazed to see him draw a bow. There's scarcely a bow in his father's shop that he can't pull to full draw. For a lad of fifteen, he's already more than a fair archer. Aye, he's not a day under fifteen," reiterated Kal, to Wilum's look of amazement. "That lad's full of surprises, let me tell you. Why, there's more muscle in that young body than many a full-grown man. And wisdom too. I'm certain that if I talked to Thurfar and Fionna, they'd let him go. In fact, it would be reassuring if he kept me company. He'd probably end up looking after me, keeping me from harm."

"Well, Kalaquinn. It seems you admire him quite as much as he admires you. I didn't realize he's well-nigh a man already. Soon, alas, he'll needs be a warrior. Ah well, go on, fetch him before his face sinks down to his knees, and then bid his father to come see me here. We'd better ask goodman Fletcher if it's all right for his eldest son to tag along with you. As for the danger, it's probably no greater for you than what we face already, except I think that things may be more perilous for your father and his companions."

Kal's brow knit at remembrance of the horror-filled skies of the previous night.

"Thraganux, the night drake," Wilum said, knowing Kal's thought. "It has not been seen in Arvon for over thirty centuries. But enough. Now go, send Thurfar to me."

Having secured Thurfar's approval, Kal and Gwyn were ready to leave the Cave of the Hourglass, both of them wrapped in a cloak to ward off the coolness of the night. Gwyn's eyes gleamed with pride, for he had been outfitted with a keen-bladed shortsword and one of his father's own bows—Thurfar had managed to bring three of his finest longbows with him—with a quiver full of arrows.

Wilum provided for a solitary picket to be posted just inside the door of the Cave. The women would take on the task of keeping vigil at the entrance, to hear any warning blast of the horn that might shatter the night air. Fionna, in her anxiety about her son, volunteered to be the first sentry. There had been a bit of a contest between Gammer and Fionna as to who should have the first honours, since Gammer was every bit as worried about her man Diggory and her nephew Galli as Fionna was about Gwyn.

Outside, all was awash in the soft caress of moonbeams, which shed an eerie slanted light on the standing stone and left the lintel of the Cave's entrance in shadow.

"Come down, Dhu, wherever you are. You never know when we might need some reinforcement, eh Gwyn!" Even though he expected it, Kal started at the sudden flurry of wingbeats with which Dhu alighted beside them from the crag above, where he must have been taking his rest. The young Holdsmen stroked him a couple of times, and with a word from Kal the bird sprang into flight. Kal continued on, aware that it was not improbable that other eyes, more malicious, were watching them. Gwyn, on the other hand, assumed a carefree air, seemingly unconcerned about the dangers that might be lurking at every turn. Even the spot where Wilum and Kal had almost met disaster held no terrors for him. Their way was made clear by the brightness of the spring moon, even though it was but a slender sickle obscured every now and then by a drifting mist of cloud. But all the same, Kal felt uneasily confined by the closeness of the rocks on every side of them along the awkward twists and turns of the path.

Soon, they left the maze of jumbled rocks and found themselves on the level of the upland plain, no more than a mile from the Well. Kal felt relieved as they stepped out into the open space. Gwyn, however, looked around and hesitated, peering at length into the darkness towards Skell Force, the direction they were headed. In the distance, they could hear the soft roar of its waters. Gwyn was suddenly overcome and began shaking like a leaf, pointing like a madman with his hand towards the Stairs. Without a further gesture of explanation to his companion, the mute boy drew his sword and broke into an awkward loping run.

"Gwyn! Gwyn, what's the matter? Slow down!" Kal ran after him, but found that he could not keep pace. "Gwyn! Gwyn!" Soon, Kal gave up calling after him and tried instead to simply hold Gwyn in sight, as he rushed after him down the footpath towards the sentries stationed at the ramparts of stone.

Kal could now discern the Well of the Seven Springs outlined dimly in the moonlight. He heard a voice shouting. It sounded like Diggory Clout's. He could not make out the words, but the tone and inflections were frantic, desperate. Diggory's voice grew louder, drifting steadily off to the right, away from the loophole and the Stairs. Kal ran faster and drew near enough now to see that Diggory had been hoisted, helpless, like a wayward lamb onto the back of something bounding up the grade toward the jagged ridge that rose above the mountain sward. Dhu, screaming, swooped low over the creature, talons outstretched, narrowly missing the jostled Holdsman, and wheeled up and around, dropping again on the beast. Well ahead of Kal, and rapidly closing with the unwary creature, charged the unlikely figure of Gwyn. Frysan and Galli made chase from the stone wall, shouting to Diggory. The moon slipped from behind a scudding cloud, and in the pale light Kal could see the grotesque contours of the gathgour beneath its burden.

Gwyn, still brandishing his sword, had come to within four or five strides of the beast. Kal saw it start at the boldness of Gwyn's challenge. The gathgour dropped the wailing Holdsman and sprang up the ridge, where, dispossessed of its prize, it filled the air with a sharp growl and leaped away with sure-footed quickness. Frysan and Galli fumbled to nock arrows to their bowstrings, but the gathgour had jumped down from its exposed point of vantage and was soon lost to sight amid the darkened boulders.

"I'm mightily obliged to you, lad. I don't rightly know where I would've ended up without you," said the shaken Holdsman. "Re'm ena, he stole up on me so nice and quiet like. But come, let's get down and join the others. It'll take more than a gathgour to do in Diggory Clout," he continued, putting a brave face on his misadventure.

"Are you all right, Digg?" queried Frysan, trying hard to fight off a bemused smile at what would have been dismissed just short moments ago as a bizarre dream fancy—the idea of the stoutly built Diggory Clout as a squirming kidnap victim flung like a child's doll over someone's shoulders.

"I'm right down fit as a butcher's dog, never been better," replied Diggory, a bit weak in the knees, affecting to dust off his breeches in order to gain pause and smooth his ruffled dignity. "Re'm ena, now you both look like grinagog, the cat's uncle. Come, Galli, wipe that smile off your face. 'Tisn't funny at all. A selcouth creature like that there gathgour, why, he could've put my light out for good. What I need about now is to get my nose into a good stout pot of Gammer's ale."

"You'll have a fair bit of a wait before there's any of that, Digg," Frysan said. "You did a fine job of chasing there, Gwyn. You're a brave lad. If it weren't for you, the gathgours would be feasting on poor old Digg. And an ample feast it would be," he said, smiling at the thought.

"Briacoil. Is everything all right?" Kal asked as he approached, winded.

"Briacoil, son. Yes, everyone's safe and sound. Diggory's just a bit shaken, but none the worse for wear, thanks to Gwyn here. If it weren't for Gwyn, I was just saying, old Diggory would be roasting on a spit, making a banquet meal for the gathgours. I never would have thought the boy had it in him."

"Nor did I, Father. It looked like he'd grown wings on his feet, the way he sped along. We were far back there yet. I couldn't see a thing. But Gwyn perks up his ears and runs off straight and fast like a fox that's been smoked out of its den. The lad has some kind of special sense about things that others can't see, don't you, Gwyn?" The mute boy basked in the glow of the accolade.

"Aye, Kal. He's a brave fellow. Did you see him wielding that sword? It's a good thing that gathgour made a run for it. I wouldn't have wanted to fight the lad, the way he was going full tilt. Not on your life. And a good thing he came. Galli and I were staring down into the black gloom of the Stairs, lost in our own thoughts, while Digg kept watch at the loophole. Then, even before we can so much as turn our heads to see what's happening, we hear these terrible screams, and, lo, there's Diggory being carried off like a sack of oats— Here now, we'd better get back down to our post and talk there."

Once at the Stairs, Kal distributed the slender branches of mountain ash to his father, Diggory, and Galli, who tied them around their necks. Frysan plied his son with questions about the Cave of the Hourglass, suppressing a moan when told of the encounter which had almost sealed the doom of Kal and Wilum. Dhu swept in to touch down, hopping over the ground behind them and up onto the wall of the Well to slake his thirst. Walking to the loophole, Galli scanned the dimly lit features of the landscape down below, looking for signs of movement. The constant background din of the waters tumbling down Skell Force meant that most nighttime sounds were lost to them.

The wind rose. To ease his stiffness and fend off the chill air,

Kal joined Galli at the embrasure. In the far-off distance, halfway along the shores of Deepmere, Galli pointed out the thin pin-pricks of light—the campfires of Ferabek's soldiers. Farther on, at the northern neck of the lake, a broad swathe of incandescence marked the spot where the town of Wrenhaven had stood. From Broadmeadows, the fires had spread to Darran Wood.

Another head jostled Galli's and Kal's. It was Gwyn. Kal greeted him, laying an arm around his shoulders. From the loophole, Gwyn stared out onto the darkened valley, happy and carefree, unconcerned, it seemed, about the dangers that now crowded the lives of the Holdsfolk.

Kal turned as Dhu cried, winging back from the Well of the Seven Springs towards him. The back of Kal's neck prickled with fear as he caught sight of three figures moving slowly towards them from up the meadow.

"Those must be our replacements for sentry duty. I hadn't realized that we've been here so long already," Galli said. "All the same, let's keep sharp, 'til we actually see who they are."

Frysan waved to the young Holdsmen by the lookout, bidding them come, and left Diggory at the top of the Stairs to meet the three who had arrived from the Cave to relieve them. Narasin and his two sons, each duly protected by a sprig of rowan, waved a greeting.

"Briacoil, men," hailed Narasin. "Everything all right here?"

"Briacoil. Everything's about as good as can be expected, Nar, what with gathgours and who knows what else on the loose," answered Diggory.

"What? You've had trouble?"

"That we have," Frysan said. "We didn't have our rowan twigs, and it was all we could do to keep them from carrying off old Digg. But Gwyn here, he drove them off. The lad came just in time, saved it all he did."

"You mean there was more than one of them?" asked Artun, wide-eyed.

"No, there was just one that we could see."

"But where there's smoke there's fire, I tell you," Diggory said. "I'd wager my best team of horses that there was a whole lot of them hiding in the rocks yonder just waiting for their mate."

There was a nervous pause, interrupted by Frysan. "But there's no need to worry now," he said. "You've each got your talisman.

The creatures will keep their distance. It's the Scorpions you'll need to keep an eye out for." Frysan turned to the breastwork and lifted the horn from where it hung on a knob of rock, handing it to Garis. "Just remember, if there's any trouble, two short, one long."

FOURTEEN

The night was becoming inhospitable. The brisk spring wind had taken on a fierce edge, wrinkling the moon-silvered channel of the Upper Skell as it left its headwaters at the Well of the Seven Springs. The hoot and cry of unseen owls from somewhere on the Saddle below rode the chill gusts up to where the retreating watchmen turned to join the path across the upland mead from the Well. Diggory grumbled to himself and pulled his cloak tighter around his shoulders, clutching it at the neck.

Kal found it hard to imagine how Wilum had fared on his own up here in the Enclosure for all those years. And not only Wilum, but all those Hordanus who had preceded him in ages past. As for himself, he was thankful to be in the company of other Holdsmen.

It was a fey place, this Hordanu's Enclosure, not at all what one might think sacred in the sense of good and holy. Strange—his impressions had been so different earlier, when they had emerged from the Stairs of Tarn Cromar onto this sequestered area. Then, in spite of all those tracks of the gathgour that had charged his imagination, an oddly bracing clarity had clung to the place, akin somehow to the crystalline purity of the waters of the Seven Springs that bubbled up from their deep hidden source.

For a moment, Kal's mind turned with wonder to the mighty Dinastor River, which flowed for hundreds of miles through highland and then lowland Arvon, emptying itself at length into Lake Lavengro at Arvon's capital, Dinas Antrum. In a real sense, though, more truly than Deepmere, these Seven Springs were the source of the Dinastor. It was suckled and nurtured here on the mountain heights, well before Deepmere took any part in its forming.

Now even this fountainhead near the roof of the world was infected with a dire corruption, this last hallowed spot, the hidden womb of Arvon's mightiest river, where the power of the Great Harmony had lingered unbroken for so long, even while the rest of the world sank into a spiralling coil of chaotic change. Small wonder, too, that the wellsprings should be tainted, when you thought of what had happened to the Dinastor's stately lowland beauties. Old Sarmel—with a touch of poignant sadness, Kal fell to wondering what had happened to the codger after that last sight he had had of him at the Sunken Bottle—Sarmel was wont to say in a vein of grim humour that in the nether parts of Arvon, where the Dinastor broadened out into a wide deep channel, the river was so sullied with sludge from the huge noisome manufactories and fuming smithies and forges strung out along its banks that you might almost walk dryshod from one side of the river to the other. That is, supposing you could see the other side through the thick pall of smoke that hung over the grimy valley of the Dinastor, once as beautiful as it was broad and powerful. "The loveliest of rivers this, this ribbon-tide of sun-flecked waters adorned by lark-exalted woods and lush and limb-burdened orchards, clinging to verdured pasturelands," Ardiel had described it in one of his more poignant lyric songs.

The wind that moaned through the looming rocks sent a dark cloud scudding across the face of the moon, so that Gwyn, who led the way, was swallowed for a moment by the darkness as if by some black-mawed beast of prey. There was a muffled thud. A volley of intemperate curses vomited forth into the night air.

"Why, it would be you, you bumbling simpleton! You clumsy moron!"

In the blackness, the little cobbler had been knocked flat by Gwyn, but did not catch sight of the others approaching until he had picked himself up off the ground and struggled to his feet. He adjusted his cloak and bustled past Gwyn, who had been left lying in the path. Kal drew near and helped Gwyn stand again.

"Briacoil, Relzor! And what brings you out here all on your own? Is anything the matter? How are things at the Cave?" asked Frysan. An edge was in his voice. The discernible lines of each man's features and frame were muted by the blanketing dark, the clouds still not yielding to the light of the moon.

"Frysan! Everything's fine. No, nothing's amiss. Wilum sent me to look for his brooch, you know, that silver thing in the shape of the harp that he wears whenever he's about something, like the Candle Festival or whatever. He says he thinks he lost it at Tarn Cromar by the Meeting Oak. He's of a mind that it's there. So, that's where I'm off to, and I'd best hurry. So step aside. There's no telling when the Boar and his dragoons might show up at the Tarn, and then where would poor old Relzor be? Aye, where would I be then? And Wilum telling me that he can't send any other man 'cause he can't spare them. And he can spare me, he says, as if my pelt was worth nothing to him," complained Relzor in a swelling crescendo of resentment. "By the welkin, come now, Frysan, make way, I say. I've spent too long already making idle talk with you. Get out of the way now! Let me pass!"

"All right, off with you then, Relzor." Frysan half stepped aside to let the man scuffle his way past them into the open meadow beyond. The moon gently found release from the drift of clouds and lit up the retreating figure, his black cloak clasped tight around him with both hands. A couple of times, he looked back, like an animal chased away from its carrion meal, and then hurried on, limping ever so slightly.

"What do you think, Fry? He's a sly hog-grubbing kind of fellow, ain't he?" Diggory said. "As flustered as a fly in a tarbox, couldn't you just feel it?"

"Aye, that's for certain. I didn't care much for all his chatter. Not his way. It's not like him to pass more than a handful of words, and those as black as tar, Digg. I don't trust him, don't trust him at all."

"Maybe we should have stopped him and taken him back with us," offered Galli.

"Then we'd be raising a fine little hornets' nest," continued his uncle. "Besides, what could he do, the stiff-necked little half-man? If he's off to Ferabek, I say good riddance. I don't know why he ever decided to stay with us in the first place, why he didn't stomp off with Enbarr and Kenulf when he had his chance."

"Puzzles me why Wilum would send the likes of him to look for the pios, if it's been lost," Frysan said.

"Couldn't spare anybody else, I suppose. We'll find out why soon enough, I expect," said Kal, while Gwyn, still groggy, leaned on his shoulder. "He really shook the poor lad's tree. And did you hear him, as if it were all Gwyn's fault? He even—"

Gwyn raised his head and began to pull at the sleeve of Kal's cloak. "We'd better get a move on. Gwyn's in another of his moods."

"I suppose we have small choice but to follow, do we Digg?" Frysan smiled wanly.

At the entrance to the Cave, they were met by Fionna. She was relieved to find her son safe and sound. Gammer had decided to take up station there beside her, awaiting her husband's return as well. The fubsy matron seized him in a huge embrace, gathering him to her bosom like a she-bear, and when Frysan explained how her man had almost been carried off by the gathgour, she placed a fist on each of her hips and grinned at Diggory, who reddened and looked to his feet.

"By the gingers, my smiling Digg. I've been expecting you to end up in the briars one of these days. No better than young Galli, you are. A fine job you made of keeping guard at the Stairs. Why, if me and Fionna was as watchful, this whole cave would be crawling with gathgours and murdering folk of all kinds. But we're made of finer stuff than that, ain't we, Fionna?"

"Ah, stop your talk, Gammer. That's a pretty question to be jabbering, when you've got a hearty trencherman to feed," rejoined Diggory, looking now at his wife with a broad smile.

Gwyn had broken from his mother's attention and disappeared, ambling off into the Cave. All but one of the torches had been extinguished, and the only other light in the main chamber, apart from the feeble shimmer of pearl-drop starlight in the opening of the smoke hole, came from the firepit in the centre of the dry stone floor, reduced now to a few tongues of fire amid a glowing nest of coals, its mounting flames long spent. Gara sat and watched the pulsing embers of the fire, softly singing "Lament for the Children," an old ballad of the Holding which told of two children who lost their way and perished in Darran Wood when it was still a trackless expanse of thick forest, haunted by bear and boar. Some of the adults were crouched around her, too tired to sleep, riveted by the old ballad's melancholy strains.

In the blackness beyond Gara, a woman keened wordlessly. A stark shapeless thing, her voice disembodied, she distilled with hushed choking sobs the sadness that erupted in painful spasms from the very marrow of her being. Exhausted as they were, however, most of the children and a good number of the remaining refugees had already drifted into restless slumber on coarse rush mats, exchanging their present sorrows for the softer world of dream shadows.

Two of the older children, their imaginations kindled, refused to sleep. Spotting Kal and Galli, they rose from their beds to ply them with questions about the cruel gathgour.

"Don't worry, little one. There's not a gathgour in all of Ahn Norvys that's apt to come within a mile of you when you've got this around your neck," Kal assured the frightened girl, lifting off his rowanwood charm to give it to her. The girl's brother, not to be outdone, pestered Galli until he too parted with his sprig of rowan. Leaving Galli to humour the children, Kal turned to search out Wilum.

"By all that's holy, Kalaquinn, come here! Quickly! For pity's sake, you'd better come right this moment. Hurry!" Frysan's shout shattered the air of repose that had settled on the Cave. The distraught voice emanated from the side chamber where Wilum kept his chest of medicaments and simples. A very faint gleam of torchlight spilled over feebly into this side chamber from the main cavern, to which it was connected at right angles by an anteroom that hid it from prying eyes.

Kal made for his father's voice. Close behind him came Manaton, Diggory, and Thurfar, stepping over and around sleeping bodies. Frysan stood in the murky half-light beside the form of Gwyn. The boy was shaking, hunched over Wilum, who lay limp on the hard stone floor. His head lolled, a bloody tangle of matted hair and gore, while his hands and arms lay crossed, as if he had been trying desperately to hold on to something. The sight hit Kal like a bludgeon blow—savage and unexpected. Others came pressing in behind him.

"He's breathing. He's still alive," said Frysan. He had his ear close over Wilum's mangled mouth. "But his breath is shallow. Bren? Bren, go fetch some hot water and a cloth. Let's get him cleaned off. Galli, we need some blankets—"

"Father, the Talamadh, it's gone! Must have been prised out of his hands. And the satchel with all the scrolls and manuscripts. It's nowhere to be seen either—"

"Relzor! By all that's holy, that's what he was about!" Frysan stood and turned away from the crushed body of the Hordanu. "No wonder he was so anxious to keep that cloak of his wrapped closely around himself. You noticed that too, eh Digg?" he said, when the other man nodded his head. "He was favouring that one side. But where did he put the sack? He can't have had that with him." Frysan looked to Diggory, while the stout Holdsman busied himself lighting one of the torches on the wall, adding new brightness to the shadowed gloom of the small cavern.

"Look at Wilum! His eyes!" shouted Kal. The battered man's eyelids flickered in the torchlight. Then with painful slowness, as if infinity were hanging on every syllable, Wilum fought to gasp words through the broken flesh of his mouth.

"'Relzor,' he's saying 'Relzor,'" Kal said, watching Wilum's lips, gathering up the halting syllables as if they were precious gems. Then, Wilum made a laboured attempt to move his head, to turn his attention to Kal. His words were barely a breath: "Get Talamadh . . . Kal, you now . . . Hordanu . . ." He struggled to frame the syllables, pausing at the huge effort it took even to shape this smattering of words. Then, screwing up his battered face, as if to summon his last stores of energy, he continued, "Hurry . . . pios . . . still have . . . some power . . . same shape." At this, the fingers of his right hand, until now tightened into a fist, eased open with palsied slowness, as if pried apart by hidden hands. The palm that lay open revealed the pios—a small silver brooch shaped like the Talamadh. He had gripped it in his fist, managing to retain it even while being forced to let the Talamadh itself go. His fingers closed over it again.

Then haltingly, in what seemed to be a jumble of ancient and present-day Arvonian, came sounds more like a pattern of exhaled breaths than distinct words: "Fat-ainn . . . Ael-ward . . . Mark . . . Stone . . . Llani-gon . . ."

His eyes closed again, and his breathing relapsed, the exhalations from his mouth so light that they might not have stirred a feather. Marina had entered the cavern, accompanied by Brendith, carrying a bowl of hot water. Gasping at the sight that met her eyes, Marina fell to the Hordanu's side and began, with the tenderest of care, to clean his broken face.

Galli had returned with some blankets and then drifted to the back of the chamber, where it tapered to another passageway that disappeared into the bulk of the mountain. Just before this passageway, pressed against a side wall of the chamber, there was a narrow crescent-shaped hole. From its lip, Galli lifted a patch of dirty cloth.

"Here, come look at this. Relzor must have thrown the satchel down here. Right here . . . I've found a piece of oilskin torn off by a sharp rock."

"The little nointer! Here, Kal, bring over one of the torches, will you? Let's have a look," said Frysan. But the limited light of the torch made it hard to gauge how far down the cache of ancient manuscripts might have dropped. All Kal could see was a black void that, for all he knew, might be two or two hundred fathoms deep. It was impossible to tell.

Kal turned from the opening and spoke to his father in a low voice. "We'd better get going after Relzor, if it's not too late already. The harp. We have to get the harp. If Ferabek gets his hands on the Talamadh, he's won half the battle. And not only that, but there's the Pyx of Roncador."

"Quite right, Kal. Re'm ena, we have to get moving, or that miserable rotter will be the end of us. But, what's this about you and the Hordanu? What does he mean?"

"I'll explain later. Now, we'd better go after Relzor. I'll go, and Galli. The two of us can track him down as fast as anybody. And we both know the Saddle like the palms of our hands. We have to get the Talamadh back."

Bren begged to be allowed to go too. For a moment, Frysan furrowed his brow in thought. "No, Bren, you stay back with us. Any more than two of you on the trail, and we might as well send a herald to announce ourselves. No, Bren, no arguments. Please, believe me, it's best this way." Frysan turned to Kal. "All right, son, enough now. Every moment you linger here brings Relzor that much closer to Ferabek. Get going, run like the wind—just a moment though!" Frysan held up his arm to halt them as they were making to leave. "Do you have your sprigs of rowan?"

"I'd almost forgot," answered Kal.

"Hurry up then. Look into that chest of Wilum's and find what you need."

"Ah good, here's a whole bundle of ash, already strung together," said Kal, rifling through Wilum's collection of herbs. He handed one of the circlets to Galli.

"Now be off with you, but be careful, mind yourselves. And you,

Gwyn, you'll be staying here this time." The mute boy's face fell. "Here, you can help us keep watch over Master Wilum, while I rack my mind and try to remember everything I ever knew about herbal remedies, which is not a lot. It would be a good idea, I think, if we called on the services of goodwife Clout. Aye, Digg, we'll be needing your good Gammer."

"She'll be glad to help, I'm sure, Fry. She knows near as much of herbing as Cloudbeard himself, I wouldn't be surprised."

Kal and Galli waited no longer. They flew from the Cave in headlong pursuit of Relzor. Dhu fell to wing from the column where he had perched by the entrance and soared into the night sky above them. They made good time along the path. Kal had grown familiar with the trail and had begun to expect some of the dipping turns and odd-shaped passageways that threaded the rocky defiles. The urgency of their mission lent wings to their feet.

Soon, they reached the three sentries at the Stairs and, in a flurry of words, gave a short account of what had happened at the Cave. The three men grew sombre at the retelling, heads shook slowly, and oaths were muttered under breath. With the benefit of hindsight, Narasin told them that Relzor did seem to bear an odd cunning mien on his arrival at their post earlier. But, thinking at the time that this was just Relzor looking and acting like Relzor, that is, shifty and faithless, he and his sons let him through down the Stairs about an hour ago, glad to be rid of him. After that, even they had second thoughts when they saw him from the loophole, heading along the flagstone walk at a clip.

"I thought it was strange," explained Narasin, "that he pushed off into the woods down the Skellside Path. Why, he didn't even so much as give the Tarn a second's glance, if that's where he says Wilum lost his brooch. Oh, if I had known, I could've planted a nice long goose-feathered shaft in that black carcass of his—"

"We'd better get after him. Briacoil, Narasin. Briacoil, Artun, Garis." Kal broke off the conversation. He and Galli climbed over the stone breastwork and left the three pickets as they ran down the Stairs.

Once Kal and Galli reached the Skellside Path, the headlong speed of their pursuit slowed, for Galli was forced into the stooped stance of the tracker. But the moon's undimmed crescent illumined the distinct impressions of Relzor's hobnailed boots well enough for Galli to follow.

Their way swung and dipped into the hollow through which the path ran. Now the moon's steady light was blocked out by the dense tangle of forest growth. A strong scent of wild mint filled the air, while a spadefoot toad regaled them with a monotonous repetition of bleating. Here Galli had to track by dropping to a crouch and feeling for the contours of the spoor.

"He's turned this way, Kal, up this path."

"Now why would he turn up this way?"

"Probably because he doesn't like this owl-eyed darkness any more than we do. I think if we follow this path it'll take us right up out of this dreary place far quicker than if we kept to the Skellside Path."

They emerged moments later onto a ridge that opened them once more to the sky. From here, the trail kept rising towards Stonehead.

"This is strange, Galli. Why's he going up? There are all kinds of side paths where he could have turned down."

"I don't know. He's a tricky little fellow. I'm certain, for one thing, that he's smart enough to know that we'd be following him down the Skellside Path as sure as day follows night. So, he's likely making his trail as roundabout as he can."

In a while, they reached a point where the path started to descend the mountain, weaving across its flank. Down the trail, they forded a stream, and Relzor's tracks were nowhere to be found on the other side.

"Why, the clever—! He's trying to lose us." Galli straightened and looked down the course of the brook.

"So would I, if I knew it was likely you were the one to be set on my scent."

Galli grunted and began ranging the banks on either side in an attempt to pick up Relzor's trail again. It took him a good quarter-hour to find it about a hundred paces downstream on the near side of the brook, where the tracks doubled back in the direction of the Skell along a dingy and overgrown side trail. After a while, this veered off onto a better-cleared pathway which swung down and ended on the edge of a lofty precipice.

"Look, that's him. Down there." Kal placed a hand on Galli's back and pointed. "He's making for the Grotto of Proclamation! That's the reason he came this way. Of course."

Galli had been so busy reading the signs of Relzor's passage through the woods, that Kal had spied him first, maybe two hundred yards below them, on a grassy ridge that bulged out from the sheer face of the bluff and seemed to end at a magnificent promontory covered almost to the edge by an arching sheet of rock and the bulk of the scarp above. The sliver of moon hung suspended in the sky over the Grotto, casting pale rays onto the landscape below. Relzor drew away from them towards the left and had almost reached the Grotto. He climbed up onto the leading edge and then paused.

"Galli, look, he's going to sound a horn."

"Here, quick, let me stop him," said Galli, slipping the longbow from his shoulder and fumbling at his quiver.

"You're too late, Galli." The deep resonant note of a hunting horn rent the stillness of the night. "Besides, chances are you'd miss him from here and then all he'd have to do is scuttle into the Grotto like a spider and wait for his sting-tailed cousins to come to the rescue." The round tone reverberated up and down the length of the valley ringed by the Radolan Mountains.

"What'll we do?" asked Galli, replacing the arrow he had drawn to his quiver. "It'll take us nearly a half-hour to scramble down there, and by that time the place could be crawling with soldiers. Quick, get down! He's looking up this way."

Kal dropped behind a tree. "That was close. I don't think he saw us though."

"We'd better be quick about this. 'Ain't no time to lose,' as Gammer would say. The sooner we're on the trail, the sooner we'll get our hands on the scoundrel. It's our only hope."

"Wait . . . there must be another way."

"What do you mean? We didn't bring any rope with us to scale our way down, and we can't very well fly down there."

"So where does that leave us?"

"I don't know. Scrambling our way down, I guess. Let's get a move on, Kal."

"Wait—! What did you say? Can't fly . . . We can't fly, you said. No, we can't fly down, but Dhu certainly can." Kal whistled a rising call which drew Relzor's attention. The two shrank back behind the cover of rock and tree, as Relzor peered up at them through the dark. He must have thought it no more than yet another of the odd night sounds that filled the air above the woods of these upland places, for after a moment he turned away again into the Grotto.

At the summons, Dhu alighted on the overhanging branch of a nearby beech tree, hopping from there onto a wind-fallen limb beside Kal.

"Look!" Galli said. "Relzor has laid the Talamadh against the wall of the Grotto. Wants to take a load off his shoulders, while he waits for his rescuers. Doesn't want to go farther into the Grotto either. He'll want to guard his approaches and keep track of friend or foe."

Relzor winded his horn once again at the brink of the ledge out into the night air.

"All right, enough man," Kal muttered under his breath. "You've made your point. Every living ear in the Holding has heard you now."

As if heeding Kal's grumbling command, Relzor swung away and placed the horn beside the Talamadh, then took up station at the edge of the Grotto, pacing it up and down in a nervous half-circle. With his dark cloak wrapped around him and the vivid sharpness of his profile, he looked like some malignant carrion crow under the baleful glow of the moon.

"Listen, Galli. We'll get the better of Relzor yet . . . Won't we, Dhu?" Kal pointed from behind the shelter of a large pine tree straight at the Talamadh. "Now wait, Dhu, wait, 'til he's facing the other way, and then off you go. Fetch me that nice golden harp in your talons, my strong and gentle Dhu, and I shall be forever in your debt."

Just then, a bobbing handful of lights caught Galli's eye, curling up the mountainside and looming larger and more threatening with every passing moment. Relzor had seen them too. His rescue force coming. He moved out to the lip of the ledge. It looked like a long column of Ferabek's soldiers, judging by the distance between the forward torches in the vanguard and those at the rear of the marching line. It would not take them long to reach the Grotto.

"Go, Dhu. Go now," whispered Kal with a gentle stroke of the fellhawk's sleek feathers, releasing the bird into the night. Dhu slipped from his perch, and with a mighty thrust of his pinions, drove himself out into the vagrant crosswinds that played along the dark face of the precipice. Pulling his wings from their full span, he plunged down straight to the Grotto. No sooner had Relzor heard the sweep of Dhu's wings behind him than he turned to see the fellhawk lift himself off into the air, his talons gripped tight around the gleaming harp, the Pyx dangling below on its chain.

Relzor's curses stained the dark night, as he shook his fists at the fellhawk, who wheeled out of the mouth of the Grotto, gaining speed as he mounted the air currents with great wing strokes back to his master. Kal found the man's fury appalling. There was something elemental about it, chilling him like an icy parody of fire radiating from a blazing hearth, strangely cold and numbing. Seething anger fed by an unsated hatred had consumed the little cobbler, sending shock waves into the night.

In a frenzy, Relzor searched the ground for a rock to throw at Dhu. But it was far too late, and for his efforts, Relzor came near to losing his balance and falling over the brink. He followed Dhu's retreating flight.

"He's seen us!" Kal said, as he and Galli abandoned their hiding places to seize the harp surrendered to them by the fellhawk. Now Relzor's wrath became even more manic and hysterical. It was like watching the desperate fits of a bird caught in a well-laid trap of lime. Dire curses and threats further blackened the air.

"Come, we'd better move, Galli. Those torchlights are coming up fast, too fast, and there may be scouts ahead of them." Kal shuddered again at Relzor's anger. What could have so cankered the man's soul? An odd stirring of pity for the misshapen cobbler rose in his heart.

Kal unfixed the chain with which the Pyx was attached to the Talamadh and tucked it in his pocket. "I don't want the Pyx clanging against the harp all the time," he said, then slung the Talamadh over his shoulder, as they began to retrace their steps back up the trail. Dhu went on ahead in short flights from branch to branch, keeping close to his master. Kal thrilled once more to feel the beguiling weight of mystery that clung to the golden masterpiece of Vali's ancient craftsmanship.

"I wonder how they'll treat him, when they find he hasn't delivered the goods," mused Galli, breaking the hush.

"Not too well, I would think, Galli, not too well at all. Ferabek's rewards for success are great, but as for failure . . . I wouldn't want to be in Relzor's shoes right now, after he's summoned every fell soul in the valley and not a cup-of-sneeze to show them, when they've come running to his horn blasts at the Grotto."

"Hush now, Kal. We shouldn't be talking. There's no telling who or what that blasted horn has drawn. You know there may be more Telessarian trackers combing the woods for us."

As it was, their trip in vigilant silence passed without event. Every now and again, when they emerged from the folded hollows of the hills onto a height or eminence of any kind, they could see flecks of light advancing in procession up towards the Grotto of Proclamation along trails they both knew well. Just as they approached the lip of Tarn Cromar, where the Skell spilled down its rock-strewn run, Galli looked back again.

"Kal, look at that." A great creature hovered over the Grotto in the distance.

"Aye, the night drake, but there it goes, I can't see it anymore," Kal said, as it descended into the dimness of the nocturnal horizon.

"It probably landed. What a fearful-looking creature, even from here."

"I feel almost sorry for him, Galli." Kal stopped now beside his companion to catch his breath atop the crest of land that brought them level with the Tarn.

"Who do you mean? Relzor?"

"Aye, Relzor. They're probably feeding him piecemeal to the night drake, I wouldn't be surprised."

"You can't be serious!"

"I am actually."

"Ah! You're too soft, Kal. My heart bleeds for the knife-faced fiend not one little bit. It's not as if he had even an ounce of pity for poor old Cloudbeard or the rest of us. And he's like now to be a murderer too, I don't doubt. Such as him deserves to be hanged from the nearest stout limb."

"Even so, Galli, even so . . . He is a Holdsman, like you and me."

"Not like you and me at all, Kal. He was a Holdsman, and one with a muckworm in his soul."

Kal sighed. "Come, Galli, enough of Relzor. On to the Stairs."

They resumed their trail past the Meeting Oak and veered behind the foot of Skell Force to climb the steps up the cliff face. When they neared the top of the stone steps, a stern voice rang out in challenge. "Who goes there? Is that you, Kal?"

"Yes, Narasin, we're back. Rest easy."

"I thought it was you. Garis said he saw you from the loophole. Says there are lots more lights down below than he saw before, and some strange beast flying through the air. They're coming from the north, he says."

"He's right. It spells trouble, although we did manage to recover the Talamadh. As for Relzor, he's about to be called to account by the Boar, if he hasn't already been, and then, I expect, they'll be come to the Stairs."

Narasin and Artun gave the two a hand over the barricade. Dhu swung low over them and glided to a rest atop the stone on which he had perched before. Narasin cowered and sucked in his breath, looking over his shoulder. "Kalaquinn Wright! I'll never get used to that bird of yours."

"Aye, Nar, that may be, but it's Dhu we've to thank for this," Kal said, shrugging up the Talamadh on his shoulder.

Kal and Galli left the bulwark and made for the lookout, where Garis stood watch, to have a look for themselves at what was unfolding in the night. Narasin and Artun joined them. Kal recounted what had happened at the Grotto of Proclamation.

"So now Ferabek knows exactly where we're all hidden," commented Narasin in a tone of resignation.

"I'm sure he already had his suspicions. Why, there's Enbarr, for one, and we were close enough to the Enclosure when he left us at Tarlynn's Coomb. It was merely a matter of time. As it is, I wouldn't be at all surprised if there was an attack by morning."

"Or even before," offered Galli. "What's to stop him attacking at night?"

"Aye, Galli," said Narasin. "We'd be like to suffer more in the confusion of a storming under darkness. It hardly gives us a chance to have recovered even a slight bit from our tiredness, while his troops are many and fresh. I'd say we're in a fine spot of trouble."

"Look," Garis said, "there's somebody down below. He's coming towards the Meeting Oak."

"By the welkin, it's Relzor. There's no other looks like him. But how did he get up so fast? He's making for the Stairs. Ready your weapons," Narasin ordered. "This must be a trick of some kind. Garis, have you got your horn ready? Three blasts—two short, one long—and we'll get our reinforcements, such as they are—"

"Garis, wait!" said Kal. "I see no other movement down there."

"They could be hiding in the woods, and we wouldn't see them, even in daylight," Narasin said.

"All the same, let's hold. What can Relzor do to us on his own? And it doesn't look like he's armed."

Narasin snorted. "That's what we thought before. What harm can that bent little man do to us, we said to ourselves. And look what happened!"

An oppressive silence fell over the men, as they waited, watching. In the blackness, it seemed half an eternity before Kal's ear caught the first harsh scrapes of Relzor's nailed boots scuffling on the stone steps.

"Here he is, I see him," called Artun, who had moved to the barricade, his bow fully drawn. Narasin ran to stand beside him, pulling an arrow from his quiver and bending his bow to full draw as well.

"P-peace. D-don't shoot. Please. P-peace." Relzor cowered behind the stone wall, breathless and pale, entreating them in a terrified stammer.

"What do you want, Relzor?" demanded Kal, who had come up beside Narasin. "What trick are you trying to pull on us now? One step more and you're a dead man."

"Aye, Kal. He thinks we're half-rocked fools, coming back here, after all he's done to put us under," said Narasin through clenched teeth, not relaxing the tension of his bowstring.

"Go on, man!" Kal challenged the cobbler. "What have you come back here for? Out with it, or I'll not keep them from pricking you!"

Relzor bent his head, glancing sidelong up at Kal, and began to wring his hands. "I-I be come . . . to ask you t-to take m-me back in . . . To beg your p-pardon . . . for all I done . . ."

"Will you listen to him? He's come to beg our pardon, as if we was base dullards. Come, Kal, let me dispatch him now, and it'll save us the trouble of a hanging." Narasin raised the bow higher to show his resolve.

"Hold, Narasin! You've got nerve, Relzor. Why should you be coming back here, after all you've done to harm us? You know you deserve a traitor's death. Your lot lies with Ferabek and Enbarr and Kenulf, not with us."

"I c-can't. He'll kill me. En-Enbarr, he told me, Ferabek's not a man to abide failure, bungling, Kenulf called it," responded Relzor, huddled against the wall of the Stairs, shaking like an aspen leaf in a stiff breeze.

"You should have thought of that before you tried to sell us down the river to Ferabek, and him having butchered so many of our clanfellows. And there's you doing the damage yourself to poor old Wilum, who may be dead by now, for all we know. Off with you, Relzor, and count yourself lucky. Re'm ena, but you're tempting me sore. Get out of my sight, before I let slip this bowstring!" ordered Narasin.

"No, wait! Wait . . ." Kal held the cringing figure in a narrowed gaze. "Lower your arrow and ease your bowstring, Narasin. Let him up over the barrier. I see no trickery here, just a man who is naked before his enemies, outdone by his own guile."

The farmer and his son looked at Kal in stark disbelief. Narasin made to object, working his mouth like a fish, noiselessly opening and shutting it. Kal's words carried an unfamiliar weight of authority.

"No, Narasin, Artun, lower your weapons. We won't send Ferabek another corpse. Besides, we might learn something more of Ferabek's intentions. Might we not, Master Relzor?"

"Oh yes, young Master Wright. Oh yes, yes, very right you are, right you are," Relzor spewed the words and snickered his choking mirthless laugh. Then, like a half-starved dog seizing on a bone, Relzor pounced on the opening that Kal had presented to him. "There's much as Enbarr came and spoke to me about. Many's the night, when all of the Holding lay asleep, we'd be planning and plotting this and that and the other . . ." He continued gabbling to himself as much as to anyone else.

Narasin unnocked the arrow from his bowstring, yet kept an eye on the cloaked form of the repentant cobbler. Kal helped Relzor over the wall, while Galli and Garis stared in amazement from the lookout post. Kal searched Relzor for weapons, and then, leaving Artun behind to man the barricade, he and Narasin marched him to where the others waited.

"But Kal, what'll we do with him, the makings of a hawk and a pigeon both, and we can't have the pigeon without the hawk? There'll have to be one of us watching the villain all the time, or someone is like to have his head dented in like Wilum's," argued Narasin. "It'll be like having a ball and chain tied to our legs, weighing us down, and we like drowning men up to our necks in water. The last bother we need is to set a guard on him all the time. Wouldn't it be best to send him back to his paymaster and be done with him?"

"Aye, Kal, I do think that Nar has a point. We're going to need every able-handed man, and woman, I don't doubt, before we're out of this bind," said Galli. Relzor's face darkened into a frown, as the tide of opinion seemed to be turning against him.

"Don't forget," Narasin added, "he's only coming to us because there ain't no other choice he's got. We're Relzor's last and only resort, and I'll wager he figures he can still find a way to turn against us so long as he bides his—"

"Look! There, look! Fireworks, like rockets!" exclaimed Garis, pointing to sparkling streamers of light that rose below them to meet the northern sky, shooting straight up, then fanning languidly into billowing bursts of colour that cascaded down, like a soft rain, until they were quenched in the sea of darkness. It was a strange sight—startling and disquieting, the more so since the moon had just then been obscured by a thick wall of cloud, pitching them into darkness.

"Can you fellows see anything? What's happening?" shouted Artun.

"Galli, you stay here and see what you can see. The rest of us, to the Stairs," commanded Narasin. He, Kal, and Garis stumbled towards the steps. Drawing his shortsword, Kal cursed himself for not having brought any light from the Cave—even just a candle.

Joining Artun, the three crouched at the ready behind the rude defensive works at the top of the Stairs, huddled there, waiting for further word from the lookout, as they peered over the barricade, watching for the telltale signs of an assault. Kal sensed someone come up to him.

"Who's that?"

"It's me, Relzor. What's going on?" whispered a voice behind him.

"What do you care! Get out of the way!" spat Narasin.

Relzor jostled closer to Kal's side, bobbing back and forth, as if on the lookout himself for the terrifying onrush of Scorpion invaders. At Kal's back, he kept up an incessant woeful chatter, peppered with self-pitying sighs and curses. For a while, Kal remained so intent on the danger emanating from the murky darkness that enveloped the narrow Stairs, that he hardly took notice of Relzor. At length, as the impression of imminent danger subsided, Kal became more sensible of the craven little cobbler clinging to him. Irritated and feeling himself violated in some way, Kal was all set to order him back from the Stairs, when Relzor withdrew, slinking away of his own accord.

Presently, Kal's eyes began to pick out more details in the darkness, and, feeling easier, he started to engage in light banter with Narasin and his two sons. With ill-defined misgiving, though. Something was not right. The fireworks were subsiding. They presaged something, he was sure, and that not good.

Sheathing his sword, Kal felt with his fingers for the reassuring curves of the Talamadh, struggling against the impeding baggage of his quiver and longbow, both of which lay slung across his back together with the harp. With a queasy sinking feeling, like a wayfarer who, after a long day's march, turns without thinking to untie the thongs of his scrip only to find it gone, Kal realized that he could not feel the weight of the harp gently tugging against his shoulder.

"The Talamadh! Where is it?" Kal cried, his voice quavering, fighting nausea, cold in the pit of his stomach.

"What do you mean?" asked Narasin.

"The Talamadh—I can't feel it! It's gone!" Kal stripped off his bow and quiver in a frantic search for the harp, as if it were still somehow there, as if it had to be there, lost in the tangled clutter of his weaponry.

"Did you drop it, Kal?" proffered Garis, noticing that Kal had stooped to pick something up.

"The strap's been cut!" Kal held the embossed leather strap that had fallen off his shoulder to the ground. Both ends of it had been cut clean through with a knife. He ran his forefinger along the even surface of the thick hide strap.

"Relzor! He had a knife hidden on him. That's why he was standing here beside me. Where is he?"

"That slinking, two-faced—!" exclaimed Narasin.

"He can't have gone down the Stairs. He must still be up here. We'll find him right enough, Kal," Artun said with bold assurance.

"Galli, quick, come here! I need you to track. Tell me where he's gone!" shouted Kal.

"Where? Who's gone?"

"Relzor, he's stolen the Talamadh again."

"Wait, what's that? Listen, Kal!" Galli called, already running towards the Stairs.

"Enbarr! Where are you? I've got it! Enbarr? Come, tell me,

man—I can't see!" Relzor's cries were issuing from somewhere to the right of them, from farther north on the grassy plain, perhaps a hundred yards away or more.

"Here, you idiot! This way, Relzor, quick now or it'll be all for naught!" goaded a second voice that sounded fainter and farther off than the first.

"Why, that's Enbarr! How did he get up here? And without us seeing him?" cried Artun.

"There's something terribly wrong here—Artun, you'd better stay here at the Stairs and keep watch. Garis, have that horn ready so we can call for help from the Cave." Kal peered into the darkness. "We've entered dangerous waters. I feel it in my bones. Come, we must be after Relzor. This way!"

The fireworks had died away now, and somewhere, not too far off, Dhu screeched into a night grown too lightless and indistinct even for his keen eyes.

"For pity's sake, man, hurry! Over here, over here . . ." Enbarr egged on the cobbler, his voice pitched higher and higher, almost shrill. Enbarr sounded closer than before, but still too distant.

The dense cloud banks that had concealed the moon parted and gave way now to thin torn wisps. The faint silvered light broke through once again onto the protruding mounds of rock and rubble strewn along the edge of the field, through which they had been tripping their way. Guided only by the eerie disembodied shouts and the dim commanding presence of a lofty line of standing stones that rimmed the ramparts to their right, they ran. Kal, trailed closely by Galli and Narasin, could see no one, and the voices had ceased, so that they seemed now to be no more real than a dream-fragment in the cool radiance of the moon's resurgent light.

"Where are they?" Kal stopped, flummoxed and panicking. "Galli, have you got a trail?"

"There's something behind that pillar over there," shouted Narasin, pointing to a towering stone nearby, very close to the edge of the plain. They froze as a black creature rose slowly from behind the outline of the stone.

"The night drake! And look, on its back, there's a— No, I see two. Two men on its back!" yelled Kal.

"Aye," Galli shouted, "it's Enbarr and Relzor. See the Talamadh! The fellow in front is holding on to it. That's Enbarr. And Relzor on behind. Can you see? The rotter!"

"Nevermind who it is, Galli. Stop them! Get your bow! Shoot them! We can't let him steal the Talamadh again. We have to get it back, we must, whatever it takes," Kal cried, while nocking an arrow himself. But, there was a quickness to the night drake that belied its imposing size, for, graceless as it was, it seemed to lift with startling ease into the deeps of the night sky, its great wings churning. Then, almost as soon as Kal let fly his shaft, the creature dropped in an almost straight dive down over the edge of the plain, so that Kal's arrow sailed harmlessly into the forest gloom that lay beneath them around the waters of Tarn Cromar, leaving the night drake itself lost to sight.

For a moment, Kal thought that he might have hit the gruesome creature, so fast did it fall from the edge, and so hideous were its wails. But, rushing to the rock-walled ramparts, he cast his eyes out to mark its uneven progress over the treetops below. The thing was clearly not wound-stricken and now flew far out of range of his longbow. Its two riders were intact, leaning back in their saddles, their heads craned in the direction of their hapless pursuers.

A stiff easterly gust blew into the faces of the Holdsmen, as they scanned the dark bosom of the valley below, grimly following the descent of the escaping night drake. Kal thought he heard the staccato cackle of laughter borne back to them by the buffeting breeze.

FIFTEEN

It was Frysan who greeted Kal and Galli on their return from the Well. He stood watch alone at the mouth of the Cave of the Hourglass. Miserable and dispirited, Kal remained oblivious to Frysan's questions. He was in no mood to talk, not even to his own father, nor to Galli, keeping an obstinate sullen silence, except for the stream of reproachful murmurs that percolated from his lips like brackish water seeping from a soggy downland spring. He muttered to himself—something about "once a knave, always a knave"—although it was not apparent whether he was angrier at Relzor or at himself.

It was Galli who stopped to explain to a puzzled Frysan what had passed at the Well. Morosely, Kal made for the side chamber, where Wilum lay drifting between states of unconsciousness and delirium, still hovering dangerously near death. All the others, adults and children alike, had finally drifted off into sleep, even Gwyn, who had been keeping quiet vigil alone by Wilum's side, after Gammer had done all she could, using her goodwife's knowledge of herbs and simples, to heal him of his wounds. Kal fell to his knees beside the broken man and began to weep. At the gentle noise of it, Wilum's eyes flickered open, and his gaze swam for a moment before focusing on Kal's face. The old man smiled almost imperceptibly, barely lifting the corners of his mouth, but his eyes closed and opened again in consoled recognition of his young confrere's presence.

Kal had lost track of the passage of time, when he finally left the still form of his mentor and crept unseen through the main chamber of the Cave. He skirted the body of sleeping Holdsfolk and drew near the mouth of the cavern. The low voices of his friend and father grew audible, and Kal hung back in the shadows, listening and watching the two men in the moonlight.

". . . so he's taken his sneaking revenge on us twice, the muck-worm wretch! I'd never have trusted him." Frysan shook his head slowly, then said, "But, on thraganux? On the night drake? Can you be sure, Galligaskin?"

"Re'm ena, but that's how it happened!" exclaimed Galli. "The beast carried them off and the Talamadh with them. It was all I could do to keep Kal himself from flying back down the Stairs to recover it again. If Narasin and I hadn't held him back—you should have seen him kick—and him being the sole Hordanu, now that Wilum's on death's door—"

Frysan fixed the young man with a stare of raw incredulity that made him falter in his account.

"It's no lie, Frysan, I tell you," Galli said in a soft voice. "Your son is now Hordanu. I heard it with my own two Telessarian ears. Wilum made him Hordanu in the boat, this very morning, while the three of us were out on Deepmere, on our way from Raven's Crag Island."

"You speak nonsense, Galligaskin Clout. This is absurd. How can you make jest at a time like this?"

"By the Stone, Master Frysan, and by all that's sacred in Ahn Norvys, above or below, I swear, it's true. You and all the other folk would probably know it was true by now if Relzor hadn't stove in Wilum's poor old skull. By Right of Appointment, Wilum called it. He said he'd announce it to all the folk in due course, excepting the occasion never came. You know well enough Kal's knack for languages. That's why Landros sent him to Wilum in the first place. Yes, I was sent as well, but we both know that was as much for the sake of friendship as anything else. And you know how Wilum's taken a deep liking to Kal and has explained to him reams of detailed things about *Hedric's Master Legendary* that most folk, even hereabouts in the Holding, scarce know about. Deeper matters than this plain brain of mine will ever be able to ken—though there are times, I know for a fact, when even Kal's been bewildered by it. And then, there's all that care that Wilum was taking to teach him lore that's been hid since the Age of Echoes, I don't doubt, or even earlier, centuries before the likes of the echobards ever set foot in Arvon."

Frysan turned from Galli and sat on the ground, leaning against the rock face of Thyus, his arms resting on his knees. He laid his bow beside him and rubbed his face with his hands. The younger man kicked at the rocky ground with his toe and continued speaking. "You could tell at every turn that Wilum was favouring Kal, giving him knowledge of things such as remain a mystery to common Holdsfolk. I don't doubt that even Thane Strongbow himself doesn't know a tithe of what Wilum told Kal. Although Kal would never admit it was happening, like he was embarrassed by the attention he was receiving. So he fell to talking all the time, like he was protesting, about how much he was looking forward to becoming a full-fledged wheelwright like his father, like you, Frysan." At this Frysan lifted his head, looking Galli full in the face.

"If you ask me plain, I think Cloudbeard was lonely, worried as he was by our good and right royal master Gawmage," continued Galli in a sardonic tone, a grin on his fair face, "and set at naught besides by so many bards that should have been paying him their respects and asking his advice and begging his judgements, him as bore the sacred office of Hedric. And laughed at as a throwback, even by certain folk in the Holding itself." Galli stepped towards Frysan and dropped to the ground, sitting beside him. "So there you have it. Your son, Kal, is now the sole Hordanu, or at least the only Hordanu as has his wits about him, although right at the moment I'm not so terribly certain about the wholeness of his mind or the soundness of his wits. Why, he was mumbling and grumbling like a surly mongrel dog all the way here." Galli's attempted humour was met by only his own chuckle.

"By the welkin, so that's what Wilum was trying to tell us." Frysan spoke low, then turned again to face Galli. "It's just that we couldn't understand what he was driving at. Even after you and Kal had left, and we supposed that all his strength was spent, and that he had begun to go out with the tide, even then poor old Cloudbeard summoned forth the energy to say it again, 'Kal . . . Kal . . . Hordanu.' His lips could hardly frame the syllables. But, for all that, they were so blunt that the point of their meaning failed to prick our thick skins.

"Aye, Galli, so our Kal is now Hordanu," Frysan said, shaking his head. "I'm thankful indeed that we have a Hordanu in the fix we're in. But to what end? Our Kal may be Hordanu, but he's a

Hordanu without a glence, without a home, and what's worse still, without the prospect of living out the next cycle of the sun, for we're trapped here, as surely as rats in some fast-flooding forsaken dungeon hold in Tower Dinas. I and the others had nursed the hope that Wilum might somehow show us another way of escape, seeing as he's no stranger to the Enclosure. Now there's not a one of us that has his bearings or the least knowledge about this cave, let alone the whole Enclosure. There's not a one of us that has the faintest notion where we should even begin looking, if we're to break free of these confounded mountains. Not a one knows what spot it would be folly or wisdom to try."

Frysan pushed himself to his feet, clasped his hands behind his back, and began treading a path in front of the Cave's entrance. He stopped and peered past the stone pillar into the gloom of the interior, then looked back at Galli. "Ha, a fit place for us to be encamped—Cave of the Hourglass, and the hourglass is fast running out of sand. Far too fast for comfort or, to face the matter squarely, Master Clout, for hope."

"And those manuscripts that I carried up the mountain in the sack. They might have had some useful bit of advice for us amid all those riddling lines. I'm dead sure they would have."

"And sure dead we'll all soon be."

"That may well be, Frysan, but, still, it's too bad about the manuscripts. They're full of ancient lore about people and places in Arvon, and probably the Enclosure too. Or else they wouldn't have been so heavy. Although, I'd give a king's fortune to feel their weight again across my back. If we could get at them, Kal would puzzle it out. He'd gain some idea where we should look, I'm certain."

"I'm certain too," Frysan said, cracking a smile at Galli's trust in his son's powers.

"But, now even the sack is gone," continued Galli. "Who knows how deep it's fallen? Perhaps all the way down to the very roots of Thyus. Who knows? That leaves us here, waiting for the Boar to finish gloating over the cleverness of his attack on the Holding. Then, when he's made ready, he can turn his attention to catching the rest of us and making a clean sweep of it. 'The Broom' he called it. Kal told me."

Frysan had stopped his restless pacing and lowered himself to sit once more against the rock wall. He leaned forward, rubbed his ankle and sighed. "All the same, Galli, we mustn't despair. There has to be a way, even if we have to venture into one of the side tunnels. From what I can tell, there are a number of them that branch out from the central chamber. It seems the place is honeycombed with them."

Galli's eyes widened in a look of questioning surprise.

"Yes, I know," said Frysan. "A dire choice, but at least that way we'd stand a ghost of a chance."

"Perhaps, perhaps. But I wouldn't give much for our chances of escape through the tunnels. Wilum talked to Kal and me about the Cave of the Hourglass not too very long ago. It was last year, I think, just after the Candle Festival, when he was setting out to travel up to the Enclosure, eager to have some time to himself to think things out, with the spring air to clear the cobwebs out of his brain, he said. It was just after Gawmage had sent him an upsetting message, another threat, but this time there was a real edge to it. Kal and I, we were all ears, Wilum was unusually talkative. Normally, he would have sent me away and kept Kal by his side, filling his ears for hours on end with cryptic verses from every dim scarce-remembered nook and cranny in *Hedric's Master Legendary*. Well, this time he was in such a state—well, he never thought to bother sending me off. I'm glad that he didn't, for I hadn't heard anything half so fascinating since my own dear Gammer—bless her—had filled me with stories of the Hidden Folk and other shadowy creatures—well, like the gathgour. Mind you, they're not so thrilling to me anymore, Frysan. I'd just as soon never again have dealings with such as them."

Galli paused a moment as if to regain his train of thought.

"Well, the Cave of the Hourglass . . . Wilum said as how once, early in the Great Harmonic Age, not too long after Hedric's time, a Hordanu perished while exploring farther into the Cave, even though Hedric had warned them—his successors, I mean. He had warned them, because he knew well enough the dangers. Even the echobards were frightened of it, and by and large they were a fearless lot. They called the caves haunted, for not a one of them ever took to exploring them, but that he failed ever to find his way again to the light of day. A maze of tunnels, Wilum called it, more tortuous than anything human skill could devise. 'Lair of Demons' in the runic language of the echobards, he said to us, one of the few things he or anybody else in Ahn Norvys

knows about runes and what they mean. One false turn was all
it took, and you might be lost forever. The echobards believed
that the passages beyond the Cave near as had a mind of their
own, drawing a person to destruction. It sort of makes you think
twice about the part of the Cave we're in now, doesn't it? I mean,
how can the rest of it be so awful and sinister, and this part of
it be all right?"

"Galli's description doesn't sound very promising, does it? But,
I have an idea that if we tried going up rather than down, we
might profit by it." Galli and Frysan started. Kal's voice sounded
firm and equable again, but with a quaver, as if there was some
great passion he was struggling to keep in check. He stepped out
into the night air, looking up at the windswept starfield above
the black mountains.

"What do you mean, son? How's Wilum doing?"

"He isn't long for this life," replied Kal, still facing away from
them, as if caught up in some dark solemn world of his own. "It
doesn't look good. His breath has begun to rattle and it's getting
even more laboured. But, he understood me, and I understood
him, I think. Yes, I understood him, after I had poured out to
him how I failed him, failed him and the Holding miserably. I, a
naive and overtrusting lout—now Hordanu. I, Kalaquinn Wright,
Hordanu of all Ahn Norvys, from the Ocean Isles of the West
to even the farthest-flung reaches of the shadowedland in the
East . . . All the while I held his hand in mine, and even before
the bitter words had died on my lips, he sought with his own
free hand to press mine, and then his eyes flickered into life,
like a dim spark thrown up from the fire that flashes bright for
just an instant and then smoulders unremarked, one of a thousand pinpoints glowing, fading, as they swirl towards the dark
heavens." Kal cast his gaze to the ground, as if embarrassed at
the poetic flight his words had taken. "W-well . . . That's what his
eyes looked like. Then, the rattling stopped, or it was masked by
another sound, a change in the rhythm of his breathing, so that
he closed his mouth every time he exhaled rather than keeping
it open. Finally it dawned on me—fool that I am—that he was
spending himself, spending the very last of his strength to frame
some word of meaning for me.

"And Gwyn, he understood. He could tell what was happening, better than me. It was all poor Gwyn could do to make me

see, so daft and slow I am to take up the meanings of things."
Kal turned to regard both father and friend, his face soaked with
the tears of quiet remorse. "'Hope,'" Kal said, almost choking on
the word. "'Hope,' the old man had been trying to say to me,
again and again, a dozen times or more, even while his hand
sought to pressure me into understanding what he meant. 'Hope,'
I said, once I had gathered my wits. 'Hope, no, Master Wilum,
I'll not let you down by losing hope, I swear by the sacredness
of the Stone and the orrthon and all that's holy,' I declared, oh,
so boldly." Kal's voice, a cry whispered and impassioned, now
cracked, broke. "I suddenly understood how, even in the teeth
of death, he had not lost hope, and that he was passing it on to
me as a gift, as a blessing, asking me to be its new bearer. I felt
a strange surge of confidence, as if the virtue had been plucked
out of his very mouth like a fruit, and its sweetness transfused
into me, nourishing me. I can't explain the feeling.

"And he knew, he knew I had bridged the gap, that I had
finally understood, for his other hand opened, revealing the pios,
as if he was bidding me take it. So, I took it and thought I saw
a smile crease the aged lines of his face, even as his eyes welled
with tears. Then the message of hope that had been formed by
the change in the pattern of his breathing ceased. His eyes closed
and he returned to his earlier hold on life, except it seemed much
more fragile. He began to look even more pallid. His breathing
became louder, more shallow. I couldn't bear to look anymore. I
felt that he had given me his leave, had got me to stop looking
back, stop living in regret. He wanted me to forgive myself, to
carry on, to look to what lies ahead."

Kal wiped his eyes with the back of his hand, drawing a deep
draught of the cool night air. He exhaled a groan, long and low.
"I left him with Gwyn. Gwyn's by his side now. You'd be hard
put to find a better nurse. It can't be long now, I think. That's
why I'm here. We've got to help him to pass on now. I mean,
you should come to say the Prayer of Passage, now, father. You're
the best of us that are left."

"But it's you, Kal, that must say the Prayer of Passage over
him," Galli objected. "It's you that's the Hordanu."

"But—"

"No! No, it's up to you, Kal. You're Hordanu now."

"Galli's right, son. He's given you the food of hope. Now, it's up to you to swallow it. Else you'd be flying in the face of Wilum's express wishes, and it's not just his wishes that are at stake here. As it stands now, the whole situation is bound up in other holy terms that we may not amend, neither I nor any other person, for they were invoked by the Hordanu himself."

"But how?" pleaded Kal. "It was all done in such haste, with scarce much time for thought on Wilum's part—or mine. How can it count for anything, when it's you, it's you that's the wisest of all the Holdsmen that are left?"

"It's you that's Hordanu, Kalaquinn." Frysan stood now and faced his son. "It has nothing to do with age or wisdom. Re'm ena, you're like a squirming lamb trying to escape the shearer's blades, my son. The more's the pity, after Wilum as near as rose from his deathbed to stiffen your backbone and give you courage and then handed you his pios as a token. Come, son, there's an old man's passage waiting to be eased."

Frysan did not give Kal the opportunity for a remonstrance, but led the two back through the sleeping cave to where Wilum lay on a couch of matted rushes. Gwyn, who sat crouched on his knees in vigil, looked up, his eyes glistening in the half-light beneath his unruly shock of hair. He leaned more closely over the dying man, listening to the even deeper rattle that now buckled his laboured breathing, eerily magnified by the walls and roof of the death chamber. It was as if the aged Hordanu had in some strange way grown in stature in the gradual disjoining of his spirit from the ligaments of his flesh, so that the place seemed fraught with inexplicable emanations of his being and other beings besides.

In the strong presence of death, Kal had to be encouraged to begin his recitation of the Prayer of Passage, and, as he started to intone the terrible piece, he felt that he was entering into a strange combat with unseen powers. He shuddered, chanting the most dread of all the turusorans, for it charted a road that no living breathing vessel of mortal clay might tread, not until its own doom-decreed time of severing. The tones rose and fell and echoed in the dark cavern.

"You, spirits of the circle of deep heaven, anagoroi most glorious, I beseech you, that you will be assistant with this mortal man that now beginneth to depart, and that you will deliver him mightily from the awaits and fallacies of his adversaries; and that it please you to receive his spirit into your company. And do thou, O Tobar, O principal, O leading, O goodest of the anagoroi, who hast from eternity been ordained to be the warder and keeper of our spirits, do thou, chiefest helper, I pray and adjure thee, do thou now aid and help our brother Wilum, as he setteth forth on his journey..."

Galli had lit a candle and held it out before him, above the failing shell of Wilum's body. At length, Kal trained his eyes on its narrow golden fillet of flame. The glow from it spread a pool of radiance over Wilum in a shallow arc that, with every flicker, sent probing fingers of hooded light feinting and thrusting at the veiling night. The primal mystery of light and darkness was being played out before them within the close compass of that death chamber. They scarce dared breathe. Each was caught by the awful gutter of the candle and the lugubrious soul-searing chant. Kal's voice grew in presence, somehow more real, more solid, more tangible. Kal had become a keening spirit, his eyes glazed, blind to the chamber, to light and shadow, to the gathered Holdsmen, and to the life-drained body over which he prayed.

It felt to him, as he droned the words of the Prayer of Passage, that he himself was being lifted out of the containing envelope of his own body, and that he was as free and unencumbered as a skylark whirling in carefree circles of flight through the vast blue sky beyond the lowering confinement of the Cave. Coupled with this sensation was the notion that he was being swept along like a leaf tossed, turned, and pushed by an overpowering current of air.

Kal found that he was not alone. There were mysterious presences close by, luminous ill-defined pillars that looked on him ablaze with a benison of glory. Kal basked in their bright warmth. Then came a change. It grew chill, and Kal felt his aerial self trembling, shuddering with a nameless dread. The light-filled creatures became thin and diaphanous. Indistinct, too, remote and unreachable, not so much because they had undergone some change in themselves, but, rather, because they were now mantled by a dark distorting medium, like smoked glass, that seemed to shift and coil, like a wisp of veiling mist. In a tingling instant of recognition, Kal knew that what he had supposed to be glass were in fact other presences—sinister misbegotten creatures, without form and chaotic, unlike the first ones he had encountered. The dark barrier of glass grew more fluid, seductive drifts of smoke sinuously shifting shape. Only these were not the whimsical playthings of nature, driven by vagrant breezes. They were real and animated of their own, now taking on one form, now another, leering at him out of the grey murk with distorted faces, so misshapen that they froze Kal to the marrow. Kal cried out once, but a strong impulse from within kept him reciting the Prayer of Passage without pause. They were closer to him, raucous, taunting and upbraiding him, mocking him for losing the Talamadh, for his failure, for clinging to hope, when there was none. His spirit smarted at the stings. The vapours had become thicker, a noisome miasma, enveloping him. It was as if he had flown into a black storm cloud from which there was no escape. He started to lose the feeling of airborne buoyancy, of being free and light. The other beautiful beings seemed to have abandoned him. One of the dark ones, leering and brazen, pulled at Kal's hair, wrenching his head down, using the long strands like a tether. And they laughed at him with throaty relish.

Kal interrupted the Prayer again with a heart-rending cry, his elation at his bird-like lightness having changed now to a desperate fear that he was plummeting down to earth, like a ponderous gobbet of lead, the curling shapes of smoke having become heavy and oppressive weights, dragging him down into murkier depths. Kal clung to the rhythmic accents of the Prayer of Passage, as if it were a talisman. Without it, he thought, he would be overwhelmed, dashed to bits on the stern pinnacles that stretched out beneath him. Kal could see them, rocky and cold and ice-covered, yawning with jagged gorges, standing ready to swallow him.

Some strange impulse prompted Kal to look behind him, even as he reeled in that dizzying freefall. It was Wilum. He could see him, surrounded by myriad luminous beings, piercing the mist with the brightness of their forms. A window of clarity was opening up in his wake. Wilum held something round and glittering in his right hand, as if to proffer it to Kal, but Kal could not tell what it was. Wilum smiled to him across the void, which was somehow obscured and unobscured at the same time. It was as if Kal was peering into another world, but only as a watcher, for there was no bridge, no way he could surmount the forces that thrust him down back to Ahn Norvys, back to the clay from

which his body drew its sinew, flesh, and bone. Wilum was calling
out to Kal, only his voice capable of spanning the two disparate
worlds. Kal could hear him, his words wafting to Kal's ears like
a healing unction.

"Briacoil, Kalaquinn. I thank thee, *Enefguthyas*, for chanting
me home to safe harbour. Fear not, *gil nas sverender*, my lord
Myghternos Hordanu."

Kal struggled to turn back, clambering against air to reach his
master and mentor. He was being flung down by some unyielding
force. There was no fighting it. Then, Kal recognized with shocking
clarity that this was Wilum's final blessing and farewell, and so
absorbed was he by it that he lost that harrowing helpless sense
of plunging through the sky earthwards to his doom. The next
thing he knew, he was lying prone on the floor of the chamber,
being gently lifted by his father.

"Are you all right, son?"

"Aye, Father, all right . . . All right, but sorry to be back here
and not with him."

"We must each of us wait for our time."

"He's gone, Kal," Galli said with solemn finality, still holding
the candle.

"I know," said Kal, groggy and uncertain, like a man waking
from a dream, except that he felt, to the contrary, that he was
emerging from real life into a dreamworld, dim and unlit, an
exile in a place where clay-shrouded forces contended in the
shadows. Oh, that he might have been dashed against the rocks
and liberated like Wilum into the light! It was the anagoroi who
had met Wilum, and he had run for Wilum the gauntlet of the
fallen ones, who prey like jackals on freshly loosed spirits. *Enefguthyas*, Soul Warden, Wilum had called him. And that poignant
valediction, destined, as he knew, to be vain and fruitless until
his own life had run its bounden course—*gil nas sverender*, until
we meet again.

Frysan folded Wilum's arms across his chest, to make the
ceremonial corpse symbol of crossing over, then left to awaken
his wife. At the entrance to the death chamber, he met Athmas,
Thurfar, and a handful of others woken by the doleful chant. He
nodded to them and passed. Soon, the ritual lament of mourning would fill the Cave. Wilum's long hair took on a vivid hue
of white, like a brookside bed of spring lilies, so that it shone

above the sallow welted face—a coronal of glory. Although Wilum's eyes were closed now in death, there was a sheen that rose from them beneath the marbled parchment of his lids. The redness of his wounds had paled, leaving a waxen mask composed in peace. The wail rose in the stillness, a single voice swelling, now joined by another, and now another.

"May the rest of us find a like end to our journey someday," Kal said to Galli and Gwyn, who were left with him beside the husk of Wilum's body.

"That's a fine thing to wish on friends, to have their heads knocked in by the likes of Relzor."

"I didn't mean that, Galli. I meant, look at him, look how peaceful he seems. No cares to bother him in this world or the next."

"Well, for now, we'd better be about our own cares, for we have our feet still very solidly planted on the soil of Ahn Norvys. At least I do. It's too early yet to be chanting the Prayer of Passage for the rest of us that want to stay here and keep our hides for a while longer yet. What we need now is some plan of action."

Kal sighed heavily, gathering himself back to the world of flesh and blood by act of will. The need to survive superseded the need to grieve. As the women began to file past him into the death room, he turned to Galli and pointed out into the main chamber.

"What I thought was, that, if we still have that rope and grapnel, we could do some exploring and see what's up above the Cave of the Hourglass here."

"That's a fair piece up, Kal."

"Well, the rope's long enough. We could use it to get a grip on the edge of the smoke hole in the centre of the Cave, lift ourselves up to the upper chamber and then use the rope again to latch on to the topmost opening. What if we can find a way out there above the roof of the Cave?"

"An excellent idea and well worth trying," said Frysan, who had returned. "I'll get the rope and grapnel again from Athmas."

Soon, the three were staring up at the stars that twinkled down at them from the clear patch of night sky through the double tier of smoke holes in the middle of the Cave. The fire had all but died, giving them an unobscured view. Gwyn kept his own strange vigil for Wilum, and even his affection for Kal could not dislodge him from it. So, he stayed with Wilum yet. Around them rose the ululating moans of keening Holdsfolk, woken from their sleep to pour out their grief for the slain Hordanu.

It took them a few throws to affix the grapnel onto a butting edge of rock. Galli took hold of the rope and tugged on it. The grapnel bit into the stone above their heads and held. Slowly, Galli applied his weight to the rope, until he pulled himself a few inches from the ground. He let go of the rope and dropped to the floor, rubbing his hands together.

"So, then, I suppose it's me that climbs. Re'm ena, but it seems a fair piece up," Galli said, looking to where the rope hung from the lower smoke hole.

"I'll climb," said Kal, seizing the rope.

"You? But you're the Hordanu."

"Which makes it my responsibility, Galli." Kal pulled himself onto the rope, wrapping his feet around it beneath him.

"But if you fall—"

"I won't." Kal began climbing.

"Let him go," Frysan said, then patted his son's leg, where he dangled from the rope. "But do be careful, Kalaquinn, we surely can't afford to lose you now."

Grunting with the exertion of it, Kal inched in jerks up the rope, 'til at last he reached the first smoke hole some dozen or so yards above their heads.

"By the welkin, but it's dark here," he yelled down to them, squatting on the lip of the upper chamber. "I can't rightly tell where I can or can't step, if I'm not to fall off into some sinkhole, and then you'll never hear from me more." The rope disappeared, tugged up the hole behind him. "I hope this sprig of ash does what it's supposed to do too, in case the gathgours are around. Well then, I'll just throw this up to see if I can't catch onto that chockstone. It's a farther ways to get to the top than even it was to get here— Aye! what's that? Something flew at me here." Kal yelled, reeling off balance.

"It's a pigeon!" cried Galli, looking up at the bird that had sent Kal ducking and bobbing at the edge of the smoke hole. Kal squatted at the edge of the smoke hole and saw the thing fly a circle in the cavern before fluttering to a rest in the wicker cage, cooing plaintively.

"It bears a message." Frysan had walked to the cote and reached through its opened door to lift out the bird. "It's been hurt, the poor thing. It's bleeding from one of its wings, and I can feel its heart thumping. The bird's had some scare," he said, cupping the cowering bird in his hands and taking it to the hearth fire, still glimmering a feeble light from its bed of coals. He untied the banded scroll from its leg, placed the delicate creature on the ground, and began reading the opened message by the uncertain glow. Galli edged closer.

"It's in Wilum's own hand," said Galli. "I recognize his writing well enough. What does it say?"

"'We are invaded by Ferabek. The Stoneholding is lost. Will meet you at Cot as soon as possible.'" Frysan handed the thin slip of paper to Galli, who took it and read it to himself.

"This is a message to that Aelward fellow. Wilum was telling you about him, when we were leaving Raven's Crag Island." Galli looked up again to where his friend stooped over the opening above them. "Aye, Kal, do you remember how he went out for a moment, before we left the keeil, and mentioned something about a message?"

"I do, yes. But the poor bird never made it, or if it did, there was nobody there."

"Wilum said it had been some time since he had heard from Aelward."

"Do you think Dhu might have harmed it, Kal?" asked Frysan.

"No, I've taught Dhu not to attack doves or pigeons on account of Wilum's keeping them. Keep that message, Galli, I want to see it."

Frysan picked up the wounded pigeon and replaced it in the wicker cote. Some of the children, awakened by the wail of lament, had gathered to look at the little creature. Frysan gave them stern instructions not to touch the bird, because it was hurt, but to find it grain or crumbs and a vessel of water. He lowered the dovecote on its rope. Kal smiled as the children scattered to scavenge provender for their charge—a comforting distraction for them in this time of distress.

Frysan returned to the centre of the chamber, lifting his hand to Kal, pointing in mock agitation. "Go on then, Kalaquinn. There's nothing to be gained by gaping down at us. Up you go! Carry on! Courage. We'll be right beneath you to mark your progress—"

"Or catch me if I fall," Kal said, turning his attention from the two below him to the hole above. With a slow, fluid sweep of his arm, he threw the grapnel up to the second smoke hole at the very highest point in the upper dome of the Cave. He cast the climbing iron once, and then again, each time having to guard against its falling back and knocking him on the head or gouging his flesh. Three times the hooked metal grapnel fell clanging beside him in the darkness before the thing caught. Kal made trial of it carefully, putting weight on the rope, until he was more or less sure that it would hold him.

Then, he pulled himself onto it and up. It proved a much more hesitant ascent than his first climb, and more laborious too, for he was uncertain about what awaited him up above on the outer rim of the Cave. With painful trepidation, he reached the cavern's apex, and pulled his upper body over the edge of the smoke-blackened opening. He let go the rope, which hung down through both smoke holes to the cavern floor below him, and took a deep breath of the outside air, cool and almost intoxicating after the stale must of the Cave and the exertion of his climb.

Dangling, he held tight to a handhold, a crack in the solid rock that edged the opening. He felt, with a tentative sweep of his free hand, that his arms were resting on a table of rock that would probably support his full weight. Very slowly, he hauled his whole body over the edge, easing himself onto the flat rock. For a long moment, he lay listening, his face pressed against the cold stone of Mount Thyus. At length, he rolled over, sat up, and looked around. He drew a sharp breath, for the sky was cloudless, and the thin moon shone liquid silver on the mountainscape about him. Whichever way he turned, there rose rugged spires, fantastic crenellations, that heaved themselves to prodigally dizzying heights and plunged wantonly into deep unplumbed abysses. Facing him, on the other side of a gulf that seemed infinitely deep, there trickled a crystal streamlet, wedged into a rocky tier of Mount Hecla, like a strand of gems in a protective casket, but so far away that its murmurs were stifled. Below the snowline, thick masses of forest reared against the slopes, each tree like a rider bracing himself stiff when his horse plunges down a gully. Behind him, a razor-edged ridge dipped from his stony perch and rose again to meet the sheer heights of Thyus, snowcapped and glimmering in the moonlight, that towered over him.

Kal stared into the very heart of the Radolan Mountains, which ran like a spine down the western flank of Arvon, separating the land, time out of mind, into highlands and lowlands. And more frightening still, he found that the outside of the Cave was shaped no less like an hourglass than the inside, for the rock fell away from him smoothly on all sides. Only the ledge on which he sat, and the knife's edge ridge of stone connecting the dome to the stark side of Thyus broke the curve of the rock. This ledge seemed to have been cut out of the Cave's outer dome deliberately, perhaps as a lookout during the Age of Echoes. Kal shifted his weight with painstaking slowness. His stomach was knotted, and he felt giddy from the heights, not relishing the thought of working himself back onto the rope.

He leaned forward and peered down the hole. "There's no way out from up here, let me tell you, unless you're a bird or a gathgour. And no way back down, I'm as like to find out," he cried down to the two Holdsmen below, trying to dull the edge of his growing anxiety, wondering how even the gathgours for all their nimbleness could challenge the time-sculpted smoothness of this granite dome, an uncertain island in a wilderness of angles and steeps. From every direction around him, the mountain canyons echoed back his words, and in that moment it came to him how exposed and vulnerable he was. He longed to be back down with Galli, his father, and the rest. While the echoes died, the keening moans drifted up to him, like a distant music, making him feel very much alone, small and insignificant, on this spectacular but treacherous roof of the world.

The wind picked up, its chill fingers tugging at his tunic. Kal turned, feeling for the grapnel lodged in the rock at the edge of the smoke hole. This was the worst part, trying to get back down, much worse than it was on that tree at the Perch earlier in the day. If only it was just the tree he had to descend now! With its many branches, the thing was all footholds. How was he going to get into position to let himself down into the Cave again without losing his grip and breaking his neck, or worse still, slipping off the edge of this smooth half-globe into the emptiness beyond?

As Kal corkscrewed his body around, edging himself closer to where the grapnel bit into the granite, the wind grew fiercer, in draughts that made him catch his breath and cower. The buffeting of the wind caused him to throw his right arm back and with it clutch at the edge of the smoke hole, while he lay on his side, huddled on the ledge, which seemed now to grow smaller and smaller. Exposed and helpless, he waited for the gusts to subside.

It was while lying on his side that he saw the night drake. The first grim sight of it chilled his heart, freezing his limbs with horror, as it threaded the corridor of the Radolans that opened solemnly to the south. On the night drake's back, Kal thought he spied the outline of a rider. It appeared he had not been seen, for the creature drifted away from him. But, suddenly, it wheeled around.

Now there would be no agonizing wait to screw up his courage, like a swimmer making his first plunge in spring, daintily testing the bracing waters of Deepmere. He was given no time to indulge his new-formed fear of heights, for the great creature bore down on him under the silver light of the setting moon. One vault over the side was all it took, and Kal was grappling with the rope, sliding down it to the floor of the Cave so quickly that he burned his palms in the descent.

SIXTEEN

"It was just a glimpse I caught, but, I swear, it was Enbarr I saw riding the thing, like it was a winged horse. The way he did when he escaped us at the Seven Springs with Relzor."

"The trouble is, you didn't wait long enough to find out. I've never seen a body move as fast as you did down that rope."

"As you would have, Galli, if you'd been in the spot I was. I could feel its breath, I tell you. Its tongue was like a giant snake's, hissing. And fire, there was fire flaring out of its nostrils, it was so keen to swoop down on me from the sky. I tell you, I could feel it bearing down on me."

"I didn't see any fire coming from it, when Relzor stole off with the Talamadh. I wish it had. We might have noticed it better creeping up on us in the dark with Enbarr, and it would have saved us a sore pack of trouble." Galli nettled Kal, while Frysan looked on, chuckling to himself at the exchange.

"All right, enough, Galli, but this time it was spewing fire, I tell you. And its eyes were big red round things, like flaming hot coals!" Kal glanced up again as if to assure himself that the night drake was not peering down on them through the double opening that loomed above their heads. "Look, quick now, Galli, there it is! Father, look! Re'm ena, but the thing's gone."

By the time Galli and Frysan lifted their heads, it had disappeared, although it had left in its wake a faint downdraft of air that teased the smoking embers of the fire at their feet. Another moment passed, and the fearsome creature overflew the Cave again, as if searching for the place where Kal had evaded it. The thing passed low. One more pass and the beast alighted on the rim of the smoke hole itself, its silhouette framed against the night sky, as knobbed and gnarled as the weathered butt of an old oak, gripping the chockstone, where the grapnel remained anchored. The foul reek of fetid carrion pervaded the air. Down it peered into the Cave. They could feel its eyes in the darkness, beaming predatory hate, dumbly inhuman and vicious. The three Holdsmen fell back, as the creature emitted a deep moaning cry. The keening ceased, and children began to shriek in sheer terror. Frysan called on the other men to gather the Holdsfolk into the empty sidechamber, bidding them take light and try to calm the children.

"Now we've found out where the mice are cornered, haven't we, Thraganux?" They heard the voice, loud and derisive, but could not see the body behind it, for it was hidden from sight on the saddled back of the night drake. It was unmistakable, though. Enbarr's voice dripped with the purring unction of triumph and power. "Not very welcoming, are they, Thrag, to scurry indoors when they see us coming? And we were just coming to speak our greetings. To give them the heartfelt thanks of my lord Ferabek for the wonderful gift that they've made to him of the Talamadh." His laughter rang in the chamber. "How exceedingly generous a token of their esteem and warrant of their fealty. And now if they but gave themselves up peaceably to my grateful Lord, the Boar, how much easier it would be for all concerned, wouldn't it, Thrag? Rather than play this dangerous game of hide and seek on the mountaintops. Besides, there's not a place they could flee to where we wouldn't spot them, isn't that so, Thrag? If they gave up young Kalaquinn Wright, how happy we would all be. Aye, how very happy," Enbarr continued with relentless spite, conversing slyly with his terrible mount.

"Do you hear me down there?" Enbarr's tenor changed. The disembodied voice was now one of violent challenge, as hard and steely as a thrusting lance. The edge of gloating triumph had given way to one of unqualified anger and, Kal sensed, frustration—yes, undoubted frustration—for there was something that was keenly desired yet by Enbarr and his master, something they still craved. Enbarr's tone was less cocksure, less smugly sinister, and so, in an odd way, more human.

"You have 'til break of day to deliver Kalaquinn, son of Frysan

Wright, or you shall all be put to the sword. Don't let that fool Wilum foster your illusions. You have but to throw yourselves on the mercy of my gracious lord Ferabek, and you shall have your precious Stoneholding back, your wayward little pocket clanholding, your highland jewel. Do you hear me, Wilum, you hidebound throwback, you stubborn . . ." He stumbled and stuttered, mumbling out of raw frustration and anger.

"It's all your fault, this chafing at the bit, this delay at a doom that knows no escaping. Or did Relzor make a proper end to you, as he claimed he did? And the rest of you, surely you have more sense than to listen to a dithering old idiot? Surely, you are not all bent on holding out? It is suicide! Do you hear? Suicide! And for what reason? To satisfy a stubborn old man who plays at being Hordanu? Release Kalaquinn Wright to us at the foot of the Stairs of Tarn Cromar by the rising of the morrow's sun, and the rest of you shall live to see another day and many more days besides. There's no resisting the might of my lord Ferabek's hand, as you shall see, for you're trapped up here with no place to run. You're trapped, do you hear me? Trapped!"

The words echoed through the cavern.

"But you may yet do my lord Ferabek's bidding and survive, aye, and you may flourish even. Either that, mark you well, or you and your children will be dashed against the Rock of Gharssûl. So you must decide, and decide soon. All you need do is unfurl a flag of truce at the Stairs of Tarn Cromar and send a messenger down with young Wright, and your hides are saved. Do you hear me? Do you hear me, I say? Speak! Loosen your tongues or let the Enclosure be your tomb!"

"Aye, we do, Enbarr," yelled Galli, "We hear you. Every twisted word. Begone with you, you traitor, with your head crammed full of long-winded lies. Better still, come down and I'll gladly knock them out of your head for you."

Frysan took up the defiant cry, shouting with all his might up into the vacant air of the Cave's top chamber. "Surely, you take us for backward dolts, to think that we believe a single word of what you've said! And even if we did believe you, do you suppose that a Holdsman, of even the slightest bit more mettle than you possess, would succumb to your blandishments merely to add a few days or even years to his span of life? "

But Enbarr did not make answer nor await a further exchange, for the night drake slipped his talons from the open roof of the Cave and climbed up into the sky with his rider.

"Go back to your master and tell him that while there is yet a man or woman of the Holding drawing breath, we shall not yield! Not now! Not ever!" Frysan roared, shaking, red-faced, his fist raised.

"It's no good, Father. He's gone." The far-off, parting cry of the night drake, soaring now high above the Cave, drifted down to the Holdsfolk. "And now he knows exactly where we are." Kal looked away from the circle of night sky above to his father beside him. "Not that it matters much anyhow. Enbarr was right about us being cornered and there being no place to run."

A deep and fearful hush had descended on the cave, broken only by the choked sobs of one or two children not yet exhausted by fear and, presently, by the murmur of whispered conversations. From the side chamber, the Holdsfolk emerged and, as if to establish some semblance of the normal in the face of their straits, moved about the familiar activities of life—children were comforted and laid again to sleep despite their fretfulness, another torch was lit, and someone stirred up the remains of the fire, laying more fuel on it, until it leaped brightly again in the centre of the cavern.

The women, while yet keening, had begun dressing Wilum's body for burial, as was the immemorial custom in the highlands. In the morning, they would inter him somewhere in the Enclosure, providing they were still alive by then. The commotion in the main chamber had been violent and had drawn the women from their corpse-duties. All of them, both men and women, had heard Enbarr's demands and sensed Frysan's air of hopeless dejection. There was a feeling of oppressive uncertainty in the Cave, spreading among them like a pollution. Thurfar had turned his hand to the fire again in an attempt to further push back the gloom that no mere firelight could dispel. Their restlessness grew.

"Don't you think, Manaton, that we ought to consider Enbarr's proposal?" whispered Gara to her husband. "I'm thinking of the little ones. Let them have a chance at living."

"I know what you're all thinking and whispering, too, amongst yourselves"— Devved's deep voice broke through the uneasy buzz of furtive conversation—"that it'd be better, perhaps, to make treaty with them Scorpions as Enbarr's taken up with. That if they want young Kal Wright, it'd be best to give him up for the remains of us, especially these young ones, for it don't matter much what happens to the likes of me, I tell you honest, for I've had my sum of days on this highland clay of ours." Devved paused and looked around himself at the hushed people. The dispirited tiredness of the Holdsfolk was palpable, as was their willingness to consider whatever means were at hand to escape the end they had reached. Now that Wilum, their Hordanu, lay dead, their last link with what remained of an older order seemed gone, and a creeping futility and resignation had spread through the Cave.

"Are you so foggy that you can't tell a rotter by his headmarks, or do I have to touch you with my hammer to knock some proper sense into you? There ain't no trusting Enbarr nor his cousin Kenulf. I'd sooner trust a fox to guard my henhouse, I know that for a fact."

"By my ten finger bones, but I'm a rank fool if Devved's not right on the mark!" said Diggory Clout. "Why, we'd all be like them knaves as run things in Dinas Antrum to trust in them false-forged hollow words of Enbarr's, him as has betrayed most all our clanfellows and his own to the Boar and his bloody Scorpions."

"And what's more," said Galli in a low voice, "Kal's now the Hordanu. Wilum made him Hordanu earlier today. Re'm ena, but it's so. The guardianship of the Talamadh and Wuldor's Howe has been given over to Kalaquinn Wright," he affirmed. A look of quiet incredulity met this news. "Wilum was going to tell you all himself, but never got the chance. You may be sure that's why the Boar wants us to hand Kal over, although how he knows that he's been made Wilum's successor is clean beyond my reckoning. Maybe it's that Thrygian sorcerer of his."

The public announcement of the election of a new Hordanu was always a solemn moment in the Stoneholding, and often nature itself conspired with the event to make it singularly joyous, alive with the mystery of change and new beginning. The old folk of the Holding, steeped in their own experiences and the lore of generation upon generation of their ancestors, most often likened the occasion to one of the bright fresh days of midspring, even when the election happened in the dead of winter. New energies seemed to flow lavishly into the Holding and Wuldor's Howe on the accession of a new Hordanu. Even now, a subtle sense of present witnessing spirits pervaded the Cave of the Hourglass.

All eyes had turned on Kal. Frysan stepped forward from beside him, sweeping with his gaze the faces of his fellow Holdsmen. "Aye, it is so." He broke the spell of wonderment, as Marina choked a cry. "You can feel it. It was what Wilum was trying to tell us. And you know it was Kalaquinn who chanted the Prayer of Passage for him. It is Kalaquinn who is our High Bard, our Hordanu." Frysan then turned to face Kal and fell to a knee, his head bowed before his son. "Hail, my lord Myghternos Hordanu." His voice resonated in the charged atmosphere of the cavern. The last syllables of his homage hung in the air, faded, then all fell silent.

He rose and faced the Holdsfolk again. "And now we'd best get some sleep, or we'll not have the strength to do a thing, even if the ground beneath us were to gape open to show us a way out of here. I've no doubt but we'll be needing our strength before too long. As for myself, I'll keep watch here for a while yet. The men at the Stairs are like to be signalling to us anytime, and then it'll be time for all of us to make our fighting stand. Let your swords and bows lie ready to hand. Does everyone know who's on the relieving watch?" There were nods from the three men slated to relieve Narasin and his sons at the Stairs. "Good! It won't be long now, I'll wake you when it's time."

He had dismissed them before anyone could say or do a thing. In stunned quiet, the group broke, people returning each to their place of rest. Kal wore a look of bewilderment. Frysan smiled and placed an arm over his shoulder. "Come," he said, "you should get what rest you can, too. The call to arms will come soon enough."

"But don't you think we have a while yet, 'til daybreak at least?" asked Kal.

"Aye, son, if you think that Enbarr was telling the truth. There's not a word that comes from that man's mouth that has any hold in it. More slippery and full of twists and turns than an eel, especially when he's after something. But enough, go and get some sleep."

Once again, an uneasy stillness cloaked the Cave. All the men and women seemed quickly to fall into as deep a slumber as the children, for now, at last, they were simply too tired to let worry keep them from it. All except Kal, who bade his father and Galli goodnight and lay down beside his mother and Bren, racking his brain for the faintest suggestion of a clue that might aid their escape. What had Wilum told him in days gone by that might be put to use? And underlying this, there was a further nagging question that his mind rebelled to address. He tossed and turned, heaping thought upon thought, until he supposed that the very heaviness of his reflections might press him into the weightlessness of sleep.

Tiring of his fruitless efforts, he arose wearily and stepped to crouch beside the remains of the cookfire, which still glowed feebly. He pulled from his pocket the tiny scroll that Galli had given him, unfolded it and held it an an angle to catch the faint orange light of the coals. His eye fell to the graceful flowing script his master's hand had set on the small leaf of onionskin. "The Stoneholding is lost . . ." Wilum is lost, he thought. He let the thin paper slip from his fingers onto the embers, where it blackened, smouldered, and smoked for a moment, before it flashed to flame, then glowing, it dwindled and was spent.

He crept to the side chamber where Wilum's body lay in endless slumber. Perhaps he might bequeath to Kal some of his vast store of forgetful sleep, or forge, by the very presence of his body in repose, some fresh meaning from their predicament. All the hope that he had felt earlier oozed from him, like a slow-bleeding and mortal wound. He needed Wilum's help. The question he had in mind now was not one he could resolve—a dire question—and Kal knew that it was beyond his own competence to decide. As holder of the ancient office of High Bard, he now bore a grave responsibility.

In the death room, a pine-pitch torch still guttered a pale wavering light, letting the shadows weave a death mask for the old Hordanu, who smelled fresh and clean from the ablutions the women had performed preparatory to his being buried. Kal found himself all alone with Wilum's body, which lay on the couch where he had died. Kal half-expected to see Gwyn, who had been clinging to Wilum the whole evening, from the time of their first discovery of him after the attack by Relzor to when Kal pronounced the Prayer of Passage. Kal looked twice to make certain he was not mistaken, for there was a wraith-like hidden-ness about Gwyn, an indistinctness and slightness of form that seemed to merge with a dark night or a foggy mist, imparting to him an elusive want of shape and visibility. It was strange. Where could the lad be? Kal did not remember seeing him in the

main chamber in the aftermath of Enbarr's ultimatum. His eyes
had sought him then, when everyone else had crowded around
the sullen hearth fire.

Kal slipped back into the large chamber to check if Gwyn
had not somehow eluded his notice to curl up in a corner. He
lit a torch and crept between the bodies of exhausted sleepers.
"Where have you got to, my little Mommick?" Kal whispered. He
stumbled over Thurfar, who mumbled something incoherent and
rolled back to sleep. At the entrance to the Cave, he asked his
father if he had seen Gwyn. Like Kal, however, Frysan had seen
or heard nothing of the boy.

"Don't worry, son. You've but missed him in the poor light.
It'd be better if you got some sleep rather than worry yourself
about Gwyn. We have a hard time ahead of us yet, with a sore
fight against Ferabek's Scorpions awaiting us at the Stairs, if we
mean to keep them at bay. And here you are, wearing yourself
out looking for Gwyn."

"Aye, but I've been sleepless too with supposing that our chances
are slim, slimmer than a snowflake's on midwinter's hearth." He
paused and looked out into the night before speaking again. "It's
me they want, that's clear enough. What if we give them what
they want, and then the rest of you will be quit of them?"

"It would be fool's work, Kal. You'd better take off your blinkers
on that score. And I don't say this because I'm your father and
you're my son. Don't suppose that I would scruple to allow you
to make a sacrifice of yourself, if in the balance your mother and
your brother and all the others here could find themselves saved.
But, I've heard tell of the Boar often enough. Even in the Holding,
he's cast his long shadow, for there's not a traveller comes our way
but quavers when he speaks of the Gharssûlian League, and how
its iron rule has grown amain, not only in those far places that
lie beyond Arvon, but in our own downlands, most particularly
in Dinas Antrum. How can anyone not feel the aftercurrents
of his slightest move, when he's forged, by the might of a hand
that knows no scruple, the deadliest alliance of forces that Ahn
Norvys has seen since the time of Tardroch? Besides, Kal, you're
more now than just my son. You're Hordanu, and don't pay heed
to those that doubt you, as they doubted Wilum."

"Doubts? Even now? Even with all this evil they've unleashed
on us?" asked Kal.

"Aye, especially now, when they've seen in which quarter the tilted balance lies. To get some peace, they think, as if peace were something that came dropping slow and easy, like an overripe plum that doesn't need to be plucked, but comes down on its own." Frysan heaved a sigh against the palpable weight that had settled over them. He faced his son squarely and said, "No, Kal, if being Hordanu in the selfsame line of Hedric means anything still, you must carry on. At any cost except dishonour, you must save yourself. Even if I and all of us here go down to defeat by Ferabek's awful butchery, you must save yourself. You owe it to the office you now hold, to every Hordanu who's preceded you, to every bard who sings the orrthon, to all of Ahn Norvys, even to the Great Harmony itself. And you owe it to Wilum and to those mightier spirits in whose company he now stands. I felt it when you were reciting the Prayer of Passage, Kalaquinn."

"Felt? Felt what?"

"That you were like a lodestone, attracting to yourself . . . I don't rightly know what. But something mysterious and powerful and the seed of something greater. It was laid open to me and shrouded all at once. But one thing's sure, I could feel it in my gut . . . the strangest feeling."

"What was it, Father?"

"That what you had, I shared in—nay, more exactly, that I had passed it on to you, and that you shared it with me, as a son. As my son."

SEVENTEEN

He'd have one last look around for Gwyn, and then he'd try to get some sleep. Kal had taken his farewell of the slender dark-haired figure standing watch at the entrance to the Cave. His father had a strange fey air about him tonight—unusual for him. Kal shrugged. Must have been his soldier's sense, duty-bound to action, honed again to a fine edge by the dark tide of events that had engulfed the Holding. And much indeed depended on his vigilance. At least he had Dhu for company. The fellhawk had nestled himself in a comfortable cornice in the rocks above the mouth of the Cave.

Kal felt overcome by exhaustion, a deep bone-weariness, his eyelids so heavy it seemed a wonder that he had managed to feel so alert and unsleepy just scant moments ago. He had been reassured by his father's presence, that quiet self-possession that rendered him master of any task or situation, whether it was repairing a broken wheel, or setting a fractured bone, or sitting guard over the few remnant survivors of the bloody slaughter that had swept over his native clanholding.

For the first time, Kal had noticed a broadening of the streak of grey that silvered the raven-black hair on the back of his father's head, just above the nape of the neck. This patch of grey was a birthmark of his, one that he had passed on to his son Kalaquinn, though not to Brendith. Kal smiled. Ah, Brendith, dear brother Bren, sleeping soundly right through the terrifying visit of the night drake. Knowing him, even the Trump of Narses couldn't rouse him from his slumbers. Galli was just the same.

Indomitable sleepers, the both of them, even now in this moment of highest danger, when all their lives seemed to be hanging in the balance, awaiting the inevitable assault, awaiting the grim blasts of the hunting horn.

From inside the entrance, Kal slowly swept the cavern with a careful eye, pausing over the dormant forms, holding each for a moment in his gaze before moving to the next, searching again for Gwyn. He was nowhere among the body of Holdsfolk rapt in sleep. This was his second time searching for him here. Kal frowned and shook his head, then stopped beneath the smoke hole by the fire's dying glow. He pulled at his chin and let his mind stray, finding it impossible to shake the pitiful image of his father's fragility and haggard wornness. An oddly sorted weight of compassion and insecurity had fallen on his heart. Enbarr's threats down the smoke hole seemed to still hang in the air above the broken remnant, a dull ring in Kal's ears punctuated by his own heartbeat. How would they survive—these few, now his concern? These so few . . . His heart throbbed. How could he carry them? Chandaris, still on a stretcher, here by his feet, whimpering and restless in his sleep. And Laloke, to whom he had given his rowan, and her brother, and his own brother Bren, and mother . . . Galli . . . Marya . . . Gwyn. And Gwyn—where had he disappeared to? Kal's gaze returned to the great pillar by the Cave's mouth. Creases of worry had lined father's face, creases he had never seen before—deep fretting runnels, like ravines set in ageless rock worn by the unrelenting course of time.

Suddenly, Kal's feeling of tiredness was sloughed off. How could he sleep, while father kept watch alone? He would find the wayward Mommick, wherever he was—he had to be somewhere—then join Father again to keep him company. Kal pulled a fresh torch from a small pile of them that lay to hand beneath the wickerwork dovecote, with its lone pigeon, cooing mournfully in its ward of deepened darkness. Kal held the torch to the feeble coals, smouldering yet in the firepit, and it leaped into life.

"What's that? Is that you, Kal? Everything all right?" Athmas looked up blinking from his pallet, startled from his fragile sleep by the unexpected burst of light.

"Hush, Athmas! Nothing to be alarmed about. Go back to sleep. Don't worry."

Kal had hardly turned away from Athmas before the man had

relapsed into the measured rhythm of his rest. Behind him, one of the children cried out in the grips of a nightmare. Kal glanced back that way, and with a sharp pang mumbled a prayer of protection under his breath. All fell silent once again, except for the rattle of snores and the plaintive croodling of the wounded pigeon.

The torch illumined Kal's way to the side chamber wherein lay Wilum's body, enveloped by the close-clinging blanket of darkness, now that the single taper in its sconce upon the wall had failed. Even before he reached it, Kal sensed the sweet-smelling oil with which the women had anointed the old man's head. He stepped around the corner into the chamber itself, where all the nooks and crannies caught the probing glow of fresh torchlight, unveiling the thick pall of darkness.

Still no sign of Gwyn. He half-expected to find the crippled boy had slipped back to hold his station by the slain Hordanu during the time he himself had been speaking with father. Gwyn was like that, a notorious fixture at a death bed, when he seemed, his eyes glazed over and impassive, to enter into silent communion with the hidden world of spirits, who were said to throng the farther mist-wreathed shores of Lake Nydhyn, the Birdless Lake.

"Oh, that mist-headed Mommick!" grumbled Kal, as he turned to leave. In the wheeling torchlight, a small twinkle caught his eye. Its sparkle blinked out at him from the ground at the far end of the room. Whatever it was, it reflected the light that streamed unevenly from his torchbearing hand, for as soon as he moved his arm to the left, away from it, there was nothing to be seen but a gloomy patch of blackness. There it was again, when he drew his arm towards it once more—as slight as a single fading firefly. Kal moved forward. The thing lay just inside the entrance of a passageway that radiated out from the tapering end of the chamber. To the right of it, at chest height, gaped the hole down which Relzor had shoved the sack of manuscript scrolls, before fleeing from the scene of his terrible crime. Strange to think that a mere few hours separated life from death, that a short while ago Wilum had lived and breathed and given counsel to his decimated clanfellows. Now he lay there lifeless, while Relzor gloated somewhere down in the valley below, safe under the protection of his newfound master.

Kal stooped to feel the ground with his fingers and found something small and round, hard to the touch. Two such things. He picked one of them up and recognized it as a marble. Two marbles, by the welkin! In the centre of each of them were embedded two crossed flakes of silver—the reason they had reflected back the light of his torch. The floor of the passage had turned soft here, earthen rather than rocky, and Kal thought he felt a breeze playing ever so slightly through the tunnel, tugging gently at the oily flames that curled up from the pine pitch of his torch.

There were footprints, fresh ones, soft-shod. They were Gwyn's, Kal could tell, judging by the impress of his club foot and the highland cut of the footgear, just as he was sure the marbles belonged to the boy. Kal shot a quick glance down the tunnel. Gwyn's tracks continued on into the unlit murk, disappearing into the black beyond of the passageway. What could he be doing, the crazy pixie-led Mommick? Kal's mind turned to the countless rueful stories of men led to their lonely ruin deep in the labyrinthine bowels of the earth by the beckonings of hidden folk, who in their subterranean lairs nursed their ill will towards creatures of light. Gwyn knew he was not to leave the confines of the Cave of the Hourglass. Why had he gone into the tunnel? Certainly, he was a curious lad, but it was not like him to disobey.

Kal lit a second torch, which he left in its bracket on the wall near the opening, and took a few tentative steps forward, taut and wary, sweeping the passage with his eyes. As far as he could tell, the tunnel continued on straight in an oblique direction towards the left, without dipping or rising. There seemed no harm in going on a bit farther. What if Gwyn was in trouble? He might even be lost already. Kal paused a moment to listen. There was nothing but a deep silence. For an instant, he lost his nerve and glanced back to the chamber, bathed in the soft torchlight, supposing that it might not be ill-advised at this point to fetch Galli or Bren or Thurfar Fletcher. But then, why disturb them from their sleep? Surely, Gwyn would not have gone far. He must be close by. Besides, the way back was straightforward enough. He would venture just a bit farther, and see what he could find on his own, before he turned back.

He followed Gwyn's tracks for another sixty paces, looking back time and again to the torchlit mouth of the passage. The footprints were evenly spaced, but a shorter stride than Gwyn would normally have taken. It struck Kal as odd. It was as if Gwyn was walking tentatively, in slow measured paces. At the verge of his torchlight, Kal saw a staggered step in the tracks. The lad must have stumbled. As Kal approached, he saw a second set of tracks between Gwyn's misstepped footprints, still progressing at an even and unbroken pace, just as Gwyn's had until now. Of course, it dawned suddenly on Kal, Gwyn had been following someone else's tracks down the tunnel! But whose? Kal stooped to look more closely. The strange footprints were a man's, unshod, but small and narrow. Gwyn had followed the footprints of the stranger, walking in them, making a game of it, his own heavy footfalls obliterating the smaller prints, until here, where he had stumbled.

"Gwyn, what were you thinking? Where have you gone?" Kal spoke into the darkness farther down the tunnel. He stood and hurried along, fear for his young friend goading him on.

Now the ceiling sank to half its previous height. Kal was forced to stoop, bent over, while thrusting the torch out ahead of himself. Still Gwyn's tracks, sometimes overlapping the stranger's, stood out, shadowcast in the soft floor. Kal had keyed himself to them like a bloodhound, when he came to a fork in the tunnel.

The tracks had disappeared on the threshold of this underground crossroads, the ground having become hard, like the stone floor of the main chamber. He thrust his torch inside each of the branching tunnels, looking for some clue as to where Gwyn was headed. Kal was all for having a try at the right-hand route, for it seemed to him that the last traces of the footprints were skewed in that direction.

Then again, in that moment, he caught the small glinting reflection of light, now familiar to him. It was some four or five strides on, inside the left branch of the fork. Kal pushed in and stooped to seize the tiny glass ball, its silver flecks winking in the torchlight. "Aye, he's surely lost his marbles," Kal whispered in the close passage. "Must be a hole in the lad's pouch. Or he's left a trail— Yes, the clever fellow!" He lunged on through the gap with the marbles clutched in his palm and in ten more paces was relieved to be able to lift up his back and stretch his frame to its full height, for the ceiling rose here, even as the walls widened.

Kal looked again at the marbles glinting in his hand. There was no more trail of footprints to follow on the hard tunnel floor, but Gwyn had gone this way. There was no doubt. The tunnel just ahead cut sharply to the left, disappearing around a bend.

He looked again at the marbles he held, stooped and placed one in the centre of the path by his feet. The way back. He broke into a jog, the torch before him bobbing as he shot around the corner. The floor disappeared. Kal caught himself short at the lip of a yawning hole. He teetered, his arms windmilling, letting go of marbles and torch.

The next thing he knew, his feet had slipped, and he was in a free fall, his arms and legs flailing in the empty air. The torch plummeted down, cartwheeling before him, lighting up the ghastly underground cavern into which he had fallen. In sheer terror, Kal screamed again and again at the top of his lungs. It was a timeless moment, drawn and stretched out of proportion, a moment that held an exquisite distillation of horror for Kal, who felt his life balanced on the shapeless boundaries between time and eternity.

He would be dashed to pieces against an underground rock or impaled on the needled point of a stalagmite. Wheeling in the air, he braced himself for it. The light vanished. His body struck something soft and yielding. There was a splash and then silence. He was immersed in a weightless blackness. Water. At least it felt like water. He struggled to regain the surface, not even sure which way was up, his unprimed lungs aching for air. He was dazed, and the totality of the darkness around him was overwhelming. Disoriented, Kal treaded water for a moment to clear his head. Then, when he had struggled free of the straitening cobwebs of shock and found himself intact, a dreadful panic, fostered by the coal-black lightlessness, seized him. Here he was, floundering in deep water with no idea how he might even begin to make good his escape from it. And it was warm water—odd for a pool buried deep in the mountains. Like bathwater, not right somehow. Perfect for some fell creature of the dark. And it was fast-flowing, sweeping him along in its current. Kal found himself too stunned to swim against it. An acrid smoky smell filled his nostrils, and it took him a moment to realize it must be the doused torch.

All at once, almost before he'd had half a chance to catch his breath, he found himself cast down another terrific drop, thrust down a pitch, steep and sudden. It was savage, a world of turbulent rushing fluid sightless sound that swept away all vestiges of control from him, pushing him farther into the innermost parts of Mount Thyus, sealing him in its dark mysterious tomb.

Again, it seemed from the sudden headlong violence of the fall that death awaited him. Again, he was plunged into a depth of water in utter darkness. He broke the surface, gasping for air. This time there was no fighting current to contend against beyond the pool churning beneath the roaring flood. At once, Kal began to tread water. His mind struggled to grasp some wisp of reassurance, struggled to encompass this further battering descent into a lower level yet of the black netherworld into which he had been pitched. With a great effort, he tried to fend off the despair that pulled at his heart. A feeling of frenzied desperation swept over him with redoubled force, like an irresistibly powerful tidal surge. He could not tread water forever. He must reach firm ground or perish in the attempt.

"Help!" he yelled out repeatedly, in crazed half-awareness that it could only be a gesture of futility. "Help . . . help . . ." The echoes were deep and ample in their resonance. It must have been a huge cavern. He was a tiny figure in a vast landscape, its shape and extent inscrutable to him. And what if all the sides of this cavern were steep and admitted of no handhold or ledge, precipitous walls enclosing an underground sea? There would be a gradual weakening, a slow barely perceptible sink into the everlasting waters of forgetful death. And if he did manage to crawl free of the water? What hope in the world would he have without the blessed gift of light? Not a glimmer of it here. Not even a suspicion of it.

It was the darkness that made everything doubly and trebly hopeless. The damnable darkness. Heavy and oppressive. Kal felt hedged and choked by it, as if it were a sensate malevolent creature, a bizarrely endowed spider, which caught its hapless victims by emitting into the air a miasma of inky blackness, spinning it out with the merciless efficiency of a predator from its bodily store of darkness.

Kal turned back to the only source of sound about him. He thrashed around underneath the chute of water down which he had spilled. He tried climbing back up to the vaulted chamber, where he had first stumbled to his doom. But the footing proved too steep and slippery, and the flow of water too strong and fierce. At length, he began to feel blindly with his fingers around the rocky margins of the rushing waters that tumbled down from above him.

If only he'd summoned Galli or Bren first. He cursed his

foolishness. If only Mommick had stayed put. Then there would have been no doom of darkness to swallow him up. If only . . . if only . . . if only . . . With a woeful sense of his own littleness, Kal marvelled at the combination of circumstances that had laid the groundwork for his fateful plunge into darkness. He pounded at the black face of the rock with his fist, asking why, again and again, asking why. It was exhausting, all this raging, coupled as it was with his feeling of powerlessness. At length, the sterility of his railing against fate came home to him, and he left off pounding the rock. His fury spent, Kal began to sob quietly, giving himself up to convulsions of self-pity.

Time passed and he regained a fragment of self-control. He searched by feel for a low spot where he might get some hand-hold and lift himself up onto a ledge. For the first while he met nothing but sharply defined vertical abutments of intractable rock, no matter how high he strained to reach with his hands. He grew tired and dispirited once again, more disconsolate now than angry or hysterical. Again he sought to sate the pangs of loneliness and desolation by screaming, screaming until the flux and reflux of his echoed cries grew cloying and unwelcome to his ears, a vain mockery of his desperate straits.

"If you want me to do your work, if you want me to be the guardian of your Howe, you've got to save me. Why make me Hordanu if I'm to perish here in this rotten hole?" he cried, resting a while by grabbing hold of an outthrust knob of rock that came to hand. With this outcry, Kal's sense of abandonment subsided, his passion abated. Phrases and melodies from the orrthon welled up in his heart. He sang quietly, his voice ringing over the dark waters in strange harmony to the ceaseless thunder of the unseen cataract. He grew quiet again and resigned, then scuttled on, like a crab, following by touch the sheer sides of the underground lake. Somewhere soon he would find a way out of the water. It seemed to him that slowly he was turning some kind of a corner. He had swum so far now that the sound of rushing water no longer filled his sense of hearing. This unnerved him, for now above the gathering silence he could hear the limpid echoes of his own splashing and thrashing around in the water.

At length he discovered a break in the walls of rock—a place for him to rest. It came as a shock to him at first to leave the warmth of the pool. The air was cooler. Kal shivered and wondered if he might not be better off back in the water. He must move to keep warm, explore, wend his way back to the light somehow. It seemed to him initially that he had found a good stretch of passably clear ground, for he was able very carefully to stand and walk without bumping into rock. But where, where might he go in this blinding blackness without stumbling and falling into an even deeper pit? He had not resolved a thing, it seemed, by dragging himself out of the water.

Kal stood in the still darkness, dripping. In the pocket of his breeches, something bulged uncomfortably against his skin. Kal awakened to it and remembered what it was. On an impulse he dug his hand into his pocket to clutch the Pyx, drawing it out slowly, the only remaining connection to his past life in this pit of darkness. No sooner had he pulled it free of the sodden fold of his pocket than the whole place was transformed, suffused with a wondrous iridescent glow. The half-moon of the Pyx shone in Kal's hand, its greenish tint of chrysoprase casting a shimmering gossamer of colour on the darkling scene, like a summer's moon that has sucked up the greening resplendence of ripening crops in order to shower it down again from the sky above. It was a friendly light that hinted by its softly tinted warmth at the verdant meadows of the upper world, like a splendid lantern of moonspun brightness.

Kal was astounded to be able to scan the area around him, marvelling at what he saw. Walking along a ledge that rose around the rim of the large pool, he could make out stalactites sparkling like slender crystal vases from the ceiling above the water, which lay in eerie repose here in the very bosom of Mount Thyus. The stalactites added their slow-dripping burden of water to the larger flow that rushed from the upper level down which he had slid just a short while ago. He had walked back far enough now to see and hear the spot, and was amazed to realize how far he had fallen and how strong was the water that flowed down the course. Even so he decided to try remounting it, now that he had light, and gingerly made his way along the wall of the cavern to the edge of the chute. He held the Pyx aloft. The broad torrent of water flowed down a steep slope from a large opening not twenty feet above where he now stood on the narrow ledge. The water roared past him down the stone face and fell crashing into the surface of the black pool shrouded in darkness below.

Fiddling for a moment with the chain of the Pyx, he fixed it around his neck and then scrabbled from firm ground into the downpour, clawing at the bed of the rushing waters, desperate for purchase in the slick course of its fall. The light of the Pyx swayed and wavered in the buffeting surge, like a storm lantern battered by wild concussions of wind and rain. Kal could scarce draw breath above the spray. He had nothing to grab on to, just a slick sheet of stone that the flow of ages had worn down to a polished smoothness. He slipped, try as he might to climb higher. His fingers tore at the wet rock, but he could find no purchase. His foot slipped and he was swept away, falling headlong back into the eddying pool that footed the waterfall.

But the light? The light! What had happened to the Pyx? Kal found himself plunged into a sea of darkness again, many times more frightening now that he had been given a taste of saving light. With the bitterness of stark fear in his mouth he clawed around his neck with his fingers. The chain, but no Pyx. The Pyx had broken free of the chain. Kal grew frantic. A madness swept over him. He thrashed about, wild for a hint of the Pyx's gentle gleam. Nothing. Nothing to be seen. Pitch blackness. The pouring spout of waters filled his ears with its din. He had to find it. He had to, or else die. Taking a deep breath, he dove where he supposed it must have sunk. The warm water swirled around him. It tugged at his clothes, binding them around his arms and legs. Kal felt closed in, confined, as if slimy tendrils had curled around his limbs. For a dreadful moment he supposed it was yffarnian water ivy. But he was too desperate to care. He fought to push himself deeper. He caught sight of a faint tumbling pinpoint of luminescence down deep below him off to the side and receding into the murky depths. His pulse quickened. Another instant and he might not have noticed the glimmer of its light at all. No time to surface for another breath of air. He must try to reach it now, before it faded from sight. Kal feared his lungs would burst even before he could touch the Pyx.

The surge of panic dispelled all calculation, his circumstances giving him no choice. Fear propelled him towards the glow of the Pyx. There, he was almost there. The Pyx floated, tumbling slowly before him, so close. His hand reached out to clutch it. Another arm's length . . . The Pyx his again . . . Nothing else mattered . . . His head grew light. His lungs were ready to burst. He had to have air. And then, his consciousness slipping and senses reeling, he no longer felt the need to scream for air, no longer ached sharply for it. His whole being began to succumb to a louring cloud of narcotic blackness. So this was what it was to die . . .

His thoughts dissolved into a haze, even as his fingers clamped themselves around the cold half-moon of light. In that instant, his body tumbled, was caught up and swept away in the grip of a surging wall of water—an irresistible underwater current carrying him in its flow farther into the depths of Mount Thyus.

EIGHTEEN

A light shone kind and radiant, piercing the numbness of his senses. An extraordinary light, broidered with unearthly softness, like the quintessence of birdsong captured at the fountain of some fresh eternal dawn. Kal supposed he had died, and that his soul had been ferried across the Birdless Lake, beyond which he had found himself entering the courts of deep heaven itself.

He coughed and sputtered, searching for breath, and felt water trickle out over his mouth and chin, then realized that the breath of life was being blown back into him. Another's mouth was cupped over his own, engaging and disengaging with it in a rhythmic cadence, like a bellows stoking a faltering hearthfire.

Little by little, the cloudy film of unconsciousness left his eyes. The shuttered windows of his soul began to reopen, and he became sensible of a chatter of voices, speaking in a buzz of strange evocative accents. He coughed again and slowly came to his senses. Lifting himself up on his elbow, he blinked, looking with openmouthed wonder at the knot of grave-faced folk who crowded around him. Clearly, they were no less astonished at the sight that met their eyes than was Kal himself, busy as they were whispering to each other, with here and there a discreet gesture in his direction.

One of them, a young man, stood closer than the rest. Kal thought he must be the person who had revived him. Kneeling on one knee beside Kal, he now offered the dazed highlander his hand. Kal took it and stumbled to his feet. He was drenched, soaked to the skin, and the fingers of his right hand were gripped tight on the smooth half-round of the Pyx of Roncador. At the recollection of how close he had come to losing it, he clutched it tighter still. Somehow he was still alive. Or was he? Were these the fabled courts of deep heaven or another eerie world that he had entered? He would have pinched himself to test his own reality, had not his clammy and uncomfortable wetness seemed to him proof enough.

"Ah, splendid, strangely come anuas! You have recovered well from your dousing and have suffered no damage on your sodden journey. But I must not be so rude a host as not to present myself to you." The small man paused solemnly, alert to Kal's befuddled state. Kal struggled to follow the words, recognizable to him now as the old language. How very odd and even humorous, to hear the venerable language of *Hedric's Master Legendary* and the orrthon spoken colloquially in this way, as if it were language of the commonest coinage.

"Wh-who are you?" stuttered Kal in his thickest highland brogue.

"I am sorry. I do not understand what you mean. Your dialect perplexes me," said the man in the same archaic tongue with which he had greeted him. "We be folk of the hammer, who speak our first-conceived earth-begotten mother tongue and none other do we speak, for there's a well-oiled unguent shiftiness in knowing aught other tongue. Many tongues for roving feckless vagabonds that care not to mind the fires of their own forges. But not for us hammerfolk of Nua Cearta plying in peace our smithy's craft." The little man broke from his long explanation, turning his eyes again on Kal. "By Vali's Hammer, though, how is it now that your face does wax more and more familiar to me? Where can I, who have never before set eyes on anuas, have seen you?" The man twisted his face in thought and scratched his head.

"What is your name? Where am I? How came I to be here?" Kal's words tumbled out in stiff hastily framed questions cobbled together in his mind from the clumsily remembered stock of Old Arvonian.

"I am Prince Alcesidas." The young man bowed deeply before Kal. "Magan Hammermaster, my sire, rules o'er our people in this our underground place of fosterment, this our Radolan Mountain kingdom, which is hight Nua Cearta, after our ancestral Burren Mountain forgelands of the Coolcower Alps, the most beautiful grottoes in all of Ahn Norvys, from which we were driven. It is here that our forebears did fix anew their smithies and founded again the scuttled royal seat of my father's fathers. You do find yourself in the royal audience chamber in the deep roots of the mountain you may call Thyus, but we Folamh. Here we plucked you from yon swan pool beside the royal dais more dead than alive, so choked with water in your gills that I did not think my breathful assays would work your release from the grappling hooks of Dark Lord Death, who does haunt the margins of our home with a bolder and more puissant insolence."

"I am deeply obliged to you, Prince Alcesidas, for the saving of my life. Indeed, I am forever in your debt," returned Kal, his tongue tuning to the shape of Old Arvonian, as he looked around himself at greater ease. His immediate fears were now somewhat allayed, although he found himself astounded by the quality of the light in this stately cavern where Magan Hammermaster held court. He glanced to see from where it came, even as Alcesidas pressed him for his own name and origins.

"I am Kalaquinn Wright. I am a Holdsman, from the Highland Clanholding of Lammermorn, the eldest son of Marina Wright and her man Frysan," he explained with a half-abstracted air, as his eyes wandered upwards to the branches of the mighty tree which rose in the centre of King Magan's audience chamber. From this extraordinary tree there hung countless luminous orbs shaped like apples, but apples so radiant with an indescribably mellow incandescence that they seemed as tiny fragments of the sun itself. Indeed, if it were possible, they were even more brilliant than the sun, more habited with life somehow, shedding gaiety and brightness on the scene like a shower of molten goodness.

Suddenly, there was a commotion of redirected attention, as Alcesidas and the others turned to see who was entering the audience hall through the large bronze doors that swung open at the farther end of the expansive subterranean chamber. It was not King Magan who entered, as Kal had anticipated, as also had the gathered hammerfolk, judging from the astonished gasps erupting through the small assembly. Rather, there entered two men dressed in light coats of mail. Their helms, strapped to their bearded chins by leather thongs, were each inset with one of the apple-like fruits of the kind that hung from the overspreading tree in the hall. Their shortswords drawn, they used them to goad a familiar limping figure.

"Gwyn! Gwyn, here, I'm here," Kal called out in blithe surprise, as if the red-haired mute boy were not suffering the duress of two sharp sword points. The armed guards made no attempt to stop their charge from loping towards Kal. His face lit up. "Dear wayward Mommick! Am I glad to see you alive and well and all in one piece! Though I can't say that you didn't keep me guessing. A fine time I've had trying to find you." Kal hugged a bewildered Gwyn to himself.

Alcesidas was busy speaking to the two guards who had escorted Gwyn into the hall. The rest of the hammerfolk appeared to be torn between listening to Alcesidas's keen interrogation and gazing spellbound at the strange-looking anuasoi who had come into their realm with such suddenness. They, in their turn, were no less wondrous a sight for the two Holdsmen, who had never with their eyes beheld the small folk of the hammer, although the legends and lore of Arvon were filled with references to them.

Especially intriguing were the women, all of light complexion, with rosy cheeks. Fair to look on, each of them. They wore low headdresses crimped with intricate patterns of sparkling beadwork, while their flowing white linen dresses were no less delicately ornate with inset jewels. The men of the hammerfolk, on the other hand, were far more plainly clothed, save for the jewelled belts which girded their rust-coloured tunics. Their faces, while equally fair to those of their women, were solemn, and many were thickly bearded. Both men and women had narrow feet, wrapped in footwear made of a strange diaphanous material that accentuated every bone and vein.

At length, Alcesidas ended his insistent examination of the two guards. He returned his attention to Kal. His features had turned severe. "You know each other, I see. But the trouble is that I do not know you. Two anuasoi who have wandered into Nua Cearta in the space of one watch, while in all the cycles of the seasons that my people have lived in exile here not one, nay, not one anuas has ever been graced by the golden light of our caverns. You must explain yourself, Kalaquinn Wright. How do you come to be on Mount Folamh, you and your lame and speechless friend, who did so meekly follow the helm lamp of one of our guards. There is too much that is out of joint, too many dim and shadowy forces and even the very substance of evil withal that are pressing on our forgelands which only now, after four centuries of Candlefeisath, begin to have the feel of home."

Alcesidas frowned darkly and stroked his thinly bearded chin. "Excuse me if I put not too fine a point on it, but I am fearful lest you be spies in Shadahr's munificent and devious employ. That would be darksome and ill-fitting. Not good at all. No, not at all good. But ah, here comes my sire, the king, and with him Meriones, who will doubtless proffer wise words of counsel."

Alcesidas wheeled around and stepped forward to greet his father, who had entered the audience hall, accompanied by a gaunt-faced man. The latter was dressed in a long robe of rich earthen brown fixed tightly to his waist with a knotted cord. He was a bard, for over his shoulders hung a cloak of the same brown tone, fixed at the throat by a sparkling pios. King Magan cut an impressive figure with his regal bearing, a golden diadem wreathing his head, and a finely woven white tunic hemmed with an array of gems illumined in the queer light of the chamber.

The whole company made obeisance in deep bows and curtsies as the king approached. All other conversations ceased, while the king, still flanked by the other man, spoke to his son and nodded once in the direction of Kal and Gwyn. Then the king moved on past his subjects to a raised marble dais at the far end of the hall, where he took his seat on a cushioned leather chair with a high back, framed in fretted oak and flanked by smaller chairs. As the king sat himself down, all the assembly moved as a body past the wonderful light-bearing tree towards the dais, where they waited, silent and attentive.

Passing close by the central tree, Kal ventured to look up and was almost blinded. The tree, alive and in full leaf, stood in the middle of the great room and rose up from a gently sloping mound, which was mantled with a neatly manicured lawn of the most vivid green. Elsewhere, flower beds bursting in brilliant geometric displays of colour lined broad ochreous walks of flagstone that interlocked in almost seamless joins.

Alcesidas remained with Kal and Gwyn, while the bard seated himself on a chair to the immediate right of the king. He had a severe sallow face with sunken eyes that sorted ill with the broad open faces worn by all the other hammerfolk. It seemed that he was a trusted counsellor of the king. The sharp-set bard conferred in animated whispers with him, making deferential nods and smiles. Skirting the left side of the dais, to the right of King Magan, was a large pool of water on which two swans of dazzling white plumage floated with a majesty scarcely less regal than that of Magan himself. A plashing fountain that rose in concentric circular tiers adorned the middle of the pool, which was fenced in on its near side by a low stone wall. Its outer rim, on the other hand, met the jagged irregularity of the rough rocky walls that ascended into the dim recesses of the cavernous ceiling, which was draped in darkness, impervious to the light-filled globes hanging from the tree.

King Magan had a mellow, kindly, open demeanour. Kal warmed to the man as he straightened out his flowing beard and fussed with a fur-fringed purple cape, a kind of robe of state that he evidently donned whenever he mounted the throne chair. When the king had finally performed all his adjustments, he beckoned to his son, who left the two Holdsmen and approached the dais. "Come, tell us, Prince Alcesidas, what you have learned of these anuasoi who have come unexpected to our domain."

"The dark-haired one, who is hight Kalaquinn Wright, we fished from between the swans here more dead than alive, swept down, no doubt, from higher pools," he explained with a gesture. "While the other, who is mute, or so pretends, was found in one of the galleries within the heights of Folamh. He followed Hodur like a heedless puppy, gawping at his helmlamp, as if it were your jewelled crown he was beholding. Hodur relates a strange state of affairs, for he says that there are many anuasoi in the Hordanu's cave and that he saw the Hordanu himself lying dead on a rough-made bier with this mute boy in attendance on him. There was fear in the air, Hodur said, as palpable to nose and eye as the smoke and steam that shroud our forges. He could almost touch it, he said, filling the air, together with the scent of gathgour. Except for this boy. He was as cheerful and frolicsome as a new-born lamb in the high tide of spring. Hodur says that the gathgours have left their customary lairs and lurk boldly in the rocky shadows of Folamh. He himself grappled with one a scant few hours before he happened on the Hordanu and this boy."

"What means this, Meriones?" asked King Magan of the severe bard at his side.

"Perhaps you should rather ask this young man, sire, for, unless mine eyes mislead me, he did follow the meaning, at least, of the Prince Alcesidas's words. Did you not, Kalaquinn Wright, if such be truly your name?"

Kal nodded his assent to this soft questioning voice, which had a wonderful sweetness, like dripping honey, gentle but not cloying.

"Mayhap you could explain in addition how you came by the pios you wear and that vessel which you hold?" Meriones pointed to the Pyx of Roncador in Kal's hand.

"It-it is . . ." Kal fumbled. "It is a story which is full of treachery and deeply sad tidings and I doubt me that I could in my limping accents render it as it is fitting to render."

"You speak the Old Tongue passably well . . . passably well. Indeed, more ably than your humility, whether false or true, does lead you to suppose. Does he not, Meriones?"

"Indeed sire, I daresay too well by a half. You might bid him carry on. Let him explain who he is and how he came hither."

"Well then, Kalaquinn Wright, tell us your story. You shall find us an indulgent lot here in Nua Cearta, not hard to please, but more wary than was our wont, none more so than my trusty Meriones, and that not without reason, as my son, the Prince Alcesidas, has recently learned and you shall learn as well."

"If he does assuage our fears, sire, which I have much hope he may, for he has an honest open face that wins me in my despite," added Meriones with grudging magnanimity.

"In the first place, before I start, I thank you, Alcesidas, for to you I owe my life. I call you brother now, more dear to me than my own life," began Kal, surprising himself by the reasonable fluency with which he was speaking the language of ancient epic and song. There was a deep hush now that fell on the hammerfolk. Still deeper grew the silence when he explained in his next breath that the Talamadh, the golden harp that bound together the heavens and the earth, had been stolen and that he, himself, was sole Hordanu by Right of Appointment, now that Wilum was dead. A ripple of shock and incredulity passed through the assembled folk.

"Tell us, Master Kalaquinn, how this came to pass," said King Magan, as Kal paused to take stock of where he might best launch into his narrative. Now it dawned on him, though still dazed from his near drowning and the wonder of his awakening, that it was desperately urgent for him to win over these people together with their king and bard. Somewhere above this tranquil audience chamber, in the Cave of the Hourglass, his father and mother and Bren might even now be awash in blood. At this point his clear-mindedness made him more anxious, causing him to trip ungracefully over his hard-sought hoard of Old Arvonian words, as he requested the aid of the hammerfolk in saving the remnant folk of the Stoneholding from the impending danger of a final assault on the Hordanu's Enclosure. He asked that his people be harboured in Nua Cearta for refuge.

This was followed by more prompting questions from Meriones, who maintained a haughty and abstracted air of scepticism. Kal pieced together the story of Ferabek's surprise attack on those who dwelled in the Holding and how only a handful of them had survived to follow the Skell up to the Hordanu's Enclosure. He described the treachery of Enbarr and Kenulf, as well as the murderous betrayal suffered by them at the hands of Relzor, the cobbler, who bludgeoned to death the Hordanu.

"And even now they mass at the Stairs of Tarn Cromar, preparing to finish the awful work they have begun, Ferabek and his Black Scorpion Dragoons, while Enbarr, mounted on the night drake, keeps vigil over us in the 'windswept spaces of the great night sky,'" concluded Kal with a stock phrase from "The Lay of the Velinthian Bridge" that just happened to match the thought he was struggling to express. His ability in Old Arvonian was proving, it seemed, more than adequate, for the king and Meriones, not to mention the whole company, were clearly held fascinated by his story.

"But what token do we have, sire," asked Meriones, breaking the short interval of silence which came over them after Kal had finished his account, "that he does utter truth and is not a fair-speaking Burren Mountain weasel sent to spy on us by our ill-shapen cousin Shadahr."

"But Meriones, he came to us half-drowned," Alcesidas said. "How came it that this was planned beforehand? It does surpass the reach of even Shadahr's guile to raise from the watery dead his simpering lackeys."

"That part may truly have happened to him by his own misadventure, seeing that outside of our own people nobody knows all the winding ways of Nua Cearta," countered the bard.

"You seem to speak truth, Meriones, and I am sore perplexed. But if this anuas speak truth as well, we must needs help him and his people, for they are a chosen folk, the anuasoi of the

Clanholding of Lammermorn, the stock from which the keeper of the Talamadh has for century upon century unfailingly come."

"If he speak truth," Meriones said, holding Kal in a steady gaze. "Oftentimes it is the most bare-faced, the most astounding lie that sways and seduces the unsuspecting heart—"

"But if you are wrong . . ." King Magan said with knitted brow.

"My lord," said the Prince, stepping forward, "is there not a way that we might test the temper of these anuasoi, one by which our fathers always tried doubtful messengers? It was you that taught me it, Meriones, when you did sternly bid me learn the legends of our folk. For even the great but treacherous Vali, when he returned with outward semblance of contrite heart to our ancestors, his own Burren clan, did submit to this ancient trial of his trustworthiness."

"Which he failed, nimble as his mind was, so that he was expelled as being a liar and a traitor, and made his way back to the enchanter Conna-gwyhn, leaving behind the mighty Talamadh, wherewith Ardiel did reharmonize the heavens and the earth," added Meriones.

"You do refer, Prince Alcesidas, to the Test of the Riddle Scrolls?" asked Magan.

"Indeed, sire, seeing as our forefathers were able, in their flight from the malice of Sör, to bring these with them, a small portion though they be of the original inheritance. Behold, as never in the past hundred years, a perfect chance to put them to use."

"The Prince does proffer a fine suggestion, sire. The Riddle Scrolls are with good cause named the Scrolls of Truth, since the one who has evil or treachery in his heart could never, as age-old custom has it, supply the correct answer to any of their hoary perplexities. May I counsel, sire, that they be brought forth to us, so that we may see whether anuas is as anuas says," said Meriones.

"If he is, we shall welcome him and his own with joy and feasting," the King said, then turned to fix Kal with a level stare. "If not, we shall feed him to the gathgour."

"What is this talk about riddles? What is this trial you mean to put me through? I am not a fluent speaker of your language and would fare ill by any wordplay. Are my words not believed?"

King Magan held Kal in his gaze, unflinching, for a long moment before turning aside to issue quickly worded orders to two men in livery. All the hammerfolk, both men and women, began to eye Kal more suspiciously than ever, except for Alcesidas, who made reassuring noises, muttering, "Do not worry, friend. I know you for what you are. Do not fear!"

This did nothing at all to mollify the Holdsman, who felt the anger rise in his gorge at the silly obstinacy of these posturing little people who were so close and so suspicious. By the cloak of Tobar, it was clear enough to anyone with even a modicum of unclouded judgement that he and Gwyn were simple honest souls. Especially Gwyn. And they in desperate need. This was ludicrous! "But I am Hordanu. My story is true, I tell you, and my people are in danger. Where is your welcome to guests and strangers?"

"Hush, Kalaquinn, hush," urged Alcesidas. "You do your cause precious little good by your insolent behaviour. As hosts to those discovered to be friends you shall find the folk of the hammer outdone by none of the peoples that in Ahn Norvys do make their dwelling-place. Quiet your tongue now, Kalaquinn. The Riddle Scrolls are brought."

The two manservants had returned to the dais. One of them carried a bronze stand with three legs, while the other bore a plain pinewood casket that seemed to have suffered the wear and tear of ages. The casket, charred black in places, was set on the stand, and King Magan bade Meriones open it and choose a scroll. Meriones undid the rough-fitting clasps and riffled through the stiff dry scrolls that filled the inside of it, unrolling one and then another to scan their contents with a quick eye.

"If I know Meriones at all," whispered Alcesidas, "he will pick something quite obscure, so that there will be no doubt but that the guidance of deepest heaven has put you in mind of the answers."

Kal's spirits plunged at this suggestion of a test. At that moment he wished that he were back at the Cave of the Hourglass or better still at the Stairs of Tarn Cromar with Father and the others, making a last brave stand. At least that way he would be there for his own folk, providing them with another set of strong arms to help stave off or stem, at least, the fury of the Boar. The way things stood now he seemed trapped in what would no doubt prove a fruitless game, in which he was bound by his ignorance to be defeated.

"Behold, sire," said Meriones at long last, brandishing one of the scrolls that he had unravelled with a pleased grin on his face. "These three pretty little riddles shall test the mettle of our Hordanu, as he claims he is."

"Begin then, Meriones," said Magan with a wide sweep of his arm.

"Do you, Kalaquinn Wright, stand ready to give answer and so be judged by these, the Scrolls of Truth?" asked Meriones, turning to the Holdsman with a question that smacked of ritual formality.

"If my knowledge of your language does equal the import of your word puzzles," said Kal with a cool eloquence that belied his feelings.

"I see no problem on that account. Your finely honed understanding of our tongue has betrayed itself to us ere now."

Kal's skin prickled with the sharpness of anxious excitement. But all the same, a part of him remained curiously peaceful. He found his mind clinging as its last resort to the sublime jewel-like words of the orrthon's Great Doxology with a wild tenacity, like a shipwrecked sailor gripping with blood-drained knuckles at a buoyant spar shaft. He knew he rested now at the mercy of these incredulous folk, who were set to dismiss him as a liar or worse, if such were his doom. Another less resigned part of him was so daunted that he felt his wits turning to unresponsive treacle.

"Let us begin. The first riddle reads so. Heed the question well, young and subtle anuas!" Meriones's gaze fell from Kal to the scroll he held open before himself with both hands. " 'What is that which is reborn after its birth?' " he intoned.

Kal's wits felt paralysed still, devoid of their reasoning powers. The question seemed to him just so many random sounds without any patterned order, although he recognized every word of its quaint Old Arvonian phrasing. How could he answer? What did this riddle mean? "Thou, Wuldor, art great . . ." he reiterated again in his mind, as if the Great Doxology was the sole reassuring scaffolding for coherent thought, a key with which he might unlock the door of this impenetrable enigma. The silence that surrounded him was terrifying and oppressive, the weight of eager scepticism and distrust almost suffocating. How long would they abide the numbing of his wits, before they cast him and Gwyn again into the darkness of Nua Cearta's outer wards—to the gathgours, as they said?

He was halfway through yet another recitation of the Great Doxology when he felt a lightening of his spirit, a lifting of anxiety, as if his being were entering into a fresh and unearthly region of transparent clarity, where other presences stood close at hand, felt but unseen. It was as if he was overpowered by a wisdom beyond his own, and in that instant he said:

> "'Day's eye burns with Wuldor's might,
>   Gifting blessed life and light;
>   And in day's shadow, silver-bright,
>   Fair Ruah's lantern guards the night . . .'"

Meriones glanced up sharply at the young Holdsman.

"The moon!" Kal said. "It is the moon, which going all around takes birth anew! That is it which is reborn after its birth."

"By stroke of luck you do hit the mark," commented Meriones. His tone sounded almost disappointed. The bard leaned toward Magan and whispered something in the king's ear, then recovered himself and gave his attention once more to Kal.

"Now let us betake ourselves to the second riddle of our three-some," Meriones said and lifted the scroll in both hands before his eyes. "'What,' Kalaquinn Wright, 'is fleeter than the wind?'"

Again, Kal felt possessed by a knowing, a certitude not of his own power, and without hesitation spoke lines that were only vaguely familiar to him.

> "'In parting, divers ways we wend,
>   And distant though we brothers be,
>   E're time and travail make amend,
>   Restoring this friend-fast company,
>   Know ne'er are we too far apart
>   To be in song, in thought, in heart—'

"The mind! The mind is fleeter than the wind," answered Kal without breaking stride, as if to underscore the aptness of this answer to the second riddle.

"Truly, chance attends you," snorted the jaundiced Meriones, his slender nose wrinkled in disdain. The appearance of aloof suspicion that the bard was trying hard to maintain, however, was belied by a nervous wonder that filled his eyes. Again he leaned toward Magan and whispered.

"What?" the king said, pulling away from his bard and looking at him. "Ardiel's what?"

"'Ardiel's Leave-taking,' sire," Meriones said, his head still bent toward the king. "He quotes from the final speech of Ardiel to the Seven Champions of Ruah."

"But what does that mean, Meriones?"

" I know not, my lord." The bard shook his head. "To answer correctly is one thing, but to recite lines from the most ancient and obscure texts, and not just once, but twice now . . . Well, I—" Meriones glanced again at Kal, as if he had forgotten that the Holdsman stood there listening. Meriones drew himself up. "Now," he continued, and lifted his head to look down the length of his nose at Kal, "the third to complete the three. 'What is that which swells with its own impetus?'"

> "'The loveliest of rivers this,
>   This ribbon-tide of sun-flecked waters
>   Adorned by lark-exalted woods
>   And lush and limb-burdened orchards,
>   Clinging to verdured pasturelands.
>   There is none that I love more than this,
>   The loveliest of rivers.'

"It is a river that does swell with the affluxion of its own impetus," replied Kal summarily, as if he were a clever schoolboy being drilled on simple questions of reckoning.

All affectation of scorn and distrust now disappeared from the bard's face, transformed into a brightness of awed acceptance, the severe cast of his features melting like the limp rags of a morning mist uncloaked by the sun's emerging fingers.

"You cite from Ardiel's 'Song of the Dinastor' . . . Truly, these bull's-eyes are more than merest chance does strike. Truly, by my hammer and the light of the avalynn, you are who you say you are. I should not have thought it so by my own reckoning. I bid you welcome, my lord Hordanu, and I beg your forgiveness for my distrust. With such honour have we never been graced in the centuries of years that have seen us here in these forgelands of our exile, nor even in those many more lived by our people past, dwelling in our Burren Mountain homeland. What a blessing indeed that is wrought us in our heart-longing exile—"

"Pray, excuse our doubtful estimation of your story, Master Hordanu," said King Magan, interrupting the effusive bard, "but these days, as you shall hear, even the home of our migration, Nua Cearta of the Radolans, is overborne with sinister uncertainties."

"I do not blame you, sire." Kal himself scarcely believed that he had survived the ordeal of the Riddle Scrolls. He bowed to the King. "Your prudence and that of your trusty counsellor do win my esteem and my respect, for they show forth the depth and breadth of your wisdom. But now, sire, that I have won your trust, I beg your aid for those who are on death's dark shore. Please help my folk."

"Well and truly spoken, Master Kalaquinn. We shall talk more anon. Now first things first. Alcesidas, take half a score of our well-armed warriors at once and with Master Kalaquinn guide back to our illumined caverns his people, the beleaguered anuasoi of the Clanholding of Lammermorn."

"Come, Master Kalaquinn, and you, too, my limping friend. You may blithely unfurrow the ample creases of your brows, which speak your anxiety more eloquently than ever artful mouth could frame," said Alcesidas, grinning from ear to ear. "We'd best not linger overlong, lest Ferabek burst through your fragile forward post at the Stairs of Tarn Cromar and overwhelm your folk ere we've had half a chance to lead them all to safety here in Nua Cearta."

Prompted by a discreet whisper from Alcesidas, Kal bowed deeply to King Magan, as did Gwyn, whose tousled red hair flew from the nape of his neck like a ragged sheet of bunting. Meriones smiled benignly at the sight, and Alcesidas left the chamber with the two Holdsmen in tow, even as King Magan received a full report on some newly planted avalynn saplings.

NINETEEN

The Crown Prince of Nua Cearta pressed himself against a boulder and peered around its edge to survey the moonlit mountainside. Behind him, his hammerson companions stood now with Kal and Gwyn at the mouth of a narrow passage that gave onto the slopes of Mount Thyus. The hammerfolk called it Folamh, "the Hollow Mountain," Kal had learned, in remembrance of their rugged ancestral caverns of the same name nestled deep in the Burren Mountains to the east of Arvon. That was one of the few things that had registered on Kal from Alcesidas' good-natured and continual banter. During the trip from the realm of the hammerfolk, the thought that they may have mounted this rescue operation too late had filled him with a nagging dread. Now it occurred to him that, in his distraction, he had paid no attention to their route up through the seemingly endless succession of tunnels and caverns that honeycombed the murky bowels of Thyus. Yet, late or not, he had come back to the surface and to the aid of his people, and with him he had a dozen grim-faced hammerson warriors and their prince.

"Alcesidas, where are—"

The Prince silenced Kal with a raised palm, not looking back. Kal's pulse quickened. The fresh air wafting toward him felt intoxicating after the dank darkness of the caverns. He breathed deeply and a tingle ran the length of his spine, then he shuddered as if a shadow had passed over him. This was a fey place, indeed, and even more so now, given the pressing danger of almost certain annihilation that faced his folk at the hands of the Boar and his minions. He wondered how many remained alive, if any, back at the Cave of the Hourglass, in the high reaches of the Hordanu's Enclosure.

"All seems well," Alcesidas whispered, glancing to his companions, "leastwise on this slope of the mountain. I hear not a movement on the path above. Come, we go this way." Alcesidas beckoned Kal forward and shuttered his helm lamp for him, his own already closed. Gwyn fumbled with the unfamiliar mechanism on his helm until one of the hammersons stepped forward, grinning, slapped the mute boy's hand away, and fixed the lamp for him. The group filed behind Kal. Alcesidas had clambered up a low rock face using rough-hewn handholds. In but a moment, they had all scrambled over the edge and were standing on level ground again, looking out over the mountain terrain.

The mountainside fell away at their feet, bathed in the faint silver light of a failing moon. A breeze sent torn shreds of clouds scudding across the sky. Kal blinked, the wind in his face making his eyes water. He had hardly more than a moment to drink in the sweet coolness of night air and the deep night sky before Alcesidas crept through a narrow space between walls of rock to their back. Behind the hammerson prince stole the hammerson swordsmen, silent as wraiths in their tunics of twilled black cloth. Each man had a small bundle of rowan switches tied around his neck, and each had his weapon held ready. A few of them wore packs, filled, Kal knew, with rope and spikes and other equipment proper to their haunts. Kal had seen the men produce their equipment from the bags, use it, retrieve it, and stow it again with remarkable speed and deftness. They were a hardy folk, endowed with large reserves of stamina. In the passage up from Nua Cearta, Kal had found himself pushed hard to match their relentless pace in a bewildering network of tunnels and vast caverns that undermined the mountain's fastness.

His senses alert, Kal dogged the shadow-cast figures of Alcesidas and his men over the stone-strewn ground and through a cleft in the pressing walls of rock. Clearing the gap, Kal regained his bearings, immediately recognizing the path that led to the Cave of the Hourglass. He could tell now where they were—just up from the shattered ledge where he and Wilum had come close to being heaved down the sides of Thyus by the boulder-throwing gathgour. The party turned and padded silently up the trail until they came to the sculpted column standing before the Cave itself.

"Halt! Who goes there?"

Though spoken only loud enough to be heard, the challenge rent the stillness, and in its abruptness sounded as compelling as a lungful blast from an alarm horn. A lone figure stepped from the shadows at the mouth of the Cave and stood in defiance of the intruders, feet planted apart across the path. He held a longbow at full draw, pointed at Alcesidas.

"Who are you?" Frysan commanded a response from the short man facing him at little more than a dozen paces.

"Father . . . Peace. Lower your bow." Kal sidestepped from behind Alcesidas, and slowly moved toward Frysan, his arms held out at his sides. "It is me, Father, Kal. And this is Alcesidas, a friend—a friend fast and true." Kal continued moving toward his father, who relaxed his pose and lowered his weapon, as he shook his head in confusion. "Aye, a friend, as are these . . ." Kal gestured with a sweep of his arm to the hammersons who stood at his back. "And Gwyn, of course."

"Kal?" Frysan said, relieving the tension of his bow and pulling the arrow from the string. "How did—how did you manage to get past me here, and me none the wiser? I thought you were inside the Cave with the others. And these? Who are these fierce-looking lot . . . ? Re'm ena, but you've thrown my mind into confusion!"

Kal turned his head to speak to Alcesidas. "This is my father," he said, "Frysan be he named—"

"Ah, yes, Frysan Wright, and Marina be his wife, your mother. He is the leader of your people?"

"Well, in the slaughterdom wrought by the Boar, our thane was lost. Frysan is the best left among us. A soldier, brave, tried and true."

"Does he speak the Old Tongue?"

"Yes." Kal nodded and stepped aside. "He speaks passingly well."

The hammerson prince stood toward Frysan, lifting a hand. "I greet you, Frysan, in peace," he said.

"And I you, stranger." He studied the short man.

"Stranger? Let it be so no longer." The hammerson prince grinned and bowed his head to the Holdsman, "I am Alcesidas, Crown Prince of Nua Cearta, the domain of Magan Hammermaster, my sire, which undergirds this mountain that you call Thyus, but we call Folamh. I was apprised of your plight by your son, Kalaquinn, so strangely arrived to our caverns, and we have come to—"

"Frysan, what's happening?" Devved emerged from the Cave, sword in hand, roused to battle fury. "I heard voices," he said. Behind him pressed Galli and a handful of other Holdsmen awoken from their sleep, among them Bren, Kal's own brother, all brandishing bows or swords and ready to fight for their very lives in the face of the Black Scorpion threat.

"Stay your hand, Devved!" Kal raised his arm, bidding the Holdsman halt. "These are the folk of the hammer. Friends. They've come to take us all to safety, to their realm deep in the heart of this mountain."

From his look, it was obvious that Devved was not mollified by Kal's explanation.

"This is Prince Alcesidas," Kal said, gesturing towards the hammerson, who inclined his head gravely. "He is the son of King Magan, their lord. He has come—"

"Listen!" cried Galli.

From below rose the windings of a horn, ominous in the night, echoing in the distance from the mountain slopes surrounding them. It sounded again.

"Two short, one long . . ." said Kal. He shot a look at his father. "There's a breach at the Stairs."

"Aye, we're under attack." Frysan grew tense once more, alert, and cast a glance back to his fellows in the mouth of the Cave, and beyond them into the dark recesses. "Alarm! Alarm!" he cried. "To the Stairs!"

"Who's on watch duty there?" Kal demanded.

"Athmas, Manaton, and Thurfar," Frysan said, stepping forward with his sword drawn. Now others had come from the Cave—Diggory and Gammer, as well as Kal's mother Marina and some of the women of the Holding. They bore hastily collected utensils—knives, staves, and cudgels, whatever could be found in their haste and extremity—and had a fiercely determined air.

"Come," Frysan said, "we go!"

"No, my father!" Kal laid a hand on Frysan's arm, staying him. "You must remain here. You must rouse and gather together our people. There is no telling what dire danger draws nigh, how close we are to being overwhelmed by the enemy. Assemble the remainder of our folk. You must descend with them now, with all haste, to the home realm of Prince Alcesidas. You will be safe there." The Holdsmen looked on with surprise. Kal had spoken out to his father in the Old Tongue. "By your leave, Alcesidas," Kal continued without pausing, turning now to his hammerson companion, "will you supply a pair of your able hammersons as guides to my father and these folk of mine, so that they can make their way in speed to Nua Cearta, while we go in aid of the three men on watch?"

Alcesidas nodded to two of the hammer warriors that flanked him and spoke briefly to them. "It is done, Kalaquinn," he said, as the two detached themselves from the group and moved to join Frysan and the Holdsfolk gathered before the Cave.

"Devved, you stay with your son," said Kal.

With his well-muscled frame, like a thickset mastiff labouring to break free of its leash, the blacksmith struggled to restrain himself. Again distinct blasts of the horn drifted to their ears from the beleaguered men below, rising in pitch, the tones insistent.

"But, Kal—"

"We've no time for arguments." Kal cut him short. "You too, Diggory. You stay. And Bren, mother and father will need your able hands." Kal's younger brother frowned in disappointment. "The rest of you come now. Quickly, to the Stairs!"

"But, Kal," Galli said, "Can we afford to risk losing you? You should stay behind as well—"

"While my people risk losing their lives? No, Galli, we are to rescue now, not fight, and I will rescue all of the people that have been left in my care. I will . . . I must!"

Kal turned and ran, Alcesidas's men parting way for him as he led the charge down the curling path, touched only faintly by the radiance of moon and stars.

The windings of the horn grew ragged in their measure. At the same time, they sounded louder and closer, no longer distant. Kal ran harder. The soft thunder of many feet running close behind him egged him on ever faster. Soon he and his companions were midway down the path that led to the meadow of the Seven Springs. The horn blasts were almost immediate now. Kal turned a corner in the rocky defile, and a man appeared ahead of him. He held a horn in his hands, doubled over and catching his breath. He was flanked by two other men.

"Thurfar!" Kal cried, rushing to the Holdsman gripping the horn. "What's happening? You're wounded!" Kal gingerly touched the blood-smeared cloth at the shoulder of Thurfar's homespun jerkin.

"Bah, but a nick, Kal. A crossbow bolt—a couple Scorpions testing our mettle, middle of our watch." The trimly bearded Holdsman straightened, panting, still recovering his breath. His pleasant open features were ashen, drawn by strain and fear. "Only two or three of them, it was. They skittered back down the Stairs soon as we let loose a flight of arrows. Now they've come back, them and their mates, a huge number of them. Heard the clatter of them at the foot of the Stairs and saw them starting up. They'd of broke our wall quicker than quick. No way to hold them off, just us three. No way." Thurfar shot a nervous look at his companions. "We reckoned it best to retreat."

"That or leave our corpses for the crows to feed on," Athmas said, his voice quavering. His wiry frame seemed more stooped than usual, and his white-knuckled fingers worked restlessly, curling and uncurling around the hilt of his sword. "They're coming, sure enough. What are we going to do?"

"And who are them here with you, Kal?" Thurfar said, casting a side-long glance to the hammersons gathered behind Kal.

"Friends," said Kal. "Rest assured. Friends who can lead us all to safety. You did right, Thurfar. Let's go back."

"And quickly!" Galli called out from an embrasure in the rocks nearby. "The place is thick with soldiers down below." Kal and Alcesidas ran to the point of vantage, where side by side with Galli they spared a moment to gaze back down on the Seven Springs, the lip of Skell Force glistening in the first blush of dawn. The makeshift stone barricade at the top of the Stairs had been broken down. The night drake, with his mounted rider, was framed for a moment against the background of the early-morning sky. The creature swept low over the open area around the Seven Springs, while in the vanguard of the thickset Gharssûlian invaders, as elusive as shadows, tall and lithe, were a handful of Telessarian trackers, attended by a baying pack of bloodhounds.

After their hasty survey, the three men turned from the embrasure and rejoined their comrades.

"In all truth, I've little love for your upper world," Alcesidas said to Kal, as the group hurried back to the Cave of the Hourglass. "Too vast, too open for my liking. With all due respect, my lord Myghternos Hordanu, I'm always glad to get quit of it."

"Then let us," Kal said, "and with speed."

When they reached the Cave, save for the shattered mortal

remains of Wilum, the place was deserted. In the soft light of their helm lamps, now unshuttered, the smouldering fire beneath the smoke hole and the lingering smell of food gave the area an eerie desolate feeling. On the stone walls, two torches sputtered. In order to keep it safe from desecration, Kal had Galli heave the slain Hordanu's body over his shoulder in order to bring it along with them for decent burial in the kingdom of the hammerfolk. At the same time, the vital satchel of manuscripts, maps, and scrolls that Relzor had dumped were quickly retrieved by a nimble spidery fellow, who was let down a long length of rope into a steep-sided sinkhole.

With calm and efficient haste, Alcesidas and his men outfitted the Holdsmen who needed helm lamps and then directed them to the passageway down which Kal had followed Gwyn.

"Why do we not return the other way, the way we ascended from Nua Cearta, below the Cave here?" Kal said, as they gathered before the tunnel.

"Why, do you perhaps fear the road back, Kalaquinn?" Alcesidas laughed. "You need not swim your way into our good graces this time. I promise."

"No, I—"

"Come, come, Kalaquinn, I jest. To be serious, however, I think it too dangerous for us to retrace our steps. We have not the time. If we continue from here, we'll rejoin the rest of your group soon enough. It's best that we stay together."

"What of the Telessarians we saw? They are trackers beyond peer in Ahn Norvys. Do you think they will follow us into the Hollow Mountain?" Kal said.

"Who is to say? They may do so. Though I believe it would be to their mortal peril. The caves and tunnels so densely undermine the mountain that I doubt not they would be lost forever. If one does not know the underground ways . . ."

"Still, I think it foolish to slight their skill," Kal said. "Let one of your warriors carry the body of my lord the Hordanu, Wilum, and let me and Galli keep guard over your rear flank. We have had some experience of their ways."

Alcesidas considered the suggestion for a moment and shrugged. "As you wish, Kalaquinn," He said, then directed, with a gesture of his hand, one of the hammersons to remain with the two Holdsmen. "So you don't get lost, which would be to your mortal peril." He winked, turned away, and led the party into the passage and out of the Cave of the Hourglass.

They passed the first branching passage, and Kal felt a twinge of dread as he cast his eyes up the diverging tunnel into the darkness. "My wrong turn," he whispered to himself and chuckled. "And a good thing I took it, else we'd all be as good as dead now." He fell silent, pondering the escape that he and his people had managed, hoping that it would succeed. At the end of the column, he hurried to catch up to the others, who pressed on at a remarkable pace.

For a while, their way led through a bewildering maze of tunnels that probed deeper down into the mountain, but remained largely free of obstacles. At length, moving swiftly, they caught up with their comrades, and in a wide chamber the whole party stopped to rest and reorganize itself.

There was a palpable sense of relief—the remnant of the Holding had slipped the Boar's grasp, and there was no sign of pursuit. They had found an escape. Kal looked at his folk. In the wake of fear, fatigue had begun to take its toll. He passed among them as they rested, offering a word of consolation to one person, exchanging a jest with another, to all seeking to convey some sense of encouragement in the face of their jeopardy.

Soon enough, and too soon for many, they sought their way again. Kal and Galli resumed their place at the tail end of the long straggling line. Now the journey grew many times more treacherous. Often the passageways proved so narrow that the opportunity seldom arose for them to walk even two abreast. At times Kal would hear the frightened cries of children and even adults and knew that they were about to skirt some awful chasm or be launched across a yawning gulf one by one in a strong wicker basket hung by the hammersons on an improvised bridge of rope, fixed into the rock by stout spikes. Other times they came to sheer underground walls that were scaled first by one of the warriors who would fasten a lead rope.

After some time, Kal could not imagine any tracker, even the most wily and artful Telessarian, equaling the agility and skill of these hardy mountain-dwelling folk, who showed so much patience with this bedraggled collection of anuasoi—heartsick demoralized women, querulous children, and exhausted men. It was a much less straightforward route they were taking now than when

Alcesidas first led him up above ground for the rescue. Then their journey was all a conscious and unvarying movement upwards to the heights of the Cave, although they experienced one or two tight squeezes, where Kal felt like a bung in a beer barrel. Here, though, they were forced to make several dizzying climbs that seemed to be taking them farther up into the mountain, higher away from Nua Cearta. Kal found himself speculating how long the journey would take. In the file ahead of him a couple of the children whimpered from hunger and the damp that chilled them to the bone.

They entered a large and spectacular gallery of sparkling crystalline rock, vaulted with a glence-like dome, but with myriad pillars, sinuously sculpted, Kal supposed, by the uncanny art of hammer and chisel, not by the random action of ancient underground streams—all done in such a way as to take on the semblance of living creatures. Some of the glittering figures looked small and bestial, some larger, more akin to men, while others resembled mad gesticulating giants armed with club and sword. It was a fascinating pantomime, a revel of sardonic grimacing faces, alive with the subtle suggestion of movement. Alcesidas called a halt here, where there was enough space for them to break out of their single file. Frysan inquired about the petrified forms.

"We know not by whose hand they came to be, Master Frysan. They were found as you see them, when our people first arrived in these parts. Meriones, our bard, says that they serve as an ill-humoured warning to those who venture farther into that passage yonder," pointed Alcesidas, "which is the reason why we make this pause. We embark now on what we call the Ellbroad Bridge, for that it is a narrow path, at most an ell in width, that crosses over a fathomless abyss. Moreover, this bridge is well nigh two goodling bowshots long. There are some of our hammersons who do call it the Look Not Down Bridge, for that it is best to look straight ahead when one crosses it, which is exceedingly good advice. I caution you not to peer over the sides of the bridge. To make certain there is no mishap, I bid you anuasoi to rope one another each to each about the waist. Here, Dalboron," the Prince bade one of his subordinates, "give Frysan your cordage."

Alcesidas arranged the order by which they would cross the fearful-looking bridge, deciding that he and four of his men, one of them carrying Wilum's body, should be first. Following him would be Devved's wounded son, Chandaris, carried on his stretcher by a fresh pair of hammersons. Then there would come Devved himself, as the lead of the two rope anchors on either end of the file of Holdsfolk. The other anchor was to be stout-limbed Galli, with all the other men, women, and children coming between him and Devved, each one roped to the other, children staying close to their parents, the men space evenly throughout. This way, if there were to be any mishap, two of the strongest Holdsmen would be holding the crucial rope ends. Behind Galli came the rest of Alcesidas's detail, one by one, sure-footed and not needing to be linked to one another. Last to come was Kal, keeping an eye open for pursuit, still chary of the Telessarians that might be trailing in their wake, despite Alcesidas's assurances to the contrary. Kal had insisted, however, that Gwyn join the others, lashed together for safety's sake.

As the Holdsfolk were being roped together, Kal noticed that there were two other smaller passageways, besides the main one, leading to the Ellbroad Bridge, branching off obliquely from the chamber with the strange statues. Out of curiosity, during a lull in the bustle of preparations, Kal asked Alcesidas where these passageways led and was told that both of them wound their way farther into the topmost bulwarks of Mount Folamh. The opening to the left, he explained, pointing in that direction, led to a tunnel, which skirted the edge of the chasm spanned by the Ellbroad Bridge.

At length, they stood ready to make the crossing. A couple of the children began crying again, just at the moment when Diggory Clout had backed off, refusing to step out onto the bridge, whining cravenly that he was "mortal 'fraid of heights." Others were starting to catch his infection of fear, until Gammer stepped in and rang him a fine peal. Even her firm hand, however, did not stop him from muttering nervously, and wishing rather foolishly, under his breath, that he had stayed in the Holding to face the Black Scorpion Dragoons or that the gathgour had succeeded in carrying him off.

"'Twould be better than this, I tell you, Gammer. You know that I can't abide high places. It's little short of a miracle that I've been able to come this far."

"Then you should've been born in the Dungheap and married one of their moon-eyed hens," she countered. "Get along with you now! And in silence, mind you. Can't you see you're making it worse for the young ones. Shame on you, Diggory Clout!"

Soon the folk of the Holding were all embarked on the Ellbroad Bridge, a slender band of stone, far narrower than an ell in places, a structure that nature itself had flung across the vastness of this pit. Its arched shape, like that of a grotesque rainbow, served to make it even more intimidating. Strange noises, like the scuttling of rats and deep growls, drifted up to them faintly from below, resonating off the stone. Alcesidas bade them sternly in Old Arvonian not to pay these any heed. Frysan translated this and other instructions for his clanfellows, whose ear for the ancient language was not as good. Galli was the last of the rope-bound Holdsfolk to step out onto the Bridge. The helm lamps, of which the hammerfolk had brought an extra store, provided ample light for them to see and watch their step. After Galli came the rest of the Prince's men, sure-footed and unafraid, encouraging him in their good-natured way.

Kal, who came last, set foot on the bridge and felt a queasy knot of fear and regret tugging at his inner parts. It was such a tiny and finespun thread of rock for such a gaping span. Did they know for certain it would bear the weight of them all? They would be sitting ducks while making their crossing. He shot a look back, but there was still no sign of pursuit. He should have let himself be roped to the others. Alcesidas had offered to take this last spot, but deferred to Kal when the latter insisted. Kal was after all the Hordanu. It was clear that they placed the office in high esteem. The man ahead of him looked a strong, capable fellow. They had placed him by his side on purpose—a guard to guard the rear guard.

It was all foolhardy bravado on his part—this thing about being the rear guard—done mostly to impress Alcesidas, show him he could be a tough-fighting Hordanu, a warrior like Hedric long ago.

In no time, Kal convinced himself that it would be sheer luck if he kept from losing his balance and tottering over into the black void that seemed to grip him with cruel sensate fingers, threatening to drag him down into the abyss and certain death. To screw up his courage, he kept telling himself that the width of the bridge gave ample room for him to walk on safely. Be bold, he urged himself. But the farther along the bridge he advanced, the more frightened he became, the more lonely at being positioned in the rear and unroped. What he would not do to have a corded lifeline tied to that man ahead of him, so sure-footed, so seemingly careless!

Just when he thought he would be forced, by his mounting anxiety, to swallow his pride and cast himself down on all fours to crawl along spider-like, the bridge trembled. Almost before he could react, piercing the shadow-wrapped stillness, there came the terrible scream of a despairing man being thrown off his feet into the impenetrable darkness. The reaction of his fellows came swiftly, even before the voice of the hapless man had thinned and receded to nothingness. Strident shouts of alarm echoed through the air of the cavern. Someone yelled Wilum's name. Dark figures crowded a long ledge that overlooked the Ellbroad Bridge from a spot almost directly above the column of warriors and Holdsfolk—to the left. Whoever it was, they bustled at their murderous business, heaving their shoulders into another large rock, preparing to hurl it down.

"Back, young anuas, back! Make way, or they will unrig us all here!" cried the warrior nearest Kal, as another heavy missile grazed the spot where the two of them stood transfixed. The rocky span shuddered again. A boulder tumbled past, thundering down against the side walls of the chasm. Kal thought he heard his mother screaming for his father, but it was impossible for him to know for certain, as he bolted back down the bridge. Goaded by the prodding shouts of the hammerson, he traversed the hundred yards of narrow stone at a flat run, until he regained the chamber with the sculpted figures. Their carven faces leered and seemed to express sardonic amusement at the sudden plight of the company.

Kal's breath stuck, and he fumbled for his wits. He had better do something to stop whoever it was. It couldn't be Ferabek's Telessarian trackers. The glimpse he had caught of the attackers told him that they stood too short for that. Within seconds the warrior who had urged him back off the bridge had come up alongside him, his stout battle sword drawn.

"This way, Master Kalaquinn, our murderous cousins are here. Let us be on them." He brandished his sword towards the passage that Kal had asked Alcesidas about earlier. The hammerson led the way up the tunnel. With a sudden spasm of fear that gripped cold his gut, Kal sensed others close behind him. He spun in time to set the beam of his helm lamp on two men dressed alike in odd garb surging at him with halberds ready to impale him against the bulging flint of the sloping passageway. He yelled an alarm, but the man ahead of him had already turned a corner. He slid his sword in a fluid movement from its scabbard and lunged ahead panic-stricken, to catch up with his companion, looking for his aid to meet these attackers. The halberded figures followed close on his heels.

He heard a shout, then the clash of steel over grunts and cries. Turning, Kal saw three of Alcesidas's warriors mowing down his pursuers from behind, not giving them the chance to swing around their halberds in the closeness of the tunnel. Already one of them was gasping out his last breath. The other had dropped his halberd, drawing his sword to engage his assailants. But as it was, he proved no match for the three who faced him and ended by crimsoning the rocky floor of the passage with his blood. There was no time for words of gratitude, as the four of them broke into a run up and through the snaking curves of the passage, looking for the parapet from which, as from a lofty siege engine, the enemy was raining down death and destruction. Ahead of them resounded the clangour of steel on steel—and voices.

"Yield now! Yield, or we shall make your corpse a sieve for to strain your slavish guts down on your brothers below!"

"Never shall I yield to muddy-mettled knaves! The temper of your swords does match the mottled white of your livers. One hammerson from Nua Cearta has more weight than a score of you Burren bellows-boys!"

Kal and the men with him clambered over a series of awkward ridges that rose sharply and fell, then rose and fell again, while the passage broadened out into a larger area. Countless stalactites hung like stony icicles, dripping water sullenly onto their leather-helmed heads. In the pooled lamplight stood the lone warrior who had preceded them on the attack. He was cornered now, in a tightly angled nook, which protected his back from the two foes who were trying, now one, now the other, to pierce the defence he threw up with deflective parries of his weaving sword. Their halberds gave them an advantage, which only the besieged man's extraordinary deftness matched. Six men besides, habited like the others in hose and jerkins of dull metallic grey, were grunting and groaning with the effort of rolling a large lopsided rock up a makeshift gangway, which they had rigged with cantilevered beams over the chasm.

"Hie, dispatch the others first," cried the cornered fighter. "I shall deal with these buffoons. Quick, before they drop that block over the edge, or I warrant it will shatter the Bridge to dust."

Kal and his companions leaped towards the gangway to face the six, who scrabbled down to meet their attackers. The gangway, already flexing under the bulk of granite, creaked and swayed with their shifting weight. The enemy had opened full wide the shutters on their helmets, allowing the beams of their lamps to sweep the oncomers. At first all was a blinding confusion of light. His heart beating like a drum, Kal launched himself forward upon the men together with his three companions and lunged with his sword at the first of the foemen who drew near him. It was an impulsive uncalculated move. The man sidestepped the thrust neatly and moved to cut Kal down from the rear as he staggered to regain his balance. But Kal wheeled around quickly enough to parry the blow to his shanks. Now he grew more wary and respectful of the hale sure-footed skill of his foe, who was joined by one of his comrades.

Two now faced Kal. They eyed him from beneath the glare of their helm-lamps, teasing him with feints and sudden movements that were pulled up short and then resumed. On either side of him he heard the clash of arms, mingled with the sighs, groans, and grim cries of wounded fighters. There was no way for him to tell how his allies were faring in this lethal contest. The sweat of fear and exertion poured down his face, burning his eyes. He longed to wipe himself with the sleeve of his tunic, but dared not let down his guard. These two were not stripling lads he was facing.

Kal knew that they had taken stock of him, could tell that he was green, not a tried warrior, as like as not to make oafish mistakes. All the same, his sole advantage was that, given his height, he overreached them with his long arms. They were wary. They tested him with interrupted probes by one or the other of their swords. They sought to divert him to one side, that he might lay himself bare, aiming to strike a vicious blow, unravelling his entrails with a well-swung sword. What these men lacked in reach, they made up for, not only by their quickness and agility, but by the forge-wrought might that powered their thick arms and wrists. Kal felt its brute force in the hit he had been barely quick enough to deflect. They were toying with him—smiling, feinting, pressing.

He inched his way backwards. There must be a way he could dispatch one of them and be left with just a single combatant to cope with. Even then, though, he'd have more trouble than he could handle. In the raw terror that gripped him, he found his situation oddly amusing. He shuffled another step back. He had no idea where they were driving him. The cornered warrior whom they had discovered taunting his attackers was lucky that he had found a niche from which to fend off his enemies. Still Kal drew back. Not even the footing he needed and two master swordsmen on him.

He felt he must be approaching the edge of the vast pit. He grew increasingly tentative now, as he tried to feel the ground behind him, taking small jerky steps. It was becoming ever more dangerous. His adversaries knew this. They hemmed him in and grew bolder in taking his measure, darting in swiftly under his defences and then back again outside his reach. They were taking their time to close for the kill. From the ragged edges of his concentrating mind he could make out their smug smiles, their sneering contempt.

"Aye, you're having great fun, aren't you?" Kal taunted them. His own voice sounded unfamiliar to his ear—smooth, measured, almost placid, belying the tumult of panic that lay beneath. "Yes, indeed, you smirking mongrels, you—"

His right foot felt nothing but air. Kal's blood froze. The man to his left now pressed to the attack, heedless of any possible countermove on Kal's part.

"Now we shall level you, anuas," he cried, as Kal fought to regain his footing, sweeping his foot around in a forlorn attempt to sidestep his opponent. There was something there. Something jutted out from the edge, something that his foot only just touched. A baleful tongue of sharpened steel came slashing towards his midriff. Now Kal had no choice but to stand his ground, what little there was, teetering over the brink. His attacker let go all self-restraint, as did Kal, who brought his blade down on the man's sword arm, severing the wrist and knocking the blade flying into the darkness of the abyss.

Kal was thrown off balance. A savage stroke of the other foeman's weapon whistled past his head. The Holdsman's sword slid from his hand, clanged once against the stone, and fell ringing into the chasm. Kal slipped. He heard a scream, his own. Scrabbling with his hands, he clawed at the solid thing his foot had just now scraped.

There was a handhold. There—the wooden struts supporting the gangway. Diffuse circles of light illumined the darkness around him. At the foot of the Ellbroad Bridge, the Holdsfolk standing huddled there had trained the full beams of their helm lamps onto the gangway, shouting to him, many screaming in horror. An arrow whistled close overhead from below, clattering off the stone wall high above the ledge. They had no clear line of sight past the solid wooden platform and Kal himself who dangled below it. He knew no more arrows would follow.

The man who had lost a hand to Kal's blade howled, beside himself with pain and rage, trying to stem the blood that spurted from his wound. Moving to the edge of the gangway, he looked to dislodge Kal from the structure. Clinging fast to a beam of the gangway with his left hand while sitting on its edge, he began kicking at Kal with his heavy boots. Pain exploded, white behind Kal's eyes, as the man hammered him in the side of the head with his heel. Kal screamed in agony, and his hand slipped from the thick plank, which left him dangling by one arm. Another blow to his head just missed him. Struggling, he swung his hand up again to the beam and eased his way farther out under the gangway. He had to escape. He had to escape not only the blows of the wounded man, but the other attacker as well, who could be heard laughing and shouting encouragement to his mate. The gangway, about two yards in breadth, swayed, as Kal moved farther along the beam letting his body hang over the void beneath him.

The wounded man stretched to afford himself more reach, to give himself one more go at the stubborn anuas. He had exposed himself to the bridge below and another arrow hissed through the air. With a soft thud, it pierced him through the shoulder. Now Kal, rather than edging away from the vicious kicks, swung himself back towards his startled attacker and caught the foot under his arm.

"Haree-hoo-sai!" Kal bellowed and pulled with all his might. The man found himself helpless to resist, batting the wooden structure with a handless arm, trying to find purchase. Screams reverberated off the sheer walls as, limbs flailing, he tumbled headlong into the chasm. The highland war cry still rang in the cavern and was taken up afresh by the Holdsmen on the bridge below.

Kal's temple throbbed with pain. His arms ached, but he dared not pull himself up. He would be easy prey for the swordsman who prowled the gangway still. The whole structure bounced and shook. What was the fellow doing? Where were the others? The structure swung. At any moment, it would break from its moorings on the massive wall of the abyss, crumple under the boulder, and career into the depths. The war cry gave way to shouts and screams. It sounded like a warning, but the clamorous voices were indistinct, unintelligible.

The platform lurched and pitched. It was the man above. He was trying to dislodge the boulder by jumping up and down on the planked ramp. He was trying to slide it from its precarious balance over onto the Ellbroad Bridge. A momentum was building as the structure wobbled and rocked. Terrified, Kal bobbed up and down beneath the beams. He tried to move closer to the rock wall. Kal yelled to his three companions, but he had no idea where they were or how they were faring. He heard the shuffle of feet tramping the planks above his head. There were the sounds of a skirmish and then the chilling cries of yet another man thrown down into the ravening blackness that gaped below.

The bounce and sway of the gangway slackened, then stopped.

"Hail, Kalaquinn! You have found a pretty place to hang yourself from. Let me lend you my arms to lift you from your unsettled perch." Kal was greeted by the familiar face of a hammerson, battle-begrimed but smiling, who leaned his body over the edge and held out his two sturdy arms, as stout as tree limbs. Beyond him, Kal saw the three other warriors, tattered, torn, bloodied, and somewhat the worse for wear, but to all appearances safe and sound. A cheer rose from the bridge below, as Kal was pulled up onto the wooden platform. The five men now turned back to the ledge and down the passage to the pillared chamber.

TWENTY

"Attention, attention, I beg to have your attention, honoured anu-asoi guests!" Alcesidas's request put a damper on the bustle and clamour in the dining hall. Cradling steaming mugs of rosehip tea, the Holdsfolk were capping off a midday meal that had been prepared for them with sumptuous care. They had taken their repast in a rambling one-storied building, which sat at the end of a cobblestone laneway in a cavern so enormous that only the dull metallic hue of the vaulted sky told them that they were not in an aboveground world. After their rescue by the hammerfolk they had been brought to this place.

To most of the gathered Holdsfolk, what Alcesidas was saying would be meaningless, but his words sounded vaguely formi-dable and served to command attention by their very shape and texture, resonating as they did with the antique cadences of the orrthon.

Another man accompanied Alcesidas. He was quite evidently an oldling of the people, for he had gaunt deeply creased cheeks on which were planted a thicket of hoary whiskers resembling nothing so much as a weedy plot of ploughland left fallow and caught in the grip of an autumn frost. This old fellow was unusu-ally bent over, stooped and shrivelled into a fleshless husk, like a rugose winter apple left clinging to the twig.

"Hush, hush, Prince Alcesidas bids you pay him heed." The old fellow's voice rose above the dying clamour, in accents that were those of quite passably fluent present-day Arvonian. He showed, however, a touch more formality and polish in his diction than was normal, for it was spiced with a hint of crisp upper-class Dinasantrian beneath the raspy hoarseness of age.

"Many thanks, Rimut," said Alcesidas, nodding to his wizened old companion, when he had all the curious faces of the upper-world folk cocked in his direction. "Ah, Master Kalaquinn, be not puzzled. Keep your seat and rest your weary legs," he added smiling, when he spied Kal push himself up from the board that was being continuously laden by bustling servers with baskets of fruits and honeyed pastries. "This is Rimut. He shall interpret for us into your own language. It is his great pleasure to do so. Moreover, it shall save your much-racked wits, Master Kalaquinn, for other deeper matters with which my sire and Meriones are certain to tax your mind and your tongue at eventide. You shall find Rimut more than equal to the task of rendering our meanings plain, both yours and ours, I doubt not. He has provided our sole acquaintance with the world beyond our forgeland realm in these hundreds of years that the hammerfolk have dwelt in the sequestered peace of Nua Cearta. With the waning of the Great Harmony, our king's grandsire bade Rimut learn the speech and ways of the people that do trod the soil of Arväon so as to convey the happenings of the upperworld to our knowing. This he did, dutifully, posing as a merchant of gems and precious smithcraft for some fifty years, even until the murder of your king Colurian and the abduction of his Queen and heirling prince. Dark had grown the times, and darker still since then, when we did again retreat into our hidden realm. But even now does our foul cousin Shadahr, scion of the malignant stalk of Sör the Usurper, press our peace with his incursions and loathsome alliances . . . But we shall not delve into that now—therein lies a longer story, full of the serpentine twists of fortune, and it best waits for another more fitting moment in time's march, Master Kalaquinn, when we are taking our ease over a beaker brimful of mead with the wise bard Meriones. As for the present moment, I wax overlong and tax your fellows' indulgence. So be pleased to let Rimut convey my sentiments to these your assembled companions." Alcesidas shifted his gaze from Kalaquinn to the folk at table, silent now, except for the homely clank of tea mugs, the earnest swish of garbed servitors, and the occasional whisper of child to parent and parent to child.

"I am Alcesidas, and this is Rimut, who shall be our word-changer during your stay with us," he continued now, pausing a moment in order to allow Rimut to assume his role of translator again after the private aside to Kalaquinn. "I am the eldest son of Magan Hammermaster, who rules over the caverns of this kingdom of Nua Cearta and the hammersons and hammerdaughters who herein dwell." Rimut repeated after the Prince, labouring over his words in a halting way that had more to do with his age than his lack of facility with the modern Arvonian of the Holdsfolk. "King Magan extends to you his greetings and welcome, and he invites you to come join him in the Hall of the Stars this very evening, as the light of the avalynn dims into dusk, so that we may make merry and feast together, hammerfolk and anuasoi, as we have not done in many a long turning of the seasons.

"I shall leave Rimut here as your guide, your eyes and ears and tongue, and bid you make free of our domain, those of you whom curiosity beckons and to whom weariness is of small account. Visit our farms and our forges, our quarry pits and our armouries. Our folk and all that we have are at your disposal. You shall see that we are not delinquent in our hospitality, awkward and strained though our first meeting with your waterlogged Hordanu may have been— Nay, I should rather say our Hordanu, inasmuch as he is High Bard of all of Ahn Norvys both above ground and below and belongs to all who chant the ancient lays of the orrthon with a sincere and unblemished heart," declared Alcesidas with a benign smile, pausing after every phrase to let Rimut keep pace. For their part, the remnant folk of the Holding were assuaging the final traces of their hunger, basking in the golden midday beams of the avalynn tree which overspread the square just outside the large windows, filling the small hall with its filtered light. Even the children had become quiet and still in the sleepy contentment of the scene.

"For the nonce I bid you briacoil, doughty anuasoi, as an earnest of our common bond, since this ancient word of greeting and farewell remains one of shared sameness in your tongue and in ours," concluded Rimut, dutifully echoing Alcesidas who motioned now to Kalaquinn, as answering shouts of "briacoil" rose up from the sated Holdsfolk. Some of the men sidled up to Rimut, burdened with queries about even the little they had seen thus far of the fascinating underground kingdom of Nua Cearta.

"By my ten finger bones, is there aught of night here, or do yon trees shine all the hours of the day?" inquired Diggory Clout, his stout frame quite overshadowing Rimut. Alcesidas and Kal drew themselves aside. Kal smiled as the little man began to speak to the growing knot of Holdsmen. They might have been at the Burrows on any one of the countless evenings that Goodman Clout and his mates had gathered about the kitchen table to swap stories of ploughing, planting, and pasture, and endless boast and bluster. A piece taller and Rimut might have passed for Landros.

"The avalynn follows a cycle of light and darkness that copies in its small way the succession of night and day which is a distinctive note of your own rising and setting sun." Rimut was surrounded now by a gaggle of curious Holdsfolk, plying him with a countless round of questions.

The others drifted towards the open door following the children, emerging into the refreshing seclusion of the courtyard without, where benches were set beside well-tended beds of vivid spring flowers and bushes—musk violets and hedge roses, striped jacinths and geraniums, star flowers and red martagons. It was as if a flowery remnant of the Holding in the fullness of spring had been transported underground for their delight—an idle attempt to take the edge off their brooding fateful sadness, even as they revelled in the amazing sun-like warmth of the avalynn's golden fruits. Although they were now comfortable and secure, beyond danger for the first time since the Holding had been attacked, they fell to remembering those of their own who were not with them, those who, indeed, would never again be with them this side of the Birdless Lake, that stagnant mere, which had been broached for them by the ferocious steel of Ferabek's Black Scorpion Dragoons.

The silence of profound sorrow clutched at their hearts. Their mourning was now beyond tears and wails of protest against loss. It was a dark numbing grief. At this point, Marina broke into a dirge of such a haunted register, so deep with anguish, that the very globes of the avalynn seemed to throb in sympathy. Even those yet indoors turned away from Rimut and cast a glance outside. All the men, women and children fell still, silent, except for her. The tones rose and fell as a pure distillation of their sadness. As one, the Holdsfolk wept, the prick of the lament lancing the boil of grief which would otherwise fester and poison the heart of the people. In the intensity of that moment was wrought the work of mourning, mourning the lost—their countrymen, their beloved, and their Hordanu.

The bittersweetness of the melody lingered, hovering in the air even as its music faded. The Prince was visibly struck by the strains of the deeply moving dirge.

"Strange things attend my mother's song. Indeed, her great-great-great-great-uncle was once Hordanu," explained Kal, carefully counting to make sure he had arrived at the proper degree of kinship. "One of the most gifted ever. Gamelyn, as he was hight. His whole being was rapt by music. He did breathe it as another might breathe air. Much evil did he stay in Ahn Norvys, although even he could not stem the incoming tide of rupture and falling away. So Master Wilum told me, rest his soul . . . Albeit his body will never be laid properly to rest, now that he lies unreachable in that pit beneath the Ellbroad Bridge, whatever may remain of him, at any rate." Kal fell into a reflective silence.

Slowly the drone of conversation resumed and Rimut was soon again mobbed by the query-laden folk. Kal and Alcesidas remained apart from the rest, shadowed by the limping figure of Gwyn.

"I had hoped, Master Kalaquinn," said Alcesidas, paying no more mind to Gwyn than did Kal, "to be your especial guide this day, before we come together for this evening's feast in the Hall of the Stars, to show you something of the modest sights of Nua Cearta. But our border rangers report strange and untoward signs in the tunnels of our northern marches, where up 'til now naught has happened to alarm us. It has been our eastern approaches for the most part that have suffered probing thrusts from Shadahr's scouting parties, as I know well, having been captured by one of them but a few nights past, well nigh to the cost of my life."

"How is that, Alcesidas?"

"I and one of our border rangers were set upon by a good score of them, ambushed I should rather say. The two of us, Ansgär and I, had been lured beyond a well-ensconced guard post by the pleading piteous voice of a man who had seemingly fallen by accident into a pit. He spoke like one of our own, and in that unsuspecting moment of naive trust we did not suppose at all that the matter could be other than it seemed. Thus far Shadahr's faithless forgemen had not made their presence known to us, except through faint traces of tracks and other slight signs that puzzled our cave-crafty rangers. Indeed only once did a forward patrol of ours espy by chance a skulking band of Shadahr's minions from an unseen hidden place. That is why we strengthened our guard posts in all the tunnels of the marches, exhorting our border rangers to even greater vigilance. Would that I had followed this counsel more closely myself!" Alcesidas indicated the door, and the two, still followed by Gwyn, rose, bowed their heads to the group, and made their way outside. Kal blinked in the mellow avalynn light.

"What happened then?"

"Alas it was I who proved to be least vigilant, and it was Ansgär who did pay the dearest price, giving his life in an attempt to save me from being captured. I too was fain not to give myself up except at the cost of my own life, struggling as I did with all my might and main. But they were too well prepared, with strict instructions to take us live as prisoners for questioning, so that Ansgär's death was a mistake and not intended on their part. The bellows-boy who did give him the fatal stroke was like to pay for this misstep with his own miserable carcass. And well he knew that this would be so, for he quailed and quivered the whole way back to their main quarters. As chance would have it, it was he who had played the part of bait to me and Ansgär. I did pity the wretch, even though he bore on his head the blood guilt for poor Ansgär. I shudder to think of it even now. Ansgär dead and myself trussed up tight, being led a captive, a royal hostage, to Shadahr's field headquarters in these Radolan Mountains. Down we marched, down towards the valley floor of Lammermorn, deep into the dateless caves and tortuous runs that riddle the under regions of your small nestled clanholding that has stood so many ages peaceful and inviolate. Alas for what I saw! Vast earthworks and ingenious sluices, newly filled lakes and pools, spilling their overflow into fathomless steeps and gorges. Great feats of delvers' skill employed to dam up and divert the springs that feed Deepmere." They stopped beside a small garden, awash with brilliant colour, and sat on the grass. The children played nearby on the verdant lawns, and Gwyn, kneeling in the path, pulled his pouch of marbles from his pocket and poured them onto the ground in front of him.

"So that explains why the level of the Mere has been dropping. But to what end?"

"Indeed, we know not, but surely one that is vile and wicked. However, they have not choked it yet. There are sources that are undammed yet, most especially the Seven Springs that nourish the Skell. But to stop up the source of the Skell they shall have to conquer Nua Cearta, inasmuch as the Seven Springs lie within our domain. And this conquest they are essaying by fits and starts to make good, aided and abetted by Ferabek, with a fund of resources that is beyond our command."

"Ferabek! I am not overly surprised."

"You do follow my story passably well, Master Kalaquinn Wright. The Old Tongue seems not to addle your head and put you off," remarked Alcesidas. "I may converse with you as I would with a fellow hammerson. Nay, more, a kin brother of the same rooftree."

The riddles had been a watershed. It seemed to him now the most natural thing in the world to hear the venerable language spoken, more natural even than the colourful earthy highland brogue of his upbringing, which he used in tandem with the more polished diction that had been imposed on him and countless other schoolboys over the years. The old language touched him deeply. By a strange paradox it had become at the same time exotically strange and reassuringly familiar. He felt like a wayfarer, who, far from home, in some lonely waste, has come upon the moss-covered ruins of a glence in a forest meadow that he half-recognizes from a dream that has haunted him from childhood. The ancient words came tripping naturally off his tongue as if they were more hallowed here in the bowels of the earth, more homey and maternal, more fitted to his mortal nature. It was a feeling that had come to him before, but only fleetingly, during a recitation of the orrthon, when the glence stone seemed to him to radiate strange powers rooted in the earth. But here in Nua Cearta there existed a more constant feeling of hallowedness for which he could find no immediate explanation. Perhaps it was because he was no longer simply Kalaquinn Wright, but Wilum's successor, the Hordanu, Guardian of Wuldor's Howe and its ancient mysteries, of which the Old Arvonian tongue was not the least.

"I am most highly flattered, Prince Alcesidas, for that my slender knowledge of your venerable tongue is all book-learned."

"All the more are you to be applauded for your ability to speak it. And pray, do drop the title Prince and call me Alcesidas plain and unvarnished, inasmuch as we are friends."

"I thank you for the name of friend, which I am full aware you do not proffer lightly, as do our greedy-gutted wheedling anuasoi who traffic with Ferabek in the Dungheap, as we have come these days to call the lowlands of our folkdom. And you too, my friend, please call me Kalaquinn plain and unvarnished. But come, do continue with your story, Alcesidas. I am on tenterhooks to learn of how you slipped your dire predicament."

"Oh so, by the veriest skin of my teeth, Kalaquinn! Indeed it may be said in a manner of speaking that it was Ansgär who saved me."

"Ansgär? Was he not killed when the trap was sprung?"

"Indeed, Kalaquinn, he was." The hammerson prince sighed heavily before continuing. "You see, the foul Burren forgemaster Shadahr was expected to arrive within hours to review for himself the ingenious work of damming and undermining that had been done by his bustling army of colonizing retainers. In view of this, Shadahr's stoat-faced taskmaster, Stoläm, thought it prudent to await his master before undertaking to interrogate me in earnest. What is more, he had surmised from the cut of my weeds and the cast of my face that I was no common hammerson whom he had caught in his ambushment, even though I refused stoutly to tell him who I was. He merely laughed and said that Shadahr would have his will of me with or without my leave.

"You should have seen his complacent drooling, Kalaquinn, his wry sneer when he bade his underlings to lock me up in their dank lightless dungeon, where crawling things did torment me, drawn by the smell of fresh blood from the shoulder wound that I had received whilst I was being taken. I scarce dared relax my guard for even the smallest hairsbreadth of a moment and found myself wishing passionately that my spirit had been sent with Ansgär's across Lake Nydhyn or that Shadahr would not be late in coming. The silence and the darkness were like the tomb, a horrible stillness. And Stoläm had not the need to station a turnkey to keep watch over me, so strong and impregnable was the vault in which they had laid me." He paused, caught in the moment again, then went on. "Exhausted as I was, I must have dozed off, for the next thing I knew there was a jangle of keys and the door of the dungeon swung open with a creak that awoke me with a start. They have come for me at last, I thought, with an unreasonable surge of relief. But no, imagine my surprise to see beneath the prying beam of a helmlamp the figure of the very man who had dispatched the hapless Ansgär, all alone and looking very much dishevelled, and wounded, as if he had been in a fight. There was a frightened hunted manner about him, for he kept glancing over his shoulder, as if in fear of being followed.

"'Up, up, Magan hammerson,' he urged. 'Do not fear. Up, up, or it will be the worse for both of us before this night is through. There is no telling when they will find the keys gone and the guardhouse untenanted by living flesh. I am hight Staelef, and I repent me sorely of having killed your companion. Understand that it was either him or me. Do you be sure that it was not my wish to slay him, since now on his account my life is forfeit. It be beyond a doubt he will order me to be fed to his tunnel wolves. Thus I throw myself on your mercy, Magan hammerson, howeverso you be hight. I know the tunnels and byways hereabouts. I shall help you escape back to Nua Cearta, so long as you do take me with you and promise me sanctuary in your kingdom.' 'Is this another piece of shameless trickery?' I asked in disbelief, now standing to face him in the glare of his helmlamp. 'To what end would I trick you now? Here now, take this broadsword of mine and thrust me through, to make a summary end of it. Sooner a good clean stroke to speed me off than the jeers of my comrades garnished by the fangs of hungry tunnel wolves.' He was in the veriest earnest. 'Well, then, Staelef, we shall join forces and you shall enjoy sanctuary in Nua Cearta,' said I, swallowing my violence of distaste for the slayer of Ansgär and disdaining to give him my name. But I had precious little else to lose and I could see that the poor trembling wretch was in fearfully desperate earnest, as indeed was I."

Kal winced. The image of Relzor's cringing form at the wall atop the Stairs floated before his mind's eye.

"And so he handed me his dagger, a fine jewelled one, well worthy of the craft of a hammerson, and then the two of us crept out of that foul place, with Staelef leading the way, his broadsword drawn and ready for whatever chance might put in our way. About two score paces on, we passed the small eight-sided guardhouse where Staelef had dispatched the lone guard and obtained the keys to the dungeon. Here we turned into another long tunnel that passed dangerously close to one of the larger caverns. Staelef drew the shutter of his helmlamp as we stole past that bustling place, in an agony of fear lest we be noticed. But, thankfully, there was none to mark our skulking progress.

"Staelef opened the shutter of his helmlamp again and on we went, 'til we reached a heavy oaken door, mortised into the granite of the passage. He swung it open and I followed him through, whereon I was startled by a din of fierce howling coming at us from the darkness ahead. I drew back, but Staelef, undaunted, strode boldly onwards, bidding me step smartly and not to falter. The sinister chorus grew louder and more threatening, while Staelef strode on in silence. This kindled the flame of my mistrust. I began to fear that Staelef had a notion to play me false." Again Relzor's face leered before Kal's mind. He tried to blot out the image, rubbing his brow and eyes with the palm of his hand, listening as the Prince continued his narrative.

"Indeed, I was sore troubled. 'Yes, my pets,' Staelef began to say. 'We shall give you meat, but not at my expense. Yes, you shall have your fill.' He laughed so loud and incautiously that I misdoubted the wholeness of his mind and grew anxious lest we be discovered. Then, as he swept the light of his helmlamp forward to the left side of the passageway, which had broadened out into a chamber, I saw what made my heart skip a beat. Behind a palisade of iron bars, only roughly visible in the murk of their rocky cage, there leapt and pawed a massed throng of bodies, their sleek grey forms merging together, with only their bright feral eyes and snapping fangs to distinguish them one from the other. Well I remember, Kalaquinn, a sour choking smell of urine and fetid pelts. These were Shadahr's tunnel wolves and ravenously hungry, it was clear. I gave them a wide berth, for I was in no small fear of those angry muzzles that tested the gaps between the bars as far as they might. But not so Staelef, who began to fumble with the circlet of keys that he had taken. He found the key he wanted, one with a wolf's head incised on it, and bade me to go wait for him at the door which closed off the upper end of this chamber, a good half of which had been partitioned off as a cage for the tunnel wolves. Brandishing the wolf's-head key, he admonished me to keep the upper door open in readiness for him, and to be prepared to close it in all haste.

"Thrusting the key into the door of the cage that held the tunnel wolves, he turned it once until it clicked open and then ran towards me. With feverish swiftness we swung shut the huge wooden door behind us. And not a moment too soon, for there came a chorus of hideous growls on the other side and furious scraping noises. We could feel dull thuds that made the door shudder, and I realized in horror that they were throwing their bodies at the wooden barrier in a rage. Staelef stood there for a moment, quite unconcerned. 'Do not worry. They shall soon tire of this and find the door by which we entered standing open and beyond that much warm flesh to stay their hunger. In the meanwhile we shall be halfway to Nua Cearta.' Then he took the lead, as we scaled our way back up towards the valley floor of Lammermorn, through caves and lairs that delve the earth beneath Deepmere, both those of ancient origin and the ones freshly dug by the Shadahr forgemen. We were able to stay clear of the small encampments they had set up to aid their work, for Staelef knew their locations quite well.

"The most dangerous moment came when, at length, we had nigh reached a chamber beneath Owlpen Castle, for we were attacked by two of Stoläm's scouts who had taken part in my capture and who had recognized me as well as Staelef when they espied us from the other bank of a broad river that we were following. We supposed at first that we had shaken them. But not so. They lay in wait for us, and sprang on us as we approached the Castle. One of them was dispatched by Staelef, although not before he himself received a mortal hurt. The other pursued me to beneath the Castle and, more wary of wounding me sorely, clipped my arm with his sword—a flesh wound, as it turned out, that bled like a river in spate. My spirit swelled up with remorseless anger at the sight of my blood. Grabbing tight hold of his arm, I shook the sword from it. We grappled together at close quarters, teetering closer and closer to a pool that I saw to be filled with yffarnian water ivy. I succeeded in tossing him into the unyielding grip of its tendrils and fled up a set of stairs that were clearly a secret passage into Owlpen Castle, although not before I had examined Staelef for a sign of life, to no avail—"

"The Pool of Retribution! The trail of blood— It was yours? We first saw it by the Pool and along the ways through the Castle."

"Yes. And it was fortunate that I happened to light on the devices of the passageway readily enough, else I had been captured once again by my enemies. In the Castle I rummaged about—"

Alcesidas paused for a moment, and then his face lit up as if he had solved a problem that had been perplexing him. "Re'm ena, I have it. It is that portrait in the Castle. That is where I have seen your face."

"I am afraid I do not understand you, Alcesidas. There are old pictures and portraits stored at Owlpen Castle, I know, of kings and Hordanus and other folk that have filled important roles in Arväon down through the ages. Master Wilum showed them to me once, years ago, when I was yet a small boy. They fill a musty wardrobe behind the Overlord's Chamber, stacked one against the other in a row. When I was given a glimpse of them on that sole occasion, Master Wilum was so overcome by a watery rheum from the eyes and a fit of uncontrollable sneezing that he never saw fit to go into that wardrobe again. I know that he did not, for when I asked him about them again some years later, he told me that he did not think the old pictures and portraits important, that this passion for portraiture was a thing of recent vintage in Arväon, a sorry vanity for preening varlets. So I know not whereof you speak, Alcesidas, for I have not set eyes on any of these things since that one time."

"Let it pass, then, Kalaquinn. All the same, the resemblance is beyond strange. Would that I had read the legend carven on the bottom of the frame! But there was scarcely time for that, when all my thoughts were of escape in all due haste. Now returning to my story—"

The hum of voices grew suddenly louder. The press of Holdsmen around Rimut had spilled out into the courtyard, some remaining with the ancient hammerson, some drifting to where their families took their rest amid the gardens and lawns.

"Where was I now?" Alcesidas continued, as the two young men pushed themselves off the grass and turned to rejoin the group. "Oh yes, I looked everywhere and, as chance would have it, found a coracle, with which I rowed myself across Deepmere and then wended my way first up to Folamh and then down into the safe haven of Nua Cearta where now we rest and speak, and where my father Magan holds his regnal seat, and where we shall feast tonight in the Hall of the Stars."

TWENTY-ONE

That he had not yet enjoyed one blessed minute of sleep for two nights running did nothing to dampen Kal's wide-eyed astonishment as he began his tour of Nua Cearta under the patient tutelage of Alcesidas. Clearly, the Prince was cherished and well-loved by his people and with good reason, for he showed himself to be unfailingly kind and amiable.

Their first stop was at the royal stables, where King Magan kept his carriage horses and fine spirited steeds bred for the thrill of the chase. All of the horseflesh was of a breed fitted to the needs and size of their masters. Alcesidas had hoped at first that they could make their rounds in a magnificent black coach, finely worked and polished, crafted in delicate lines of wrought iron. Both its doors were adorned with Magan Hammermaster's royal crest, an avalynn arrayed with blazing orbs of pendent fruit and set within the outline of a snowcapped mountain. But this splendid coach proved to be uncomfortable, too small even for Kal's slender frame. Besides, there was Gwyn to reckon with as well, his unwillingness to disattach himself from Kal making them a party of three.

Alcesidas resolved the problem handily by having one of his grooms commandeer a broad hay wagon, pulled by two dappled grey horses with broad shoulders and hindquarters. The horses were well-suited to their masters, both horse and master giving the impression of a foursquare solidity that sprang from the rooted bulk of the earth itself, one with it in a way that the taller Holdsfolk, for all that they were bound to the soil too, could not match.

Grabbing hold of the reins, Alcesidas let Kal take a seat beside him, the Holdsman plying him with questions above the clip-clop of well-shod hooves along the cobblestone roads that webbed the countryside beyond the royal palace buildings, which were situated at the focal centre of the subterranean kingdom. Dominating the royal enclave was a set of gleaming white edifices that were founded on such a lofty earthen platform that their roofs merged with the ceiling of the immense main cavern. One of these structures, with its makings of a spherical dome, had all the outward appearances of a glence, while its companion building was rectangular, fitted at each corner with turrets. Each turret was six-sided and overtopped the walls of the building, rising to meet the underbulk of Folamh. The approach to these buildings was through a series of stepped terraces connected to each other by four flights of white marble stairs, which, as far as Kal could discern, marked the cardinal directions. The terraces girdled the foundational ground in concentric circles. Planted on each level were avalynnia, the ground around their smooth trunks awash with the colour of all manner of flowered shrubs and plants and spreading creepers. His curiosity piqued, Kal asked about this impressive sight, but Alcesidas demurred and bade him wait until evening.

Gwyn had taken his seat behind them on the flat bed of the wagon, with his legs neatly crossed. How child-like he was in one respect, and yet how old he seemed in demeanour and address, as if he was in constant communion with some other more elemental and ancient world. Most people remarked on his eyes. Kal thought that he had never encountered eyes that were so transparently deep. Yet at the same time they seemed to overflow like a fountain bubbling from a deep-founded well.

The air about them gleamed bright and clear, more brilliant than even the most light-filled summer's day that Kal could remember in the upper world of the Holding, which was lit by a solitary daystar. Here, on the other hand, the many avalynnia shone like myriad upon myriad of self-contained suns that rendered all the colours of nature's raiment more lustrous—the crowning green of the forest trees more vivid, the earth hues more rich and brown. It was springtime as well in Nua Cearta, where the vegetation turned to seasons that mirrored those of the upper world.

On their way out, the three met up with a group of Holdsfolk on foot, mostly younger men and women, their curiosity stronger than their fatigue. They were being given a walking tour by a talkative Rimut, who took a moment to rest his lean little frame on his staff and greet the wagon riders with a friendly quip. Passing Rimut and his party, the three approached a copse that was throbbing with life, filled with wood pigeons and songbirds. Alcesidas explained that this was called South Wood, on the other side of which lay a deer chase especial to his father's heart—the heart of an avid huntsman.

Beyond South Wood along the road, they began to encounter neatly ordered farmsteads with bright painted roofs and branching laneways dyked by turf and stone that were overhung with ivy. Even so, between the settled clearings, there were broad tiers of thick woodland that mantled a picturesque succession of soft humpbacked hills which in the farther distance were broken by great overtopping smudges of metallic grey—the massive pillars called menturya or "stone roots," Alcesidas explained, for they upheld the weight of Nua Cearta's vast rock ceiling. There were pastures too where diminutive cattle and sheep cropped the sweet green grass, and they saw fields being planted with wheat and rye amid a network of irrigation channels. Every other farmstead, it seemed, had a barn-like building with a distinctive flame-red roof. Kal was told that these were individual forgeworks. At a couple of these farmsteads they stopped the wagon and turned from the roadway to tour on foot. Presently they came to a mill whose wheel clacked merrily in a swiftly flowing stream that meandered through verdant water meadows decked with delicate cowslips. Here again, Alcesidas suggested that they make further exploration on foot.

At every place they visited, there were warm endearing smiles and wishes of good health to greet the Crown Prince, who had so recently managed to escape the clutches of their treacherous cousins. Underneath the hearty sentiments, though, Kal could sense a spirit of anxiety and concern. They were, for all that, a genial race of folk, modest and unassuming, bound to simple lives on the farm or at the forge in a world set apart and made habitable by the extraordinary endowments of the avalynn.

Kal had heard, of course, about the hidden kingdoms to be found in the hollowed core of the Burren Mountains and had read about them too in the *Master Legendary*. The hammerfolk had been great and indispensable helpers in Ardiel's fight against Tardroch as night raiders and scouts, and the Talamadh itself had been fashioned by Vali, the greatest of their craftsmen. But in this stern grey age of limping harmony and faltering order more and more Arvonians, in the lowlands especially, were discounting the hammerfolk as no more than the fabulous creations of Hedric's quaint imagination, another of the hidden peoples bound to the world of myth and the world of myth alone. Yet here they were, the hammerfolk, undoubtedly real and very much alive, giving the lie to the narrowness and self-absorption of the world of the anuasoi, who were so quick to doubt that which they could not see or touch with ease in the drab confinement of their worka-day lives.

"I am truly struck with awe, Alcesidas, at the brightness and homeliness of Nua Cearta and its folk," Kal said, as the Prince enjoyed a lusty quaff from the foaming tankard of rich brown ale that the bustling hammerdaughter had served each of them. He and Alcesidas were sitting in the tidy cozy kitchen of a well-tended farmstead whose fields sat on the very edge of the underground kingdom.

It seemed to Kal that Nua Cearta sprawled over miles and miles of landscape, and that for the most part it coincided in extent with one large continuous cavern, broken only by the great supporting menturya. Kal followed the Prince's happy lead and pulled deeply from his own pewter tankard. There was something robust and hale, even earthy, about the flush-faced hammerson enjoying his cups. Kal half-expected Alcesidas to break out into a rollicking drinking song. Thirst had parched them both in their tramping about the neat and pretty countryside, where throstles sang from blooming hedgerows of whitethorn that separated field from field under a vivid firmament of chalcedony and agate, jasper and carnelian. Everywhere, placed at a strategic distance from one another, were avalynnia, shining little islands of light that chased away the perpetual darkness that would otherwise have smothered Nua Cearta.

Alcesidas had explained to Kal how quick the avalynn tree was to flower and bear fruit, even when young and merely the size of a shrub. It was this that had allowed the hammerfolk to settle and cultivate Nua Cearta fairly rapidly after their expulsion from the Burren Mountains. Kal learned too that most of the forges here were small ones, scattered throughout the domain on family steadings that provided the folk with meat and drink. This abundance of small forges was a facet of Nua Cearta which stood in marked contrast to the monstrous smithworks of the forgelands far away in the Burren Mountains. There was, nonetheless, one adjoining cavern outfitted with a large forge for the occasional projects that exceeded the scale and capability of the smaller home-based smithies. Kal smiled at the thought of Devved. The big man must be beside himself.

Alcesidas drained his mug and looked up to see the goodwife's husband, who had made his appearance, gripping the twin ears of a huge earthenware pitcher, which he set upon the kitchen table with evident satisfaction. His knobbed hairy hands were dark and smudged and quite out of proportion to his body, yet supple, even sensitive. One could tell from the sure way he handled the pitcher and then leaned over to unlatch the window by their table.

"Briacoil, my prince, it is no short while since our rooftree has harboured your august person and you too, anuas, briacoil. I bid you especial welcome to Far Acres, since Signy tells me that you fill now the office of Hordanu."

"Kalaquinn, I present to you Volodan, the greatest of all our craftsmen here in Nua Cearta, and I doubt that even Shadahr would be able to find his equal, even if he combed every nook and cranny of the Burren forgeland itself," replied Alcesidas, doing the honours. "It was he who made Magan Hammermaster's coach, which you did admire earlier."

"My dear Prince Alcesidas, you are too much flattering. Signy will think that you are swelling my head. And now already she thinks it is a gourd that is thick-skinned and large beyond due measure," Volodan said, laughing from a florid face streaked with the grime and heat of his work. With a weary but relaxed air, the man undid the leather apron that covered his loose-fitting tunic and hung it on a peg by the door. No less smudged than his face, the once cream-coloured tunic was girdled at the waist with a rough length of cord.

"I am a forgeworker like any another here in Nua Cearta," sighed Volodan. "But enough, have done with your overgenerous praise, Prince Alcesidas, or you shall have me blushing like a forge ember. There's another sort of 'meed' that better fits my case, and yours too, I'll wager, from the dust and sweat that cover you both. Indeed, I have taken the liberty of fetching a pot of Signy's honey cider for us to savour. We must show the young Hordanu that our hammerdaughters do best their men in their work. Our smithcraft is but paltry diddling to their honeyed labours in the brewhouse."

"What, Volodan? Will you have us mix ale and cider like callow guzzlers?" teased Alcesidas.

"Surely, you have heard the Cider Rhyme, my prince? 'Beer upon cider is a bad rider, but cider 'pon beer is very good cheer!'"

"Very well, then, Volodan, your versesmithing has won us. Come, pour us a well-filled cup. We shall undertake the labour of putting your rhyme wisdom to the test, shall we not, Kalaquinn?" pronounced Alcesidas with a full-toothed grin. Kal rushed to empty his mug of ale, so that their host might replenish it with cider. The mellowness of late afternoon's avalynn light lay upon them like a blanket, a perfect match for the ripeness of the cider. From outside they could hear the joyful fluting of a meadowlark blending dozily with the rise and fall of laughing children's voices, which drifted to their ears from an apple orchard close by the forge. That's where Kal and Alcesidas had left Gwyn, who had drawn open his ever-present pouch of marbles at the sight of the two children, a boy and a girl, who could not resist Gwyn's simple charm any more than he could resist theirs.

Kal's head grew lighter. He found it harder and harder to keep abreast of the conversation. Determined though he was not to be an impolite guest, sleep pulled at him. He'd had no food to soak up the edge of the ale and the cider, although Signy had now returned with a fresh loaf of rye bread and a generous slab of old cheese from the pantry. It proved a most pleasant light meal, all the more tasty because it was garnished by hunger. Alcesidas advised him to save some room for the evening's feasting in the Hall of the Stars. Again an unbearable weight of drowsiness tugged at him. He could no more resist yielding to it than could a tree, given its final felling strokes by the woodcutter, resist being sent crashing to the ground. It was as if all the sleeplessness and exertions of the past two days had conspired to come together and take their toll at last.

The next thing Kal knew he was slowly awakening in a great four-poster bed, complete with a leek-green canopy pricked out with many brightly plumed birds like pheasants. The soft fragrant linen sheets had helped to make his sleep sweet and forgetful. Indeed, it felt as though he had been sleeping for ages. At first his senses were confused by vague hints of wakefulness and dream all jumbled. There had been shouts of alarm, the rattle of arms, and the shriek of a woman's voice. But all these snippets of conscious recollection had only just managed to enter that tiny nook of his mind which had been the last to resist the relentless pull of sleep. Ah, but he had been weary, weary beyond caring, too weary to bestir himself no matter what. And then somehow he had ended up lying in the back of the wagon, with Gwyn bent over him, while the light grew dim and the monotonous noise of bees in the yellow musk slowly faded, leaving only the regular clip-clop of horseshoes on the cobblestones, sending him deeper into his slumbers.

Kal yawned, then stretched and noticed that he was clad in just a long nightshirt. He raised himself and drew aside the curtains of the four-poster. The room was of finely cut stone blocks, and on much of its wallspace there hung vivid scenes woven into old rich tapestries. There was even a fireplace, in which the glowing coals lay ready to be banked up and stoked with the logs piled high in a chased gilt box braced by four legs alongside the hearth. A broad window opening set in a thick embrasure gave the room its allowance of natural light, now receding into an indistinct twilight. What had happened? How long had he slept? It was all a puzzle to the Holdsman. The last thing he remembered was his visit to the home of Volodan and Signy, and by then it had already been late afternoon.

As Kal, still sleepy and disoriented, sought to disentangle these questions, his eye strayed to the door of the chamber. A nervous-looking fellow stole in on tiptoe, lantern in hand, wearing green hose and a brown sleeveless jerkin over a white shirt. Kal did not need to see the avalynn crest sewn into the jerkin to recognize the livery as being that of one of King Magan's retainers. Without so much as a glance in Kal's direction, keeping his back to him, the man reached up to a sheltered niche in the wall, no more than an empty depression. Kal heard a click and rasping sound as of something being slid, and there was a sudden outpouring of light that came from an avalynn fruit suspended in the niche by a glowing filament. At this the man ventured a glance in the direction of the bed. He seemed almost as taken aback as Kal. Without waiting to be given leave by the young Holdsman, he blurted out an apologetic "briacoil" and explained that he had been sent by Prince Alcesidas to build up the fire, unscreen a chamber light, and wait by, until Master Hordanu should awaken. The footman must have noted Kal's knitted brows and puzzled countenance, for he bade him wait until he fetched Prince Alcesidas, then muttered another polite "briacoil" and hurriedly bowed and left.

Kal ambled to the window and unlatched it, swinging it open to the spring air, heady with the delicate scent of the gardens below. Nua Cearta was spectacular beyond words. As the vista unfolded before him, he realized at once that he was atop the pinnacle of layered terraces which dominated the sightlines of the kingdom. Apparently his sleeping chamber was situated in one of the turrets affixed to the building he had seen earlier.

Below him the brightness of many avalynnia was waning into a unique mimicry of twilight. The air was tinted with the pink flush of a sunset akin to the ones that Kal had experienced so often in the Holding, except that in this case it seemed to have undergone a sublime diffusion into all points of the horizon, not merely its western portion. And the granite mass of Nua Cearta's sky, bereft as it was of the upper world's nightwork pattern of twinkling stars and lamping moon gave the dusk an ominous louring final quality, like that of a dense linen shroud being pulled tight over the mortal remains of day or a great stone slab being closed over its rocky tomb.

Beautiful as it was, Kal found it somewhat unsettling. Touched to the quick for a moment by a strong and poignant sense of life's perilous sojourn on the brink of engulfing night, he gazed down at the majestic marble pile of Magan Hammermaster's palace. Cut from the very rock of the cavern, its cream facade too had been sculpted to resemble the meticulous craftsmanship of master stonemasons working block by block. This made for an altogether unique combination of artifice and nature—an emblem of the hammerfolk themselves, whose forgecraft and stonework existed so happily side by side with their agricultural pursuits. The palace, like a gigantic dove brooding with half-folded wings, was flanked by the royal mews and stables and armouries and sundry other buildings—looking like the dove's nestlings.

Beyond that could be seen the roads that traced their way outward to the hinterland of the kingdom, with its farms and mills and forges laid in a quiltwork pattern of undulant fields and forests, all settling into the blackness of a Nua Ceartan night. Along several of the roads, Kal watched flat-bedded wagons, hung with lanterns and brimming over with folk, hastening to the royal enclave, called, as Alcesidas had told Kal, Sterentref, to distinguish it from Sterenhall, the building from which he enjoyed this view. Kal noted that there were several other wagons and coaches stationed empty in a large open area that lay behind the royal stables, equipped with tethering posts and rails. Many people, too, were mounting the wide stairs up towards Sterenhall and its companion building in the shape of a glence.

Clearly discernible, as well, although not near enough to be identifiable in the gathering murk of the fading light, were Kal's fellow anuasoi, their superior height and difference in gait allowing him to pick them out from among the hammerfolk that plodded their way up the stairs.

"It is an awe-inspiring sight, is it not, Kalaquinn, Nua Cearta spread out before you at dusk? I too have pondered many a problem from that window." Startled, Kal whirled around to find Alcesidas, clad in garb befitting his station, smiling at him from the open door. "Briacoil! It pleases me to see that you have slept long, and well I trust. Indeed, I had begun to doubt me whether you had somehow been ensorcelled. We shall have need of your presence this evening. Without you our feasting would scarcely be complete, and we have waited one day already for you to have your rest."

"How long have I slept? Where am I?"

"From yesterday afternoon. I made merry asking Signy if she was not perhaps wont to spice her cider with a sleeping draught. I thought nothing would wake you after that affray you did studiously ignore with your snores and wheezings."

"What affray? What mean you, Alcesidas?"

"Come, wash here and change into your day clothes and I shall tell you what honour that crippled boy who dogs you has brought upon himself." Alcesidas pointed to a screen in the far corner of the room, on the other side of which there stood an ample bathtub of porcelain filled with steaming water and a fresh set of clothes laid out on a chair, together with a large mirror.

Above the bathtub was another strange-looking niche, like the one at which Alcesidas's groom had earlier groped. The back of it was faced with a kind of door that Alcesidas slid open to reveal a glowing avalynn fruit that provided Kal with light to see by in the area behind the screen.

Letting Kal scrub himself clean behind the partition, Alcesidas recounted yesterday's events to him. As the Prince had sat talking with Volodan—while Kal drifted off to sleep—a frantic high-pitched shriek of alarm from Signy reached their ears. Leaving Kal in his slumber, he and Volodan had dropped their mugs and rushed outdoors towards the orchard in time to see Gwyn laying down a short bow beside a figure spread out on the ground, facedown and inert. Two shafts protruded from the back of the lifeless man. Signy too arrived on the scene, favouring a forearm that had been gashed.

It happened that one of Shadahr's spies had been spotted by Signy as he crept up to Volodan's forge. She had just emerged from the rootcellar, which faced the rear entrance to the forge. Otherwise she might not have seen him skulking towards it. Shadahr's minion was keen, no doubt, on gaining some notion of the state of Nua Cearta's forgecraft—which, Alcesidas added, was far superior to that of Cearta itself. Realising that he had been discovered by Signy and that a hue and cry was imminent, he let fly a bolt at her in order to silence her and make good his escape. The shaft merely grazed her arm. At this she cried out in her alarm—which is what Volodan and Alcesidas had heard and Gwyn as well, from the orchard, where he was still playing at marbles with the two children. Shadahr's spy made to run, well aware that the game was up and his only chance lay in headlong flight, his straightest way back to his own tunnels being by way of the orchard.

Gwyn had loped to snatch up a shortbow that Volodan had left leaning against one of the pear trees, where there had been a butt set up for archery practice. Signy had watched the whole scene unfold before her. Her children screamed, as the fleeing spy ran in their direction, making for the screening outbuildings that bordered the orchard. He eyed the children, slowed for a moment, and then turned towards them, ignoring Gwyn. Scooping up the little girl in his arms, he ran to the outbuildings with her. An arrow thudded into the ground behind him as he ran, while the little girl screamed, held in his grip.

Then, before he could turn the corner of the milking barn, he emitted a muffled cry of pain. Gwyn had placed an arrow in the fleeing man's shoulder from behind. But this did not stop him, for the arrow hit the quiver slung over his back, which blunted its impact. Gwyn had gotten the measure of Volodan's short bow. Again he let fly. This time the bolt found its mark in the small of the spy's back. Dropping like a stone, he pinned the little girl beneath his body.

Alcesidas and Volodan arrived in time to help Gwyn and Signy comfort the child. Great rejoicing followed. Gwyn became an instant hero and could scarcely tear himself away from the grateful parents, who called their neighbours in for a small feast of thanksgiving, which hammerfolk are wont to do at the slightest provocation. Their coming together also provided the occasion for Volodan and the other hammersons to search the outlying fields and woods, where they knew there were entry points into Nua Cearta from the tunnels and caves of Folamh.

"So Gwyn and I loaded you, sleep-ridden and all but dead to the world, onto the wagon. We took you back to Sterentref and had you carried on a stretcher here to this room. Although you remained in a daze, we managed to dress you in a nightshirt and place you in bed, letting you indulge your keen desire to sleep."

"Once again, I am deeply in your debt, Alcesidas," Kal said as he stepped from behind the screen, now bathed and dressed, having remained attentive to every detail of his friend's account. He regarded himself in the mirror. The clothes fitted him superbly well. They had been tailored for him—white hose and a deep blue tunic embroidered with silver—and he found them trim and comfortable. The hammerfolk had even left him a fine pebbled leather pouch, which he opened to find the Pyx of Roncador repaired to its golden chain. This pouch he attached to the belt of his tunic. He looked and indeed felt like a new man entirely, refreshed by his long sleep and ablutions.

The light had become somewhat dimmer now, even though Alcesidas had, while they talked, unscreened another chamber light in yet another niche in the wall. Still, the onset of night was soft and gradual, not a suddenly falling darkness, as on a winter's evening.

"Indeed, your Gwyn has won the undying gratitude of all of

Nua Cearta, Kalaquinn," Alcesidas said as Kal clasped together the two ends of his cloak with the pios.

"And where is he?"

"Gone back to the home of Volodan and Signy with another of my grooms. Their daughter kept asking for him and refused to be consoled without his near presence. An altogether remarkable young man, I should say, Kalaquinn, as is your other boon companion, Galligaskin. We stand in deep amazement at his skills." As he spoke, Alcesidas opened a wooden cabinet by the window and withdrew from it a pyramid-shaped object with a hand grip atop it, the sides of it opaque. Pulling open some small metal doors on it, light poured out from its now transparent sides of glass. In the lantern an avalynn fruit, which hung on a glowing white filament, gave out a pool of brightness.

Holding the lantern, Alcesidas doused each of the chamber lights by drawing shut its sliding panel. He related how, recognizing Galli for who he was by his browmark, they had learned more of Galli's Telessarian blood through Rimut, and pressed him into service, getting him to scan Far Acres for further signs of the enemy, signs that might have escaped the notice of the hammerfolk. Galli ended up ingratiating himself with them by discovering the precise spot where the spy had slipped into Nua Cearta, a cleft that lay hidden under a small overhang of rock. Volodan and his neighbours went to work with their sturdy little draught horses, sealing this gap with a good many stoneboat loads of rock.

But now they were to the feasting hall, and, as he held open the door to Kal, Alcesidas explained how eagerly he had been awaiting this evening's festivities, already a day postponed.

TWENTY-TWO

Alcesidas and Kalaquinn stepped into the corridor outside the sleeping chamber, where a liveried footman bustled past them with a respectful "briacoil." In his hands, he bore a long pole tipped with a hook, which he used to lay open the shutters of the avalynn lamps that rested on the walls at intervals on decorated corbels braced to a bossed plaster ceiling. Crisscrossed with a latticework design inset with the floral emblem of a lily, the walls of the corridor opened into a gallery filled with many rows of seats looking out onto a great darkened hall. The hall was enclosed by lofty windowless walls that rested on a series of columns, which girdled the whole perimeter, except for the end with the gallery. The space between the columns was spanned by rounded trefoil arches that framed a further welling darkness, where one or two weak lights flickered.

It was the ceiling, however, which proved altogether remarkable, for it lay open to a familiar night sky—a night sky as Kal had known it in the upper world of the Holding—a panorama of stars set off by the luminous sliver of the rising moon and the twinkling brightness of the Evening Star. Alcesidas paused for a moment to explain that what they beheld was Sterenhall, or the Great Hall of the Stars. Its splendid ceiling was formed of transparent crystal.

Shadow-enrobed figures were trickling into the Great Hall of the Stars from the murkiness of the encircling colonnade, taking their places on benches at trestle boards below a dais on which were two tables arranged in tiers. Here and there the tables held a small avalynn lamp, its shutters tinted red and designed, explained Alcesidas, to spill out only just enough light by which to dine. The tantalizing smell of venison, roast fowl, and other savoury dishes heaped upon salvers that lay on groaning sideboards pervaded the Hall and wafted up to the gallery. Kal's stomach clenched with hunger pangs.

Alcesidas shepherded Kal along to the far end of the gallery, where they descended two flights of stairs and entered one of the dim colonnades that flanked Sterenhall. Other silent figures, murmuring to one another, glided by them from other entrance-ways dimly lit by the same diminutive avalynn lamps that had been placed on the tables in the Great Hall, their glow as soft as moonlight.

Following Alcesidas through one of the arches, Kal stepped into the Great Hall of the Stars. He gazed up at the ceiling, his breath taken away by the sheer clarity of the heavens spread out above his head. Never had he seen the stars or the moon as vivid as from this extraordinary hall. It was as if the dome of the night sky had been somehow amplified within the walls of the chamber, making the heavenly bodies more real and lustrous, almost graspable, their immensity fitted in some strange wise to the compass of mortal men.

Alcesidas bade Kal follow him to the dais, as they threaded their way through the milling throng. Servitors scurried about with amazing nimbleness, balancing platters from which they filled the various sideboards in preparation for the feast that was at hand. Now, as he and Alcesidas mounted the stairs of the dais, Kal could see some of those who had been seated there in that elevated place of honour—a whole clutch of Holdsfolk. He discerned the figures of Diggory Clout and Gammer, bantering back and forth in their customary way, flanked by their daughters. Kal hailed Galli, seated beside Marya across the table from Kal's own mother and father and brother. Alcesidas waited while Kal stopped to greet his family with warm embraces. Happy to be reunited with them, Kal made to sit down in the empty space beside Galli, but Alcesidas urged him on to the upper tier of the high table.

At the very centre of the table, on a high-backed chair of ornately carved oak and deeply embossed leather, sat Magan Hammermaster, stooped deep in conversation with Meriones, seated at his right hand. Meriones gestured up into the night sky, pointing keenly to some detail of it, and then fell to expounding some other point to King Magan. One of the small avalynn lamps was propped up on the table before the two of them, casting an eerie glow across their bearded solemn faces. King Magan wore his crown and looked very regal even in the weak light, while the watchful eyes of Meriones swept across the Hall, scanning the pillars of the darker colonnade, where armed guards discreetly kept watch.

Behind the armed men, from deep within a dark gaping arch of the adjoining colonnade, there glared a blazing hardwood fire in an enormous stone hearth. A double swinging door that adjoined the hearth was in constant motion, for it led to the vast kitchens of the Great Hall, where the festive food was being prepared by a whole battery of bustling cooks, bakers, brewers, turnspits, sweepers, and scullions.

"Briacoil, Master Hordanu. Briacoil, Prince Alcesidas." It was not surprising that Meriones, with his restless hooded eyes, had noticed the two of them first, lifting his brows at their approach. Acknowledging them, he let his face soften into a welcoming smile. King Magan followed suit with warm words of greeting, and then turning to his left he presented Kal to a slight vivacious woman, who wore a golden coronet similar to Magan's, but smaller and inlaid with a more brilliant arrangement of jewels. In the smooth regularity of her features Kal could see Alcesidas. The elegant set of his mouth and chin, the delicacy of his nose, were copies of hers.

"Enchanted to meet you, Master Kalaquinn. They told me you were young, but not so fresh-faced. Youngling to be Hordanu! I've always pictured you in my mind's eye to be old and venerable and full of years—Hordanus I mean—and bearded like some of our hammersons, albeit taller, in the way of anuasoi."

"Dear Hammermistress, I humbly crave your pardon for my youth, and I beg Your Royal Majesty to be assured that I am your utterly complaisant servant in the weighty matters of age and facial adornment. However, the remedies are not mine to sue for, but stand rather in nature's unbidden gift. All I may do is hope that the years as they unfold may efface the deficiencies of my youth and thus ingratiate me with your august majesty."

"Most aptly and diplomatically put, Kalaquinn!" said Alcesidas with a clap of his hand on Kal's shoulder.

"How smoothly he has bearded the lion—or lioness, I should say!" roared Magan.

"Indeed," Meriones said, a sparkle in his eye beneath a raised and bristling brow, "surely his way with words gives the lie to his importunate manner of coming hither."

"Well spoken, Master Hordanu." Almagora Hammermistress bowed her regal head, breezing on in a voice high-pitched but not unpleasing, which sounded something akin to the twitter of sparrow song. "I spoke too soon, I see, and let appearances deceive me. And your brave friend, what a pure untrammelled pleasure, a most charming young anuas, even though his tongue be bound by muteness and his understanding of our language be somewhat clouded." Gwyn sat beside her, absorbed in whittling a block of wood with a small knife. To his left sat Volodan and Signy.

Throwing back his tousled thatch of hair, Gwyn lifted his head and broke into a broad smile, holding up the wood block that he had been shaping. It caught some of the ghostly red glimmer of the avalynn lamp.

"Would you not say, Father, that it is an amazing likeness of Mother?" Alcesidas grinned.

"Re'm ena, but it is, son. A startlingly true one, I should say." And such it was, for the long, delicately sculpted lines of it captured the unfettered bird-like quality of the little queen, who, when she saw it, emitted a pleasant piping laugh, the sheer joy of which did much to smooth for a moment the solemn frowns that had puckered the huddled shadow-scored faces of her husband and Meriones. Kal, whom King Magan bade sit in the empty seat beside Meriones, had conceived an immediate affection for her.

The two places to Kal's right were empty, although one of them stood reserved for Alcesidas, who had been sent by his father to check on the state of affairs in the kitchen. Meriones remained deeply immersed in conversation with the king. This gave Kal pause to look about the Hall of the Stars and breathe in the atmospheric magic of its half-toned darkness, so subtly embroidered by the stretch of sky above him. With preening neck, the star form of Alargha the Swan floated in the heavens.

Kal gasped, realizing what moments earlier must have drawn Meriones's attention. Tonight the Swan's star-points shone with a brighter, more vivid glow, like exquisitely cut gems, more clear and distinct than he had ever remembered them to be—so alive and unfettered she might almost have alighted in the Hall itself. As for the Swan's eye, it pulsed with such a glow that it left the rest of her outline faint and dull. He had never seen the Swan so beautiful. Meriones turned to Kal.

"What think you on this, Master Hordanu?" asked Meriones, who had noted Kal's rapt observation of the heavens.

"You are asking me, Master Meriones? Why, I can scarcely disentangle my thoughts about the affairs that have befallen me and mine this past while, let alone anything larger and more momentous, as this wondrous brightness of the Swan does surely portend."

"Still, you are Hordanu, and for that very reason your opinion holds weight."

"Indeed, Master Meriones, Hordanu by happenstance."

"Come, Master Kalaquinn, you know better than I that one never becomes Hordanu by happenstance. Come, grace us with your thoughts." Meriones tilted his head back up towards the sky, studying it. Kal followed his lead and spoke.

"Indeed, then . . . In its broad lines the Swan must represent the Talamadh as by common agreement. Its power stands now dim and faded, under mortal threat. But such starbrightness of the Swan as we mark in the heavens tonight portends that this threat will come to be foiled and the Talamadh will be recovered. But changed beyond telling, it will regain the full-fledged vigour of its music and become a mightier instrument!" Kal said this with a growing confidence.

"And the uncommon flaring of the Swan's eye?" Meriones held the young Holdsman's gaze, prompting him.

"As for the eye of the Swan, my heart divines no meaning, but then who can say?"

"Indeed, who can, if you cannot?" Meriones frowned, casting another quick glance upwards.

"That much suggests itself to my heart, whatever may be its worth."

"Doubtless it is worth more than you suppose, young Master Hordanu. I am certain that you have hit upon the truth of it. I saw the star-point of Alargha's eye pulse as you did speak."

"Even so, Master Meriones, it does seem wise to let events themselves or their near approach bear out interpretations. Perhaps that is the design behind such wondrous omens, that they should not be exact, but serve as a vague forewarning or consolation, as did many omens that occurred in the Stoneholding before the onslaught of Ferabek, although we did little to pay them proper heed."

"Except Master Wilum?"

"Indeed, one must needs say that he took them seriously and was provident."

"By special warrant of his office, don't you think?"

"So I imagine, for he was ever aware of some fateful unfolding of things, the way he held out against Gawmage and cherished the manuscripts and rolls. And this he did in the face of so much indifference on the part of his own people. Many Holdsfolk thought that he had become a moss-backed dotard."

"And he put you through your paces, too, I have heard."

"Re'm ena, that he did, Master Meriones. Or I should not be able to carry on a conversation with you in the Old Tongue."

"And so much more than passably well."

"In his keeil," continued Kal, shifting his weight onto the carved arm of his chair, leaning towards Meriones, "Master Wilum made me pore over a great many of the old lays and legends until my eyes ached and my mind reeled, while Galligaskin worked for him out-of-doors in and around the Howe, although, mind you, it must be said that I did help him to hoe the garden and clean the Great Glence and suchlike tasks. Wonderful those times were. The utter peace. Strange to think that they have gone forever and that the old man lies entombed here in this mountain. Even Master Wilum's keeil had a smell all its own. I cannot describe it, the smell of meadowsweet and leather, of polished wood and smoke and dusty vellum sheets. All of the Howe and the glencelands too always felt so very tranquil, so untouched by the ominous signs that beset the Stoneholding. It seemed so far removed from the parlous state of the lowlands and the confusion reigning in Dinas Antrum, until just the other morning.

"At that time it all changed. All changed when Gawmage's messenger violated Oakenvalley Bottom and quenched the Sacred Fire. Then it was as if everything had been shattered, as indeed it turned out to be, and I was cast into this role of Hordanu which suits my youth so ill. Would that Master Wilum had lived . . ." Kal's voice trailed off into brooding silence.

Meriones had closed his eyes, as if recollecting himself, and now opened them again, full of a new intensity. "Do not fret,

Master Kalaquinn. It is laid on my heart that you, Hordanu, are the pulsing eye of the Swan, for you remain rightful custodian of the Talamadh and keeper of the Great Harmony. Essential to the restoration of both. I say to you that your fortunes are closely and mysteriously bound with those of Ahn Norvys in these dire days. If I may make so bold as to counsel you, let your office itself be your warrant, your armour and your mainstay. You may pile years on years, 'til your head be as hoary as the snows that lie above us on the crest of Folamh, and still not achieve worthiness— Hush now, Magan Hammermaster makes ready to give the signal that will begin our feasting."

Alcesidas had come up beside the bard, whispering to his father the king, who fondled a bejewelled white sceptre that he had lifted from the table before him, which was spread with a fine linen cloth. Fewer people stood or walked in the Hall now. An air of expectation filled the place. King Magan struck one of the stout wooden arms of his high chair with the rod. Alcesidas slid into his seat beside Kal and nudged him whispering, "I think you and the other anuasoi shall find the first course very much to your liking. 'Twas I who thought of it," he added with a wink and a grin.

A deeper silence descended over the banqueters. King Magan rose and bade all his guests welcome to the Hall of the Stars, dwelling with particular attention on the folk from the upperworld who graced the folk of the hammer with their presence. These included the Hordanu himself—something unprecedented in Nua Cearta, he explained expansively. Already their anuasoi guests had been of inestimable service. With gratitude, he cited Gwyn's intervention in thwarting Shadahr's spy at Far Acres and Galli's extraordinary skills as a tracker. The hammerfolk, never behindhand in giving courage and skill their due, broke out in applause. Then, before the King could press the patience of his hungry audience by carrying on, Kal espied Queen Almagora administering a cautionary poke to his ribs.

As King Magan seated himself again, there sounded a melodious flourish of trumpets emanating from either side of the large kitchen doors. From them emerged a pair of thick-built hammersons, bearing up high on their shoulders a broad silver plate. On it rested a great boar's head with long tusks, encircled by a wreath about the temples. In the boar's open mouth there blazed the figure of a harp made of volatile, fiery camphor. Bearing the plate into the Hall itself, the two hammersons began to sing in full-bodied rollicking voice.

> "See on this plate the dread Boar's pate,
> Wreathed round in nightshade's clasp.
> He would make bold the Harp to hold
> And 'tempt great Vali's craft.
>
> He would make bold with Harp of Gold
> To unsing Ardiel's Lay.
> Come one, come all, witness his fall
> As night submits to day.
>
> Come one, come all, come sing withal
> For light will shadows rout—
> The Talamadh in glory clad
> Will sear and burn his snout!"

In a rising crescendo they finished their song, and even as they sang the last word the harp dissolved into an explosive confusion of ivory white wings and feathers, made plainly visible by the flames that had engulfed the boar's head itself. A cluster of doves rose from the shining platter, seeking the freedom of the open air above.

The hammerfolk broke into riotous and unrestrained cheering at this clever prelude to their feast, shouting, "Down with Ferabek!" "Down with Shadahr!" and "Long may they moulder in their graves!"

The Holdsfolk too, though the verse was lost on them, had nevertheless understood the play and broke clapping into cheers of amusement while Rimut made disjointed attempts to catch the lines in translation.

"Well done, son! Most excellent! And most clever!" Magan cheered, clapping, as he turned to Alcesidas, who glowed with the pleasure of having mounted this short, but spectacular, bit of entertainment.

"Indeed, how splendid, Alcesidas! Were those your well-wrought lines? Splendid! May it be a presage of the Boar's richly deserved demise!" cried Kal, as he initiated another round of applause.

The crystal goblets of the banqueters were filled with meddyglyn. The feasting folk were all busy wassailing with this pleasant liquor, when platters of food were brought from the sideboard to the tables—trays heaped with venison, beef, mutton, veal, goose, snipe, pheasant, and hare, together with dumplings, onions, and roots, steaming loaves of manchet bread, huge rounds of cheese, and bowls of fruit. The great hogsheads of mead that had been wheeled into the Hall were broached. And for those who had other preferences, there were ale, cider, and perry as well.

Kal noticed that the Holdsfolk, whose young children had been left at the well-guarded and tended guesthouse, were in fine fettle. The memory of their trials seemed to have been banished for the time being. The drollery of the boar's head and the spicy golden languor of the meddyglyn had softened them. Even Devved grew mirthful, while Garis and Artun, loading their plates with venison and dumplings, found themselves in playful banter with the Clout girls. Narasin's good-humoured "by the welkin" floated above the murmurous chatter. Kal could even hear the distinctive timbre of his own father's voice raised in jollity.

Gwyn was keeping Queen Almagora amused in his own unique fashion, by carving the likeness now of her husband from another block. The Queen looked on, fascinated by the deftness and subtlety with which he managed to capture the living face of her husband—his unknit brows set above guileless eyes, like clear windows giving onto a summer landscape drenched in unshadowed light. Almagora now asked the young anuas to carve a likeness of Meriones next. Undoubtedly that would be most interesting. The landscape of his bardic countenance, like his grimly serious manner, was gloomier, more autumnal, if not downright wintry. Volodan and Signy vied with their queen for Gwyn's mute attention.

Meriones allowed his goblet to be replenished. He used the occasion to turn to King Magan and speak to him with earnest gesture and lowered brow, as if making a proposal. The King listened keenly, inclining his head and nodding. Then, rising to his feet, he rapped his sceptre once more against the arm of his chair. Meriones stood to join him, arms cradling his harp. A hush descended on the Hall. The King paused, waiting for the murmur of conversation to subside, then fixed his gaze on Kal, bidding him rise with an upward gesture of his palms.

"My lord Myghternos Hordanu." The words, spoken with simple directness by the King, resounded through the Hall, which grew still. Not even the echoing clatter of cutlery could now be heard. "Come, come," he bade him, arms outstretched. Meriones made way for Kal, who crimsoned to find all eyes now trained on him. "Come, take this my Hall seat, my place of kingly appointment, for you are Hordanu of all Ahn Norvys. In the hallowed order of affairs, I am your liege, you are my master. My royal majesty yields to you, my lord Myghternos Hordanu."

The king conceded the spot at table before his chair and moved aside. Now Meriones stepped forward.

"My lord Myghternos Hordanu, take this my bardic harp and sing." He held out the instrument to Kal. "In flight and danger, by Right of Appointment and without benefit of ancient ceremonial, you have been entrusted with the office of Hordanu. Now, here, tonight, in this the Hall of the Stars, the time has come for you to fulfil the time-honoured custom, to do as all newly invested Hordanus down through the ages have done. My heart insists it must be so. Come, my lord Myghternos Hordanu, sing what must yet be sung. Sing for us your Lay of Investiture. You know well what hallowed flights of inspiration do ever attend this new-wrought song, what timeless truths your forebears as Hordanu have framed in verse that springs from the fresh new hope and strength of their first hours in the office of High Bard. Though this harp of mine do pale by comparison with the Talamadh, as the moon does pale before the light of the sun, take it now and sing. Let the heavens bear witness to your new song. Let the folk of the hammer and these your clanfellows, our guests in Nua Cearta, be privileged now to hearken to your Lay."

Kal took in the assembled crowd, his eyes coming to rest on the harp which the small bard presented him. Meriones insisted, pressing the harp into his reluctant hands. For a moment Kal hesitated, but then he bowed his head, understanding, submitting to the duty now before him. With a quick glance towards the heavens and Alargha the Swan, he began plucking random notes on its strings. Suddenly, he no longer felt embarrassed or shy, but strong with a confidence that came from a depth within him. The notes fell into regular measure. He started to chant:

"Three thousand times the Swan hath wheeled
Across the deep night's jewelled field.
Three thousand times did green spring yield
Unto grey fall, its days annealed
By the summer's sun.

So strengthened in sweet days of bliss,
Three thousand years of benefice,
The song-sung peace o'er Ahn Norvys
Now strains against the avarice
Of blackest Dreosan.

Hear how the dulcet harmony
Of Ardiel's great Victory
Now falters in its potency
Against a darker villainy
Than Tardroch didst avow.

Deep shadows cast from shadowedland
And shadows shadows do command—
Oh, fell the deeds wrought by fell hand,
And fell the creatures that now stand,
O'er Wuldor's wasted Howe.

The Talamadh by guile forfeit,
The Sacred Fire remains unlit,
The songlines' strength becomes unknit—
Fey portents seeming to admit
The waning of all weal.

Yet hope! For hope is life's bequest,
Emboldening the meekest breast,
To which the stars above attest.
Doth not the faintest light shine best
Amidst night's darkling veil?

A tristful heart doth hope emboss
With mettle when all seemeth loss;
It gently sifts about the dross

To seek the faintest hint of gloss
And pluck out precious gem.

But what the gem that hope doth deign
To now descry midst ashen pain?
Velinthian's still fading strain
Hath yet the power to ordain
Myghternos Anadem.

Now know wherein this hope lies fay—
Not in the Harp, but hands that play;
The one who sings, and not the Lay;
Mark, it is he who sings today,
For I Hordanu am."

Here, Kalaquinn raised his head and paused, letting the echoes
of the harp drift and hang suspended, its music prolonged as in a
dream. Again he shifted his gaze to the sky, as the stillness in the
Hall fell deeper still, augmented by a softness of light that seemed to
flow down from the stars above, shedding a mysterious radiance on
all below. Winking in the deepness of night's vault, Alargha the Swan
had become a casement opening the Hall to another timeless realm,
flooding the quivering air with a lambent glory, as if the anagoroi
themselves had graced the banqueters with their presence.

In a moment that seemed to hover on the brink of the eternal,
the eye of the Swan pulsed brighter, waxed larger in the sky, out-
shone all the rest. Kal felt his body grow light and unclayed, the air
around him a rich glow that infused his mind with an astonishing
clarity, washing it pure and clean as if by the bracing essence of a
mountain stream. Caught up in the glimmer of reflected starlight,
Kal's face and clothes became transformed, radiant. The King and
the bard beside him had also been transfigured, each assuming a
new stature and visage. He turned to his left and no longer saw
King Magan, but another royal figure, taller and younger with
golden hair, a jewelled crown circling his head, wearing a surcoat
that bore the heraldic device of hart and hind. Kalaquinn knew
this must be Ardiel, his hands extended to receive. Receive what?
From whom? The young Holdsman glanced aside to his right, but
instead of Meriones found a man of middle age, bearded, with
a solemn cast to his features, wearing the long brown cloak of a

bard, bearing before him with both hands a golden harp, holding it out from his body in a gesture of giving—Hedric relinquishing the Talamadh. Kal turned his head again, his eyes seeking Ardiel. In that moment the radiant tide of light emanating from the eye of the Swan ebbed and grew dim. Ardiel had faded from sight. Magan Hammermaster of Nua Cearta stood waiting. Kal resumed the strains of his song.

> "Hordanu born of Hedric's line,
> Hordanu born midst eglantine.
> Hordanu destined from all time
> To be Hordanu peregrine—
> To quest both king and flame.
>
> As Ardiel sage Hedric sought
> To forge and temper what was wrought
> With Vali's Harp, the peace dear-bought
> He broke asunder; rendered naught
> The strength of bard royal.
>
> Now as the Age nears to an end,
> Must fresh blessed Bard now make amend,
> By dire sacrifice unrend,
> A hard and weary way to wend,
> To bring to end all moil.
>
> To quest the king, though thoughts forbid,
> He soon must hie to deep amid
> The shadowedland. But deep is hid
> The secret of the Ardielid,
> An ancient throne to claim.
>
> When he of royal blood is found,
> Yet unanointed and uncrowned,
> To Pit of Uäm, deep spell-bound,
> Go then, the Roncador's half-round
> To fill with living flame.
>
> In Lammermorn, when kindled young
> Is Sacred Fire, and from the sung

Criochoran of holy-tongue,
No deeds therein be yet unwrung,
Ahn Norvys will be gained

By wreaths of right, the two entwined,
Upon fair Raven Head combined.
When on that blessèd brow shall find
The milk white Hart and milk white Hind,
As Wuldor foreordained—
Know Ardiel hath come."

Kalaquinn withdrew his fingers from the strings of the harp and allowed the music to subside, while the casement that had briefly swung open to a realm of timeless light and beauty was gently closed. Still, as a more lasting warrant of what they had experienced, a feeling of peace now descended on the hearts of all those present. Kalaquinn turned to give the harp back to Meriones, who bowed gravely and said aloud to all those gathered, "Folk of the hammer and honoured anuasoi guests, we have heard our new Hordanu's Lay of Investiture. As is custom and is fitting, let us now give him his meed of acclamation! Briacoil, my lord Myghternos Hordanu!"

King Magan was the first to shout, "Briacoil, my lord Myghternos Hordanu!"

As by thunder, both he and Meriones were drowned in a mighty eruption of voices, while all those in the Hall rose from their seats and took up the same refrain, lusty and heartfelt.

After several minutes of deafening approbation, Kalaquinn took his seat, the chair relinquished to him by Magan Hammermaster. This served as a signal that the time had come to resume the feast.

Filled with a new peace, the folk of the Holding were soon enjoying themselves again, their appreciation all the keener in this place of wonder, where all they needed to do was look up to feast their eyes on the exquisite embroidery of stars that decorated the vastness of the nightscape. At last the rigours and dangers of their flight as well as their uncertainty about the future were riven from their minds and hearts—unlaced, just as the carvers had unlaced from bone the succulent meats for their delight. Kal could not help wondering now and then, as he cast his eyes to the heavens, about the twofold mission whose impossible weight Wilum had laid on him—to find the lost Prince Starigan before Ferabek did and with him to reach the Balk Pit of Uäm.

Meriones, sensing these moments of brooding abstraction, would bid him unwrinkle his brow and revel with the rest. There would be time without a doubt for serious talk later. Even the demeanour of the grim-lipped bard had lightened. And jolly-faced Alcesidas too was ready to reaffirm the sage counsel of Meriones—that for the moment the future could well look after itself.

"Dear Kalaquinn," he urged, laying an arm around Kal's shoulder, "your self and your folk are safe. Be at peace! Let what is to come stay written in the sky for the nonce. Come, have another bumper of mead!"

ACKNOWLEDGMENTS

In itself, writing is a solitary, oftentimes lonely, endeavour, even in a collaborative relationship like our own. Nonetheless, we have found that our own act of sub-creation, to use that beautiful phrase of Tolkien's, has been aided and abetted beyond calculation by many, many people. We owe them a deep debt of gratitude. Without them, this book would never have seen the light of day.

First and foremost come family members—spouses, children, brothers and sisters, parents, in-laws—who never lost faith in the work, supporting us both materially and morally through the lean times.

Then there are friends like Tolkien illustrator Ted Nasmith, who has always been an unflagging supporter, even during those long stretches when the whole project seemed stalled in the doldrums. We recognize and wish to thank the many others who, in the creation of this work, provided us with support and critical feedback: Fr. Bob Wild, Fr. Jim Duffy, Dr. David Craig, Professor Guy Trudel, Tom and Jane Bowen, Neil O'Connor, Jeremy and Monique Rivett-Carnac, John and Susan Artymko, Diane Davis, Elena Afelskie, Rob Huston, James Riley, Wendy Shepherd, and Gonzalo Moran, to name just a few.

A special note of thanks is due to Joe Durepos, who introduced us to our aptly named agent Peter Rubie, a true gem, who recognized the potential in our work from the very outset and connected us with our editor, Jim Minz, and all the wonderful folks at Baen. The astuteness and critical insight Peter and Jim bring to the project have enhanced our writing, raising it to a level we could not have achieved on our own. It is our pleasure to call them not just business associates, but friends, and we look forward to a long and fruitful relationship. We would also like to acknowledge Todd Lockwood for gracing the cover of this book with his artwork.

And to all those many others, as well, who have encouraged us in this journey in ways both great and small—to you, friends, we extend our heartfelt thanks. Though too numerous to mention here, you are never far from our hearts and thoughts.

ABOUT THE AUTHORS

The Stoneholding is the result of a unique collaboration between Mark Sebanc and James G. Anderson. While the origins of the novel lie in a story crafted by Mark over several years, in its present form it stands as a tribute to the alchemy of a mutually sparked creativity. Mark and Jim have toiled together in friendship, with single-minded dedication, setting, honing and polishing the initial work to its present clarity and scope.

Mark has worked as an editor and translator, with several books to his credit. He holds Bachelor and Master of Arts degrees in Classics from the University of Toronto, and lives with his wife and children in the Upper Ottawa Valley of Ontario, Canada.

A teacher, musician, and poet, Jim earned both Bachelor and Master of Arts degrees from Franciscan University of Steubenville in Ohio. He, his wife, Lisa, and their three sons make their home on the Canadian prairies, not far from Saskatoon, Saskatchewan.